THE
BANE
WITCH

ALSO BY AVA MORGYN

The Witches of Bone Hill

YOUNG ADULT NOVELS
Resurrection Girls
The Salt in Our Blood

THE
BANE
WITCH

A Novel

Ava Morgyn

ST. MARTIN'S GRIFFIN
NEW YORK

First published in the United States by St. Martin's Griffin, an imprint of St. Martin's Publishing Group

THE BANE WITCH. Copyright © 2025 by Ava Morgyn. All rights reserved. Printed in the United States of America. For information, address St. Martin's Publishing Group, 120 Broadway, New York, NY 10271.

www.stmartins.com

Scripture quotations taken from the (NASB®) New American Standard Bible®, Copyright © 1960, 1971, 1977, 1995, 2020 by The Lockman Foundation. Used by permission. All rights reserved. lockman.org

The Library of Congress Cataloging-in-Publication Data is available upon request.

ISBN 978-1-250-83545-1 (trade paperback)
ISBN 978-1-250-83546-8 (ebook)

Our books may be purchased in bulk for promotional, educational, or business use. Please contact your local bookseller or the Macmillan Corporate and Premium Sales Department at 1-800-221-7945, extension 5442, or by email at MacmillanSpecialMarkets@macmillan.com.

First Edition: 2025

10 9 8 7 6 5 4 3 2 1

For everyone who has suffered violence and abuse
at the hands of a loved one or stranger.
You are the real heroes.

If you or someone you know is experiencing domestic violence,
call the 24/7 National Domestic Violence Hotline at
1-800-799-7233 (SAFE)
or visit the website (thehotline.org) to chat with an advocate.
For immediate danger, please call 911.

CONTENT WARNING

Some of the thematic material in *The Bane Witch* contains depictions of blood, gore, physical/sexual assault, sexual trauma, kidnapping, violence, murder, suicide, and death. For more information, please visit the author's website.

CORBIN VENERY

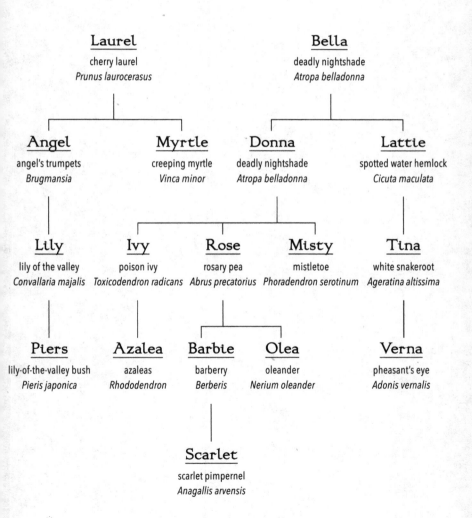

Laurel
cherry laurel
Prunus laurocerasus

Bella
deadly nightshade
Atropa belladonna

Angel
angel's trumpets
Brugmansia

Myrtle
creeping myrtle
Vinca minor

Donna
deadly nightshade
Atropa belladonna

Lattie
spotted water hemlock
Cicuta maculata

Lily
lily of the valley
Convallaria majalis

Ivy
poison ivy
Toxicodendron radicans

Rose
rosary pea
Abrus precatorius

Misty
mistletoe
Phoradendron serotinum

Tina
white snakeroot
Ageratina altissima

Piers
lily-of-the-valley bush
Pieris japonica

Azalea
azaleas
Rhododendron

Barbie
barberry
Berberis

Olea
oleander
Nerium oleander

Verna
pheasant's eye
Adonis vernalis

Scarlet
scarlet pimpernel
Anagallis arvensis

1

Bridge

I planned my death the way I design a room: heavy objects first to anchor the narrative, bones for all the crucial details—creases and corners where the devil hides—to rest upon. There can be no gaping voids of negative space where the mind lingers unattended. Just quiet pauses between elements. A story you don't know is being told as your eye is drawn from cornice to carpet. Organic but not random, harmonious but not predictable. A well-designed room feels accidental, but never hapless. A well-designed death is no different.

I squeeze the berries in my pockets, letting their juices seep into the fine lines of my knuckles and fill the soft, white crescents of my nails. The walk is silver before me in the predawn gloom, a bright paragon of architecture over the Cooper River, running headlong into the future. It dazzles, this bridge, like something from a spaceship, ready to launch me into the next place.

The first time I ate deadly pokeweed, I was five. I found those dangling clusters of glossy black berries and wine-pink stems irresistible, popping one after another into my mouth. I'd never been so hungry before. I can still feel the high August sun bearing down on my scalp, drying the juice and staining my hands burgundy. And I can still hear my mother's scream when she found me—a sound without shape, the bellow of a gutted animal. His body was a log at my feet, fallen. She slapped the berries from my palms until they stung and rushed me to the hospital, leaving the dead man behind.

I don't remember feeling ill. I don't recall the stomach cramps or the seizure she said I had. "You stopped breathing," she would tell me. "You almost died." I don't recall the man giving me the berries. "He was sick," my mother claimed. I do recall the briny flavor of his skin, the give of flesh beneath my teeth, the hot pulse of blood like iodine. I recall resting against hospital pillows when the nurse brought me ice cream, and my mother crying softly, the policemen looming columns of black.

I didn't eat pokeweed again. Until I was nine.

Death by deadly ingestion isn't common, but it has a certain drama my husband, Henry, will immediately ascribe to me, an *unnecessariness*. He always found my reactions exaggerated, even comical. As if I were in an old cartoon—helicopter arms and tweeting birds flying around my head. Stars blinking in and out. It's hard not to flail when someone is cutting off your oxygen.

The police, I suspect, will look at my past—popular interior designer who withdraws from polite society, whispered about at the odd dinner party. And there is the family history, of course. They'll find it fitting, at first. A sloppy suicide—crucial to keep Henry from coming after me. But the peculiarities will pile up, hinting that something is *off*. They'll start looking into the husband because that's what they always do.

I'm counting on it.

I blink against the fog, my shoelaces slapping the walk, rain jacket zipped to my chin. Soon, the sun will freewheel across the sky, lighting Charleston up, setting it aglow. It's a glorious day to die, an ironically tranquil morning.

I love Charleston. I love its quaint, cobblestoned history and watercolor ambiance, the unpretentious gentility of the people. I came here looking for something—charisma, hospitality, belonging. I was only twenty-three, fresh from community college with nothing but an unimpressive degree, youthful optimism, and a relentless work ethic. In seven years, I built a life to be proud of—a brilliant career, a circle of specious friends, a client list longer than this bridge. In two, Henry took it all away.

On days like this, Charleston looks like a painting, too romantic to be real, like some old debonair destination in Europe—Paris or Venice or Copenhagen. It's what made me believe over the last two years. In him. In *us*. If the light slanted just right and the breeze smelled of gardenias and palm and I didn't overcook the shrimp, we would be okay. The good days dot my memory like sand dollars on the beach. Prizes to collect, dead as they are.

I don't believe anymore.

Whatever happens when I hit that water, I will never see Charleston again, never ride in one of its horse-drawn carriages through the French Quarter or sip planter's punch under a sherbet-colored sky. This city was all I had—the father I never knew and the mother I always craved. Charleston was the place where I left behind a troubled past clouded with questions and drew myself in clear, crisp lines. But this bridge is where my love affair with Charleston *and* Henry ends.

I glance over my shoulder and quicken my pace. Behind me, the man in the black hoodie trudges with his head down. He could pass for Henry. Same height. Same build. I've been watching him for months on mornings just like this one. Henry leaves exceptionally early for work, wanting to fit in a workout at the gym and still beat his associates to the office. I would leave my phone on the kitchen island and climb out the bathroom window, so the front door camera wouldn't alert him to my coming or going, and drive to the nearby waterfront park. I'd come here and contemplate the only way out I could see. It's how I noticed him. He was here every week around dawn, in a jacket, hood hanging around his face, head down, and hands balled inside his pockets. He never noticed me. He never noticed anything. I wondered if he was thinking of jumping, too.

I put everything into place. Switched from driving in to taking two buses, knowing the next time I saw him, I had to be ready to go at a moment's notice if I wanted Henry to pay.

Then he stopped coming.

I spent a restless couple of weeks standing at the mouth of the bridge, my secret bus fare dwindling, knowing I may not get another opportunity to follow through.

This morning, my luck turned.

I see a dark speck at the seam of my pocket and remember the dully sweet flavor of pokeweed berries when I was nine. We'd moved to a house bordering a national forest, and come summer, the flowers dappled the edge of the wood like constellations. I would lie in my bed and watch them swaying gently in the dark. They turned from spectral white to chartreuse, to pink, and eventually a violet so deep it vanished in the night. When they began to drop, I couldn't stand it anymore. I waited till the moon was over the trees before going to them, unable to explain my craving. Then I grabbed a fistful and shoved it, stems and all, into my mouth. The juices flooded my gums, blander than I'd expected. I'd thought I was being discreet as I ate my way around our yard. But in the morning, my mother saw the stains along my lips and fingers, splattered across the front of my gown.

Later, the doctor would call it *pica,* an eating disorder characterized by the desire to consume substances with no nutritional value. I was given supplements and cognitive behavioral therapy and out came the little pills that made my heart race. They monitored me so closely I could scarcely take a piss without an audience. But eventually, my mom began to relax. Her new husband, Gerald, disliked the attention I was taking away from him. He coaxed her into leaving me alone for increasing periods of time. It didn't take long for me to find my way back to where the pokeweed bushes waved at me with big, frilly leaves.

Maybe I built up a tolerance after that first incident, like people who are snakebit so many times they no longer react to the venom. I never got sick, never went back to the hospital, never encountered another strange man in my forays or sank my teeth into his arm, standing sentinel over his prone form until someone found me. "He fed you. He grabbed you, and that's why you bit him," she'd recited over and over. It was easy to remember when the police came.

But it was harder to forget. The hunger—like claws raking across my stomach lining. The taste—bitter and forbidden in a way I longed for. The man—a hard face like chiseled stone, a harder fall, the rightness of it, the certainty. And the memory, a flash that didn't belong to me—hands around a slender throat, full blue lips, eyes that stopped blinking. I still don't know who she was. Or him, for that matter.

Eventually, we moved to a neighborhood with wide streets and arching oaks, and a new doctor put me on a medication that blunted sensation and emotion. My cravings dulled to a docile purr. I didn't even see pokeweed again until I was in my twenties and old enough to resist. But sometimes I would pull my car over just to watch them dance across a field, the mere sight a comfort. I never told anyone else about them, or the pica diagnosis, the man at my feet or my trip to the hospital, or why I took the medications I did. Not even Henry. Not even when the pokeweed started coming up in the yard, brazen and leggy along the back fence.

The Cooper River is a haze of green beneath me. I keep glancing over my shoulder as my pace accelerates, the center of the bridge coming into view. At its maximum height, the road deck of the Arthur Ravenel Jr. Bridge stands at nearly two hundred feet. Maybe one in ten survive the fall. I've done my research. It's a calculated risk, but a risk all the same. Though it hardly matters; I'm dead either way. Henry will kill me. In a week. In a year. He's been working up to it. I see it glinting behind the dark centers of his eyes when he fucks me, one hand always at my throat. It is his greatest turn-on. If Henry had a dating profile it would read: *Enjoys antipasti and Beaujolais, Beethoven's Piano Sonata No. 14, and fantasizing about dead women.* Sometimes when he touches me, I see their faces—the women he wants to bury, the ones who will come after. They spark across my mind like saltpeter, ashen and gasping for breath. Something in me burns to save them, has to try. I hope it is enough, this plan. At least if I die today, it is by my own hand. At least they'll be safe.

The center of the bridge in sight, I pull my fists from my pockets and crush the berries into my mouth, chewing carefully, letting the liquid roll around my tongue. It's mid-August. A brutal summer has brought the berries out early, but they're most potent closer to fall. I ate extra just in case. Henry is always so particular about measurements. As an engineer, he doesn't leave anything to chance. Therefore, I can't either.

I swallow the mash and look across the water. My heart begins to pound. Ducking my head as I walk, I double over and shove a finger down my throat. It only takes half a second for most of the berries to come back up, splatting the pristine walkway in maroon pulp. I cup my hands beneath my mouth, covering my fingers in a slimy, purple mess. I grip the railing with them, letting the pokeweed smear across it. The sun will bake this to a rich, oxblood patina.

Glancing up, I see the black reflective eye of the camera overhead.

Now.

I spin around and back up, bumping awkwardly into the rail, raising my hands and shaking them. The man in the hoodie, an oblivious player in my little drama, draws closer, and I slow down, act scared, clutch my chest. My mouth opens in a silent scream as I climb the railing. My tears are real, even if the reason isn't. I must be fast now. No second thoughts or time for doubt, for the man in the black hoodie to intervene. I have both feet over when our eyes meet.

His steps slow. He stares at me, silent and wary. I can see the sense of obligation warring with his desire to stay unattached playing across his face. I want to tell him he's too late. There's nothing left of me to save. I want to tell him about my and Henry's first date at the Peninsula Grill. How he introduced himself to me by all *four* names—Henry Excelsior Walden Davenport. How he pronounced *foie gras* like he'd been saying it since birth. How he made me read that whole menu aloud a year later while he stood masturbating over me, a foot against my neck. I want to describe all the ingenious ways he found to torture me, sometimes in plain view of others. The ways I became invisible. The people who looked away.

But there's no time.

The man's eyes widen with alarm. Mine narrow. If I could stop and explain without ruining the effect I've so carefully orchestrated, I would. Instead, I straighten my spine as I count to three, throw my hands out in mock self-defense, and leap backward off the edge, dropping like an arrow. Legs straight. Arms tucked.

I squeeze my eyes tight as everything falls away and I resist the urge to flail. Henry trained me well.

When I break the water, the force ricochets up my bones. I splinter with pain—icy and needle-sharp—in a thousand places at once. But I don't pass out.

Instead, I swim.

2

Acacia

The mouth of the Atlantic is right there, waiting to swallow me whole. I'd swim farther, but I can't risk it.

I come up near the Charleston Harbor Marina, the bridge still hovering in the growing sunlight behind me. The boats are lined up like prize Thoroughbreds in a stable, bobbing gently on the surface, white and guileless. It's a dangerous move coming into these narrow, crowded channels. I could be spotted, and I can't afford any miscalculations. Henry can't know I climbed out of this river. But I'm still too stunned to think and driven by a survivalist instinct to leave the city while I have time. The clock is ticking, and every second counts. Once my absence is discovered, I won't be safe in Charleston.

I paddle down a central channel toward the shore. A dockhand in khakis and a faded T-shirt is helping a man pump out the holding tank on his boat despite the early hour. I hear the clipped stream of their conversation and try to make myself smaller in the water, moving closer to the boat bows, ducking between them to pass undetected. I want to sink beneath the surface, but the life vest makes that impossible. Unzipping my raincoat, I make quick work of the vest's plastic buckles and pull both pieces off. I leave the vest on a nearby cross dock—we're in a marina after all—but hold on to the raincoat. Henry's seen it before. The less I leave for him to piece together, the better.

"Thanks again for meeting me," the older man is saying with an entitled tone, as if he expected it. "I want to get an early start."

"No kids this time, Tom?" the young man asks.

"The wife took 'em to her sister's place in Summerton," the other replies flatly.

I freeze as their voices near, but the water laps softly, pushing me into their field of vision. I dip low, so only my eyes are above the surface. They're across the dock from me, angled toward the craft, but any sudden movement could garner unwanted attention. I pull my arms carefully to my sides and hold my breath, my gaze steady on them as the wavelets push me by. My heart pounds erratically, tripping over fear.

"Carol's always saying she wants to come, but then she always makes plans," the man begins complaining. "If it were up to her, I'd never get out on the water. You have to put your foot down," he says to the boy, instructive. "Can't let 'em boss you. Understand?"

The kid nods, disinterest hidden behind the reflective lenses of his polarized sunglasses.

I drift by, disembodied, unattached. A phantom of the harbor. For once, I enjoy being invisible.

Just as I think I am free, the kid yawns and turns his head in my direction. I drop below the surface, praying he doesn't notice the ripples. Through the murky waves I see him stand. My lungs burn but I don't dare come up until I'm hidden on the other side of a large deck boat. I push my face toward the sky and take a deep breath.

"I thought I saw a head, a woman. But it went down again," I can hear the kid explaining.

"Manatee," Tom says with confidence, clapping the kid on the back so hard I can hear it. "You're not the first to be fooled, son."

Grateful, I don't wait to hear the rest. I slip back under and carefully propel myself forward, coming up only when they are far enough behind for me to not be heard as I move. I swim between pilings to the bank. The light is spreading, but colors blend together, lacking sharpness. I pass through the marsh grass and drag myself onto the scrubby shore undetected. I fall onto my back and breathe, my eyes searching the sky for a portent that might tell me if I've pulled this off. But the clouds stretch long and thin, diluting the blue in meaningless smears, giving nothing away. I still have a very long way to go before I'm safe.

Now the pain begins to register. A terrible ache is radiating up the outside of my bare right foot. The first thing I did as the shock of my plunge gave way, and I began to rise toward the surface, was kick my shoes off into the water. I sit up to examine my foot, and a sharp pain pierces my left side. I bite back a cry. I've cracked a rib. Maybe two.

Carefully, I study the rest of my body. My jaw aches where my teeth ground together, and my chin is rubbed raw from the impact forcing the life vest up. My nose still stings from the water that rushed into it. Water I coughed out as I first cleared the surface, the taste of mud scrubbing the pokeweed from my mouth. But I am whole, if broken in a few places. The rib will heal. The foot worries me more. It is already swelling. There's no apparent bruising yet, but it will come. I press gently along the side and wince as I near the fracture. I'm lucky this is the worst of it, lucky the force of the impact didn't blow my hips out of their sockets. But a broken foot is not a triumph. I have a long way to walk.

I press myself up on my hands, gathering my good foot below me. Wrapping my arms around my middle protectively, I turn and start toward the beach club, keeping low so as not to be noticed. The pool will soon be full of shrieking kids and women working on their tans. I crouch so the boardwalk will shield me from view of early risers. Every other step is agonizing, and yet I delight in the pain. It is the first thing that's truly mine in two years' time. And I've had worse.

The street is quiet when I cross, the fine hairs around my face already drying out. Red has begun gathering beneath the skin of my foot. By tomorrow, it will turn purple-black.

I pick my way across the golf course to the nature trail, skirting the greens to remain inconspicuous. I came here three weeks ago, stopping at a local breakfast place in case he asked, making sure to bring back his favorite for an unconventional dinner that night. Henry has always taken a guilty pleasure in biscuits and gravy, though he rarely indulges in food he considers lowborn. I took him to a Waffle House on our second date. I don't think he ever forgave me for it.

It's not much, this park. A few trees and some lookout towers. But it's enough. There's a small culvert running under the trail. I watch an errant dog walker pass before ducking down and poking my head in. The backpack I taped under here on my last trip is thankfully still waiting. It takes a moment to peel the duct tape away. I rip it from the pack once I manage to free it, stuffing the tape inside. The trees and scrub provide some cover as I tug the raincoat and tank top off, stuffing them into an empty trash bag I had waiting. I pull on the *Miami* T-shirt I bought with some cash at Goodwill a few weeks ago, its faded pink and turquoise design a welcome sight. Bending down, I peel off my drenched leggings and pull on the dry underwear and jeans I packed. Everything wet goes into the trash bag, which I tuck inside the backpack. I find a hair tie inside and knot my damp, blond hair behind my head, pulling a bucket hat down over it. Next are a pair of slip-on sneakers, also purchased at Goodwill. They're a size and a half too big—an issue I thought would be problematic. Now, I'm thankful. It's the only reason I get the right one on at all.

I emerge from the park looking for all the world like just another tourist on a hike, but I keep my head down. There's a grocery store near the bridge. I've shopped in it before. I follow the road for nearly a dozen blocks and take a cross street over. Whenever possible, I walk behind the lampposts, hoping to avoid CCTV cameras. By the time I make it to the shiny, automated doors, I'm rigid with pain. I beeline for the pharmacy and find a walking boot in the first-aid aisle. It's one of those conspicuous Velcro numbers that doubles the size of your leg, but it's my only hope of healing this right without going to a hospital. I grab a pair of compression socks, a super-size bottle of aspirin and some water, a toothbrush and toothpaste, and a hair-coloring kit in Cinnamon Kiss. I pay at the pharmacy window with cash I hid in the lining of my pack and make my way behind the store to put the sock and boot on.

The relief is instant. I slide down the painted block wall to the sidewalk and stretch my leg out before me, popping three aspirin and drinking half the water in one long gulp. The sun glares off the shiny green paint of the dumpster behind the store. I want to sit here for the next several hours, a nobody behind a nameless grocery store, close my eyes, and bask in the lightheadedness that comes with total anonymity. As if the last two years of my abusive marriage are just a bad hangover I need to sleep off. But I can't rest yet. The more physical distance I create, the safer I become. I took the thing Henry valued most with me over that bridge. Not my life, but my death. I stole his moment. He'll hunt my corpse, but there won't be one. And that will leave him restless.

There's a boutique hotel a few blocks away on the other side of Highway 17. I stayed there for a friend's bachelorette party before Henry and I met. I remember the posh, private restrooms with wide pedestal sinks and doors that lock, and I need a place to dye my hair. Maybe I can catch a ride with someone leaving town. Pulling out the nineteen dollars I have rubber-banded together—what's left after paying for the post office and Goodwill clothes, weeks of bus fare, the fake IDs, the life vest, and the drugstore items—I realize I'll have to. I couldn't risk Henry seeing these purchases, couldn't pay for them with one of our many credit or debit cards. Without the benefit of my career, my own money and accounts—all things Henry saw fit to talk me out of over our time together—I could no longer buy things without them being watched or questioned.

That cash—four hundred fifty-eight dollars—was all that was in my mother's bank account when she died, the tiny apartment she'd been renting bare except for two folding chairs, a glass frying pan and some basic utensils, a closet of old clothes, and a twin mattress neatly made up on the floor. Where the rest of her life had gone, I couldn't say. Though I suspected Gerald had a role in it.

I didn't need the money then. So I stashed it in the pocket of her favorite cardigan, the one she always used to wear when I was growing up—green with little lily of the valley flowers embroidered on the front. I would take it out from time to time and press the soft fibers of the sweater to my nose, smell her there, thick like woodsmoke, roll the dollars between my palms, and wonder where it had all gone wrong. After I left at eighteen? When I first ate the berries at five? Before I was born? Were we always destined for this—a long disappointing road winding toward fallout? If I retraced my steps, could I piece us back together, keep her here, understand? I would always put the money, the sweater, back with a shake of the head and the heavy knowing that whatever power had been required to repair our relationship, or even give us one in the first place, I didn't possess it. But I could never bring myself to spend the money. Until now.

I push up and limp over to the dumpster, tossing the trash bag of wet clothes inside. The city is waking up, and it's time to go. Returning to my pack, I take stock of my worldly possessions. A second compression sock. A bottle of aspirin. A toothbrush. A tube of Colgate. A plastic comb. An army-green bucket hat. A Rhode Island ID and its duplicate.

I pick up one of the IDs and stare at it. The face looking back at me is a woman I don't recognize. She is a free woman. A lone woman. She has no past, no future. She exists only in this moment. I am her now. *Acacia* . . . I check the ID. Acacia *Lee.* I remember choosing it for the meaning ascribed by the website I was on—*clearing in the woods.*

Sighing, I drop the ID next to the wad of money and zip up my backpack. Until today, when I ate a jarful of deadly berries and threw myself over a bridge, *this* was the riskiest part of my escape plan.

Two months ago, the paper ran an article about university students overrunning the local bars with fake IDs bought from China. I read it on my phone in the passenger seat of Henry's Jaguar on our way to the Dock Street Theatre. They were putting on a production of Tennessee Williams's *The Glass Menagerie.* Henry favors stories that feature fragile women.

"What are you reading?" he asked.

"Something about Bitcoin," I said, taking my cue from the article, which indicated that's how some students were paying for the IDs. "I don't really understand it." I killed the screen and laid the phone in my lap.

His eyes slid to mine. "You shouldn't read things over your head," he told me. "Let me handle the investments."

It was a quiet warning. He didn't like me straying into subjects more strenuous than fashion or diet trends, anything that could lead to independent thought.

"Of course," I replied. But I read the article again that night in the bathroom, and once more the next day while he was at work. It was like a toxic seed that once ingested burrowed deep inside, sprouting against my will. I had thought about leaving before. One hundred thousand times I'd fantasized about it. But Henry controlled our life together, and if I left, he would find me. Not to mention the women, the ones I saw percolating in the dark folds of his mind, the ones he would kill once I was out of the way, once he stopped fighting his urges and gave over to the monster within. As long as I was here and breathing, so were they. It wasn't enough to leave Henry. I needed to stop him.

But if I became someone else entirely. If I didn't just leave but was dead already . . . Suddenly, the world was colored with possibility. I couldn't save *this* life, but I could find my way to a new life altogether. And in the process, I could hold him accountable, put him where he belonged. I could save the others. The cogs of my mind whirred day and night, plotting. I memorized the name of the website listed in the article, but I was too afraid to use it. Instead, I rolled it over and over in my brain when I lay next to him at night, a private affair I was having with an idea. If he hadn't driven me to the woods, I might never have used it.

It was a warm night in June. He didn't come home after work. I waited up, like he wanted. I made dinner but didn't eat it. Henry never liked for me to eat without him in the evenings. If he was late, I was to wait. I decanted the wine and sat beside the fireplace watching the flames flicker across the leaded crystal, orange on burgundy. It reminded me of something I couldn't quite place. Eventually, I dozed off and dreamed of pokeweed berries.

When I woke, it was dark, the fire was out, and Henry was standing over me. "Get up," he said with bared teeth.

I did as he asked, the wine still sitting in its open decanter, dark like dried blood. Maybe it was that he didn't find me waiting. Maybe I had been snoring. Maybe something went wrong at work. Maybe the men in the break room made him feel inferior. I would never know. In the end, he didn't really need a reason beyond that he liked it.

He led me by the hair to the car and told me to get in. We drove for hours, until the houses and stores and lights grew thin and there was nothing but trees and night. It was well after midnight when he pulled off down a dirt path, stopping before a chained swing barrier. "Get out."

I didn't have any shoes on, but I knew better than to argue. He walked me up the road and had me turn onto a narrow game trail. We followed it deep into the woods to a small meadow with a stand of pines on the other side. He pointed to the ground between the trees. "Here," he said.

I stared at him. Tears striped my cheeks despite my efforts to hold them in, but I bit back any sound. I didn't know this place or how he knew it.

"This is where I will bury you," he told me. "Your body will rot here, and no one will ever find you."

I looked down at my future grave, a patch of quiet earth. If he had picked a place and dared to show it to me, we were close, much closer than I realized. I might not make the drive home. I could only hope he'd want to torture me with the knowledge first, like a cat toying with a mouse.

"I'm sorry," I said, not knowing what I was apologizing for, but knowing better than to say anything else. Correcting me was Henry's favorite hobby—the way I dressed, the way I spoke—but what he really loved was hurting me for no reason. When his control slipped and the monster slunk out of its cage and my humiliation had no bearing, that was what he lived for.

He caressed my face, then pinched my bottom lip until I cried out. "Of course, you are. Because you are a foolish, bovine woman and a sorry fuck. Now lie down."

He raped me there, on my future grave, *two* hands on my throat. The last thing I saw before blacking out were the red stems of a pokeweed bush nearby.

I was surprised to wake the next morning, back under the crisp sheets in our bed, the house silent around me. Henry had already gone to work. My mouth and neck were badly bruised, and it hurt to swallow. He was getting careless.

The next week, I used the computer at our local FedEx to place my order for a Rhode Island ID. Taking the picture should have been hard, but it wasn't. The side of the building was white as a sheet. I asked the young man behind the counter to come out with me and snap my photo with my phone. He didn't even question what it was for. I had to wire the cash through a Western Union in a nearby bank.

I watched the mailbox for weeks. Henry liked to bring the mail in when he came home from work, but packages were left at our door. Because he didn't want them stolen, he'd have me set them in the foyer until he could open them. A month after my trip to FedEx, we got a small box wrapped in brown paper. I brought it in and opened it in my closet. The IDs were tucked neatly behind a set of decorated chopsticks. I pulled up the carpet in the back corner and slid them underneath. When Henry came home later, he asked about the package. He'd seen it on the door camera he had installed the year before. I showed him the chopsticks. "They're a gift," I said. "I thought you'd like your own for when we go to Izakaya." We ate sushi regularly. Henry called it "civilized food."

He backhanded me and the chopsticks went flying. "They're beautiful," he said. "Never open my mail again."

The slam of the dumpster lid jars me from the memory. I spin to see a young man in the grocery store uniform brushing his hands off. "You need help or something?" he asks.

"No," I quickly answer. "Just resting."

"We don't let homeless sleep back here," he says.

"I'm not homeless," I try to explain, thinking how I must look. "I'm leaving anyway."

I've scooted past him when he stops me. "Hey, don't I know you?"

My heart throbs once, twice, then goes alarmingly still. "I don't think so."

He walks around to face me, cheeks lifting, suddenly friendly. "Yeah, you're that woman. You saved the guy from choking last year, the cop. They put you on the news."

Fear skates down my throat and hits my stomach with a thud. I'd acted on pure instinct that night. Adrenaline driving me out of my chair before I knew what was happening. When it was over, I'd even felt proud, believing that maybe balance had been re-stored. That by saving this one, I'd undone that terrible day when I was five. That there was something salvageable in me, some-thing worth loving. But Henry was so enraged by the attention it brought, he beat me senseless later. I close my eyes. This cannot be happening. "I don't know what you mean."

"Course you do," he says undeterred, his smile sure as the sun. "I remember your eyes. Greenest I've ever seen before or since."

3

Don

My eyes are not always green. They're more gold really, a strange sort of hazel, like tarnished jewelry, the patina of brass or copper. The green comes and goes, following a cycle I can't trace, showing up like iridescent June beetles at the right season, the glint of pond water when the light is just so. They were green when I bit the man. I remember him saying so, the way he bent over to look into my face, a sticky gleam in his eye like hard candy before he stood, his hand clamping on my shoulder, his thumb running down my trachea. And they were green when I met Henry, staying that way for months until after we were married, dulling eventually with the despondency of our life together, only to flare up at odd intervals, often when things were at their worst. Apparently, they are green now, precisely when I need to be at my least noticeable, like a beacon that gives me away. What, I wonder, are they signaling this time? It can't be good.

I hobble several blocks in the sunlight, crossing to make my way into the lobby of the smart hotel, looking entirely out of place. The desk girl wears a neat suit and is surrounded by ivory columns, though she has limp brown hair and lipstick that is too orange for her skin tone. Her face is stony when she sees me. I try to slip past, duck toward the hallway with the elegant bathrooms, but she barks out, "Miss, can I help you? Are you a guest here?"

"I'm meeting someone," I tell her. "At the bar." I point a finger in its direction as if this is irrefutable proof.

Her eyes narrow with suspicion. It's still morning. "Do you have a reservation?"

"For the bar?" I return.

I see her jaw grind. "Can I see your ID?"

I hesitate, then reach into my pack and approach the counter like it's a judge's bench, arm stretched out.

She plucks the card from my hand, studying it with hungry eyes. When she can find nothing wrong, she passes it back, a flicker of defeat across her lips. "We have a policy against loitering, Ms. Lee," she says, voice tight.

"I'll keep that in mind," I tell her.

"See that you do."

Smiling politely, I turn and head outside to the pool, passing the bathroom on the way, lugging my booted foot up a barstool. I order a glass of the house white because it's the cheapest thing on the menu and still costs half of what I have left. It's half past eight, but I figure I've earned this drink after narrowly escaping death. Beside me, a woman is tucking into her crab omelet like it's the last meal she will get on this earth. The smell of Swiss cheese and fresh chives hits me and my stomach rumbles, but I can't afford the food. When she gets up to leave, I slide an avocado slice from her plate and shove it in my mouth while the bartender's back is turned. I'd steal another, but he quickly notices and whisks the plate away.

I drink slowly, letting my eyes crawl around the pool. A man in a fedora comes down and seats himself near me about ten minutes after I arrive. I try to make eye contact, but he's uninterested, scrolling on his phone. Just as I rise to move a seat closer, he's joined by a woman in a strappy bikini and short cover-up. Awkwardly, I double back, returning to my seat with my face burning. To make matters worse, the receptionist from the lobby keeps checking up on me. I raise my glass to her, and she slinks away. I'll have to leave soon. She's not likely to forget I'm here.

It's not like this in the movies. In the movies, a pretty woman can sit down at a bar and be swarmed by interested, available men who will buy her breakfast and offer to drive her anywhere. Movies are full of shit. I count between sips to make sure I don't drink too fast. Two women in caftans make themselves comfortable on the lounge chairs—they don't look like they're going anywhere—and a third woman in a sharp black suit asks for a seltzer water with lime. I smile at her, but she responds by slipping her AirPods in and taking a call.

My glass slowly empties, every drop like the sands in an hourglass. The bartender gives me a couple of sidelong looks, but I pretend not to notice. Before the wine is completely gone, I rise and move back through the doors, darting into the ladies' room and locking it behind me. I slump against the porcelain sink with relief. But there's no time to relax. That vulture of a receptionist will find me missing and question where I've gotten off to.

I pull the box of hair color from my pack and quickly mix tube one into bottle *b,* clamping a finger over the spout as I shake it furiously. I don't part my hair in the neat little rows I remember my mother doing that time she decided to go red. Instead, I concentrate on the hair around my face, squirting the rest of the dye like a tangle of Silly String across the crown, rubbing it in with gloved hands. The instructions say to wait half an hour, but I doubt I'll get that long. Sure enough, fourteen minutes in there's a knock at the door.

"Just a minute!" I call, falling silent for the next five.

Another, more aggressive knock sounds.

"Hold on!" I bluster, hoping to buy a few more minutes.

But a third knock is followed by the sharp strike of the receptionist's voice. "Come out, Ms. Lee! It's time for you to leave."

I turn the water on high and duck my head as far under it as I can, using my hands to splash it across my neck. The sink runs the color of Mississippi mud, deep and red and unforgiving. I hear the clerk calling, "I have security!" as I use the hand towel to dry my ends, wipe up the rim of the basin, the splatters across the wall.

When I finally look in the mirror, it takes a moment to adjust.

I haven't seen myself like this in nine years, having kept even my roots at bay with regular salon visits since coming to Charleston. My hair hangs like dark drapes parted over my face, glinting with copper threads, the color of my childhood. I am transported in time, old insecurities seeping in like gas under the door, that feeling of being unwanted, worse than being alone. Inside, something stirs, unpredictable and fierce, a part of myself I do not know but recognize. Beside my hair, the sunny color of my skin suddenly looks pale, and my eyes are greener than I've ever seen them.

I wad up the dye-stained towel and shove it into the bathroom trash can, opening the door just as her fist is raised to pound again.

Her mouth drops open in disbelief. "Why is your hair wet?" she asks. "And *dark*?"

"No reason," I answer and try to sidle past her.

She glares at me, moving to stand in my path. "You need to leave." Behind her, a security guard hovers with his hands on his hips like a human barricade.

"That's what I'm trying to do," I say defiantly. "I only finished my wine a few minutes ago."

Her eyes narrow. She crosses her arms. "You think you're the first prostitute we've had in here? You a meth head?" She takes in my shirt and jeans, my booted foot. "Don't deny it," she barks at me. "James saw you."

The bartender must have noticed my poor attempts to be friendly with the other diners. The only thing I want to proposition someone for is a ride, maybe an egg. I limp around her, jerking my arm away as she tries to grab me. "There's no need for this," I tell them. "I'm going."

She follows me into the lobby, where the security guard leans over the counter and grabs a phone.

"What's he doing?" I ask, clutching my backpack to my chest.

"He's calling the police," she snaps.

I round on her, needing to calm her down, deescalate. "No, don't do that. Please. You don't understand. No police."

Her mouth turns down at the corners, and I realize I only

sound more guilty. "Don't loiter in the parking lot either," she says. "We can see you on the cameras."

My whole body goes cold. Desperate to leave, I limp rapidly toward the doors, floor slick under my walking boot, the jaunty beat of my stride impossible to overcome. Behind me, I hear the security guard call out as he hangs up the phone. Panicked, I slam into a mother with a preschooler in one hand and a suitcase in the other. "Sorry," I apologize, stooping to pick up the book I caused her to drop, annoyed that I let it slow me down.

This penchant for dutiful niceness is what landed me with someone like Henry in the first place, that made it possible for him to creep over me like an invasive vine until I was buried, submerged in his will. If I were the kind of woman to flip the desk girl off or kick the woman's book aside, I doubt Henry would have even tried. Even my mother, for all her interest in blending in, knew when to let others stew in their own juices. But I am forever trying to get gold stars, to be the good little girl it is impossible for me to be.

Outside, the parking lot is dotted with cars. I start across it, hoping to get clear of the hotel before the cops show up. The faint wail of sirens sounds a few blocks away, causing my heart to skip several beats. Even if I make it to the sidewalk, the police will be looking for a woman with this T-shirt and hair color and eye color, a giant boot on her foot. I'm in jeopardy wherever I go in this city, a walking billboard for anyone to read.

An older gentleman in a business suit is stuffing a leather and herringbone suitcase into his trunk. I shuffle up behind him and tap his shoulder, flashing my most nonthreatening smile. "Can I ask where you're headed?"

He hesitates, taking in my faded shirt—the neck rimmed in Cinnamon Kiss—and canvas backpack.

"I thought if we were headed the same direction, maybe you could use the company?" I try to sound nonchalant, but my voice hitches as the sirens approach.

He emits a small noise. He doesn't look scared, just surprised.

People don't do these things anymore, I realize. They don't ask strangers for rides. There's an app for that.

The receptionist from the lobby barrels through the hotel doors with her pet security guard, waving her arms at me angrily. "Never mind," I say quickly to the man, ducking between his car and the next.

He leans toward me and takes a deep breath. His eyes shift to the shouting receptionist.

I back away, pointing to my boot. "It hurts to stand, is all. I didn't want to wait." Tears gather behind my eyes as I turn to limp away.

He exhales behind me. "I'm going to DC. I can take you as far as that."

I turn back. "Are you sure?"

His eyes travel from my chest to my face. He clears his throat. "I'm Don. You in some kind of trouble?"

The blare of sirens is bearing down on us, and the security guard is stalking in our direction. "I need to get out of the city," I admit. "Now."

"Get in," he says, unlocking the doors of his Toyota Avalon with the key fob. He climbs into the driver's seat and starts the engine, backing out hurriedly after I close the door, before the security guard can stop us.

As we pull out of the lot, we pass a police car pulling in. I duck, pretending to dig through my backpack. When I sit back up, I let out a sigh of relief. We are zipping down the boulevard, the beaming rectangle of the hotel shrinking behind us. My fake ID isn't meant to hold up against law enforcement or background checks. I have no social security number to go with this new name. No birth certificate.

Don leans toward me, and I smell the bourbon on his breath. He sniffs my hair and his lashless eyelids flutter. "I'm Don," he says.

"You told me that already," I remind him, my stomach twisting with sudden uncertainty. "I'm Acacia. I work at NYU. I came here to stay with a friend for the summer."

"Sure you are, honey," he tells me as we pull onto the freeway. "Sure you are."

WHEN WE FIRST met, Henry gave me his four names and I gave him my one.

"I'm Piers," I said, sizing him up—the silk tie and gold cuff links, those little round, tortoiseshell frames he was so proud of. *Expensive nerd* wasn't exactly my taste in men, but my taste in men had gotten me nowhere. I was lonely. My mother had died only weeks before, taking too much with her to the grave—any hope I had of a reconciliation, the memory of that day when I was five, answers about what happened. Grief would sneak up on me in the most unexpected ways—in the middle of a movie, on the toilet, in line at the deli. I suddenly ached for her quiet hostility as dearly as one might a favored stuffed animal, that haze of fear passing over her when she looked at me. Instead, I found myself abruptly alone in the world.

At least he would impress my clients. They were all I had left.

I remember his smile went lopsided and his eyes creased. At the time, I thought he was just confused. Later, I would come to know that look. It meant he was displeased but not in a position to express it. It was a look that meant I had it coming.

"Piers *what*?" he asked.

"Piers Corbin," I said. "No middle name."

He rubbed his chin. "Is that short for something?"

I'd grown used to the reactions to my name over the years. It seemed all wrong for me growing up. Boyish, British, jutting into the air like the sharp end of a knife. I never understood why my mother chose it. In my work, it had fostered a baseless impression of rarefied heritage, one I did little to refute, that lured my clients like honeydew. The murky void of my past as enticing as a rare textile, a silk brocade of their imagining, the emperor's new clothes. But I didn't want it to have the same effect on him. It would be nice, I had thought, to have one person truly know me.

"Not at all. My mother always wanted a boy," I told him. "It seems I disappointed her from the very beginning."

His smile broadened. "A condition I am most familiar with," he said amiably. Leaning in, he added, "My mother always wanted a duke."

YOU CAN LEARN a lot about a person in six hours.

I have learned that Don is fifty-seven years old. That he's a political consultant of some kind, married to a woman named Darla who has been fighting ovarian cancer, with three grown children, all boys. One is a dentist. One just got married. One joined the navy and is stationed in San Diego. That they have always owned Labrador retrievers. Their latest model is named Silky. She's a parvo survivor.

I've also learned that Don needs to stop approximately every hour and a half to pee. That he keeps a thermos full of bourbon under the seat. That he is lactose intolerant and eats red meat at least once a day. That he and Darla have been sleeping in separate rooms for three years. That he hasn't had a captive audience like this in at least a decade. That he pays for everything with an American Express Platinum Card, except gas, which he puts on a Shell card. That his passcode at the pump is 0909—his birthday.

Somewhere between his litany of complaints on the health care system and a recitation of his wife's latest demands, I fall asleep. I must be out for two hours or more. When I wake up, we're no longer on I-95.

"Where are we?" I ask Don, who has removed his tie and unbuttoned his collar. I notice his thermos is empty.

"Don't you worry about that," he says, patting my thigh with a thick, brutish hand, bloated fingers. He's a large man, big in frame. His bald head nearly brushes the ceiling. Beneath the suit of fat encasing his body, there are muscles twice the size of mine. Sweat beads on my temples, dosed with epinephrine.

I move my leg over and his hand falls away. "I don't recognize this road."

"Taking a little detour," he tells me, grinning ghoulishly. "The scenic route."

"I'm in kind of a hurry," I tell him. "Scenery doesn't matter."

Don's yellowing eyes slide over me. There is a flash of rumpled sheets in my mind, dewy skin, a bruised knee tucked against her body as a man faces the hotel window, dragging his dress shirt over sweaty arms. *You have the room till morning,* I hear Don's voice say. *Enjoy it.* When he leaves, she starts weeping.

"Watch the road," I tell him, snapping back to the present.

"I think you know where we're going," he says. "We have a connection, you and I."

I wonder if he also had a connection with the underage girl in the hotel. If I saw what I think I saw. "I needed a ride," I say. "You're just a way between two points."

He grins, undeterred. "Come on. Don't you want to have a little fun before we get into the city? Something to remember me by?"

My palms start to itch. I'd thought once we cleared Raleigh that I could relax. That he was a sad, disgruntled man in a sour marriage who needed a good listener. "Pull over."

"What? *Now?*" He looks confused, then his face lights up. "I was going to get us a room, but if you can't wait."

"I feel sick," I tell him. "Just pull over." It's not a total lie.

The county road we're on has a narrow shoulder bordering farmland. He slows down and rolls his car onto the grass. "Acacia," he says, turning to me. "That's pretty."

I tug at the door handle, but it's locked, and he's pushed the childproof button. "Let me out," I demand.

He scoots across the console toward me. "What's your real name, huh?" he asks in a husky voice. "I bet it's even prettier."

"Just let me out here," I repeat. "I can walk."

But he's on me before I can get all the words out, his hands everywhere—squeezing my breast, unbuttoning my jeans, pulling at my shirt and face. "You smell good," he whispers hungrily. "Like gardenia bushes in the summer. They used to grow by the house where I grew up. That was my favorite house. It's gone now."

I know he's drunk because I smell like ammonia and river mud and because it's an oddly specific description. I claw at his face and arms, but he hardly notices. Another woman streaks across my mind, a fat hand flattened over her mouth. Don pins one of my arms to my side, his weight bearing down on my broken rib, causing me to cry out. His other hand is inching down my panties.

"Come on, girly. I brought you all this way. I bought you those peanuts and that sandwich, all that bottled water. What's in it for me? This is what you wanted, right? This is what you really wanted."

I turn away and scream and he jerks my face back, mouth gaping over mine, bourbon-tainted saliva slathering my lips and chin. His tongue is as strong and as determined as the rest of him. In his ardor, he loosens his grip and I free my other hand, managing a weak punch to his throat. He draws back, surprised, but his grin only widens.

"Hard to get? Hardly seems right for a girl in your position, but I'll play along."

It's the way his eyebrows fall, slumping over his eyes, that I notice first. Then his hand goes to his throat. "How hard did you hit me?"

He starts wheezing after that. His eyes bulge and his face purples and his other hand clutches his stomach that gurgles loudly. I flatten myself against the passenger door, unsure what I'm seeing.

"What did you do to me?" he wrenches out before the first spasm hits, every muscle in his neck and shoulders coiling over itself. His mouth clenches at a weird angle and his eyes roll as the seizure takes over. I see my moment and scrabble at the handle, but still the door won't unlock.

Don grimaces and tears at his door, swinging it wide and vomiting all over the gravel. It's a pained, guttural sound.

Frightened and desperate, I grab the key fob where he's wedged it in the ashtray as he doubles over outside the car. I press at the buttons frantically until I hear the familiar click and jerk the handle. The passenger door flies open, and I tumble out backward, scrabbling away on hands and feet. The cabin light flares on and the car dings menacingly as Don contorts in another peculiar spasm. This time when he vomits, I smell the blood. And he collapses.

Getting to my feet, I take shaky steps around the trunk and find him lying face-first on the ground.

"Don?" I whisper, my voice hoarse. I nudge him with a toe. He doesn't respond. "Don!" I pound his back and struggle to roll him over. When I finally succeed, his eyes are open and lifeless, his posture limp, his mouth still. No breath emanates from his nostrils.

Shit, I think. *Shit. Shit. Shit.* His vomit is the color oxblood at my feet.

Suddenly, I am five years old again. The breeze toys with the thin wisps of my hair as I squat down, poking a finger into the man's shoulder. My toothmarks dot his forearm, the glisten of spit and blood in them. I don't know to feel bad yet. There is a buoyancy inside me, something rising like heat, lifting me up. I smile and slip another berry between my lips, but I'm not hungry anymore. In the distance, my mother's voice is calling, the pitch tilted and wrong, blemishing the afternoon.

Don, I realize in that moment, is very, very dead. And still, I feel scared of him. I taste the bourbon in my mouth and wipe my face again and again. If I leaned down now and pumped his chest, put my mouth over his and blew, would he hold me there? Would he come to and finish what he started? Would I be saving a rapist?

The shame within me stirs, a mix of regret and confusion. This is a bad, bad thing. *Again.* And I don't know how it happened. I can hear my mother's voice echoing from the past: *What have you done?*

I wish I knew.

The car dings, and I recognize that even if we are on an unpopular road, we are making quite a scene. If I stand here too long, someone will happen upon us. There will be police and an ambulance. I can't risk it.

I step over Don's body and reach into the driver's seat to grab his discarded tie. I use it to tug his wallet from his front pants pocket. Nine dollars won't get me far, and I can't use his credit card without leaving a trail. Don doesn't look like he's hurting for much with his swollen belly, twill dress shirt, and eel-skin shoes, but he's only got a twenty. Looks like plastic is the way he likes to play. I pocket the cash and Shell card and throw his wallet into whatever stalky crop they're growing in the field next to us. Climbing into the driver's seat, I drop his thermos on the ground before pulling the passenger door closed.

I should feel something, I think. Something more than panic at what this might cost me. Something more than displaced shame. A man just died. And I did nothing to save him. But I don't feel sad for Don. I only feel relieved to be rid of him and grateful for his car. When I saw that policeman choke at the restaurant in Radcliffeborough, I wrapped my arms around his chest without hesitation, jabbing my fists into his solar plexus until he coughed up the chicken lodged in his windpipe. I remember the intense fear that something terrible was happening, how he might be lost. His life, however unknown to me, had a palpable weight, like gold bullion. He had a value I could taste in the room. Even after saving him, knowing he was okay, I was so shaken I couldn't eat. That was before I learned he was an officer, before I saw the fury in my husband's face, before the reporter showed up.

Watching Don die was nothing like that.

Maybe Henry has finally broken something in me. Maybe I'm no good for men anymore. Maybe I never was.

4

Myrtle

Meeting her was a shock.

I didn't grow up with family. My father died before I was born. I had no siblings. If there were grandparents, they never came for birthdays or holidays, so I just assumed they'd all died. Eventually Gerald came along, but he wasn't family. My mother clung to him out of some desperate longing for normalcy, trying to create the appearance of a true American household. But we were always just loose parts stowed together. We didn't fit. Even when it was only my mom and me. Sometimes I would catch her looking at me, as if I were a thing to be wary of.

I was nine years old and deep into the shame of my nightly forays in the woods and the resulting diagnosis when a woman showed up. I remember lounging on a plastic chaise in the backyard when she came strolling over, a thick flood of dark hair pouring over her shoulders, flashing with copper glints, like mine. She was exquisite in a pair of stiff, wide-leg pants, the scuffed leather toe of her boots peeking out, little purple flowers embroidered on her shirt, and a knit scarf wrapped too many times to count around her neck.

She stood over me as I froze, staring up into those twinkling eyes, the color of shamrocks. "Do you know me, child?"

I shook my head slowly.

"Just as well." She sighed. "Let me get a look at you." Bending down, she lifted my chin, turning my face as she studied it. I'd been at the berries again, and a thick drop of wine-colored juice sat on my lip. She wiped it off with a finger that she quickly put in her mouth, tasting. "Stick out your tongue," she told me, straightening.

I did as I was told. It was no doubt stained a blistering magenta color.

She rolled her eyes and crossed her arms. "Where's your mother?"

I pointed toward the house, the sliding glass doors that led into the living room.

Without another word, she marched across our lawn and let herself in.

Once she disappeared inside, I crept slowly behind and wedged myself under the kitchen window so I could eavesdrop.

"Can't just come striding in here!" I caught my mother saying.

"Shall I go back out and knock?" the woman asked.

"No, of course not. But what if Gerald had been home?" my mother continued.

I could practically hear the woman shrug. "I'm sure he'll learn what you are sooner or later. And then what, Lily? Have you asked yourself that?"

My mother made a disgruntled noise.

I rose on the balls of my feet and peered over the window ledge. My mother was leaning back against the kitchen sink, hands gripping the counter. Before her, the woman loomed, tall as any man and straight as a pine tree.

She picked up a coffee mug from the nearby dinette table. It was Gerald's favorite, shaped like a football, and was never far from his ashtray. "What are you playing at, Lily?" she asked my mother with a tsk. "You know better than this. We aren't on an episode of *Bewitched*. Our magic doesn't work like that. There is a price for being who we are, *what* we are."

My mother scowled. She walked over and pulled the mug from the woman's hand, tucking it against her chest. "Don't tell me how to live my life."

"Someone has to." The woman flourished an arm to indicate

the house. "This is not a life for us. You know that. *This* is not something we get to have."

"He takes care of us," my mother stubbornly insisted. "You wouldn't understand, but we *need* him." She set the cup in the sink. "You made your choices," she said quietly. "And I make mine."

"What would Grandma Laurel say?" the woman admonished. "This is my sister's fault. Angel was always dreaming of a different life when we were growing up—princes and kisses and fairy tales—running headlong into what she knew she couldn't have. She never taught you right."

"This has nothing to do with her," my mother quietly insisted.

"It has everything to do with her," the woman replied. "She was a fool. And she's made you one as well. Took me long enough to find you here, playing housewife while that daughter of yours languishes in the dark with no clue of her heritage, already in bloom, early just like you."

Suddenly, my mother spun on her. "Leave Piers out of this. She's a child."

The woman rolled her eyes again. "If only. She's one of us, Lily, and she'll overripen. It will cost her, if it hasn't already. Just like it did you."

My mother's head shot up. "Don't you dare speak of it."

The woman sighed and placed a hand on my mother's shoulder. "I'm trying to help you, Lily. Please let me."

My mother shook her off. "Like you helped my mother?" She gave a hard stare. "Thank you, but we'll help ourselves. Piers's gifts will wither on the vine. Mine have. Muscles atrophy when you stop using them."

The woman looked sad, the delicate corners of her lips curving down. "You know it doesn't work like that."

"Doesn't matter," my mother said. "We have drugs now, things that weren't available to our mothers and grandmothers. We don't have to be *this* anymore. I'm getting better every day. She's getting better every day."

The woman rubbed forcefully at her forehead. "You don't really believe that, Lily. Let me take her before it's too late. Let me teach her. I know Patrick's death has been hard on you. Sometimes, despite our best efforts, love happens. No one blames you for that. But this . . . it's bordering on unforgivable. Whatever my sister's faults, even she saw reason in the end. Let me do this for you, for *her*. To keep you both safe."

"She's *my* daughter. Not yours," my mother snapped. "How dare you come here and threaten me."

The woman drew herself up to her full height, stiffening. "She belongs to the venery, Lily. The *family*. She's not yours alone. She's also my great-niece. We have to look out for each other."

"I don't have a family," my mother said coldly.

The woman's face hardened to a beautiful edge. "No," she agreed with just as much venom. "I suppose you don't anymore. You should be careful, Lily. *Those who hunt alone often starve.*"

My mother narrowed her eyes. "I don't hunt anymore. But if I catch you near me or Piers again, I'll expose us all. You know I can."

The woman tapped a finger against her arm before finally speaking. "When he finds out, this man of yours—and he will—he dies. Do you understand?"

My mother didn't respond.

"Lily, promise me, and I won't tell them where you are. If you don't, I can't stop them—"

"Yes," she interrupted, her shoulders sagging, beaten. "I understand."

The tall woman sighed. "Educate her while there's still time. At the very least, explain what's happening to her. She's more lost than you ever were. We need her, Lily."

Angry tears slipped down my mother's face. "Go," she answered through gritted teeth, her head hanging. "Just go."

I watched as the other woman spun away from the kitchen, heading toward the door. Ducking, I stumbled a few steps into the grass before the sliding door opened and she stepped out, my mother behind her. She looked between us, her face suddenly uncertain. "Your . . . *aunt* was just leaving. Say goodbye, Piers."

I waved as she started past me. The glass door slammed, my mother retreating into the house. The woman paused in the yard, beckoning, and I approached her. "Piers—that's an unusual name," she said.

"It's for boys," I told her.

"Is that what you think?" She eyed me skeptically.

I nodded. "Mommy wanted a boy instead of me. She said so."

Her eyes softened. "Your mother loves you, child, whatever foolishness she speaks." Her fingers toyed with a lock of my hair, nearly identical to her own.

"But . . ." I whispered, confessional, "I did a bad thing."

Her eyes flared wider, flicking to the house and back. "Did you now?"

I nodded slowly, brimming with unexpected tears.

She brushed them away with the end of her scarf. It smelled of plums and rosemary. "There now. We mustn't cry over spilt milk. Was this very recently?"

I craned up at her, my neck crunching behind the weight of my head as I shook it from side to side.

Her eyes glittered like something shimmering in the dark. "Did he hurt you, the bad thing you did? Did he hurt you first?"

I gaped, my mouth a porthole—how did she know?—and shook my head again.

"I bet," she began, "that if you think very hard, you'll find he hurt someone even if it wasn't you."

The lips like death, the unblinking eyes—the woman I'd seen only in my mind, like a streak of memory, when I'd first laid eyes on him. "But I hurt him," I tried to explain. Didn't she see the danger inside me, the storm corralled by my ribs?

Bending, she said sweetly, "Things are not always as they seem, Piers. Remember that. A very little poison can do a world of good. It's all about how you apply it."

I didn't understand yet, but her words touched something small and raw inside me, soothing the inflammation.

"Tell me, do you know what a crow is?" Her long, bold form intrigued me. My mother always made herself smaller, her shoulders curled with shame and grief and things I didn't understand. This woman held her head so high I thought her neck might snap.

I nodded. "They nest in the trees behind the house."

She smiled, her lips parting beguilingly. "We are a family of crows," she told me. "Don't forget that. The other children you know, they're hawks or sparrows, doves or starlings. But you, dear girl, are a crow. Do you know what sets a crow apart?"

I shook my head.

"Crows feed on what others can't." She stared down at me. "Including other birds."

I gulped, feeling the ominous energy behind her statement.

She smiled tightly. "I live in a place called Crow Lake, as it so happens. It's in New York near the Canadian border. Do you know where Canada is?"

"Above America."

"Right. Smart girl." She smiled wider and my heart leapt at the attention. "I want you to remember where I live. If you ever need me, come find me there. Now, tell me, where can you find me, Piers?"

"Crow Lake," I said.

"Good." She gave a brusque nod and turned to walk away.

"Wait!" I called. "Who are you?"

Her eyes pierced my own. "Why, your aunt Myrtle of course."

5

Syracuse

What if I get there and she's not alive? Or she moved? I have nowhere else to go and less than thirty dollars to my name. If I show up and she's not there . . . I scrub these anxious thoughts from my mind. After more than seven hours of driving, and a few spent sleeping in a Walmart parking lot, the fuel tank is idling near empty, but I've made it as far as Syracuse. I dare not take Don's car farther. I pull into an old cemetery at the edge of the city—a lonely, rolling expanse of graves and historic vaults, the bones of people who mattered once—and park along a gravel road. If she's not there when I arrive, maybe I can find my way to the Canadian border—it's close enough. But even with a whole country between us, I can still feel Henry breathing down my neck, feverishly close, as if he's been hiding in my shadow all along.

I kill the engine, leaving the keys in the ignition, and pop the trunk. The graveyard feels deserted, these tombs too old for visitors, people who are no longer missed. Around back, I rifle through his suitcase full of business attire and men's toiletries, luxurious frivolities like a leather necktie case and hundred-dollar eye serum. I hadn't pegged him for an aging metrosexual. I grab a striped button-down with short sleeves when a small leather box catches my eye. Unzipping it, I discover it's a jewelry case. There's a flashy money clip inside, clamped around another fifty-six dollars. I guess I didn't need to put all those chips and roasted peanuts on Don's Shell card after all. There's also a gold signet ring, stamped with a compass design, a tiny blue stone winking at its center. I study the ring. It glints in the breaking sunlight, radiant. I know real gold when I see it. I quickly pocket it with the cash and close the trunk, careful to wipe anything I've touched before I go.

I climb to a tomb with gothic arches across the front and slip inside the stone pillars, quickly swapping the Florida T-shirt for the button-down, which I knot at my waist. I stuff the tee through the tomb's gate, letting it drop into the shadows on the other side, and step out into the morning. The cemetery spreads out in all directions unhindered, its green hills crested by historic mausoleums and ornate headstones. I'm not sure which direction to take. Mature trees poke through the landscape, obscuring the view, and the newborn sun washes everything ocher.

I start straight ahead when a man in a green jumpsuit with a hedge trimmer calls out to me. "Hey! This your car? You can't park here."

I pick up my pace, hopeful he hasn't seen my face. He must be a groundskeeper, maintenance on an early shift.

"Lady! You can't leave this car here," he calls. "They got rules."

I can't exactly run with a broken foot, but I shuffle away as quickly as possible, tearing through small clusters of trees and family burial plots, winding between hills and graves, trying to lose him. I have no sense of where I'm going, but eventually I scramble down a slope and into the back parking lot of a university campus, losing myself among a meager scattering of early-bird students. I can't stay here in Syracuse, where I've ditched the car. My need to get out of the city is almost as strong as it was in Charleston.

It's cool here, and my arms dimple with goose bumps as I think. I see a girl with wide eyes and a dark ponytail walking by, a latte and a stack of books in her hands. I tug at the sleeve of her crochet cardigan. "Hey, can you tell me where the bus station is?"

She slows but doesn't stop, pulling her sleeve away, frowning at me as she marches on.

Another girl is on a nearby bench, digging through her backpack. I decide she looks kind and hobble toward her. The boot is already wearing me thin and beginning to itch. I sit beside her. "Looking for something?"

She looks up, her face round and open, trusting. The kind that smiles easily. Her long dark hair is pulled back on both sides. "My vape. I can't find it. Probably left it in my room." She rises, determined to go locate it.

"Wait!" I say, before she can leave. "Do you know where the regional bus station is?"

Her eyes fall to the boot. "It's by Onondaga Lake," she says. "Northside." She pauses. "You need a ride somewhere?"

I should say no. Don taught me that. But the truth is, I'm exhausted. "I'm headed north," I tell her. "I just need to get to the station."

"Come on," she says. "You'd have to cross the freeway. It's dangerous, especially with that thing on. I can take you."

Grateful, I follow her to a plain brick building—presumably her dormitory—with a full parking lot in front. She stops beside a blue Jeep. "You need help getting in?" she asks as she opens the door.

I wave her away.

She presses out a thin smile and climbs in the driver's seat. Without traffic, we cross the city in minutes. She pulls up to the curb and puts the Jeep in park. "There isn't much up north. You got family that way?"

I nod. "Yeah, actually. Crow Lake. You heard of it?"

She shakes her head.

"It's a small town. Er, village," I tell her.

"You don't know?" she asks, one eyebrow inching higher.

I shake my head. "I've never been before," I say before climbing out and turning to close the door.

"Just watch out," she tells me, her round eyes going glossy. "They got a man up that way. Likes to choke people." She holds her hands around an imaginary neck to demonstrate.

Cold sweat trickles down my middle back, Henry's lips at my ear, curling into a smile. *Boo.*

"A killer," she enunciates. "Hiding in the mountains."

I click the passenger door closed, unable to speak, and she drives off with a wave. Glued to the curb, I try to shake my husband's phantom, the sense that even here, he is watching. But Henry can't possibly know where I am. He's back in Charleston, thinking I am dead, gliding along the bottom of the Cooper River where I belong. The man in the mountains is someone else. Another version of Henry, perhaps, sucking his oxygen from the mouths of women. Another predator. But he's got nothing to do with me.

I make my way inside to the counter to buy a ticket, praying I have enough money. "One seat for Crow Lake," I tell the woman. Above me, a TV informs the near empty station of a grisly murder scene discovered recently on a mountain trail. *Saranac Strangler Strikes Again* the headline beneath the reporter reads.

"No stop in Crow Lake," the woman says.

"What's closest?" I ask, glancing back at the TV.

"The madman of the mountains continues to terrorize the peaceful hamlets and lakeside communities of the Adirondacks," the reporter is droning. "With this latest victim bringing his body count to a total of four. Police say women should be extremely cautious, particularly along the lonely trails and stretches of road that crisscross this scenic area."

For a split second, I think I see her—the crook of an arm against the leaves, a blond ringlet twisting in a subtle breeze, her body strewn across a clearing, the surrounding trees gathered as witnesses. And then, like darts hitting a board, three more, each in such rapid succession I hardly register them. Black hair. A jutting collarbone. Freckles pale and purpling. They pass through me like wind, leaving behind a hollow cavity where they were. A place inside me that is no longer mine.

I look back to the woman behind the counter, her large earrings glinting silver under the fluorescent lights as she shakes her head. "I hope they catch that sicko soon." She meets my eye. "He strangles them first. Chokes the life right out of them before doing things to the bodies."

I swallow hard and refuse to question what she means by *doing things* because I already know. Henry's sweaty face pumps over me, eyes staring through mine until he sees what he is looking for, the bit that's missing, the danger in its place, and he finally erupts in climax. How much easier it would be for him if he didn't have all that life getting in his way.

"We can get you to Saranac Lake," the woman says. "Stops at the market on River Street."

My eyes flick to the television screen and back. "That'll work." I'll figure the rest out from there.

She passes me a printed ticket after I pay her all the cash I have left, getting twenty-three cents in change. I'm well and truly broke now. The leftover snacks from my last fill-up will have to tide me over until I arrive. Her fingers linger as I go to slide the ticket toward me. "You be careful up there," she says. "You're just his type."

"Thank you," I say as I wrestle the ticket from her, an eerie intuition crawling over me. I start to walk away before turning back. "What do you mean I'm his type?"

Her eyes level on me. "A woman," she says. "Alone."

6

Regis

The sun is disappearing when the bus rolls to a stop before the market in Saranac Lake. My butt is numb after the ten-hour circuitous route—including a healthy layover in Albany—the bus has made of an otherwise three-hour trip, and I'm beginning to shake from low blood sugar. I pause at the door of the bus and turn to the driver. "How far is Crow Lake from here?"

He appears taken aback. "Crow Lake? Thirty miles at least."

A half-hour's drive. I mentally calculate how long it would take to walk that far with a broken foot. I'm looking at the better part of the next twenty hours *if* I don't stop or slow down. My eyes coast over the hills across the lake, the inclines a foreboding portent. The concern must show on my face because the driver says, "Maybe you can catch a ride with someone."

The lump of Don's lifeless body flashes in my mind.

I clamber gracelessly off and stand back as the bus pulls away. Across the still road, and the calm waters of the lake beyond, the white-lined gables of several houses shine softly in the dusk of the trees. Boats are docked along the shore, looking like abandoned toys resting on the water. Even in the fading light, there is a rainbow of color between the elements and the architecture, and I am reminded suddenly of Charleston, my heart tightening around its grief. The feel of the mountains is unmistakable, a quiet, hovering presence, both enormous and close, like being lost and found at the same time.

Feeling faint, I make my way inside the store, fingering packs of powdered doughnuts and sticks of beef jerky with growing need. There's a large convex mirror in the corner above me to reveal shoplifters, my figure lean and curved against it. I'll never make the walk to Crow Lake without some food. I glance toward the cashier. My hands tremble. When she turns her back, I grab a handful of cheese and peanut butter cracker packets and try to shove them into my open bag. A couple fall to the floor, plastic crinkling loudly.

She spins around. "Hey! What do you think you're doing? You gotta pay for those!"

I leave the crackers on the floor and start toward the doors, but a gruff man with arms like tree trunks pushes a dolly stacked with cases of beer in front of the exit. "Going somewhere?"

"I was just—"

"Trying to leave without paying," the cashier finishes for me.

The man plucks my bag from my arms. Sticking a hand in, he pulls out several cracker packets. His eyebrows flatten into a thick line.

"I can pay," I blurt. "It's just—here." I pull Don's ring from my pocket and walk over to set it on the counter before the clerk. "I need to barter for a ride. North to Crow Lake. It's all I've got, but it's worth a lot more than some gas and crackers."

The clerk picks it up and turns it over in her palm. She looks at the man, but he shakes his head. Setting it down, she says, "Sorry, we only take cash money."

"I can take you," a deep voice says from behind. I turn to see another man come up behind me. He snatches the crackers from the beer man as he passes and sets them on the counter beside the ring. "That's a nice ring. Keep it. I'll pay."

I quickly grab the ring and put it away, feeling suddenly self-conscious. The man has a six-pack of beer and a bag of chips in one hand that he also sets down.

"You sure?" the cashier asks him.

He meets my eye. "Positive."

"Suit yourself," she says with a shrug.

I slide my crackers off the counter as he pays, taking him in from the corner of my eye. He's tall with a sandy-colored beard cut close to his jaw and an untucked flannel shirt. His nose has a slightly crooked ridge, the sign of a previous break. His face freckles along the crest of his cheekbones, tawny and worn from the sun. His eyes are gray, but not dull. Something dazzles in them, like colored stones beneath the surface of the water. They remind me of the Cooper River, the taste of mud, the feel of freedom. I want to escape behind them.

When he's finished, he holds the door for me. "Come on, my truck is just out here."

I hesitate, then walk briskly outside, anxious to get away from the judgy glare of the cashier. "It's okay," I tell him when he follows me out. "I can walk."

His mouth twitches on one side, and he sets the beer down in the bed of a nearby truck. "Not sure that's wise," he tells me. His eyes dart down to my booted foot and back up.

It's not any wiser to get into a truck with another strange man, attractive though he may be in a wholesome, mountain-grown sort of way. Even if he bought me an armful of crackers. Wasn't that Don's excuse after all, that I *owed* him? I squint past him, thinking he will leave me alone if I don't say anything, but he just stares, waiting.

Finally, he opens his door and says, "Get in. It's unlocked."

I pause, wrestling.

He leans across the seat to open the passenger door and I flinch, a reaction he doesn't miss. Undoing the glove box, he straightens, watching me through the window of his open door. "Come over here," he says, pointing to the passenger side. "Look inside."

His voice is low, gentle, and yet I move only in small, wary steps. As I skirt the ajar door, he says, "The glove box."

I take my eyes off him at the last possible minute and rest them on the open glove compartment, where a blocky handgun is lying on its side.

"Take it," he tells me.

It feels like a trick. I don't move.

His hands go up. "I just want to help you. You'll never make it to Crow Lake on foot, not with that boot, not in these mountains. I can tell you don't trust me, so take it. It's already loaded. If I do anything to hurt you, all you have to do is point and pull the trigger. Understand?"

My lips part, the air whistling between them. The gun should alarm me, but it doesn't. Instead, it is the way he makes himself vulnerable that unnerves me, like a person bowing at my feet. I reach in and close the glove box. "I trust you."

His whole body sighs. Pressing his lips together, he dips his head and climbs in the truck. "It'll take less than an hour," he tells me. "If the roads are clear."

"The roads?" I echo.

"There was a big storm up that way last night. Might have knocked over some trees. We'll see."

I slide into the truck, biting my lip as a fresh wave of pain crackles through my rib cage. I close the door and watch the lake through the window as we back out.

"I'm Regis, by the way," he says.

"Acacia," I tell him.

"Where you from?" he asks as we get onto the road.

I turn from the window to give him a tight smile. "Down south."

"Well then. Welcome to the Adirondacks." His face lights with a knowing grin. "You ever been in the woods before?"

The edge of our yard when I was a little girl flashes through my mind, shadowy and striped with pokeweed stems. "Not in a very long time."

WE DRIVE IN uncomfortable silence for the next half hour or more while I eat my crackers one at a time. Between bites, I sneak little glimpses of him, sucking each detail down with my food, where my stomach warms. His build is neither slim nor stout, but comfortably somewhere in the middle, with well-muscled arms and square shoulders, a broad, toned chest. He has the look of someone who only woke up a couple of hours ago, a little disheveled without being messy, and his presence is as solid as a boulder, as if he is tethered to these mountains, a part of them. I smell fir needles in his hair, the wiry crop of beard, like a man made of the forest with tree sap running through him. It makes me want to roll in him like leaves, pick him from my sweater afterward, laughing.

"Crow Lake, huh?" he says finally. "I can't imagine you're here for the underrated trails with a foot like that."

I shake my head, finishing off the last of my crackers. "Family."

He nods, scratching at his beard. "Not much else up here, I'm afraid. It's beautiful, but it takes a certain kind to live here."

I wonder what he means by *a certain kind.* "You live in Saranac Lake?"

"I live in the area," he says, eyes fixed to the road. "I was born in these mountains. I don't know anything else."

I'm quiet, trying to imagine what it's like to know only these rocks and thickets of trees, the stillness of mirror lakes dotting the gaps. An air freshener hangs from his rear-view labeled with the fragrance Black Ice.

"You're here at the wrong time, you know," he adds. "You should have come earlier."

"Oh?" I meet his eyes and have to look away. They are earnest and level and strong. They make me want to lean against him, to feel my muscles unwind one by one.

"Summer's almost over. The temperature will start dropping in the next few weeks. These mountains will light with a fire of orange and red and yellow. It'll be the most spectacular autumn you ever saw. Until the snow sets in. Then you'll wish you were anywhere but here." His tone says he speaks from experience.

"I don't know," I tell him. "Winter might be nice. It doesn't snow where I'm from very often."

His smile is laced with irony. He's having a laugh behind those eyes at my expense. "And where would that be exactly?"

"Texas," I lie. "Near Austin."

"Well, Acacia from Near-Austin, Texas, I'm afraid you're in for a frigid shock." He rests an elbow on the edge of his door where it meets the window.

"You don't like winter?" I ask him.

"Me? I love it. It's my favorite season. It wakes you up, really teaches you what it is to be alive. But I was born and raised here. I got ice in the veins. Newcomers usually have a different reaction." He studies me as I avoid his gaze. "But if you have family here, maybe you'll stand half a chance. I give you till Christmas."

I frown. His certainty makes me want to prove him wrong, to show him I'm his equal. I doubt I'll be ready to set out on my own in less than five months anyway. I need money, work, a plan—things that take time. But the idea of moving continuously, staying several steps ahead of Henry like a shark that can't stop swimming lest it drown, appeals to me more and more. I thought once I was out of Charleston, I would feel safe. Instead, I feel harried, a rabbit scented by wolves, never able to let down my guard.

The road turns black, the night thickening around us. Only his headlights cut through it, lighting up the pavement, the trunks of sleeping trees. I think we're nearly there when the ginger-brown bark of a red pine comes into view, its enormous trunk laid out across the road at an angle, green needles sheeting the pavement.

"Shit," he says, rolling to a stop. "We'll have to turn back."

"Turn back?" That's not an option for me.

"Can't pass till it's cleared. We can try again in the morning." Regis puts the truck in reverse and starts to back up.

"No. Stop. Just let me out here," I tell him, panic hitching my voice, pinching my throat. "I can walk the rest of the way."

He brakes and eyes the hulking boot on my foot. "You're still at least ten miles out from the edge of Crow Lake," he tells me.

"It's fine," I try to reassure him. "Really. I was gonna walk anyway. You saved me a lot of the trip." I start to open the door, but he reaches for me.

Instinctively, I lean away, my hand snapping out for the glove box, the gun I know waits inside.

Regis raises his palms. "Listen, it's really dark out here. Easy to get turned around, even with a road running before you. This is bear and moose country, you know. And worse."

"Worse?" I quirk a brow, confused.

"There's a serial killer running the area targeting women. We just found another body this morning," he says.

The news report in the Syracuse bus station. The warnings. "I thought he was the *Saranac* Strangler?"

Regis frowns. "That was just the first two victims. The third was found in Tupper Lake, to the west."

"And the last?" I ask.

"North of here. Off a remote trailhead."

"I'm not worried," I lie. It comes out wobbly, uncertain, a table missing a leg. The Saranac Strangler feels like a joke Henry is playing on me, as if he knew what I was planning and decided to beat me at my own game.

"I can drop you at the nearest motel," he says. "Pick you up in the morning, drive you wherever you want to go. Just please, don't get out of this truck. Not like this."

He is pleading like a wounded man, eyes creasing with worry. It stuns me, forces me to rethink, wonder what this means to him, what *I* mean to him, the stranger he only just met. Most people would wash their hands of me as quickly as possible, feel no responsibility, and never look back. Regis, I realize, is not most people. Regis is unique, special. The thought is like a blast of cold, fresh air. Clearing. Restorative.

I pause, take my hand off the door handle, staring at him frankly. "I don't have any money."

"Not a problem," he says, relieved, a smile inching its way over his face. "I'll pay."

But the nearest motel, it turns out, is a lodge off a county road twenty miles from here that is already fully booked when he calls. He puts his phone down, a hangdog expression pulling at the corners of his mouth, and eyes me like an abandoned puppy he has picked up after being told the shelter is full. "Don't get the wrong idea," he says after a minute, "but what if I take you to my place? Just until I can get the road cleared and drop you off in Crow Lake. I'll sleep in the truck if you want. You can lock me out of my own house."

I watch the way his brows lift and lower when he speaks, as if they are trying to send me a secret message, and the pudge of his bottom lip puckering around the words. I look out the window to where the dark is desperate to get in. A night so complete you could lose yourself in it forever.

"Acacia?" he asks when I don't respond.

My eyes meet his, wary, spooked. At worst, Regis is an unknown. But out there, in the pitch, is a monster I am very familiar with, a murderer lying in wait. After Henry, I am so tired of fighting. I don't need to run from the arms of one killer straight into the grasp of another. "Okay," I tell him. "Take me to your place. One night."

He nods briskly and swings the truck through a three-point turn, hurtling us back down the road. When we pull off into a dark cove of trees, a pocket of land hidden from the world by a wall of eastern white pine and hemlock, the headlights settle over a small, L-shaped cottage with a storybook stone exterior, quaint chimney jutting up at one end like a schoolhouse bell tower.

"This is it," he says, beaming, his own little slice of heaven. He hops out of the truck.

I'm climbing down when something catches my eye, glowing faintly near a thick parcel of jewelweed off the corner of the house. I move toward it, crouching down carefully. It's a mushroom, white as a ghost with a long stem and flat cap, smooth as stone. I've never seen anything so ethereal. The hunger I was battling, satiated at last by peanut butter crackers, suddenly flares to life, causing my mouth to fill with saliva. My fingers are inching forward when he stops me.

"I wouldn't," he calls, near the hood of the truck. "It's a destroying angel."

I look at him. "A what?"

"A mushroom. The pure white ones like that are poisonous. It'll shut your liver down in a matter of hours. You'll be dead before daybreak."

I take a step away from it.

"You wouldn't be the first to mistake it for something edible. The lack of color makes people think it's safe. It's deceptive that way, lures you in. They think the toxic ones are all bright red or orange, but it's the ones that aren't obvious that are the deadliest."

I get to my feet, meeting him near the front door.

"If you're still hungry, I can cook you something inside," he says. "I make a mean grilled cheese, best in the forty-six High Peaks."

I nod my consent as he shoulders the door open and follow him into the house, my eyes lingering only a moment longer on the moon-white skin of the mushroom splitting the dark.

Regis shrugs out of his flannel shirt, an army-green T-shirt beneath clinging to his torso. "Make yourself comfortable," he says as he pulls an iron skillet from a low cabinet and quickly gets to work on the promised grilled cheese.

I peer from room to room. He lives neat for a man. Not immaculate like Henry—there are jackets crowning the backs of chairs and at least one empty mug left in every room—but the floor is clean, the sink empty of all but a few dishes, the living room confidently arranged for comfort. My eyes travel from the gleaming wood paneling to the butcher-block table to the suede sofa. A small corner cabinet displays a few choice pieces of enamelware. The hearth has a long, half-log mantel set with German beer steins. It looks like Snow White could live here. On a side table, I find a framed picture of a young girl, shiny brown hair in braids, freckles speckling her cheeks, eyes merry. A half-burned candle sits in front. I lift it for a closer look. His daughter, perhaps?

Regis ducks his head into the room. "Ready," he says, smiling bashfully as though we are old friends, reunited at long last.

I turn, setting the picture back down. His eyes glide over it, falling, sinking behind his brows. "Sorry." I don't know what I'm apologizing for.

"My sister," he tells me. "Once upon a time."

It is a strange choice of words, as if she belongs to a fairy tale.

"You have siblings?" he asks after I seat myself at the kitchen table and bite into the gooey decadence that is melted cheese combined with toasted bread.

"No." I feel his gaze on me as I eat and carefully avoid it.

"Children?" he tries again.

I shake my head. By some mysterious divine intervention, a secret chamber inside me where every warning about Henry I never heeded was tucked away, I did not make that particular cardinal error. I send a silent note of gratitude to my innermost self, who kept watch while the rest of me slept.

"Truly a free agent, then," he comments.

It's light, not meant to carry the weight I feel in it, but his words sing through me, *a free agent*.

I inhale the sandwich and Regis takes my plate, cleans it right away, and leaves it on a towel to dry. He turns. "I'm just gonna get some things then go outside."

"You don't have to," I say. It seems wrong to make this man sleep in his truck when he's been nothing but nice.

He shrugs. "I don't mind. You'll sleep better that way." He slips into his room and back out, a throw blanket over his arm, toothbrush and tube of toothpaste fisted in his hand.

At the door, we pause, staring into each other like mirror images, the night crooning behind him.

"Well, sleep tight," he says, reaching for the knob, his hand finding my own.

I stand there foolishly, feeling the way his fingers cup mine, not quite able to pull away. The little girl from the picture is suddenly there in my mind, all front teeth and laughter, a crease across the tip of her nose. She floods me with joy, a warmth for this man like the soft light of the sun, filtered through budding trees. None of the horrible flashes I've seen before with other men—gasping corpses, crying women. Only a rippling girlish energy like pink lemonade.

He lets go and she fades away. I lock the door behind him.

I SLEEP LIKE the dead and wake with a start. It takes several long, heart-thudding seconds for me to remember where I am. The house is perfectly silent, dust motes dancing like glitter through beams of sunlight, not even the hum of an air conditioner to greet me.

"Regis?"

I walk to the door. It's still locked. When I turn back, the face of the girl in the photo smiles out at me, a little off-center. Why does he only have a picture of her so young?

At first I think it's late morning, but the slant of the light is wrong. Disoriented, I look for a clock, but can't find one. I turn on the television, only to be greeted by another news report. Not morning, *evening*. I recognize Don's thermos lying in the grass at the reporter's feet, and my intestines ball up inside me.

". . . And that's when they found the body, lying here beside the road. The man has been positively identified as Don Rodgers, a high-profile political consultant from Washington, DC. Police are still investigating his cause of death but ask anyone with information to please come forward."

Someone hammers on the door, and I hit the power button, going to peer out the window. Regis smiles back at me and I let him in. My knees knock with every step, the thermos in the grass an exclamation point at the end of the sentence condemning me. Why did he have to be someone newsworthy? However much I wanted to be a moving target so Henry couldn't find me, now I want to bury myself somewhere deep and not come out until Don's flesh is stripped from his bones and the question of how he died submerged under a mountain of ever-piling current events.

"Did you just get up?" he asks, the bright smile he carries flickering like a candle hit by a sudden wind.

I wrap my arms around myself. "What time is it?"

"It's after six," he says, peering at me as though I'm another species. "My word, what have you been through?"

I clear my throat. "Can you give me that ride now?"

He sets a paper bag down, pulls out a pack of pork chops and a couple cans of beans. "Thought you might want to eat something first."

It's sweet, but all I want is to disappear. "I'm not hungry."

His mouth flattens, twitches, and reforms itself into another, kinder smile. But I can see he's disappointed. "No problem. Let me put these away."

I use his bathroom to brush my teeth, and splash some water over my face and arms, the grime of the river still clinging to me. I used the hand soap last night to wash away the worst of the smell, but wasn't comfortable enough to take a shower. I comb my fingers through my hair and rearrange it in another tight knot. *It'll be okay,* I tell my reflection. *She'll be there. She'll help you.* For confirmation, I conjure the article and picture I found before leaving Charleston of the woman from my childhood standing beside a vintage green-and-red motel sign. The caption read: *Myrtle Corbin, owner of the Balsam Motor Inn, found the body Wednesday morning when she went to inquire about her guest.* It was seven years old.

The drive is shorter this time, the road clear. Regis explains that he spent most of the day helping the county break up the tree so it could be hauled away. He talks as we drive, amiable, light conversation, the occasional question I answer as succinctly as possible, a kind of happy white noise to fill the time until we pass the WELCOME TO CROW LAKE sign and begin to spot signs of life— a mailbox, a gas station in the distance, a tiny, bustling tavern: the Drunken Moose.

"So, where to? Do you have an address?"

"No," I tell him. "But I have a name. The Balsam Motor Inn."

His eyes narrow almost imperceptibly. "What do you want with that place?"

A chill enters the cab of the truck, putting space between us. "I told you; I have family there."

"Myrtle?" he asks, incredulous. "Myrtle Corbin is your family?"

"Is that a problem?" I can't miss the layer of disappointment under his tone.

He shakes his head. "No. No, of course not. She just never said she had family, is all."

But I lean closer to the door as we cross through the town and carry on to Aunt Myrtle's place. The sun lowers itself in the sky, as if it is racing us to our destination. My companion is suddenly quiet, almost sullen.

When I see the familiar rustic green-and-red sign that reads MOTEL in block letters come into view—neon bright in the dull evening—I grin with relief and roll my window down. Above it, a tree-shaped sign is painted with BALSAM MOTOR INN. A crescent of cozy cabins with low gable roofs, painted brackets, and tea-dark, live-edge siding are set against a thick backdrop of fir trees, a sweet, Christmassy smell dusting the air. At one end, an A-frame rises to an impossible pitch under a dark metal roof like the point of a witch's hat. Sleepy windows checker the front, their planter boxes crawling with ivy, and a farmhouse door shadowed with glass reveals a darkened interior. Two brightly painted signs hang over it, one reading OFFICE, the other CAFÉ. I feel like we've stumbled into a rundown elven village somewhere in the Bavarian Alps, the pops of green, red, and yellow reminiscent of carnivorous plants.

Regis pulls up in front but leaves the motor running. "This is it," he says, a knowing cut to his jaw.

I open the door to get out. "Thank you," I tell him. "For everything."

"Glad I could help." He nods. "Will I see you again?" he asks sharply as I close the door.

I lean against the open window. "You know where to find me."

His eyes linger over me. "Stay out of trouble." It is authoritative, a command, and also worried, a request. I wonder what trouble I could possibly find out here in the middle of nowhere. Then he pulls away, vanishing into the night.

I make my way to the door of the A-frame but find it locked. Knocking loudly, I step back, hoping she is here. Anyone, really. This is my only hope.

Inside, I see a series of small lights turn on in succession. When the door opens with a tinkle, a tall woman answers with silver-streaked hair dripping over one shoulder in a long plait. Her face is rounder than I remember, her eyes a touch more sunken but just as bright, with full cheeks beneath them and a curling smile. "Dinner was at five. We're closed now. No vacancy, dear. See the sign?"

She points, and I turn and realize that the lit sign does indeed read NO VACANCY. Only, the NO keeps flickering on and off.

"Blasted sign," she grumbles. "Try the Gooseneck, in town. They might have a room yet." She starts to close the door.

I whip out a hand to hold it open, and her eyes flick to mine, troubled. "Aunt Myrtle?" I ask. "Myrtle Corbin?"

Her face falls, contorts, rearranges itself into a whisper of recognition. "Piers? *Lily's girl*?"

The sudden relief hits me with such force I can scarcely stand. I lean against the doorframe. My shoulders tremble and the tears flow as I dash them away. "I have nowhere else to go," I whisper.

Without hesitation, she pulls the door wide. "I knew you'd show up someday," she says, motioning me inside. "Come in, child. You're home now."

7

Reyes

Women don't go missing from houses like this. Investigator Reyes put the patrol car in park and studied the house, his partner still on a call. A new colonial designed to look old—white siding and black shutters bathed in the late afternoon sun, a wide front porch with rattan ceiling fans and topiaries flanking the leaded glass door, a sculpted lawn bordered by trees. This had to be over an acre of land. The property oozed charm and money. There wasn't a leaf or splinter out of place. They were deep in the suburbs here, almost out of them entirely, but the idea of Charleston clung like an old perfume. They had brought the city with them.

A black Jaguar sat in the drive. It looked expensive, the spare tire installed on the front driver's side sticking out like a sore thumb.

His partner hung up. "This the place?"

"Looks like it," Reyes said.

He glanced at his partner. Will was old South Carolina stock, born and raised the same way his parents and their parents were. But he was a solid partner, a family man with a nose for the job and the loyalty of a spaniel. Reyes, on the other hand, was a transplant, the only son of a single mother from California who landed here after fleeing a bad relationship. He was younger than Will but he'd seen a thing or two growing up. He'd learned to keep his eyes open. And he was naturally suspicious. He balanced out his partner's tendency to draw the most obvious conclusions, and Will kept him from diving down every dead-end rabbit hole. They'd been together two years now, and Reyes valued Will's input. Their partnership had gotten off to a rocky start, Will deeming his need to question everything as obsessive and Reyes believing his partner's laid-back approach was lazy, but that had changed when a routine traffic stop turned out to be drug-related. Reyes had sensed the driver's hostility, somehow knowing a gun was there before they got a visual; his suspicion saved Will's life. But it was Will who'd talked the man down, making it possible for Reyes to overpower him and make the arrest. Will was the true hero.

Since then, Will Poole had become the big brother Reyes longed for growing up, an older male influence he could actually trust. The men Reyes had known as a boy were far from trustworthy; they were downright dangerous. And he'd been gifted with an older sister instead of a brother. He loved Lucia, thanked God she was alive and well every day, but she'd put them through hell for a time, following in their mother's early footsteps despite the pain it had caused. Their mother had been desperate when she'd moved in with the tall man, caring for two young children on her own. Reyes could forgive her for not knowing what he was until it was too late. But Lucia should have known better. Instead of schooling her, it had twisted her idea of love, leaving her vulnerable to a man like Jace, a man who had nearly killed her.

Will pulled a face. "Ten bucks says she left him for her trainer and is halfway to Acapulco."

Reyes grinned. "Let's hear him out just the same."

"What is it you always say, Emil? A call is a call is a call?" Will asked with a good-natured laugh before swinging open the car door.

Reyes hung back, staring up at the house. The windows were so clean they practically disappeared. The whole place gave him an uncomfortable feeling, like it was smiling with a bullet behind its teeth. He had a hunch this one wouldn't be as cut-and-dried as his partner thought. His mother had always attributed these hunches to God. *Sussuros del cielo,* she called them—*whispers from heaven.* After the things he'd seen, the things his family had endured, Reyes wasn't sure he believed in God, not the way his mother and sister did. But he believed in *something,* and right now that something was warning him to be on his guard.

At the front door, he stared up into the shiny dome lens of the camera as Will knocked. Everyone had their own surveillance nowadays. Maybe it would prove useful.

A white male opened the door. Late forties. Thinning, longish hair. He was tall, with lean muscles knotting him together. His face was red, as if he'd been exerting himself, but he was wearing a crisp white shirt and an expensive suit the color of sharkskin. His glasses sat squarely on his nose, eyes pale and sharp. Something about him struck Reyes, persisted in a recessed corner of his mind like the buzzing of a gnat.

"You Mr. Davenport?" Will asked.

"Yes, that's me," the man intoned. "Henry Excelsior Walden Davenport."

"You called about a missing woman?" Will continued.

"Yes." The man held the door open. "My wife. Come in."

Reyes followed his partner inside. They were greeted by an elegant foyer and an expansive den. Wide plank floors ran throughout. The navy sofas had that down cushioning that made them look so inviting. The coffee table appeared to be teak. And there was a hint of something citrus in the air. But the furnishings were decidedly masculine, the colors academic. You'd almost assume a woman didn't live here at all. He closed the door behind them.

"I became worried when I texted my wife after lunch and she didn't respond," the man told them, his face grim. "I rushed home and found this on our bed." He held out a sheet of linen stationery. It was covered in dark pink script. "Her car is still in the garage."

"Set it there, please," Will told the man, indicating a large kitchen island that overlooked the den.

Stepping up to the marble counter, Reyes studied the letter. It was brief, full of agonizing apologies and a hopeless perspective. She was saying goodbye, telling her husband she wished she could have made him happy, apologizing for letting him down, explaining that by the time he found the note it would be too late, she intended to jump, and not to look for her.

Reyes had seen a number of suicide notes in his time as an investigator, but this one stood out. Less from what it said than what it didn't. In every note he'd read before, the person professed their love for those they were leaving behind. They knew they were hurting someone by making this choice, and that's the only thing that had made them hold out for as long as they did. But this woman never said *I love you* or *I'll miss you*. She didn't even sign the letter with her full name. Just a splash of whatever strange ink she'd used and a large letter *P*.

"What is this?" Will asked the man. "This substance? She have a special pen or something? Was this her favorite color?"

The man shook his head. "I've no idea," he stated plainly. His lips turned down at the corners. "My wife was an interior designer," he said by way of explanation. "She has a flair for the dramatic."

"Did you search the house?" Reyes asked him. "Look for her?"

"Of course," the man snapped.

"I mean, *really* search it?" Reyes reiterated. "I don't mean to be morbid but sometimes people will find a hidden place within the home to take their life, one that feels safe but might seem unexpected. You went through closets? The attic?" As he spoke, Will began bagging the letter.

The man pinched the bridge of his nose, more irritated than upset. "Yes, yes. I looked everywhere. What are you doing?" he asked Investigator Poole. "That's my letter."

"We should get this analyzed," the detective said. "See if we can identify what the substance is."

Reyes nodded in support. "We'll do our best to confirm a suicide," he told the man. "But in the absence of a body, a case will need to be opened, an investigation carried out."

"An investigation?" the man questioned. "Are you implying someone took her?"

"No, sir," Reyes told him. "Just following procedure. This will likely be over very soon. Do you mind if I take a brief look around? Confirm that your wife isn't in the house?"

The man agreed, but his lips were tight against the ridges of his teeth.

Reyes wandered through the house. Now that it had been mentioned, he could see the wife's designer influence throughout the flow of rooms, a quirky, almost unsettling touch that made them stand out, yet was immaculate in its execution—an oddly shaped mirror or an unexpected color of curtain. Things the average person wouldn't gravitate toward, or even know how to find. The element of surprise. It reminded him of the note. But in stark contrast to her obvious presence in the design, she was strikingly absent everywhere else. No framed pictures of her. Nothing personal or with her name on it. Not even a bit of jewelry or pair of shoes lying around.

Whenever he came to a door, he opened it and checked inside. But nothing appeared out of place. When he reached the master bedroom however, the bedsheets and blankets had been torn from the mattress and strewn across the floor. The doors to large his and hers walk-in closets were hanging open. His was impeccably organized, arranged by color and season, outfitted with cherrywood drawers and racks. Hers had likely been the same, but the clothes were now torn from their hangers, the drawers spilled open onto the carpet. He turned and found the man watching him from the doorway, eyes narrow and cold. He never heard him approach.

"Is it always like this?" he asked, watching the man's jaw tighten.

"Most certainly not," he answered quietly. "I found it this way when I arrived."

"This could indicate a struggle," Reyes told him. "It could shift the focus of the investigation."

The man shrugged coolly. "A tantrum more like," he said. "My wife is prone to fits."

"Fits?" Reyes asked.

The man smiled stiffly. "She was unwell. Emotionally unstable. We moved out here to protect her reputation, give her privacy," he said as he entered the room. He bent down and picked up a green sweater with little white flowers on it. His knuckles whitened around the knit. "I thought it would help. She had a large circle of friends and clients in Charleston who didn't understand. She was embarrassed."

Reyes nodded. "Can you provide evidence of her mental condition? A number for a psychiatrist or a prescription?"

The man strode into the attached bathroom and back out, handing Reyes a bottle of pills. Much of the label had been obscured by a water stain, the print blurry and faded, but he could clearly make out *Davenport* and *Paxil*. "She also took Ritalin. Had since she was a child. But she must have stopped taking these in the last year. They haven't been refilled in over six months."

Reyes tucked the bottle into a pocket. A sudden cessation of psychotropic medications was known to cause emotional unrest, severe and even fatal in some cases. Whatever his reservations about the letter, this would appear to support a suicide. "I'm sorry for your loss, sir." He headed back downstairs.

"I'll write a report," Will told him as he entered the room. "Submit this for analysis, prints, etc." He lifted the bag with the note inside.

Reyes turned to the man, Henry. "Did you locate any of her personal effects? Purse? Wallet? Phone? That sort of thing."

He gestured toward the kitchen, where a satchel-style bag in milky leather rested on a stool. "Everything is there. Even her phone. But it's useless. I checked it already."

"You have the code?" Reyes asked.

Henry's eyes narrowed slightly. "Of course."

Reyes walked over and lifted the purse with a sigh. It didn't bode well, her leaving behind the intimate, necessary things. "We'll take this as well, go through the contents, have anything of interest evaluated."

"If you must," the husband replied.

"I noticed a camera out front," Reyes told him. "We'll need access to that footage. What time did you leave?"

"Early," the man told them. "Like I always do for work. There's nothing on the footage. I checked it already."

"Still," Reyes replied, "we'll need to verify that, clock your departure. Where do you work?"

"Why?" the husband asked. "What does that have to do with anything?"

"We'll need to confirm your whereabouts." Will stepped in.

"An alibi?" he questioned warily.

"Not exactly, Mr. Davenport. Just procedure." Will met his eye but kept his tone soft.

"I assure you I had nothing to do with this," the man responded flatly, but the corner of his eye twitched.

Reyes felt invisible hackles rise along his neck and shoulders. "Which the camera footage and your work will surely confirm," he reminded him.

Reaching inside his coat pocket, the man slid a matte black business card from a gold money clip and passed it to them. "You may speak with my administrative assistant, Johanna. She can confirm my arrival," he stated.

Reyes nodded as he took the card, and the man walked them to the door.

"We'll be in touch," Will said.

The man nodded. "As soon as possible, please."

Reyes held out his hand, and the man's handshake was firm, tactical. As he pulled back, the detective couldn't help but notice the dot of pink staining the cuff of the man's sleeve. "What's that?" he asked.

He looked confused.

"Your sleeve," Reyes told him, rippling with alarm. "That stain is the same color as the ink on the letter."

Even Will's face scrunched with curiosity.

"I've been handling it since I arrived," the man said. "It must have come from that." For a second, the placid exterior seemed to slip, and his face lit with genuine wonder and something else . . . *fear.*

Reyes nodded, watching him. "Must have."

They walked away without looking back.

In the car, Reyes turned to his partner. "Did something about that guy strike you as off? He's rigid. Almost unaffected for a man who may have just lost his wife to suicide."

Will puffed out his lower lip. "He's not my cup of tea, but his story makes sense enough. You contact the secretary. See if it checks out."

"I will." Reyes eyed the house as they backed out of the drive. "I don't know what it is," he said, "but there's something he's not saying."

"WHAT ARE WE doing here?" Will asked.

The bridge stretched before them like a silver expressway. "This is it," Reyes told him. "The bridge she names in the letter. I thought we should walk it. Maybe she's still here, contemplating. Or maybe she left something on the walkway. If we can confirm the jump . . ."

"Then we know where to look for the body," Will finished, glancing at the river. "Let's go."

They took their time scanning the pavement, the water below them, looking for anything that might indicate she was there.

"It's odd, isn't it?" he asked Will, pondering the note.

"What is?" Will was focused on the ground, looking for something of use.

Reyes squinted. "That she would name the specific bridge *after* she told him not to look for her. If you didn't want someone to look, wouldn't you leave that out?"

Will shrugged. "The bridge is kind of a given. She probably knew that and figured it didn't matter. Or maybe deep down she did want him to come after her."

He nodded. Will's explanation was plausible, but it still didn't sit right. Nothing about this did. He'd felt a nagging, uncomfortable recognition of that man, though he was sure he'd never met him before.

Reyes was beginning to doubt they'd find anything when the stain came into view, near the pinnacle of the bridge. "You see what I see?" he asked his partner as they approached the maroon splat dried out against the bleached concrete.

Will frowned. "Such a weird color."

"What is this?" Reyes asked. "Some kind of juice?"

"Vomit," Will answered him, pointing to some pulpy bits. "She was sick here."

"Scared?" Reyes asked.

"Maybe," Will said. He looked over the edge into the water. "Wouldn't you be?" He glanced upward at a nearby camera. "We'll need that CCTV footage to confirm if we don't find a body."

"We might need it anyway," Reyes said, still staring at the colorful stain. "We should get a sample of this."

"Really?" Will asked with a raised brow.

"Make sure it matches the substance on the letter. What if it's something she ate? Something . . . I don't know. Toxic? A kind of safety net."

Will looked unconvinced. "A safety net for a suicide? She wanted to die, Emil. What would she need a safety net for?"

"That's what I mean," Reyes said, scratching a bit of the pulp up with his pen, depositing it into another bag. "In case the fall didn't kill her, or she chickened out. Something to make sure she died no matter what."

"Like an overdose of sleeping pills or something," Will said, catching on. "You seen a medication this color?"

"Besides cough syrup?" Reyes gave his partner a quizzical look. "No. I doubt it's medicine."

"What then?" Will asked.

Reyes shrugged. "Something else. Some kind of plant maybe?"

"Looks like fruit punch," Will told him. "I'll never drink Minute Maid again."

Reyes laughed. His partner had an unusual sense of humor that kicked in at the oddest times, a side effect of the job. Processing the things that they had to led to some uncommon coping mechanisms. "That's it," he said, handing him the bag. "You're a genius, man. It's probably a berry of some kind."

"A berry?" Will didn't follow.

"Something wild," Reyes told him. "Something deadly. And a lot of it."

Will stared over the railing at the Cooper River, eyes bugging at the water. "Jesus. What was this woman trying to escape that she effectively killed herself twice?"

The smooth, red face of her husband, Henry Davenport, flashed through Reyes's mind. He'd known men like Henry before. Well, not *exactly* like Henry, but close enough. His mother's boyfriend when he was young—the tall man—could put her in the fetal position with just a look. And his sister . . . With his help, Lucia had managed to free herself, start over, stay safe. But her scars weren't the kind that just etched the heart. In her last run-in with her fiancé, he'd carved her face open with a broken beer bottle, beaten her to within an inch of her life, and left her for dead in a motel room off the I-20. By some miracle, she'd regained consciousness and managed to call her brother. Reyes drove more than seven hours to collect her and take her to the nearest hospital. It was there they first learned she was pregnant. After that, Lucia came to live with him until the baby was born and they were certain Jace wouldn't come back to finish what he'd started. Years later—Mia was fast approaching six years old—Reyes still panicked whenever his sister didn't immediately answer the phone. He winced thinking how easily Lucia could have ended up like this woman. *What was she escaping indeed.*

On the walk back to the car, he wrestled with the surname, the hard, pale exterior of the man, Henry, and the large, looping *P* from the suicide note, each insignificant on its own, but together they weighed on him with familiarity and dread. Heaven, it seemed, had gone from whispering to screaming. He glanced at Will. "What was her name again?"

Will looked at him sidelong. "Davenport. Why? You're getting that constipated look on your face, Emil."

Reyes ignored him. "Her *full* name."

Will glanced at the mobile computer. "Piers Davenport. No middle name."

A wave of heat flushed across Reyes's chest, and his throat tightened around an imaginary blockage, the old sensation still living in his cells when he couldn't draw a breath, the day he nearly died. "Do we have a picture?" he asked hoarsely.

Will quickly pulled one up from the internet. "We do now."

Reyes stared into the burning green eyes he remembered so well, though they were softer here, on-screen, than they had been in person that day. He felt his heart and his stomach meet somewhere inside his abdomen, everything shifting with the force.

"Jesus, Emil. You okay? You look like someone gut punched you," his partner said.

"I know her," Reyes let out slowly, the steady squeeze of her arms around his ribs like an ache now. She was a part of him. That's how it was when someone stood between you and death. They stayed with you, like a scar next to the heart. "She saved my life."

8

Crow Lake

Myrtle seems nervous, turning off the lamps and sconces one by one, their little red shades darkening to plum. At the last, she pauses and eyes me from across the open room, her face haloed in its light, warped by wicked shadows. "I must confess, I'm a little surprised you found me. How did you do it?"

My own eyes are adjusting, trying to take in the details of where I find myself. The walls are paneled in honey-stained wood that matches the several small cedar tables and log chairs, their backs burned with the image of a tree. A kitchen takes up the rear of the room; and an L-shaped counter made of rough wood, bark, and twigs is situated left of the entrance. A black spiral staircase pierces the back of the café. To a sleeping loft, perhaps. And a wall-mounted TV hangs to the right. Overhead, a couple of old wagon wheels dangle from chains, lanterns suspended from the outer rings like rustic chandeliers.

I clutch my backpack awkwardly. "You told me, remember? You said you lived in Crow Lake. You made me promise not to forget."

She breezes past me on her way to the front door. "Yes, but how did you know I would be *here*?"

I tell her about the article I found, memorized.

She eyes me with pride. "Clever girl."

"You live here?" I ask, taking in the cozy lumberjack interior.

She laughs. "In the café? No. You're lucky you caught me. I was just making sure the coffee makers were set for the morning.

I always do it at close, but second-guessing myself has become a bad habit in my old age."

We step outside and she locks the door behind us. "Follow me," she instructs as she starts around the building toward the woods. The night is rich with smells and sounds, alive and awake in a way few places are. It feels almost illicit to stand among this much nature, outnumbered. The sky is riddled with starlight, the trees a wall of black beneath it, as solid and unbreachable as any man has built. As she nears them, I ask, "We're going in there?"

Myrtle stops and turns toward me. "Don't tell me you're afraid of the dark?"

I shake my head despite my reservations. I've stepped off a bridge. Surely, I can handle a patch of woods at night. But these woods are not a patch, they're a sea, rolling over mountain and hill, valley and glen, blanketing the state in a thick carpet of leaves. And they do not know me. I am a stranger here. A sheep in the lion's den.

She steps through the brush into the void.

Pausing at the edge of the forest, I look up, letting my eyes skate up elongated trunks to the ocean of stars beyond, the only thing greater than this wilderness. I am caught between infinities. There is a split second of knowing that once I pass through this barrier, I can never go back. My mind shakes the thought off like a dusting of snow, and I step in.

I quickly realize we are on a narrow trail, scarcely perceptible in the night. But Myrtle seems to know her way; her steps never falter. I do my best to place my feet where she placed hers, stumbling when I get it wrong. But she doesn't chide me for it.

"I was sorry to hear about your mother's passing," she tells me as we wind deeper into the forest. "I loved Lily despite our differences."

Slowly, my eyes are adjusting. The shapes of leaves emerge from the blackness, the subtle colors they wear. I even manage to avoid a few switches before they smack into me. But it's the smell that really comes alive, rich and sweet as incense, the many notes of a perfume. Some hit me up front, others linger, waiting for me to notice. It is a performance, the scent of the forest, interactive and dynamic.

"She killed herself," I blurt.

It's the first I've spoken of it to anyone. I told Henry she died but never how. I was too ashamed, too afraid he'd think less of me. I didn't realize until this moment how desperately I need to unburden myself. How trapped my grief has been inside me these last three years, like the steel sphere in a pinball machine, ricocheting off every surface, doing more damage.

Myrtle stops and stands stock-still, the earthy, southwestern pattern of her wool robe the only reason I can see her at all. "I know," she says quietly.

"I still don't understand why," I say as we start walking again. But I feel, deep in my bones, that it is because of me, because of that day. *What have you done?* Her voice slips around inside my skull, an echo that never ends. And now I have done it again. "I could have helped her," I tell Myrtle. "I had money. If I'd only known she needed it. She didn't even tell me Gerald was dead. She was so proud."

We approach the straightforward frame of a log cabin. From the porch light I can see it's painted dark brown with lively green trim and a red front door. It perches in the forest like something from an old folktale. Myrtle clomps up the stairs to its small porch and sets her hand on the knob. Glancing at me, she says, "Your mother was many things, Piers. But in the end, I don't think she was proud at all."

I swallow and follow her inside.

The interior of the cabin is like something from a movie set—glowing log walls and a stone fireplace, a rack of antlers over the door, braided rugs and handwoven baskets. I drop my backpack onto the buffalo plaid sofa and pick up a hooked pillow featuring a bear surrounded by red berries. Myrtle busies herself in the small but open kitchen where folksy twig accents mark the wood cabinetry and an old Hoosier cabinet stands against one wall, cluttered with enamel canisters. "Are you hungry?" she asks.

"I had crackers," I say, sinking into a willow armchair with worn-in cushions. "Yesterday."

She frowns and begins making me a sandwich—tomato, spinach, and herbed goat cheese, bread so thick with whole grains it practically sprouts. It smells divine. When she brings it to me and I start eating, her frown lines deepen. "Good God, child. When's the last time you had a proper meal?"

Embarrassed, I set the sandwich down. "A couple days," I tell her through a full mouth, not counting Regis's grilled cheese, not sure if I should mention Regis or the grilled cheese I had there.

Truthfully, I quit eating much at least three days before I made the jump, nerves killing my appetite. Only when Henry was watching did I pretend to eat anything. But Henry never liked me to eat overmuch, so it was easy to fool him. It wasn't weight that he cared about but control. "Don't forget yourself, Piers," he would tell me. We would have whole meals out where every bite I took was preceded by a glance in his direction, the silent but obvious look of approval on his face. When that look shifted, I set my fork down no matter how hungry I felt. The one time I didn't, he took me home and held my face in the pillow until I wet myself. I learned after that.

Her eyes slide to my booted foot. "You're in trouble," she says plainly. She looks concerned but not surprised.

"Not anymore," I tell her. Henry will never find me up here, miles from the comforts of urban living. I felt unsure until I arrived, but being tucked into the forest like a chick beneath the wing of a hen, so much unadulterated nature pooling for miles and miles—I can't imagine it. And by now he's found my note, knows I'm dead. Even without a body—it could have easily washed into the Atlantic—he won't know to look at all if I did my job right. I permit myself a modicum of relief.

Myrtle leans back into a leather armchair, watching me eat. Beside her, a stack of old books glow arsenic green. "It's been a long time, Piers," she says quietly. "Why now?"

"I don't go by that anymore." My eyes meet hers. I'm not ready to talk about Henry yet, about why I came, how I got here. And while she's family, Aunt Myrtle is a stranger to me. I look down at my sandwich, appraising. "You can call me Acacia."

"Can or should?" she asks.

I don't say anything, and she nods. "You didn't answer my first question."

I swallow my bite of sandwich. "I told you. I have nowhere else to go."

She looks at my fingers denting the bread, a few still stained maroon from the berries. Our eyes lock. She remembers. She *knows*.

"There was a man," I say.

"He still breathing?" she asks, watching me.

"Yes." Technically, Henry is alive. But Don is not. I'm not sure how much I can tell her. But I cannot tell her that. She cannot know it's happened again.

"He know where you are?" she asks this time.

I shake my head as I take another bite. "I never told him about anyone but Mom."

"Why the name change then?" she presses.

I'm so tired. I just want to eat this sandwich and pass out somewhere soft and warm. But I can't show up on her doorstep after all these years with nothing but an empty backpack and a broken foot and not expect questions. All in all, she's being incredibly understanding. I can't imagine anyone else taking this half so well. Then again, I can't imagine anyone like Aunt Myrtle. She's a breed unto herself.

"He's dangerous," I tell her, my voice barely a whisper. "He thinks I'm dead. It was the only way."

She stares at me as I finish eating, then rises to take my empty plate. "Come on," she says, heading toward an open doorway at the far end of the room.

"I can stay in one of the cabins by the road," I tell her, not wanting to put her out any more than I have. "Just until I get on my feet."

"Don't be ridiculous," she says ushering me into a comfortable bedroom with a simple iron bed covered in a jewel-toned quilt. Two pillows in plaid shams rest on top. A floor lamp with an old hide shade is already on in the corner as if it were waiting for me. "You're family."

"It might be safer," I tell her truthfully. I don't expect Henry to come looking for me, but two years with him has taught me to always look over my shoulder.

She smiles in the soft light. "We don't fear men in this house," she tells me. "Men fear us."

WHEN I WAKE, it's a quarter past noon, and Myrtle's cabin is empty. I find the bathroom and take a long, hot shower, washing off days of filth and fear. I have to sit under the water because of my foot, now a grotesque shade of eggplant. After, I wince when I run a towel across the bruising around my left rib cage. I've been taking small breaths and aspirin to manage the pain, but it's not enough. Still, a doctor will ask questions. They might see a news report and put two and two together. I wonder if Aunt Myrtle knows someone trustworthy.

In my room, I find a pearl-snap shirt on a velvet chair in the corner, along with a pair of denim overalls, a fresh pair of cotton underwear, and thin wool socks. My other things are gone. Myrtle must have realized I didn't even have a change of clothes. The overalls are a tad long, but I roll the hems up. I'm just grateful to be clean.

I limp around the cabin, taking in its homey details. The designer in me delights in its quaint, romantic take on wilderness living, the wood ceiling and vintage Audubon prints, the tramp art frames and cross-stitch tablecloth—mushrooms with ferns and birds—and clumps of dried flowers and herbs. On a table by the sofa, I find a framed black-and-white photo of several women. I recognize Myrtle at once. She can't be more than sixteen, her dark hair shining. Beside her stands another woman, nearly as blond as my mother was. She's not as tall as Myrtle but just as assured, and they share the same jutting chin, square shoulders, and oval faces, the same glimmer of defiance in their eyes. Behind them is an older woman whose hair is pulled back off her face, her slim black dress severe in shape. And they are flanked by two more, a graying woman in white pearls and one who looks to be in her twenties with a sweater draped over her shoulders. They could be any group—a bridge club or a charity board—but there's something restless behind their eyes that unites them, something feral.

Feeling brave, I step outside and marvel at the difference a little daylight can make. In the sun, the woods around Myrtle's house are thick and gloriously green like something from a storybook, charming even, with trees that tower over the cabin and branches that run nearly to the ground. Ferns fan out across the turf, and decaying logs play host to mosses and shelves of fungus. Near the porch, a tender knot of white emerges from the dirt, spotless and enticing. A destroying angel, as Regis called them. More glint in the undergrowth like tempting fairy lights, weaving their way through the woods around the cabin. A spike of warning lances through my center like pain. Do they always grow so abundantly?

A red squirrel makes angry noises in my direction as I start down the trail. I don't have Myrtle to guide me, but the path is evident enough, and once I clear the trees, the A-frame café sits only paces away. A large black Lab is lying in the sun near the front door. He barely lifts his head. Stooping, I can't resist giving his head a good rub, delighting in the way his tongue lolls out happily. I asked Henry for a dog, but he couldn't abide the smell. I place my nose on top of the Lab's head and breathe in deep. He smells like comfort.

Inside, I find Myrtle behind the counter separating the kitchen from the dining room. A couple sits at one table with a little girl, and a man drinking coffee at the bar watches me as I enter. "Thank you for the clothes," I tell her as I approach.

"Your others are in the wash." She points to indicate the small addition jutting off the left side of the A-frame, a laundry and bathroom for the guests. She smiles as she refills the man's coffee cup. "Acacia, this is Ed, one of my boarders. Get used to his ugly mug 'cause you're going to be seeing it a lot. He lives in cabin five, likes to drink up all my coffee with his dog, Bart, whom I see you already met."

I brush the dog hairs from my arms and smile at Ed as I take my seat at the neighboring barstool. "Hi."

He nods. His eyes are close-set and sunken, camouflaged behind wiry, graying brows that hang over them like untrimmed climbers. A long nose and sloping cheeks end in a thick parcel of white beard. A trucker's cap sporting a patch embroidered with a wide-mouth bass sits high on his head like a crown. "You renting a cabin all by yourself?"

"Acacia is family," Myrtle tells him. "She's come to stay with me for a while."

"You don't say," he drawls, looking me up and down. "I think I see the resemblance now that you mention it. She's not your daughter, is she Myrtle?"

My aunt shoots him an unreadable look. "A niece," she says, "of sorts."

"Huh." He doesn't seem to know what to make of that.

"We're an old family," she continues. "A lot of branches on the tree. We keep in touch."

He nods slowly.

A blond woman breezes into the café, smiling at us as she approaches. She can't be a day over forty, pretty in a simple kind of way. "Myrtle, you're a lifesaver," she says, beaming. "That vinegar-soaked tennis ball trick really worked! I can't thank you enough."

Myrtle smiles. "When I know, *I know*. If only everyone around here listened to me like you did," she says, shooting Ed a look. Turning to me, she adds, "Beth Ann had a raccoon living under the front porch chewing up her stairs. So, I gave her a few tennis balls, told her to soak them in vinegar, and roll them right under there. They hate the smell."

Ed cocks a suspicious eyebrow. "Those wouldn't be Bart's tennis balls, would they, Myrtle?"

"I'll buy ya more," she tells him. "Beth Ann, this is my niece, Acacia. She'll be staying with me for a while. She needed a little R and R, and I told her some fresh mountain air would set things right."

The woman turns to me, one hand brushing her straw-colored locks back from her face. "Welcome! You know, I moved up here a couple of years ago from the city. Got tired of all the pollution and noise. Best decision I ever made! You're going to love it."

I haven't had a female friend in two years. And really, I never managed to forge those bestie bonds most girls do in childhood. But she's so open and energetic, I can't resist smiling. Maybe, in this new life, we can be friends. "Thank you."

She pats my arm. "We'll chat soon. Well, gotta go, Myrtle. Those turnips aren't going to plant themselves. Just wanted to say thank you since I was passing by."

Ed watches her as she leaves. "Remember when you didn't think she'd last a month?" he says.

Myrtle smiles warmly. "Once in a while, it's good to be wrong." Then, she adds, "Anyway, try not to be too much of a pest with Acacia here, eh, Ed? Keep that hound of yours from baying at the moon all hours."

"Aww, Myrtle, Bart never causes no trouble. You know that." He turns to me. "Best boy that ever walked on four legs. I can promise ya that. You afraid of dogs?"

I shake my head, giggling. "No, sir. I love dogs. Never had one, but always wished I did."

He brightens. "Well, Bart belongs to everybody around here. Ain't that right, Myrtle? She don't like to admit it, but she loves that dog as much as me," he says, throwing a thumb in her direction. "You know, I had a great-aunt with tuberculosis. She stayed with us for a whole year when I was a kid. Slept right out on the porch when the weather was warm enough. Cleared her lungs right up. We got on good."

Myrtle cocks an eyebrow at Ed like he's lost it. "Uh-huh."

He swats a hand at her. "All I mean is, lots of people come up here to heal what ails 'em."

"And what's your excuse?" she asks slyly.

He thrusts his lips out, rubs his beard. "Ain't nothing wrong with me these mountains can't fix."

Myrtle scowls. "If that were true, my firewood would be chopped by now."

He grumbles, standing. "I'll spend the whole day on it tomorrow, Myrtle. Promise."

"*Tomorrow?* What's wrong with today?"

He stretches his legs. "Old Bart and I got a busy afternoon of fishing planned. Gotta get out while we still have time."

"Ed, I need that firewood. Preferably before the first freeze, or we're both gonna count this our last winter." She gives him a pointed look.

He swats a hand at her again. "I told ya, I'll get to it."

"All right then," she caves. It's clear she cares about him, despite his orneriness and procrastination. "Catch a big one, Ed," she tells him. "Bring it back if you want me to cook it up for you later."

He waves as he heads out. "Will do, Myrtle!"

When he's gone, I turn to find a hot cup of coffee waiting for me. "His wife died a decade ago," she tells me, watching them through the window. "She was the earner in the family. Ed hasn't worked since he fell off a roof and broke his back in his early forties. He's lucky to be alive. But he couldn't hold on to his property without her income. Then the drinking set in. I let him stay here in exchange for upkeep around the place."

"That's kind of you," I tell her.

She shrugs. "Ain't nothing to it. He's one of ours, is all. And we look out for our own around here." Suddenly, her face falls, the smile dissipating like smoke. A serious look glints in her eye. "He comes in daily for the conversation. And he pokes around the place doing odd jobs for me. But he's not nosy. He knows when to mind his own business, understand? He's no threat to you." She says this last bit as if she's worried of what I might do.

"He seems nice," I reassure her, "like the cantankerous grandpa I never had."

She shrugs again. "He gets lonely." Then she gives me a little wink. "The lonely ones always find their way to me. I put them out of their misery."

I'm not sure what she means by that, but I'm too busy slurping my coffee to ask. "I take it you're not married?"

She laughs in a low voice. "We aren't all like your mother. I know my place, and it was never at a man's side."

"Never married, then." I take this fact in, chew on it. "And no kids."

"I had a son," she's quick to correct. "Couldn't keep him. It was a long time ago." Her eyes don't meet mine. For a few minutes, we sit in uncomfortable silence. I feel guilty for bringing it up.

"You sleep okay?" she eventually asks.

I nod.

Myrtle takes in my appearance, the rolled cuffs and hang of the overalls. "When this family leaves, we'll close up and drive to Malone, get you some clothes. You can't keep wearing mine."

"But I don't have any money," I tell her.

"I know," she says, reaching out to smooth the hair around my face. "This round will be on me. And you need to see a doctor about that foot."

I flinch. "I don't know if that's wise."

Her eyes narrow. "An urgent care clinic. You'll be in and out quickly. They won't ask questions."

I nod my assent, and she carries a pitcher of water over to the table with the family to refill their glasses.

"Guests," she tells me when she returns. "Cabin three. They'll be gone in the morning."

"Do you get many this far north?"

"We stay full enough in the summer," she says. "But it will slow down soon. Kids will go back to school, and people will prepare for autumn and the cold that comes after. They're less inclined to travel then, which is just as well. Except the skiers. I have ten cabins altogether. Right now, not counting Ed and Bart, they're all full, but tomorrow after that family leaves, we'll have an opening. Next week, likely a couple more. By next month, we'll sit at half capacity, and winter will be slow. But I like it that way. The quiet suits me. It's the right kind of life for a Corbin."

She makes it sound like I come from a family of recluses. Frankly, I wouldn't know. And my mom, for all her desire to look like the perfect nuclear family, never really mixed much with people. Gerald was her everything, which is almost as sad as my and Henry's marriage.

"Not like your big-city life, I guess," she says. "Must be strange for you."

I smile tightly. "Charleston had its perks, but I didn't really get out much the last few years." When I glance up, she's staring at me. "But that's all in the past now." I don't really care where I am at this point as long as Henry isn't here. "Can I ask you something?"

"Shoot," she tells me, pulling out a tub of egg salad and some bread.

I take a breath. "Why didn't you ever come back? After that first time, I never saw you again."

Her eyes look sad as she answers. "Your mother wouldn't have liked that," she says. "It was for your own good."

"I was so alone," I say into my coffee cup. "Meeting you was the only time I felt like I belonged."

Until Henry. I remember the way he took charge on our first date, ordering for me, answering whenever the waiter asked me a question. I was so naive, so desperate to be someone's. I believed it was a sign that he cared about me. It was the first time I truly felt valuable. But after we were married, it changed. Instead, I felt like something he possessed. Those early gestures were never about me; they were about him, his need to dominate. Maybe, if Myrtle had been a part of my life growing up, I wouldn't have been vulnerable to Henry.

She squeezes my hand. "I should have come to find you after Lily died. I'm sorry."

"Why didn't you?" I ask.

Her face crumples and she quickly turns around. "Too many bad memories, I guess."

9

Mushrooms

When the news breaks, I feel hands circling my throat.

The first few days in Crow Lake, Myrtle allowed me to rest. I spent my time in bed, reading books from her stash of racy romance novels, trying and failing not to think of Regis—strong hands and the sandy shadow of his beard—and drinking cup after cup of a questionable tea she kept brewing for me. She made good on her promise to take me to Malone, where I got an overdue haircut, reshaping the long sheet of my hair into something edgy and just past the shoulders with face-framing layers, a new phone, and enough clothes to ride out the summer and fall without worry. And where a rattled doctor confirmed my cracked ribs and gave me an X-ray revealing an avulsion fracture of the fifth metatarsal on my right foot. He offered to write me a prescription for the pain, but beyond that, there was little he could do. After that, Myrtle's home brew regime began.

At night, we'd sit on the porch in the dark, soaking in the clean scent of fir trees and sipping from our mugs. When I dared to question the bitter aftertaste, she admonished me with a cluck of the tongue. "Family recipe," she insisted and got up to pour more. But then she would tell me stories about the motel and the guests she'd had over the years—the time a woman delivered a baby in cabin two, and the rock star who stayed in cabin four after leaving rehab, trying to avoid the press.

A week later, she put me to work.

Most days, I dust and make beds, vacuum the cabin floors.

I help with laundry—bedsheets and towels—and give a hand in the café whenever I can, carting plates and glasses, wiping down tabletops, washing a few dishes, simple things. We got crutches per the doctor's orders, but they hurt my hands and I stopped using them. Besides, my foot is healing quickly, hurting much less by the day. Maybe there's something to Myrtle's tea after all.

The guests dwindle as September approaches, but we stay busy at the Balsam Motor Inn. The café sees the most business at breakfast. And really, *café* is an overstatement; Myrtle doesn't even keep a menu. She has a blackboard by the front door where she writes what's available for the day, and a help-yourself spread that she puts out on the small bar every morning—fruit and boxes of cereal, shingles of toast with butter packets, a pitcher of orange juice. But she keeps the waffle iron hot and mixes batter daily. And the maple syrup is in ample supply. At lunch, she offers one kind of sandwich along with peanut butter and jelly for the kids and individual bags of chips. For dinner, there might be a soup or a casserole on offer. Between our guests, people from town with slim pickings, and drivers who are passing by, there's always a few folks inside. I don't like being visible to people who might leave and take a mental picture of me with them, but I can't hide out in her cabin forever while she clothes and feeds me like a child.

A couple of times, I wake in the night and find her gone, the front door open, forest beckoning. Once, I saw her turning down a path in the dark, Ed's dog, Bart, at her heels. I wanted to follow, but my foot made it impossible to do so quietly. The absences unnerve me, like breaks in a chain, interruptions that should not be there. But I don't ask her about them.

One night, I bring the picture from her living room out to the porch and hand it to her. "Who are they?"

She wipes the glass with her shirttail and looks at me as I sit down across from her. "Do you remember your grandmother?"

I shake my head.

Her lips purse. She points to the blond woman next to her in the picture. "She was my sister, Angel. You met her, but I guess you were too little to remember."

"And the rest?" I press.

She studies their faces. "Well, you know me. This woman behind us is our mother, Laurel. Your great-grandmother. She was remarkable. It's a shame you never got to know her. And this lady in the pearls is her sister, Bella. The other one is Bella's daughter, Donna, who has an older sister, Lattie, who's not in the photo." Myrtle smiles. "So many years ago."

She passes it back to me and I run a finger over their faces. "I wish I could meet them," I say to myself.

But she hears me. "I suspect you will. Eventually."

THE NEXT EVENING, the news report airs on the small flat-screen television mounted on the wall. Myrtle keeps it on continuously for the guests but mutes it because the noise drives her crazy. We're dealing with the last of the supper crowd, a whopping total of seven people. Tonight's special: New York–style chili and saltine crackers. It's a hit with several of the single men in town. Ed downs two and a half bowls on his own, and I slip him an extra sleeve of crackers when Myrtle isn't looking. He winks his gratitude. The more food in his belly to soak up the beer, the better. I'm wiping down a table when she turns up the volume on the TV.

"Her body was found next to this firepit, no more than ten feet from her house," the reporter says, a woman with short black hair and sharp cheekbones. "Like his other victims, she'd been strangled. This marks the Saranac Strangler's fifth victim and a deadly turn in his MO. Only a couple of weeks since his last murder, the Strangler seems to be ramping up his activities, trying to sate a growing bloodlust. Additionally, this is the first victim found on private property. Is the Strangler getting sloppy? Or growing bolder?"

I feel it strike me like a blunt object, the flash of wet, pale hair, her smell—lavender shampoo and fear. Pee soaking the ground. It's gone as quickly as it came, but I put a hand to my throat just the same. There is something starkly familiar about this one, though I can't place it. I think I hear Henry laughing and spin around.

Myrtle is looking at Ed. His mouth hangs open. "Is it just me, or do you recognize that firepit?"

"Looks like the one at Beth Ann's place. She keeps an old tractor tire rim in the stones just like that," he confirms.

My chest clenches. Beth Ann—turnips and raccoons and sunshine smiles—the friend I always wanted but never had. She dropped in that first day after I arrived.

Myrtle's face falls. "I was afraid of this. I told her she should stay with her brother in Vermont, just until this Strangler business passes."

"This is the same Beth Ann I met?" I ask, setting a bowl and spoon in the sink behind the counter, hoping I'm wrong.

Myrtle frowns. "Yes. She worked as a freelance writer and had the benefit of being able to live anywhere, which is why I wanted her to leave. No point taking unnecessary chances. But once mountain life gets ahold of you, it's hard to let go. Even for a few weeks."

"She was doing so good," Ed mentions, hanging his head. "Even you said it had been a long time since you'd seen a woman on her own take to these parts so well."

Myrtle drops a dish towel to the counter. "No husband, no kids, no one to look out for her. I tried to convince her to pack up and go someplace else. Come back when she's happily married. A woman like that gets lonely up here with nothing but trees for company. How's she going to meet anyone? Huh?"

"You seemed to make it work," I point out, but Myrtle only huffs.

"That's different," she insists.

I don't see how, but there's no arguing with her. I've already figured that much out. Ed, for all his extra years of experience, still has not.

Myrtle turns to him. "He's close. He's been dancing around us this whole time, but Beth Ann was one of ours. That means the Strangler is in Crow Lake." Her eyes fall on me.

I turn my attention back to the news report as I push in chairs at the table I just bussed. The reporter is sharing a forensics profile of the killer, hoping it might spark some leads.

"The Saranac Strangler is believed to be a man in his thirties or forties. Known for the meticulousness of his previous crime scenes, he is thought to have an overarching need for order and control. His victims suggest a history of difficult relationships with women and a preoccupation with power and dominance. Though he leaves no DNA trace to corroborate the theory, it is believed his sexual fantasies are entangled with his need to kill, and it is suspected that these murders may be his only course for relief."

Myrtle walks up behind me as I let out a choked laugh.

"Something funny to you?" she asks, her voice low.

My teeth clench and I busy myself wiping at imaginary spots on the salt and pepper shakers. "I know the type, is all," I tell her.

"Homicidal maniac is a *type*?" she asks, incredulous.

I turn to face her, my eyes cold. Somehow, this news makes it feel like Henry is winning. "It is for me."

Her lips flatten against one another. "Come with me," she says.

I follow her to the back of the café and slowly up the winding staircase—careful of my boot—to the second-story room. She unlocks the door and turns on the light. I recognize what must be the pantry, storage for all the food and equipment she uses in the café and guest cabins. Shelves line three walls stocked with canned tomatoes and powdered coffee creamer and large plastic jars filled with spices. Clean towels and tubs of laundry detergent fill another whole unit. "It can get hard to make it in or out of this town in the winter. It's good to keep stores, just in case."

I nod, knowing that once my foot fully heals, I'll probably have to come up here and haul things down for her. The front wall by the door has built-in cabinets made of knotty pine. I glide my hand down them, running my fingers over the smooth tiles of the counter, feeling an odd pull to the last cabinet on the top. There's an extra sink up here, I notice. And some kitchen supplies—a mortar and pestle, a coffee grinder, a food dehydrator. Nestled amid the stock of food and supplies is an upright futon with two pillows and a throw blanket on top.

"For the occasional straggler," she tells me, nodding toward the futon. "It's smart to keep an extra bed around here."

She starts to reach for a large bag of salt. "I've got to get this down. Help me by opening that bin."

With my cracked ribs, I can't really muscle the bag, so I take the lid off the waiting plastic bin and pull out the old bag to throw away.

"This man," she asks as we work, "the one you say is danger-ous, that thinks you're dead—he chokes you?"

I swallow. "Sometimes," I admit.

When she looks at me, her eyes burn. "He ever kill anyone?"

"Not yet," I tell her, moving to lean against the counter. I fold my arms and look away. These are hard things to admit to myself, much less someone else. I can't imagine a woman like Aunt Myr-tle being hurt by a man like Henry. But she doesn't judge me. In fact, she's remarkably placid.

She sighs. "But he's been working up to it? Practicing on you?"

I nod. The women I've seen coming, the ones I hoped to save, flip like flash cards through my mind. These are not women Henry has killed. They are not even women he's met yet. But somehow, I know they will be. Unless . . . My eyes flood with tears, hot and spiked with shame.

She gently grabs my chin, lifting my face up. "You look at me, Piers Corbin, when you talk about him. You understand? Don't you ever hide your face in shame again. Did anything unusual ever happen during these episodes? Before or after? Any urges?"

"Urges?" I echo, sniffling. "Like what?"

"Never mind," she says, looking a little disappointed. "You'd know them if they did." She steps back, studies me. "Stay here until you calm down. No use alerting anyone down there that you're upset. The less they know about you, the better."

I nod.

She starts for the door, adding, "Stay out of the cabinets. Those are my personal stores." And then she's gone.

The room is blissfully quiet. I pull a tissue from a box, blotting my face, then wiping my nose. When I'm ready, I turn to go back down, but a feeling of intense curiosity compels me toward that far cabinet on top. Aunt Myrtle said to leave it alone, but the feeling wins out. Inside sit several unmarked jars of varying shapes and sizes. Most look like they began their life as something else—spaghetti sauce containers or pickle relish. One in particular catches my eye. It's filled with something dried and wrinkly, off-white in color, that I can't take my eyes off. Slowly, I reach for it, the glass cool in my hand as I grip the lid and twist. Once it's off, I take a deep inhale of the earthy, moldy scent. My lungs practically hum with desire. My mouth waters. Everything in me is tingling with need. I know this feeling. I've felt it as a little girl staring at the pokeweed berries. The memory floods me with mortification, all those heavy, dark feelings I carried as a child, unwanted, misunderstood. The thud of the man at my feet. The lump of Don on the ground.

I screw the lid on tight and replace the jar, closing the cabinet and stepping away. Whatever else Myrtle is keeping in there, I don't want to know. Her secrets are her own. Mine are already enough to bear.

I SPEND THE next day working hard to ignore the pull of that storeroom cabinet and its devilish jars. When I close my eyes at night, I see the dull gleam of its contents, the rich scent filling up my lungs. Myrtle notices my agitation, the way I can't sit still, my need for movement, but she doesn't say anything. The need is insatiable, a constant whine at my back, an itch I can't reach. It clouds my mind when I try to read and distracts me in the café.

Even Ed comments when I trip over his dog on my way to the washing machine, turning to apologize profusely to Bart, who is simply delighted to receive attention.

I'm embarrassed and annoyed that my condition—pica—has reared its ugly head. As a child, I couldn't explain it. My mother always looked at me with such disappointment, as if she'd been given a freak for a daughter. Even the doctor seemed particularly vexed by my case, not sure what to make of this girl and her deadly obsession. But that was just it. It wasn't deadly to me. Once they left me alone, eating pokeweed made a certain kind of sense. It felt so natural, an instinct I should follow, like drinking water. But as an adult, I understand how peculiar and unsettling it is, how it must look to those on the outside. And I can't afford to stand out here. Nor can I risk appalling Aunt Myrtle, whose good graces are keeping me alive at the present moment. I suppress the urge.

But by the second night, I can no longer take it. I toss and turn and finally rise when I hear the front door open. Myrtle is going for one of her nightly walks. I pull on some shorts and scoot onto the porch, watching her disappear into the shadows, and then I bolt for the café. She keeps a spare key hidden in an old coffee can full of dryer sheets in the laundry room, which she leaves unlocked for guests to use at their discretion.

I make quick work of finding it and let myself in without turning on any lights. In the dark, the café is a muddle of shapes, silent like a heart that's stopped beating. The spiral staircase rises like a spine at the back, and I clunk my way up it to the storeroom door. The door doesn't budge, but luckily I have a sneaking suspicion that proves to be true—the front door key also unlocks this one. Grateful, I dart to the cabinet. The jar I'm looking for glows softly in its recesses, an invitation. I twist off its cap and reach inside, pulling up several fingers' worth of the dried plant, shoving it into my mouth. The taste is buttery at first, only subtly bitter, and a bit like chewing on Styrofoam it's so dry, but my eyes flutter with pleasure just the same. It's some kind of mushroom, desiccated and chopped up. I should stop with one bite, but I can't. I reach in again and again, letting myself savor the strange texture, the pungent, wood-like flavors. By the time I put the lid back on, I've made a sizable dent. I tuck it behind several of the other jars, in the hope that she won't notice, and leave the café, locking up behind me.

Slipping the key back into its hiding spot, I rush to the cabin, praying she's not back yet, and breathe a sigh of relief when I see the front door is still open. I stop in the bathroom to quickly rinse my mouth out. My eyes pulse an unnatural green in the mirror. Climbing into bed, I sleep deeply for the first time since I found the jar. But my dreams are vivid and unnerving with an Alice in Wonderland twist. Giant mushrooms tower over me, their stalks a dazzling white. Tags hang from their caps, swaying gently. I reach up to turn one over and find an old Bible verse, a line from Genesis I heard during my mother's brief foray into church—*From any tree of the garden you may eat freely; but from the tree of the knowledge of good and evil you shall not eat, for in the day that you eat from it you will surely die.*

THE NEXT MORNING, my mouth feels extra dry and weirdly numb. I dress quickly and decide to leave the boot off for the first time, my foot still tender but far less swollen. Myrtle watches me enter her little kitchen and sits a cup of coffee before me along with a dish of sugar cubes.

"Where'd you go last night?" she asks, and I wonder how she knows.

My eyes meet hers, guilt pooling behind them. "There was a guest who stopped up the toilet in the public bathroom. I went to help plunge it."

She sips from her cup. "That's odd."

"What is?" I drop two cubes into my coffee and stir.

"That they would come all this way in the middle of the night to tell you." She looks down her nose at me. "Usually, they just let it overflow."

It's not a pleasant thought.

"Which cabin?" she asks.

"Hmm? Oh. Four, I think."

She smiles. "I'll have to thank them when I get the chance."

I smile back. Cabin four is checking out this morning, but I don't bother saying so. One look tells me she knows already. I could throw it back in her face, ask her where she goes creeping off to half the nights, but I don't really want to rock this boat. I need Aunt Myrtle. Whatever was in that jar, I won't be eating it again.

Fortunately, the day is a busy one and Myrtle doesn't get another opportunity to rake me over the coals about my nightly whereabouts. I'm far more focused today than I have been, pulling sheets from beds and mopping up the laundry room floor and cleaning out the toilets of the empty cabins. Myrtle has one strict policy—cleanliness. Especially when it comes to bathrooms. Her cabins are small and understated inside, but they're cute enough and more importantly, they're sparkling clean. Toilets and sinks get cleaned every day in occupied cabins unless they hang a DO NOT DISTURB sign on the exterior knob. But even in the unoccupied cabins, toilets and sinks get cleaned every other day. I did try to point out that no one was using them, therefore it was an unnecessary waste of product, but Myrtle would hear none of it.

The café is unusually full. The continental offerings at breakfast get wiped out, and five people from town come in for waffles. Lunch is BLTs and it seems like just about everybody and their brother wants one. Dinner is a classic tuna casserole with garlic bread. I worry we'll sell out of the two whole trays she's made. I'm refilling waters when the unfamiliar couple comes in. It must be nearly seven by now. We don't have a regular closing time. Myrtle typically just locks up after the last dinner guest has left or been run off. Tonight, we're running later than usual.

He strides through the front door like he owns the place, seats himself at a table I only bussed minutes before. But she lags behind, refusing to make eye contact, her dress several sizes too big for her frame.

I take the pitcher of water back to Myrtle in the kitchen.

"Go see what the travelers want," she tells me. *Traveler* is what she calls anybody coming in off the road.

I nod and make my way over. "You here for the tuna casserole?"

"You got a menu?" he asks, voice rough.

I point to the chalkboard Myrtle uses. "You're looking at it."

He peers across the room at her writing. "I want the BLT."

"Sorry," I tell him. "We ran out of bacon at four o'clock."

He looks up at me, and I recognize the haughtiness in his expression, that same edge Henry always had, as if he were a head above everyone else in the room. As if I am lucky to be in his presence. "I don't like tuna fish," he says slowly.

"Well, we can make you a peanut butter and jelly," I suggest. "It's what we give the kids."

He glares at me, licks his bottom lip. "Fine."

I turn to the woman. "And for you?"

For the first time, she looks up, and that's when I see the swollen cheekbone, shiny and purple, the broken vessels and bruising under her eye. Suddenly, the large dress makes sense. The injuries beneath it are probably worse than her face. She can't bear anything against her skin.

"She'll have the same as me," her husband or boyfriend interjects. He eyes her across the table. "I don't want to smell fish on you in the car."

My hands begin to tremble. I wipe them across the front of my shirt.

"Tonight would be great, sweetheart," he says, shooting me an irritated glance.

In it, I see her body crumpled on the floor, see the trajectory of his leg as he kicks her, watch her bleed across the carpet, the baby lost to her now. My blood surges, a whoosh sounding in my ears.

"Sure." I bite the word off at the end and walk slowly to the kitchen, passing Myrtle on the way. She's been roped into a conversation with two of Ed's friends, who spend most of their free time at the Drunken Moose. Their favorite subjects are the weather, guns, and fishing.

"And coffee!" I hear the man shout across the café at me.

My shoulders jerk and I duck behind the counter to pour his cup, hands shaking the whole time. I know this man. He's not Henry's exact match, but he's of a kind. And I know an abused woman when I see one. She's lucky he let her come in here at all, looking like that. He probably figures no one knows them, so they won't be confronted. Guys like him count on people's need to maintain the status quo. Or he's become so arrogant he's lost touch with the fact he's committed a crime. He'll speed out of here when he's done, probably hold her down while he rapes her tonight for having the gall to look me in the face. I stare into the black void of his coffee and see all the pain Henry has ever caused me. Anger flushes across my skin like heat, and I begin to perspire. My stomach twists. It's not nausea exactly, but a need for release. My lip curls. Leaning down slightly, I work my tongue, gathering saliva, and spit a long drip into his cup, stirring it with my finger for good measure. Someday, I'll find a way to fight back that really counts for something, but for now, this little gesture brings a modicum of justice.

I set the coffee before him, burning with every step. I place a glass of ice water next to her. I want to touch her shoulder, tell her I *know*. But that would only make it worse for her. I walk back, preparing to make his sandwich, when Myrtle steps in front of me.

"I've got this," she says, grabbing the handle of the fridge. Her eyes dart from me to their table. "Why don't you go outside, check on the bathroom, make sure there's plenty of toilet paper."

"But there's so many people—" I start to say.

Myrtle narrows her eyes at me, tucks her chin. "Go outside, Acacia. Cool off. You look . . . flushed."

I think she knows what I'm feeling. She must have seen the woman, too. I nod and stalk out into the cool air, not even stopping to pet Bart. I dally in the bathroom, restocking toilet paper and changing the trash. I wash my hands and splash water across my face. And then I kick around in the grass behind the café, waiting for my internal body temperature to regulate, for the tremor to leave my hands and the burn to leave my skin. It takes several long, slow breaths as I look up to the sky, stars beginning to spill across it like glitter.

It's so beautiful here it hurts, a deep ache in the chest like your heart is stretching, too small to take it all in. These mountains hold me in a fertile embrace, a mystical undercurrent pulsing just beneath the soles of my feet. I never fancied myself the outdoorsy type, but here I feel connected to something I've been missing my whole life. As if these mountains and I are made of the same stuff. As if I am closer to the bobcat and the timber wolf and the black bear than I am to another human being. It helps that I can't imagine Henry here, in a place so rugged and wild, so free. He would detest the natural order of it, the lack of right angles. It makes me love it all the more. I can see why Myrtle came here and never left. I may never leave myself.

Convinced I've taken enough of a break, I head back toward the café. I'm just walking up to the front door when I see the man from the road through the window. He stands, takes an ungainly step as if his legs don't quite work, and turns to the side. His stomach swells before my eyes and he clutches at it. His skin burnishes with a sickly urine color, the whites of his eyes turning yellow like aged paper. He stumbles forward, vomiting violently across his shoes, and I see the wet stain grow along the back of his tight jeans as he shits himself. The woman with him begins screaming as he collapses, taking another table down with him in a great clatter of dishes.

I am frozen with one hand on the door. As he falls, my eyes meet Myrtle's across the café, and in them, I see fear.

10

Sheriff

I didn't create the monster, I just married him. But I met the woman who did.

After he proposed and I accepted, Henry explained that he came from an old English family, a relic of the British nobility on his mother's side—Eleanor. She'd technically been born and raised in the United States but clung to the social etiquette of her ancestors. It had made his childhood especially challenging. He adored his mother, but she was cold, and she didn't mingle with people outside her own family. He wanted to invite her to the wedding, but he had to be sure she wouldn't encounter any guests "beneath her station." As it turned out, all Charleston was beneath Eleanor's station. So, we married alone, with only her arctic blue eyes and disdainful pout to witness it.

The ceremony was minuscule, under the wide branches of oak trees at a historic site with just the three of us in attendance.

She walked up to introduce herself after the nuptials in a black lace skirt and jacket set, dark crimson lipstick rimming her smile. She had Henry's lean build and thin hair, but her eyes were lighter, like those of a corpse. "You must be the bride," she said as she looked me over.

I smiled nervously. I wanted so much to make a good impression, to please Henry in this way. I knew what his mother meant to him, despite their troubled relationship.

She turned to her son. "Her hips are too narrow. Has she any people? Any heritage? Can she even give you children?"

He dropped my hand. "Mum, please don't be rude. Piers has been very successful here in Charleston."

She glared at him, opened her handbag, and pulled out a pair of white gloves. "You know I hate when you call me that, Henry."

His face reddened. "Sorry, Lady Mother."

My mouth dropped open.

With her gloves finally on, she held a hand out for me to take. I grasped her fingers and gently shook them once before letting go. She peered at me. "Eleanor Frances Astley Davenport. You may call me Eleanor. Not Ellie or Nell or Fran or Mrs. Davenport. Certainly not mother-in-law or anything of the kind. To Henry, I am Lady Mother, never Mum. Though he persists in his childish infatuation. To you, only Eleanor. Do you understand?"

I nodded, speechless.

"Close your mouth," she told me. "You look like a codfish." She cast her frigid gaze on Henry. "I had such high hopes when you were born," she said with a touch of wistfulness. She turned to me again. "You will be welcome at Excelsior Hall on holidays and when expressly invited. Never in between. You are to mind my son in all manner of things, is that clear?"

I looked to Henry, aghast. But he stared at me as if this were all perfectly normal.

"You haven't any reason to trust your own judgment, being of low birth with no real position in society, so it should prove easy for you. Be an obedient, dutiful wife and I'm sure this union will succeed. But if you are willful," she continued, "if you are negligent of my son or indecorous in your behavior, if you disappoint him . . ." Her eyes flashed. "Well, you will find him to be well-trained in the art of discipline. I saw to that myself."

I stood there, horrified, unsure how to respond when Henry finally spoke up. "Piers, show some dignity. Find your tongue."

"Yes, ma'am," I finally uttered, too shocked to say anything else.

"Shall we luncheon then?" she asked. "Is she respectable in public?"

Henry slipped his hands into the pockets of his trousers. "She will be agreeable. I assure you, Lady Mother."

Eleanor sniffed. "Very well then. Proceed."

I spent the next hour and a half feeling like I was in another time, maybe on another planet. Henry and his mother discussed the stock market, the state of the British royal family, the upkeep needed at Excelsior Hall—which I had gathered was their crumbling family home in Virginia, one she hung on to with great effort after his father disgraced them with several bad investments—and the perils of steeplechasing, a horse racing event I'd never heard of. When I asked for a glass of champagne to celebrate, Henry took it away while it was still half full and gave it back to the waiter. He ordered me the roast chicken, taking pains to make sure they did not cook it in too much butter. Eleanor ate only a wedge salad.

When lunch was over, she kissed her son on the cheek. "Don't waste time," she told him. "You have a duty. Fertility is likely her only virtue, and it has a shelf life." Her eyes cut to me and back again. "Grandchildren are all you can give me now."

"Can we drive you to the airport, Lady Mother?" he asked her.

She waved a hand. "Don't be absurd. I don't need assistance. I remain perfectly capable of maintaining my own affairs. Let's hope you do the same." She leveled her gaze on him before turning to me. There were no cheek kisses, not even another handshake, just a cold, "Piers."

We watched her get into a car and drive away.

"She won't even stay the night?" I asked.

Henry rounded on me. "Could you say nothing? Seriously, Piers?"

I swallowed my words. "I—I'm sorry. I was nervous."

He glared at me. "You know how important this was for me," he said angrily.

I gaped. "Henry, she insulted me! At every turn! On my wedding day! And you stood by and said nothing. You let her speak to me like that."

He grabbed me by the arm and tugged me to the car. "Get in," he said, pushing me toward it.

Shakily, I climbed into the passenger seat. We didn't speak the whole ride home. I cried silently, wondering how the happiest day of my life had gone so terribly wrong. I believed then that it was Eleanor's fault, that she brought out the worst in him. Later in bed, when he began to undress me, to kiss my neck and breasts, I convinced myself it was over. She was gone, and things would return to normal. Henry would dote on me, cherish me, take care of me. He would forget her outlandish advice and accusations. He never apologized, but by the time he was inside me, I didn't care. I mistook his sexual attention for affection, a gesture of reparation. He was hungry for me that night, so eager and insatiable, ferocious with his thrusts. "No one will ever love you like I do."

I remember the way his hand wrapped around my neck as he came, almost tender, how it slipped over my own mouth as I moaned with pleasure. "Hush," he told me, looking down. "Don't spoil it."

Eleanor died six weeks later. She suffered a fatal heart attack. Her maid found her sprawled across the wool rug the next day, but it was too late. The night Henry got the news was the first night he hit me. I remember him putting down the phone slowly and turning to look at me.

"What's wrong?" I asked, noting the strange fall of his face, his slack jaw. "Did something happen?"

He walked toward me, staring, eyes brighter than usual. "You did this," he said quietly.

"Did what?" It was late and we'd just finished moving into our new house the day before, the one he bought by surprise and convinced me would make us happy. The one I never wanted. I was wearing a tank top and pajama shorts, a loose sweater thrown over.

"What did you do?" he asked.

I stared at him, baffled, my mother's words only a beat behind his—*What have you done?* I was five years old again. Confused and culpable in ways I didn't understand.

And then he screamed, "What did you do!"

He lunged at me, and I tried to run, but he caught me by the hem of that sweater and yanked me to him.

"Henry, please!" I cried. "I don't know what you're talking about. I don't know what you mean!"

But he was gone, something demonic filling the pale depths of his eyes. He grabbed my face, squeezing it in his hand, shaking me as he called me names. "This is your fault! You're worthless. Barely good for a fuck, you know that? She's dead because of you! Because you can't give me a child. You can't do anything right!" He punched me hard in the stomach and I doubled over, unable to draw a breath.

I hadn't confided in Henry that I'd had an IUD inserted the year before. I didn't realize when we married that he'd want children so soon, but I had no intention of getting pregnant yet.

"Please, Henry. I'm sorry. Please let me help you," I wept.

"I don't need your help," he growled as he shoved me down, grinding the side of my face into the carpet. "You can't even help yourself."

I slept curled up beside the coffee table that night, where he'd left me. When I woke, he was gone, but there was a blanket over me and a note that read, *Dinner at 7:00.*

THE CAFÉ ERUPTS in chaos. Myrtle shouts at Ed to call 911 before tearing across the room and getting one of the Drunken Moose regulars to help her roll the man over. "Start chest compressions!" she orders him. "It looks like an allergic reaction. I'm going up to the storeroom to see if I have an EpiPen." Her eyes fall on the sobbing woman who came in with him. "Someone get this woman some ice for her face," she barks and the other Drunken Moose guy heads for the freezer. "Anything to calm her down." She looks down at the man doing chest compressions. "Don't let him die," she breathes.

He looks up. "But, Myrtle, it's too late."

"Then bring him back!" she shouts before spinning toward the back stairs.

By now, I've made my way inside, skirting the mess and the madness with wide eyes.

Myrtle grabs me by the hem of my shirt and I instinctively wince. She lets go but takes my hand. "You're coming with me," she says under her breath, herding me to the back and up the staircase in front of her.

Once in the storeroom, she slams the door behind us. "What did you do?" She shakes me by both arms, and I crumple, my face washing with tears as my heart races through my chest. I suddenly find it hard to breathe, and my inhales sound like I'm sucking them through a sieve. I'm hyperventilating.

Myrtle backs me toward the futon and sits me down. She kneels before me. "We only have a minute," she whispers. "This is very important. Do you hear me, Piers?"

I nod my head.

"I have to go back down there soon. That poor bastard was dead the second you laid eyes on him; they won't bring him back. But that's neither here nor there. I need you to empty the cabinets of all the jars, do you understand?" She rises and swings open the far door, the very same one I was in last night. "Bury them in the salt," she tells me, pointing to the large plastic bin I helped her fill. "Bury them deep. You hear me? No one knows about this. Dry your face, and when you come back down, stay calm."

I feel like a small child being scolded. I cover my face with my hands. "I spit into his coffee," I tearfully admit. "That's all. I—I don't know what happened. I don't understand."

Myrtle pulls my hands away. "Piers, look at me."

My eyes meet hers and in them, past the fear and the panic, I see strength. She may be the first person in my entire life I can truly lean on. "This is not your fault."

"Okay," I whisper through rattled breaths.

She goes to the door. "Remember, bury them deep," she says over a shoulder.

"Myrtle?" I ask, shaken. "How do you know? How do you know it wasn't me?" If I'm not to blame this time, then maybe I'm not to blame for Don or the man when I was five.

She turns to me before she leaves. If I didn't know better, I'd say she looks proud. "Oh, honey, this may not be your fault, but you killed him sure as I'm standing here."

Her words wash over me in a tide of anguish. Don's panic-stricken face flashes through my memory. The salt lick of flesh in my mouth at five. I keep seeing the man downstairs stumbling, his belly swelling impossibly large, the sickly golden change in his skin, the sudden drop. I force myself to breathe through the terror. I did this. I killed a man. A bad man, to be sure. But there is something called *due process* in this country, something called *innocent until proven guilty,* something called a *jury of your peers.* And if I am responsible for that dead man lying downstairs, then I am responsible for Don, too. For that man when I was just a child. I am a criminal, hapless but deadly. An accidental murderer.

One could argue that as a child I was innocent by default, that Don was self-defense, but the man downstairs, that arrogant prick who liked to beat up on women, never laid a finger on me. And that makes me guilty beyond a reasonable doubt.

Suddenly, Myrtle's command comes barreling back to me. I rush to the cabinet, hastily pulling the jars out, as many as I can hold. Carrying them to the salt bin, I shove them down one at a time, salt up to my armpit. It takes a few rounds to get them all. There must be more than ten. Fortunately, some are quite small. They all fit easily into the container, and while the salt level rises, it doesn't spill over. When I'm done, I run a hand over the top to hide the indentations where my arm had been, smoothing out the salt. I make sure to shake any excess off my sleeve before leaving the room.

Slowly, I creep down the stairs, using my injured foot as an excuse to draw it out. People are standing around in small clusters, whispering to one another. The man doing chest compressions has moved aside for Myrtle to take his place. The abused woman is sitting with a dish towel full of ice pressed to her face, sniffling quietly. The energy, for all its hysteria minutes ago, has shifted to subdued.

My eyes fall on the dead man. His face is gruesome to behold—staring, tainted eyes and vomit smeared across his chin. The only thing worse than the sight is the smell. Myrtle is right; he's long gone. But she pumps away, looking up to meet my eyes just once. Her face is unreadable, but I know she's given up on reviving him. Everyone has.

I find an empty seat and slide down into it. My mind cannot work out the connection. With Don, I knew the pokeweed was to blame somehow. It must have lingered in my system, contaminated my mouth or skin, something he came into contact with during his attempt to rape me. But even so, wouldn't he only have encountered a trivial amount? An inconsequential trace? Surely not enough to be fatal.

This is different. The pokeweed I ate is long gone, passed through urine and sweat, washing me clean. It can't be responsible for what happened to this poor asshole. *I* can't be responsible, unless . . .

Unless Myrtle's cabinet stash is just as lethal. Unless whatever I devoured during my midnight pica excursion wasn't harmless but devastating.

My eyes fall on her bent form, the agitated thrusts of her arms, the resignation in her face. Her long, silvering hair is clipped behind her head, falling gracefully over her shoulders even now. *We are a family of crows,* she told me once as a young girl. *Crows feed on what others can't, including other birds.*

I am seeing Aunt Myrtle with new and terrifying eyes.

The sound of a siren cuts through my abstraction. An ambulance rolls into view and comes to a stop. Paramedics leap out and rush into the room, moving Myrtle aside. She explains what happened as they work, what everyone witnessed. I know nothing about saving a life, but it looks like they're giving him all the usual procedures despite their resigned expressions. They load him onto a stretcher and head outside, the wife or girlfriend tripping behind. "He needs a hospital," one of them says to Myrtle.

He needs a morgue, I think.

Behind them, two fire trucks pull up, lights whirling. Relief steals over me as the body is whisked away. I slump against the back of the chair, letting out a long, slow breath. I dare a glance at Aunt Myrtle, who looks similarly relieved, leaning against one of the standing tables, a hand to her head as she allows herself a much-needed break.

But a white law enforcement vehicle with green and gold stripes parks at an angle outside the café, and just as quickly as we'd let down our guard, we erect it again. A uniformed man steps out, the brim of a hat obscuring his eyes, and marches inside.

I rise from my chair, my gaze meeting Myrtle's for a split second before she greets him. "Sheriff Brooks," she croons, smiling momentarily. "Thank you for coming."

As he looks up, I nearly tumble back into the seat behind me. Gray, fathomless eyes rake the room before settling on me. His lips part as he removes his hat, the shorn beard tidy along his jaw, and his shoulders strain against the fit of his shirt, a vein in his neck pulsing. It's Regis, who gave me a ride from the market in Saranac Lake, who made me a grilled cheese sandwich and let me sleep in his house. Who held my hand a beat too long standing at his door. I can't reckon the misfortune in having shared a night with a cop in between murdering two different men and staging my own death. Everything in me goes icy cold as I recall him noting Don's ring, which I so recklessly offered for a ride out of town.

Myrtle steps between us. "We haven't touched anything yet," she tells him. "But I have a full night of cleaning and sanitizing before I can open this place up again. So, let's make this quick."

"Sure, Myrtle," he agrees with a small smile. "I'm just gonna take a statement and a few photos if that's okay with you. We can bring you in for questions later if it seems necessary."

She begins recounting her version of events. Beside her, the two men from the Drunken Moose keep interrupting with their own details, eager to share their stories. Regis glances up continually between the three of them, jotting things on a notepad. Finally, Myrtle snaps at one of the men. "If I'da wanted your help, Terry, I woulda asked for it. Last I checked, I can speak for myself just fine."

I notice Regis trying to conceal a smile. "Thank you, Myrtle," he says when they're done. "Mind if I ask around, talk to some of the other patrons."

She shrugs. "Be my guest. We all saw the same thing."

He nods and starts my way.

Uneasy, I begin stacking chairs and pretending to wipe off tables. Myrtle's right about one thing—this will be a hell of a mess to clean up. I dare a peek over my shoulder and see Regis chatting with a few other people, but it doesn't take him long to find his way to me.

"Acacia Lee from Near-Austin, Texas," he says. "We meet again."

I nod. "You didn't tell me you were the sheriff."

"Didn't think I needed to," he says. "You commit any crimes in Franklin County recently that I should be aware of?"

I laugh nervously. "Aren't you a little young for a position like that?"

He shrugs. "Not according to the citizens of Franklin County, who elected me after Sheriff Jackson died five years ago."

I nod my head, feeling like submission is my best policy.

"I'm from this county," he says after a moment. "People here know how seriously I take the job. They trust me."

I imagine his rugged good looks didn't hurt when it came time to run, but I don't mention it.

"But I'll tell you a little secret if you promise it doesn't leave this circle." He leans in. "I thought I was a bit young for the job myself."

I grin as his breath tickles my cheek. "Your secret is safe with me."

"You changed your hair," he says. "I like it."

I blush, feeling the heat creep over my cheeks. "Thanks," I say with a genuine smile.

He starts to smile, but carefully clears his face, remembering where he is, *why.* "Acacia, why don't you tell me what happened here tonight."

"M-me?" I stammer, somehow unprepared though I had to know this was coming.

"You were in the café when the man collapsed, weren't you?" he questions.

I clear my throat. "Uh, outside actually. I mean, I was just coming back in. I saw it happen through the glass of the front door."

He turns to look out the front. "Interesting vantage point. Far as I know, you're the only one to have it. It'll be helpful to know your account."

I shrug, put a hand on my hip. "Same as everyone else's, I'm sure," I tell him. "He stood up, didn't look right. Started grabbing at his stomach, got sick, and fell over."

Regis's gentle eyes bore into mine with sudden intensity. "Define *didn't look right.*"

"Oh, you know. He, um, well . . . his stomach kind of swelled up, and he turned this funny color. He looked real scared."

"Did he?" Regis scrawls something across his paper.

"That's when he fell. And then the woman started screaming."

His eyes meet mine. "The woman?"

I swallow, mentally kicking myself. "She came in with him. Must have been his wife or girlfriend. She'd been . . . *hurt.*"

He drops his arms, squinting. "Define *hurt,* Ms. Lee."

"Her face was bruised," I tell him. "I think he must have hit her."

He stares at me. "That's a big assumption to make," he says.

I look down, avoiding his gaze. "He seemed the type. But that's just my opinion."

"The type?" Regis crosses his arms.

When I meet his eyes again, I think he can see the unspoken words in mine. "I've been around men like that," I say. "He was bossy. And she didn't want to look at me."

He nods quietly but doesn't press me.

"You can ask Myrtle," I add quickly. "She gave the woman ice for her face after the guy died."

He casts a glance over his shoulder at my aunt. "Did she? Funny, she didn't mention the woman."

I realize I've messed up, but it's too late to take it back. "It was a lot," I tell him. "She's shook up."

He cocks his head. "Never known Myrtle to be rattled by much of anything."

"Well," I try to explain, "a guy died right in front of her."

He gives me a tight smile. "Wouldn't have been the first time," he says coolly.

If I could bite my own tongue without drawing attention to myself, I would.

"Thank you, Miss Lee," he says before stepping away. "You've been very helpful."

11

Bane Witch

Ed reaches for a glass speckled with sick, and Myrtle grabs his wrist. "Go on, Ed," she tells him. "Get some rest. Acacia and I can handle this."

It's after ten o'clock, but we finally get to work cleaning up. I quietly collect a trash bag, reach for the same glass, notice Myrtle doesn't stop me.

"Throw anything he touched away," Myrtle says to me. "Anything he threw up on."

Ed stands, puzzled. "You sure, Myrtle?"

She nods. "Absolutely. I don't need anybody else keeling over in here. You already got a bad back."

He gives her an irritated look. "Never stopped you from bossing me around before."

She only chuckles at that.

"You're older than I am," he reminds her as he scoots to the front door, but he bends to rub at his dog's ears when Bart runs over to greet him, and I know he's glad to get away for the night.

We stack the remaining chairs against the far walls and scoot the tables over, righting the overturned one together. I pick up dishes from the floor that aren't tainted, taking them to the sink. Once we've collected everything to throw away, Myrtle has me double bag it and take it to the trash cans outside. When I return, she's shaking a spray bottle of water mixed with bleach, a mop in one hand.

"Get the bucket. Fill it extra hot. And bring a roll of paper towels," she tells me.

I'm not looking forward to cleaning this up, but it's the least I can do after killing a man in her establishment. At least it's not blood. But as I lean over the floor with paper towels a moment later, I decide blood would be better.

Myrtle props the front door open, and we work in silence until the floor and furniture have been thoroughly sanitized many times over. When we're done, we take turns scrubbing our hands and arms from the elbows down at the kitchen sink. It's practically midnight when we finish up.

"I think that's it," I say, exhausted and ready to take a scalding hot shower and collapse into bed.

But Myrtle frowns. "No, not quite." She starts for the staircase. "There's one last thing we have to take care of. Get the door."

I walk over and close the front door.

"Lock it," she tells me, and I do as she asks, then follow her into the storeroom.

She pulls a small hiking backpack from one of the lower cabinets and drags it over to the salt bin. "Retrieve the jars."

"I thought you wanted them hidden," I tell her as I stand over the bin, uncertain.

"That's what we're doing," she says, reaching down into the salt herself and coming up with a jar that might have once contained pimentos but now holds a bevy of tiny, dried white flowers. She sets it in the backpack. "This was only temporary. We need a more permanent solution until this whole investigation blows over."

I follow her lead, reaching down and pulling out jar after jar until we're sure we haven't left a single one behind. Myrtle zips up the pack and shrugs her shoulders into the straps. "Come on."

"Where are we going?" I ask. "It's late."

"Isn't it obvious?" she says, grinning at me. "On a hike."

I keep just a few steps behind as Myrtle leads us deeper into the forest than I've ever been. I get a sense we may be headed to one of her nightly stops. I have so many questions coursing through my mind that I've no idea where to start. My tongue sticks to the bottom of my mouth, useless.

Finally, Myrtle asks me a question. "So, what did you say to Sheriff Brooks? He looked . . . intrigued."

"Nothing," I'm quick to tell her. "I mean, nothing unusual. I saw what everyone else did. I told him that. But . . ."

She stops and looks at me, her eyes indecipherable in the darkness. "But?"

"I mentioned the woman who came in with the guy who died," I confess. "Was that wrong?"

Myrtle laughs then shrugs. "Of all the wrongs committed tonight, that one is the least of our worries." She starts walking again. "He seemed real familiar with you."

"He gave me a ride from Saranac Lake." I duck around a branch sticking out into the path, leaving out the bit about my overnight stay. "I ran into him at a market. Didn't know he was a sheriff, or I wouldn't have accepted."

"Probably better you did," she says over her shoulder. "I haven't seen him look at a woman like that in years. Might be our best defense under the circumstances."

I don't want to admit that the idea sends a misguided thrill shooting through me. He's an attractive man, the first I've met in a long while with a demeanor that actually appeals to me, not just mentally but on some intuitive level. But after Henry, I can't imagine sharing my life with a man, letting someone in again, trusting him. I know the world isn't populated with men like Henry, that there are good, decent men out there who make wonderful husbands and partners, loving fathers and respectable colleagues. I just don't think I have anything left for one of them. I don't think love is an experience I get to have.

I clear my throat. "Are we going to talk about what those circumstances are?" I ask quietly, stepping over a large rock.

Myrtle grunts, and my frustration grows. But before I can complain, she stops. "Here we are."

I look around. We are off the path, standing among a mix of balsam firs and red spruce trees. Ferns tickle my calves, and the ground is uneven. Before us rises a low hill. Through the branches, I can make out patches of stars. Not far off, I hear the trickle of water. "And where is that exactly?"

Myrtle stoops, brushing at leaves and needles and pine cones on the hill. Her fingers latch on to something and give it a hard shake. Forest fodder goes flying, and she tosses a sheet of camo netting aside and then a tarp. I hear a hollow sound, the clang of metal. She grips something in the hill and pulls it upward and back. I realize it's a door.

"Tarp helps to hide the entrance and keeps it waterproof," she tells me. She drops a foot into the hole and starts down.

I stand in the dark, in shock.

A second later, she pokes her head back out. "Well, come on. I want to get some sleep tonight."

Stepping in, I realize there's a steep, ladderlike staircase that leads down into the hole. I take each step carefully, but Myrtle lights an LED lantern once she's inside. She dims the light, but it's enough to make my descent easier. I arrive inside a small room, large enough for a cot bed at one end, a worktable and storage shelving at the other.

"What is this place?" I ask her, turning around.

"This," Myrtle tells me, "is my hideaway. It's important in our line of work. A little place like this can mean the difference between a long and happy life under the radar and burning at the stake."

Our line of work . . . I am prickly with unspoken meaning. She's not exactly referring to hospitality. "Did you make this yourself?" I ask her, amazed. The walls and floor look like poured concrete. It's solid and comfortable, a feat I can't imagine a single person, let alone a single woman, accomplishing.

"I had help," she says, dropping the backpack on the work-table. "Sadly, he didn't make it."

I spin to face her, even more on edge. "What do you mean by that?"

She starts unpacking the jars onto some shelves near the table. Her eyes slide to mine. "Exactly what I said. He died just after the completion, which was great for me and too bad for him."

I suck in air, not believing my ears. She says it so cavalierly that it makes my hair stand on edge.

"Don't look so offended," she says wryly. "He had it coming."

I practically choke on my own breath.

Myrtle pauses and turns to me, setting a hand on her hip. "You feeling sorry for him?"

I don't know how to respond.

"Well, don't," she says. "His name was Stan. Had a little girl back in the nineties whose room he liked to creep into every night from the age of seven onward. A child that age shouldn't know certain things, like the taste of her daddy's sweat. He was a sick man who ruined a life that wasn't his to destroy. I did the world a favor. But I got my money's worth out of him first. If you ask me, he went down easy. He deserved a lot worse than I gave him."

My fingers curl into fists at my side and then straighten again. "H-how did you know that? About his daughter?"

"I got my ways," she says darkly, giving me an appraising look. "I imagine you do, too." Once she's put the jars away, she turns to me. "Let's get something straight. No one knows about this place, and I intend to keep it that way."

"No one?" I repeat.

"Well, except Bart," she concedes.

"The dog?"

"He's impossible to hide things from," she tells me. "But he's not talking anytime soon, so I figure he can be in the club—a kind of honorary member."

"There's a club?"

She smiles. "Figure of speech."

I wrap my arms around my waist, completely lost. "Myrtle, what's going on here?" I whisper. "What happened to that man tonight? What are you telling me?"

She presses her lips together with pity, then steps over and pushes down on my shoulder until I sit on one of the narrow steps. She takes a seat on a small twig stool across from me. "Piers, honey, there's something you should know about us. Something your mother should have told you a long time ago."

"Crows," I whisper.

"What?"

"You told me we were crows. When I was a little girl and you came to see me, that's what you said." My mouth feels dry around the words.

"And so we are," she agrees. "Do you remember why I told you that?"

"*Because crows feed on what others can't, including other birds,*" I repeat. I've never forgotten her words in all these years.

"That's right," she says reassuringly. "You've done that before, haven't you? Eaten something other people couldn't eat, not without it making them real sick."

"Pokeweed." It might be the very first time I've spoken the word aloud. Saying it feels like a release, like a marble I swallowed years ago has finally come back up.

"Your mother preferred castor beans," she tells me. "Swore by it for a time. A *short* time, mind you. My sister, Angel—your grandmother—liked lily of the valley, which is where your mother got her name. I just so happen to be partial to a little fungus called the destroying angel. I think you've heard of it? Tasted it, at least."

Something inside me roils, bucking against a truth I've been denying for so long I don't know how not to. The mushroom near Regis's house comes back to me, its enticing glow. And Regis telling me to leave it alone, that it would kill me before sunup. The trail of them around her cabin, like a constellation.

"Of course," she goes on. "I don't like to limit myself, especially here where there is so much life. And I have a particular gift for . . . shall we say . . . making my own blends? So, far be it from me to chastise you for getting into my supply. It's just, you might have told me. We could have prepared."

"Prepared?" I can hardly form the word.

"Now, we have to clean up this mess. Oh, they'll think he picked the mushroom up long before he got to my place. Destroying angel usually takes several hours to work. But it's a risk having so many witnesses and Sheriff Brooks sniffing around here. I've been very careful to establish myself in this community. I have a good thing going. I don't need Angel's and Lily's mistakes haunting me. And yet here you are." She gives me another appraising look. "The venery will be angry I kept you from them, but I had to be sure. Now I'll have to call a conclave to sort this out."

"The *venery*?" I remember the word from the day I eavesdropped on her and my mother.

She pats my knee but doesn't answer. "At any rate, speaking of names, did you come up with *Acacia* all on your own?"

When I don't respond, she goes on. "The acacia tree produces a cyanogenic poison to discourage indulgent herbivores. Did you know that? It's no wonder you gravitated to it. But it's your real name that I want to tell you about. You should know that it is very special. You weren't named Piers because your mother wanted a boy, though she did. We'll get into that some other time. No, my girl, you were named for *Pieris japonica*—lily-of-the-valley bush. Delicious berries, I'm told. Sadly, responsible for multiple deaths in children every year. I wish people would stop landscaping with stuff that can kill them. Of course, that would only make our job harder."

I shake my head, trying to make sense of what she's saying. "The man, tonight. The one who died. I did that when I spit into his coffee because . . . because of what I ate in your jars?" I point at the shelves, which I now realize are lined with countless jars like the ones in the storeroom. "That was destroying angel mushroom?"

"Delicious, isn't it? Such a shame the general population will never get to taste it."

I stare at her, horrified and titillated all at once. "What about when I was a little girl? The man at my feet, I did that, too?"

Her brows arch tellingly. "Ah. The *bad thing.* I was wondering when that might come up. Yes, I'm afraid you were initiated into our gifts rather young. I imagine he was your first."

"My first?"

She smiles. "But certainly not your last."

I feel nauseous. I don't bring up Don; I don't need to. It's evident that his death is also my doing.

"It must have been terribly confusing for you," she goes on. A sympathetic hand pats my knee. "What horrors did you see when you looked at him? Far too young for such things, but nature will take its own course, I'm afraid. Like it did with your mother. Don't trouble yourself over him any longer, child. I'm sure you didn't fully grasp it at the time, but you were only doing what you were born for. And in the end, the world was better off. The women you spared would thank you if they only knew to, I'm sure."

I bracket my head between my hands, trying to stitch it all together.

"There, there," she soothes. "It's like I always say, *a very little poison can do a world of good.*"

My eyes meet hers. "But I killed them. You're saying I'm a murderer."

Myrtle clucks her tongue in disgust. "You misunderstand me, my dear. A Corbin, *yes.* A murderer, *no.*"

"A killer," I whisper.

"That, too," she agrees amiably. "Every family has their traditions."

"Aunt Myrtle . . ." I stare at her in disbelief. "What are we?"

She takes a deep breath. "You're not just any old girl from any old family, Piers. You never have been. You're a bane witch. And it's time you start living like one."

12

Black Hoodie

The woman on the other end of the line was hiding something. Her voice was soft, as if she were holding back, afraid to be too loud. And she answered his questions with as few words as possible. He could just barely detect the trace of an accent.

Reyes pinched the bridge of his nose and breathed in. He needed to stay calm if he was going to draw her out. "I know you said he didn't leave until after lunch, but was he on time arriving the morning of the fifteenth?"

"Mr. Davenport values punctuality," she responded. She didn't sound annoyed exactly, just uncomfortable. "He's a very exact man."

He frowned. It wasn't an answer; it was a deflection. "I see."

Reyes leaned back in his seat. This was going nowhere. He thought about his partner and how Will might handle it. Will had a quieter way of questioning people, less direct, more open-ended. Reyes decided he needed to change direction, come at her from a new angle, knock her off her guard. She was scared. He was certain of that. Whether it was of him or her boss, he couldn't say. "What else can you tell me about Mr. Davenport?"

There was a pause, a sharp inhale. "Sorry?"

"What's he like to work for?" Reyes pressed. In his experience, there were two things everybody loved to talk about—themselves and other people. If he could loosen her up, get her talking, make it feel more like a conversation, maybe he could get a straight answer about Henry Davenport's arrival at work on the morning of

August fifteenth. Ever since he'd learned who Mrs. Davenport was to him, this case had become his top priority. If she killed herself, he needed to understand how a woman who was lauded a hero less than twelve months ago, who saved a life without thinking, would choose to take her own. Even if it wasn't his business, he needed to know *why*. They were linked, their lives intersected and intertwined at a point neither of them saw coming. No matter his particular views on God, or lack thereof, Reyes didn't think that was coincidence.

And if she didn't kill herself, he needed to know what happened to her. He needed to give her justice. It was the least he could do. He owed her his very breath.

The woman cleared her throat. "My job is very rewarding."

"I'm sure it is," he confirmed. "I'm just curious what Mr. Davenport is like as a boss." He'd made a point to call *after* he watched Henry Davenport drive away from the office, assuming rightly he'd get more out of his administrative assistant that way. "It's Johanna, right? Is that German?"

"Dutch. My family is from Rotterdam." She paused again, as if deliberating. "Mr. Davenport . . . He—he's not unkind," she began, which he took to mean that Henry wasn't kind either. "Just impersonal."

"I see." Reyes shifted in his seat, jotting down a note. "Go on."

"He's a perfectionist," she added. "A very driven, ambitious man. Very focused. I've learned a lot from him."

Sure you have, Reyes thought with an eye roll. He wondered if the pretty Dutch assistant was doing more than taking dictation and fielding calls for Henry. "Is he . . . respectful?"

"In what way?" she pressed.

"Of you? Of women?" He hoped she had the courage to answer him honestly.

"He's never been inappropriate, if that's what you're implying," she rushed to answer.

"Your relationship has never strayed beyond professional?" he asked. He tapped his pen against the steering wheel. It wouldn't be the first time a man killed his wife to make way for his mistress. "I assure you, this is strictly confidential."

"No," she insisted. "You don't know him. He's not like that."

Something in her tone made him curious. Her words had more weight than they should, like they were filled with sand. Grating. "What do you mean?"

"I don't think he likes women very much," she blurted. "Not that he's into men, just . . . he's more critical of the women in our office. He's short with them—*us*."

And there was the crack he could wriggle into and pry open. "Short how?"

"Agitated by them. Maybe even . . ."

"Go on," Reyes pressed.

She swallowed. "Maybe even disgusted."

So, Henry wasn't the type to shtup the secretary and bump off his wife to get her out of their way. Which meant either Reyes had misjudged him from the beginning, or he was worse. "And does he have friends? At work, I mean. Does he spend time with colleagues outside the office?"

"Never," she said sharply. "He's very private."

"Has he ever spoken of his wife before?"

"As I said, he's very private," Johanna said.

"Of course." She was growing impatient with his questions, probably feeling like she'd said too much. *Easy, tiger,* he reminded himself, backing off. Knowing when to apply pressure and when to ease it were crucial to this job. And they were not his strong suit. He waited, letting the moment stretch out between them like chewing gum.

"But I have spoken to her on the phone once or twice." The administrative assistant rushed to fill the void. People generally disliked silence—Reyes loved it. "And I met her once when she came to surprise him for lunch on their anniversary. I don't think he liked it very much. He's not really one for surprises. She never returned."

"How do you mean?" Reyes asked her.

"Oh, well, he's just very precise. Detail-oriented, you might say. He likes things a certain way. Some would call it controlling, but . . ."

"What would you call it?"

She sighed. "Orderly."

"I see." Reyes jotted the word *orderly* down in quotes.

"In the extreme," she added.

Interesting . . . "What was she like, Johanna? Mrs. Davenport?"

"She was lovely," the woman gushed.

He had to agree. Even now, he could smell the honeyed scent of her lotion and see her green eyes smiling at him, wide and glossy like glass marbles. He hadn't been attracted to her in the biblical sense, but he'd found her magnetic. He felt, in that moment between them, as if he'd seen into her, and it was what he'd registered there that drew him—a pulpy brilliance within her, like flower petals made of light.

"A little shy, but that was understandable under the circumstances."

"What circumstances?" Something about her niggled at Reyes, like a sensitive tooth, smarting to the touch. He found himself compelled to learn more about her, even if it didn't seem relevant to the case. He just *needed* to know, had since that night. But she'd been so quick to dismiss him after, her smile fading like the moon at dawn, almost as if she were horrified by what she'd done. He never quite understood it, and his professionalism had kept him from checking up on her, instead relegating his curiosity to a specific sort of hero worship and pushing himself into stoic detachment after. She didn't owe him anything. She'd already saved his life.

"Well, she was still healing," the assistant told him. "A car accident. Her lip was pretty swollen from the airbag. It seemed to make speaking hard."

Reyes dropped his pen. The man's cold eyes flashed through him. He'd heard plenty of excuses like this, grown accustomed to them after witnessing his mother's and sister's experiences with abusive men—an unexpected fall, a bike accident, the dog knocked them down . . . On and on they went. Lucia had gotten particularly creative, at one point claiming she was clearing off a high shelf when a pair of pliers had fallen and struck her in the face. He understood their fear, the need to cover up the truth at any cost. He'd seen the way they were punished if they let on, how little protection the law afforded them. It was survival. In a way, he admired his mother's and sister's fortitude. He couldn't free his mother from the tall man's tyranny as a boy, she had to do that for herself, but it's what led him to become a cop. And he took the domestic violence calls they got very seriously. Even Will had to admit that Reyes had pushed him to take as much action as the law would allow them. Unfortunately, the law didn't allow for much. And now his fears about Henry Davenport had been confirmed. Maybe not directly, but Reyes knew how to add. Controlling husband plus busted lip plus missing wife—*plus* what he'd seen on the bridge footage earlier—equaled a crime.

"Thank you," he told Johanna. "Can I call again? If I have any other questions?"

"Yes," she replied. "But only after six."

He checked the clock on his dash—*6:33 P.M.* "Of course," he said. "I'll remember that."

He didn't hang up right away. Instead, he waited, instinct telling him she was on the verge of breaking.

"Investigator?" she squeaked.

He smiled, grateful. Silence was the one card he could play that never failed him. "Yes?"

"You did say the fifteenth, didn't you?"

"Yes, Johanna."

She sighed. "I believe Mr. Davenport did arrive later than usual that day. Something about a tire."

Did he now? Reyes took a breath, remembering the spare he'd seen on the Jaguar. It could check out, of course. Maybe he pulled over to change a flat. But it would be hard to confirm. And it could just as easily be a clever disguise for his tardiness. He kept his voice steady. "How late?"

"Almost an hour," she admitted, her voice growing very small. "Please don't tell him I told you," she breathed into the phone.

"Confidential, remember," he reminded her before hanging up.

The station was only a short ride away, and he was eager to share what he'd learned with Will. He found him at his desk behind the partition, slurping a Cup Noodles.

"How do you eat that shit?" Reyes teased. "Didn't your mother ever cook for you?"

Will scowled up at him. "Don't knock it till you've tried it, brother. Cup Noodles are a classic. Now what do you want?"

Reyes grinned. "I spoke with the assistant—Johanna."

Will's face twisted with confusion. "Who?"

"Davenport. The missing person case. The woman from the bridge, remember?" Reyes should have expected this. They'd been called out to an assault and battery charge in the third degree at a bar last night, and the suspect had fled the scene. Will was preoccupied with finding him before he managed to cross state lines. And unlike Emil, he felt the Davenport case was an open-and-shut suicide, even though her body had yet to be recovered. Though with the Atlantic so close, that wasn't unheard of.

"Right." Will nodded. "So, does the husband check out?"

"He was at work, but he was late coming in."

"How late?" Will asked.

"Enough. And the secretary mentioned something about a busted lip."

His partner frowned. "He looked fine when we saw him."

"No, the wife." Reyes told himself to be patient. Will would catch on eventually.

The investigator sat forward. "You mean the day of? This woman saw her?"

He shook his head. "No. Some time before. But it's suspicious. If this is a domestic violence case—"

Will waved a hand. "Let me stop you right there, Emil. Even

if you can prove this guy beats his wife, which I doubt you can, it doesn't have any bearing on her whereabouts. It could just as easily support her decision to jump as it could indicate anything else, including foul play."

Reyes grinned down at his partner.

"Why are you looking at me like that?" Will set his Cup Noodles down. "You know it makes me nervous when you get that shit-eating grin on your face."

"Come with me," he told Will. "I got something to show you that will change your mind."

Will stood up and wiped his hands on a napkin, following Emil around to his own desk. Reyes sat down at the computer and pulled up the footage he'd been studying from the CCTV camera. He dialed it back to the right moment.

"Just watch," he told his partner before hitting play.

The image was silent, but soon enough the Davenport woman came into view. She was looking frantically over a shoulder before she doubled over and got sick. Rising, she spun around and began backing up into the railing, putting her hands out in self-defense.

"What the hell . . ." Will muttered, squinting at the screen.

"Just wait," Reyes told him.

Together, they watched as she climbed over the bars, sobbing, pleading with someone still off camera. A second later, he appeared. Tall. Lean. A black hoodie obscuring his face and hair. He watched her, pursuing, and then stopped. Something transpired between them, shorter than an eye blink. But Reyes could see the way her face fell, resigned, and how unaffected the man was. A moment later, she dropped. The man stood frozen to the spot before he approached the rail and looked over.

"You see that," Reyes pointed out. "He's making sure."

The man stepped back. He kept his head down, angled away from the camera. He didn't run—a man like Henry, Reyes thought, would never run—but walked briskly away.

Reyes stopped the footage.

Will whistled. "Did we just witness him force her over that bridge?"

"Looks like it. And remember that pink dot on his shirt sleeve?"

His partner pinched the bridge of his nose. "Are we sure? Couldn't this have just been some guy walking along when she jumped?"

"You saw the way she was acting," Reyes told him. "That look like she wasn't coerced to you? And he saw her do it. He double-checked. If he'd been a bystander, why wouldn't he call that in? Wouldn't you? Wouldn't anyone?"

"You got a point," Will conceded.

"I checked the footage every day for the next week and a half *and* two weeks prior to this date. This guy never returns to the bridge. He's not just a walker."

"Okay," Will said. "So now what?"

Reyes leaned back in his chair. "Now we're investigating a murder, not a suicide."

His partner looked nonplussed. "Of course, we are."

"Also, I found these in the purse." Reyes picked up a pair of matching post office box keys. "They were tucked into the lining. I'm gonna swing by in a couple of days and check it out."

"You think her mail is going to tell you something?" Will asked him.

Reyes shrugged. "Maybe. You never know. Why keep both in one place? Besides, it'll take more evidence than this grainy video to indict him."

Will shook his head. "You're like a dog with a bone. You need to listen to me, Emil. I know this woman means something to you, but you need to keep your head no matter what it looks like."

Reyes jolted back. "What are you saying? You saw the same thing I did on that screen."

Will exhaled. "Just . . . don't go off the deep end, okay? You have a way of getting overinvolved. And this . . . *this* is personal. You shouldn't even be on this case."

"So?" Will was being overly pragmatic. It didn't matter how Reyes knew her, how he felt. The truth was the truth, and it was staring them in the face.

"So . . . we need a body," Will said. "Convicting someone of murder when there's no body is harder than threading a needle with a shoelace, video or not." He pressed his mouth into a shrug and tapped Reyes's forehead. "Just keep your cop brain on, okay? Promise me. Don't let the lizard brain take over."

Reyes swatted his finger away. "Whatever. I know what I'm do-ing. We need to be careful," Reyes told him, a serious edge creep-ing into his tone. "I don't trust this Davenport guy, but we need his cooperation. If we let on for a second that we suspect him, he'll try to cover his tracks. Maybe run. You find out anything on that substance from the note and the bridge yet?"

"They're a match," Will confirmed. "Something called poke-weed. The berries contain multiple deadly toxins and organic chemicals including phytolacca, saponins, and lectins, which cause significant GI distress. People in Appalachia have tried to use pokeweed as a folk remedy for decades, which results in hos-pitalizations and deaths every year. Vomiting is among the side effects. Historically, it's been used for dye."

"Are you thinking what I'm thinking?" Reyes asked.

"I don't know, Emil. I'm generally scared of whatever you're thinking."

Reyes laughed. "I think it's time to pay Mr. Davenport another visit."

WILL SUGGESTED CALLING first, but Reyes thought it would be better if they caught him off guard. It was a golden afternoon—a Saturday, so they could be sure he was home. The house practi-cally shimmered in the sun it was so white. Reyes had a feeling that if asked, Henry would say white was his favorite color.

The door opened, and Henry Davenport stood before them in

a pressed shirt and slacks, a neat leather belt at his waist, black loafers on his feet.

"You going somewhere Mr. Davenport?" Reyes asked. "Did we catch you at a bad time?"

The man's mouth fell open, but he quickly shut it. "No. I was just preparing to eat lunch. What can I do for you, officers?"

They had, as a matter of course, informed him that his wife's body had yet to turn up. But Reyes assured him they had confirmed her jump from the Arthur Ravenel Jr. Bridge. "We'd like to take another look around if that's okay. Maybe collect a few more items."

"I don't see why," Henry spat. "She's dead. You said so yourself. She jumped. Must we continue this charade of an investigation?"

Will took a step forward. "Mr. Davenport—may I call you Henry?—we're just doing our jobs. We have a couple of small things we'd like to follow up on. Some . . . *questions* have arisen as to the nature of your wife's death. Nothing to concern you, but we'd be remiss if we didn't perform a routine follow-up. You understand?"

Will always had a way with the difficult ones. His baby face and Pillsbury Doughboy build made him appear softer than he really was. People tended to trust him, or at least feel less threatened. Reyes, on the other hand, ran three miles every morning and lifted in his time off. His square jaw signaled high testosterone and his eyes had a penetrating quality that made others uncomfortable, as if he could see through them. He'd been working on turning down the intensity of his personality to do his job more effectively, but pairing him with Will was one of the best decisions their chief of police had ever made.

"Questions?" Henry looked intrigued, his right eyebrow lifting.

Reyes saw an in. If they led him to believe they were investigating the possibility she wasn't dead rather than the possibility she was murdered, he might be more forthcoming. "We can't confirm anything just yet," he said softly, almost in a whisper, like he was bringing the man in on a confidence. "But, between you and me, it's entirely possible a body won't turn up. We just . . . we need to investigate a little deeper to know for sure."

Something behind the man's eyes shifted, a flickering shadow that slithered away. He cleared his throat and lifted his chin. The door swung wide. "Please, gentlemen. Come in," he said.

Investigator Reyes stepped inside, interested to see so little had changed in the wife's absence. As his partner talked the man up, Reyes walked through to the back of the house, drawn by the large picture windows. Sunlight poured into the room, but not a speck of dust could be seen. It wasn't the interior of the house that interested Reyes though. His eyes were busy searching the backyard until he found what he was looking for. He didn't even need to step outside to spot the brightly-colored stalks growing along the fence line, dripping with elongated clusters of shiny, dark berries—pokeweed.

13

Venery

I crash through the woods like a rabid bear, tearing at limbs and slapping at fronds as I try to keep up, shouting questions at her back. "What do you mean I'm a bane witch? What *is* a bane witch? Are you saying my mother just failed to mention this important detail during my entire upbringing? Are witches even real? Where did we come from? How does this have anything to do with me killing that man?"

Finally, she whirls on me. "Keep your voice down!" she hisses. She grabs my elbow and begins dragging me down the path. "Have you no survival instincts whatsoever?"

I trip along beside her, feeling for all the world like a seven-year-old child being scolded by her nanny. "You can't just say something like that and then shimmy back up the ladder into the night like nothing's changed!"

"I didn't think you'd go screeching behind—" Her face suddenly falls. She stops so fast I bump into her.

"What the—"

She puts a finger to her lips, eyes wide as she stares into the blackness surrounding us. Then I hear it, the distinct rustle of leaves in the distance, steps that stop nearly as quickly as she did, as if we are being followed.

"Fool girl," Myrtle whispers, pulling me toward the cabin with a burst of speed I didn't know she had in her. She doesn't stop until we are safely inside, the front door locked behind us.

I watch, bewildered, as she moves around the house, turning

out all the lights and staring out the windows like she's looking for something. Not thinking, I flip on a small lamp on the sofa table, and she spins around, flapping a hand.

"Put that out!" she demands.

I click it off, sheepish. "Sorry." She creeps toward the glass, her eyes moving side to side. "What are you looking for?" I ask in a soft voice.

"Not sure yet," she replies, still vigilant.

"How can you even see out there?" It's so dark beyond the windows that I can barely make out the nearest tree, let alone anything deep in the forest.

When she glances at me, I notice the way her pupils constrict, abnormally large in the dark before shrinking. But it's the way her left follows the right that unnerves me, leaving one eye black and the other green for a moment. "It's hereditary," she explains before turning back to the window.

I wrap my arms across my chest as we stand in silence, the night outside permeating the house around me until I feel like I might fall into it. The hush between us stretches paper-thin, the tension holding us each in place, taut and unmoving. Myrtle seems to be zeroing in on something. Her head inclines toward the glass before her. I feel like I might snap, the questions growing inside me with every passing second. I am on the verge of speaking—or screaming, I can't be certain which—when a deer suddenly steps out of the nearby brush into a patch of starlight beside the cabin. Myrtle sighs. Her head drops. She turns from the window and sinks into a chair, heavy with relief.

By her behavior, she was expecting something else. A threat.

I make my way to the sofa and lower onto it, so flustered I can hardly draw breath. Myrtle clicks on the lamp beside her, the one she fussed at me for only minutes ago.

"You'll have to ask your questions one at a time," she says, pulling out her cell phone and laying it in her lap. "That's the only way I can answer. And consider them well. I would like to get at least a wink of sleep tonight. I'm not staying up indefinitely to satisfy your curiosity."

"Are we okay?" I inquire, nervous after the night we've had, after seeing her so panicked.

She sighs, a touch of exasperation in it. "Is that one of your questions?"

I shrug. "You seemed scared. What were you expecting to come out of those trees? Because it wasn't a deer."

"I don't know," she tells me, reaching for the photograph of the women I'd asked her about several nights ago. "Any number of things. The Strangler for one. The sheriff for another."

"The Saranac Strangler?"

Her lips pull taut. "Is there another around here I should know about?"

I frown.

"He's close," she finally says. "Getting closer by the day."

"How do you know?" I ask her.

Her eyes sharpen on me. "Tell me, when that man came in tonight, what did you see when you looked at him?"

I shrug. "An asshole."

Myrtle frowns. "Beyond that. What did you see that no one else in the room could?"

"The woman," I admit. "Bleeding. She lost her baby because he beat it out of her."

Myrtle nods knowingly. "*That* is how I know. Our magic has a way of whispering to us. It's not always the same for everybody, but it is never wrong. I don't know why the Strangler is here, but I have my suspicions," she says with an uneasy glance in my direction. "And you can never be too careful, not when you're one of us."

"One of *us* . . ." I let my shoulders finally drop. "And what is that? What is a bane witch exactly?"

Myrtle's lips tug up on one side in a coy smile. "What do you think it is?"

I rub my hands over my face. "Someone who can eat poison, I guess. Someone who *is* poison."

She flips the framed picture over in her lap. "You're a bane witch. So am I. So was your mother and her mother and so on. Yes, we can eat poisonous plants without feeling the effects. Our magic reserves the toxins safely in our bodies until it's time."

"*Time?*" I ask. "Time for what?"

She studies me as if she is evaluating whether I can handle the answer. "Time for them to be released."

"I don't understand," I tell her. "How does that work? How is that possible?"

She purses her lips. "I'm not a doctor, Piers. I can only tell you what I know. Tonight, when you saw that man in the café, aside from what you saw, what did you *feel*?"

I grip the cushion beneath me. "Angry," I admit. "Edgy. I wanted to do something. I wanted him to hurt the way—" I pause, anxious about sharing this part of myself.

"The way?" she presses.

"The way I've been hurt. The way he hurt that woman." I look down at my knees.

She nods. "What did that feel like in your body? The anger? The desire to *do* something?" she asks me.

I remember my stomach turning on itself, the heat and the sweat and the tremble in my hands. Like I was barely containing the feelings. Like I wanted to explode. "It felt like pressure." I meet her eyes. "Everywhere inside me. Like something was building. It burned."

She nods again, slowly. "Because something *was* building," she agrees. "You were ripe—ready to release your venom. The prey was before you and you could sense it. This is what you were made for, born for."

"Prey?" I shake my head, confused. "Rabbits are prey. Mice. Deer. That man was an asshole. He was no victim."

She waves a hand as if brushing my words aside. "*Prey* is a euphemism, that's all. Don't get hung up on the word. The point is you fed before that man arrived. Something in you knew he was coming. It wanted to be ready. And your magic drew him to you, left him vulnerable, provided an opportunity, so that you could do what you were put here to do."

"Which is?" I'm almost afraid to ask because the answer is ringing through me before she forms the word, but I need to hear her say it.

"Kill." Myrtle watches to see how I react. When I don't immediately freak out, she goes on. "Or protect, depending on how you want to look at it. But in some cases, our case, the two are interchangeable."

"*Protect.*" The word is awkward in my mouth. I've never been able to protect anyone, not even myself. Henry made that abundantly clear. And yet, isn't that what happened with Don? I protected myself in that car somehow, or my magic did. *Magic.* An even harder word to wrap my head around.

"Our . . . *instincts,* Piers, are carefully synchronized. It might feel random at times, but it never is. You broke into my stash the other night. Don't deny it," she insists when I open my mouth to argue. "I was watching you, waiting in the dark to see what you would go for. I could read the signs on you the last few days, unable to focus or be still, you were practically vibrating. I knew you were feeling it—the hunger—and if I gave you an opening, you would probably take it. But I had to be sure. When that man came into the café tonight, that's when I knew for certain."

Her words feel like they're racing ahead, answering a question I haven't asked yet. I hold a hand up. "I don't understand. Why not just tell me? Why not explain what was happening to me? If I'd known that pica runs in our family, it would have saved me a lot of shame over the years."

She tsks at the word. "Forget that diagnosis. You don't have a disorder. You aren't deficient. You are operating exactly as the magic designed. But I couldn't know that until I saw it for myself. I just wish I'd gotten to you before you spit in his coffee."

I recall her blocking my path on the way to make his sandwich, how she insisted I go outside and cool off. The realization is cold like ice against the skin and bright with shock. She knew then what I was capable of. She just didn't realize she was too late. I fall against the sofa's backrest, reeling. "You knew. You could have stopped me."

"I did try," she says defensively. "My timing was off, is all."

"You think?" I spit at her. "Why let it go that far, cut it so close? If you already knew about me eating the . . . the . . . whatever mushroom."

"Destroying angel mushroom—*Amanita bisporigera.* A personal favorite of mine. It's very effective, as you saw for yourself. Though a bit messy perhaps. Anyway, that's neither here nor there. I couldn't be certain everything was functioning normally until I observed your allure. Of course, now I've seen the full cycle, so there's no room for doubt," she explained.

The casual way she discusses the gory death I just witnessed—a death I caused—is unnerving. I push my horror aside to focus on the facts. "My what?"

"Your allure, dear. It's how we call our victims, what drives them to us. How do I explain this?" She taps a finger against the back of the photo frame in her lap. "Like magnets!" she finally says. "You are one pole, he another. It's an invisible force mostly, but sometimes when they are close, when they need a nudge, it kicks into overdrive, overriding their senses. They'll experience you in a particular way that appeals to them—a smell or a feeling, even a feature of your face or hair."

Don's strange comparison of me to the gardenia bushes of his childhood home floods my memory, the way he kept leaning toward me, like he was drinking in my scent. Understanding washes over me, prickling across my skin in eerie waves. I don't know myself. I never have. How much of my life has been lived in the shadow of what I am, my ignorance creating a disconnect that I filled with shame and doubt and pain?

I meet Myrtle's eyes. "But I didn't call him. I don't even know him. I just know his type—" Something in my mind begins to turn, an engine igniting in the cold void. I can't quite bring the pieces together on my own, but I can see how they fit. I furrow my brow.

"Don't you, though?" she asks darkly. "A bane witch knows her victims the way a mother knows her baby before she's ever held it. It's intimate, primitive. You knew the moment he stepped through my door who he was, what he was capable of. You knew what he had done and would likely do again. And everything in you responded to it. That is your gift *working*, Piers. That is your destiny."

I wrap a hand across my forehead, stunned. I consider the way the man looked up at me, full of vanity and pride and rancor. The way he spoke with spite sharpening his words. The way he took up space that didn't belong to him, like a challenge. The way he reminded me of Henry, even though on the surface they were worlds apart. But the core of him was the same kind of rotten. And I knew that particular stench. I smelled it the second he arrived.

Myrtle is right. I *called* him. I don't know how, but I did. And now I know why.

If I drew that man to me tonight, did I draw Don? Was he more than a random man in a parking lot, an easy ride, a means to an end? And what did that make Henry? Had I married someone I was supposed to destroy, allowing him to destroy me instead?

"If it's any consolation"—I hear Myrtle cut through my thoughts—"my first died in a spray of bloody emesis on the floor of a New York deli. That was before I made it this far north. I was young then, only fourteen."

I look up at her, my jaw slack and face pale, full of revulsion.

She grins. "I licked his spoon," she says with a wink. "Dunked it right into his bowl of soup. Then sat in a nearby booth with my lunch until I could be sure the job was done. That was the best pastrami on rye I've ever had," she adds wistfully, popping open one of the little latches that hold the back of the frame on.

I visibly gag and her face falls. "TMI?" When I don't respond, she leans forward. "Bend your head over your knees, dear. That's it. Wait for the nausea to pass. This will all feel like second nature in no time, you'll see."

I sit up, taking a deep breath. "You were fourteen?" I manage to get out. "When you killed your first man?"

She pops another latch on the frame. "Nearly fifteen. Of course, Angel—my sister, your grandmother—was thirteen when she took her first. She was always showing me up. Your mother was even younger. Too young, really. It's not good for us to bloom before puberty. I think that was the root of a lot of her problems. And then there's you. Five is unheard of, perilously young. I've kept that little detail to myself. I couldn't know how they would react. But you've survived against all odds, even with Lily never training you. There's something extreme that runs through your line. A defect, if you ask me. Too much power isn't healthy. To think you just kept feeding and feeding after that. All that poison and magic building up with nowhere to go. It's a wonder you didn't explode."

Her words shatter me. I didn't explode. Instead, it all turned inward. I learned to hate myself for what I was. I poisoned myself instead of someone else and ended up in the arms of a man even more toxic than my family line. A man whose idea of love is deadly. There is a strange irony to it. A horrified laugh burbles out of me. "You wanted to take me," I say, my eyes wide and disturbed. "All those years ago. I heard you ask her to let me live with you, to let you teach me."

"I did," Myrtle confirms. "But she refused."

"You should have taken me anyway," I grind out, tears forming at the corners of my eyes. One leaks out and rolls down my cheek. "It would have been better. For everyone."

She pops another latch and appraises me. "Perhaps. Perhaps I failed you as much as she did. But I couldn't cross your mother. I had to play my hand carefully."

I wipe at my eyes. I don't want to cry for her knowing she kept this from me, let me believe I was broken, leaving me with nothing, not even the barest understanding of who I am. But my mother is a wound in my heart that will never heal, no matter how I resent it. "Why? She couldn't have been that powerful. She never killed anyone. She was weak, mixed-up. And she abandoned me."

Myrtle looks pained. "Whatever passed between you, Piers, your mother loved you."

I shake my head. "No. You misunderstand. I'm not talking about our estrangement. She abandoned me long before that. Don't you get it? She let those doctors poke and pry at me. Let them gawk at me like an exhibit, a puzzle they couldn't solve. Let them pump me with medication until I finally became so destitute that I decided there wasn't any point and stopped taking them. By not teaching me to kill, she left me to die. And all the while, she knew. And she never said a word. Not. One. Word."

Myrtle pops the last latch on the frame and looks up. "Lily was many things," she says ominously, "but she was never weak. Confused, yes. Even deluded. But she was so much stronger than you know. This life, Piers, is not without suffering. Your mother had more than her fair share. It was a testament to her strength that she didn't crumble sooner, that she held on to some sliver of dignity and sanity, of herself, until the bitter end."

I grind my jaw. "She had no dignity. She gave it all to Gerald." Was it really any wonder I ended up with a man like Henry?

Carefully, Myrtle lifts the back off the frame. "You're wrong," she says quietly. "In the end, she proved that."

My head shoots up, eyes slitting at her words. "What does that mean?"

"Your mother believed she was *helping* you. It was misguided, I know. I did try to warn her. But she was experimenting with things we'd never had access to before. I couldn't know that she was entirely wrong. For many years, I thought she'd figured something out. That she'd spared you. At least, that's how she would define it. I lied when I said I didn't come for you after she died. I've kept close tabs on you and Lily over the years. The internet has made that much easier of course, but we've always had our ways in this family. But I saw you living a life free of all this. Unburdened. Unhindered. I knew the drugs Lily was taking hadn't done enough to change her, but I thought maybe she'd gotten to you young enough—"

"What drugs?" I glare at her.

She looks surprised. "The same she gave you. The ones the doctors prescribed. Of course, she fed them a lot of malarkey about fake symptoms in order to get them, but it didn't seem to matter. They're pretty eager to hand those particular pills out these days."

"My mom was taking Ritalin? She was taking Paxil?"

"Among others," Myrtle supplies. "They helped, I suppose, for a time. But you—you seemed to lose all sense of the hunger, you stopped blooming, no longer ripe. The allure wasn't even working. You moved away, got an education, found work, made a name for yourself. You seemed . . . *happy*. If I had shown up on your doorstep, told you that you were an ancient weapon magically designed to be a defender of women and children by taking the lives of predatory men, an instrument of justice and vengeance older than time, a poison eater, I would have ruined it all. I would have devastated you. I couldn't do that. We decided it was best—safer, even—to leave you where you were, keeping a careful eye of course."

Not careful enough, I think. But then, that's Henry's genius: hiding the rot behind a mask of charm, a veneer of carefully crafted perfection. "*We?*"

She picks up her phone, punching in a number she reads off the back of the photo. "The venery, of course."

Her speaker is on, and I hear the other line ring through the room. There is a click, and a hushed "Myrtle?"

Aunt Myrtle sags into her chair, her age suddenly showing in a way I hadn't noticed before, in deep grooves around her eyes, the slack of her arms. "Lattie. Get your mother," she says. "I'm calling a conclave."

"Now?" the other woman chirps.

"You have a better time in mind?"

The woman clucks her tongue. "Fine, fine. What am I to say

this is about? You know Donna, she's loathe to leave California without a damn good reason."

Myrtle smiles. "Oh, I've got a good reason all right. Tell her it's about Piers."

"Lily's girl?" the woman drawls.

"She's with me," Myrtle says, meeting my eyes. "And she's taken her first mark."

14

Matriarch

The woman looks lost. From the cat-eye slant of her sunglasses to the ruby satin of her chunky-heeled sandals, to the little ruffle around her ankle socks and puff sleeves on her canary yellow baby doll dress and even the sun-tipped strands of her long, tousled waves—she looks more like she stepped off a hipster runway than into a café in the Adirondack Mountains. Her look is street with an unmistakable devil-may-care aesthetic, but I know money when I see it. Every piece she's wearing is expensive. And she's too young for all that swagger.

She lowers the sunglasses down the bridge of her nose and takes in the room.

I stand there with a pot of hot coffee in one hand like I've just seen an orangutan play the piano. Beside me, Terry from the Drunken Moose is at a table, scarfing down his bowl of Wheaties. When he sees her, he drops his spoon, splattering milk all over himself.

A smile plays across her hot-pink lips.

Even Bart is slobbering up the glass outside, wishing he could follow her in. Stupid dog.

Ed walks up next to me. He must be on his fortieth coffee break of the day and it's only two o'clock. I have come to realize that Myrtle used the word *upkeep* very loosely when telling me about her and Ed's arrangement. He's more like a glorified pet. Ed has Bart, and we have Ed. "You lost?" he asks as he squints one eye in her direction.

"Do I look lost?" she replies.

He doesn't know how to answer that. His mouth pulls to one side like his brain is diverting energy from the rest of his face to formulate a response. Finally, he says, "You don't look found."

If I could crawl under Terry's table and disappear, I would. It's been a while since I moved in my usual Charleston circles, sipping champagne in a silk cocktail dress at an art opening as I worked a room, looking for new clients. I wasn't fearless, but I had finesse and I knew how to use it. But I never possessed the kind of confidence I see before me now. She has to be several years my junior, probably in her late twenties, and yet I find myself instantly regretting the cable-knit sweater and stained jeans I dragged on this morning. Also, how is she not cold? It can't be more than fifty degrees outside.

"Can I help you?" I ask, certain she's taken a wrong turn somewhere, like back in Manhattan, and just kept going.

She pulls the sunglasses off and stares at me. "Are you her?"

"Uhhh . . ." My mouth falls open.

She walks in a slow circle around me until she's back where she started. "I like it," she says, stepping toward me.

"Like what?" I ask, completely dumbfounded.

"No, like, it works for you," she says with emphasis. "This whole mountain-girl-barista thing you've got going. Rugged but sensual, you know?" She leans in toward my right ear so only I can hear the next part. "Let's hope it's enough."

As she leans away, her eyebrows arch, but I can't read the meaning behind her expression. I only know her words have chilled me to the bone. Myrtle didn't tell me much about what to expect from the venery, only that this gathering is vital to my survival. With pinched lips and worried eyes, she pressed into me the understanding that this is no mere family meeting but an inquisition. My fate will be decided by these women, my own family. Women with the power of death in their lips. Before I can respond, Myrtle cuts in.

"Azalea?" Her voice rings through the café as she descends the back staircase. "Is that you? Already?"

The girl breaks out in a wide smile and breezes past me. "Aunt Myrtle! I left as soon as I heard. Caught the next flight out of Portland."

I turn and watch Myrtle wrap her in a warm hug. "You must have flown out at midnight."

"I don't really sleep," she says. "At least not at night. I'm more of a catnapper really."

"Come," Myrtle tells her. "You must be tired. I can put you in cabin two to rest before everyone else arrives."

Myrtle leads her toward the door. "Watch the café," she orders as she passes. "I'll be right back."

I flash her a look that says *Seriously?* After all, I accidentally murdered a man here less than twenty-four hours ago. But she waves it off.

"Ta-ta!" the woman calls, waggling her fingers over a shoulder as they stroll into the afternoon sun. I watch them disappear behind the door of cabin two, my heart beating fast.

"Who the heck was that?" Ed asks, staring toward cabin two.

"Azalea," I tell him like I've known her all my life.

He looks at me. "One of yours?"

"Apparently," I reply.

She's only the first, I realize a moment later. There will be more. How many, I don't know. Myrtle went straight to bed after making the call last night and has said very little today, aside from having me phone several incoming guests and refund their deposits so the cabins would be available for family. I gave them all some lame excuse and endured being cursed out about half a dozen times before 10 A.M.

"You've a strange family," Ed says, taking the coffeepot from me to refill his cup.

I can't argue with that.

❧

IT'S THE SIX-YEAR-OLD who unnerves me the most. She stands at her mother's side when they arrive, watching me with guarded eyes—something no one under ten should have. When I offer her our standard peanut butter and jelly, she regards me coolly and says, "You're the one Mommy calls a complication."

"Scarlet!" her mother admonishes. "Don't be rude."

But Scarlet only looks pleased with herself.

I smile tightly into her mother, Barbie's, face. "Cute."

"It was a long flight," she offers weakly.

As it turns out, Azalea is the least of my concerns. They continue to arrive over the next twenty-nine hours, the bane witches, trickling in like flies off carrion, each more eccentric than the last. They all cast a wary eye my way, but it's clear they know who I am. It's an unusual feeling to be surrounded by strangers who know you. I expected some kind of familiarity, a familial bond that would kick in like blood memory to lend me a sense of trust or at least recognition. But by the end of the next day, the only thing that makes it clear they are family is the restlessness behind their eyes, a shifty, hungry look they all share no matter their age or personal style.

I gather from the whispers that the clan matriarch is coming, "Is she here yet?" and "Have you heard?" being repeated in hushed tones near Myrtle's ear over and over throughout each day. Aunt Myrtle answers them with a shrug and a brisk shake of the head, but it's clear she's on edge. At one point, I pull her aside.

"Who are they talking about?" I ask her.

She purses her lips. "Aunt Bella." Then she inclines her head. "*My* aunt Bella."

I swallow, recalling the women in the picture she named. "You mean . . . ?"

"Your great-grandmother's sister." Her eyes are pointed, driving home the implications.

"Jesus . . . How old is she?"

Myrtle sighs. "One hundred and two."

I recoil. "Is it even safe for her to travel?"

"We'll find out," she says with a shrug. "Apparently, she insisted."

Her words are little comfort. And it begins to sink in just what a big deal this is—*I* am—for a centenarian to come all this way to weigh in. It only makes me more nervous. While it might look like a family reunion on the surface, I am being evaluated. Opinions will be aired. Votes cast. Decisions made. And though Myrtle hasn't said as much, I get the feeling a lot more hangs in the balance than if I'll be invited to the next potluck.

As if things aren't already tense enough, Sheriff Brooks shows up an hour before close. He sits at an open table, watching me rush to serve bowl after bowl of chicken and dumplings to our unusual crowd, along with a few regulars and two travelers in for a quick meal. He's nearly impossible to ignore, the warmth radiating off him like a heat lamp, my blood cold and needy. Every time I see him, something inside me stirs a bit more. It takes a while for me to realize it is desire. I haven't felt it in so long. Instinctively, I understand this to be beyond inconvenient. When you have just learned you are responsible for the untimely deaths of three men, developing a piping hot crush on the local law enforcement is not exactly ideal. And Myrtle is always watching, along with the rest of them now.

When I finally get over to him with a cup of coffee and a water, he asks me to sit down.

"Now?" I question.

He glances around the room. "You got something better to do?"

I tug at my earlobe, a nervous gesture, and perch on the edge of the opposite chair. He's in uniform, which doesn't help. Not the official, authoritarian vibe it gives off or the way the starched shirt emphasizes his square shoulders, the chiseled slope of his jaw. Tawdry scenes from Myrtle's collection of paperbacks flicker through my mind with increasing speed. I flush from my thighs to my eyelashes and have to reach over and take his ice water, gulp several mouthfuls down.

He stares at me. "Weird crowd tonight," he says, rolling his eyes around the room of clearly out-of-place women.

"Aunt Myrtle is hosting a thing," I say offhandedly, hoping that will satiate him. "It's, um, good to see you. I didn't get a chance to say it the other night; I was still in shock. But it is." They are words I'm certain I should not say under the circumstances, but they spill out across the tabletop like a mouthful of seeds.

He glances at his hands, the soft down of his lashes flickering against his skin, and then peers at me. "Acacia, I . . ." The breath rushes out of him as if he has lost a fight. "I didn't come here as a social call."

"Oh." I draw my hands into my lap, fingers interlocked, and wait for him to say more.

He looks around, leans forward. "I think you should be careful."

My knee starts jumping under the table. "You mean because of the Strangler?"

His head shakes and he inhales, regroups. "I thought you'd want to know the gentleman from the other night didn't make it," he tells me.

I take a breath. "That's, um . . . that's too bad."

"Yeah," he says. "It is."

"Thank you for telling me. I'll be sure to pass the word along to Myrtle." I start to rise.

"I'd hoped to ask you a couple more questions," he says before I can make my escape.

Thwarted, I lower back down to the chair. "Sure. Go ahead."

He pauses. "Don't you want to know how?" he asks, leaning an arm across the table.

"How?" I repeat, not sure what he means.

"How the man died. What killed him."

"Oh, right." I laugh nervously. "That *how*. I thought you meant . . ." I don't actually know what I thought he meant. I clear my throat. "Never mind."

Something slides across his features, the softness there only moments ago now slick as oil. Regis has left. It is just the sheriff sitting before me now. He watches me with a poker face that only makes me want to babble more. "Poison," he says slowly.

The word sits between us like something barbed. An accusation. A hand grenade with someone's finger on the pin. I clear my throat again. "P-poison?"

"Uh-huh." He leans back. "From a deadly mushroom."

I arch my brows and nod as if I am appraising this information. "Wow."

His tongue runs over his bottom lip. "The same, actually, as the one you tried to pick that night after getting out of my truck. Do you remember? I told you it would kill you before sunrise. Destroys the liver."

"Right," I say, glancing around the room. A woman in pink slacks is watching me from the far wall, a gold chain belt slung across her hips and a cashmere cardigan draped across her shoulders. She seems to know there is more to this conversation than friendly chitchat. I feel like she's assessing my ability to manage the sheriff, ready to scurry off and report my shortcomings the second I turn around. "What a coincidence."

"I'd say so," he responds. "I spoke with the woman at the hospital, too, the one you told me about. Turns out she's his wife. Only married a few months. She confirmed that he hit her. Seems your instincts are spot-on. Maybe I should give you a job at the department."

I laugh emptily and he smiles at me. "I don't think Myrtle could spare me."

"Maybe not," he says. "The wife also told me you served the man his coffee right before stepping outside. That it was the last thing to touch his lips before, well, you know. You didn't mention that."

"Didn't I?" I suddenly feel like the room is heating up by a few dozen degrees. I rub my palms together under the table, trying to disperse the sweat. I have to remind myself this is the same man who let me lock him out of his own house. "She's right, I did. But I—I wouldn't know, you know, if that was the last thing he had. I was outside, like I told you."

"Doing?" he asks now.

"Laundry," I blurt. "Changing stuff over from the washer to the dryer."

He doesn't look convinced.

"And restocking the toilet paper," I quickly add, as though it will make a difference.

"Right, okay." He taps his sunglasses against the table. "It's odd, don't you think, that you and I had that conversation outside my truck right before we end up on either side of this investigation."

"Investigation?" I don't recall him saying anything about an investigation before. At the time, it had all seemed very routine. Clearly, something has changed. My eyes slide to the woman in pink slacks, still staring my way. I have got to do better than I'm doing if I want to impress this conclave or venery or whatever the heck it is. Sheriff Brooks is not my only threat at the moment. Leaning forward, I let my hair fall over one shoulder. "You said yourself I wouldn't be the first to think it was edible. The lack of color and all."

He inhales, a grin tugging on the corners of his mouth. I can see him wrestling with himself behind those suede-gray eyes, the man and the cop. "That's true," he concedes.

I shrug. "They must have pulled off the road before they ever got here and picked it."

"The wife says they didn't stop except for gas."

"She's lying," I tell him. "Something like that would take hours to work."

His eyes narrow ever so slightly. "*Work*—that's an interesting choice of word."

It takes all my self-control not to screech with frustration. "It's just a word," I say. "Maybe she did it herself, the wife. Maybe she wanted out after he used her face as a punching bag." I feel a little guilty throwing this already battered woman under the bus, but it's a diversion. Regis can't get anything on her because there's nothing to find.

"Maybe," he says ambivalently, but I can see I've got him thinking.

I reach a finger forward, run it smoothly over the gold frames of his sunglasses, let it brush against the skin of his knuckles, electric. "You know, Regis, if you wanted to see me again you could have just come by. Questions or no, I'm always up for a cup of coffee."

I do it to knock him off his horse, but the moment we touch, I find that I mean it, that I want nothing more than to sit over a cup of coffee with him and stare into those eyes, giving my secrets away.

He breathes deeply, as if steeling himself against something. His eyes find mine over the table, a carefully controlled yearning in them. For a second, we are back at that night by his door, an ocean of feeling between us. "I'll keep that in mind," he says, slowly withdrawing the sunglasses.

I lean back just as Myrtle comes over. "Sheriff Brooks, you here on official business or to monopolize my pretty niece?"

He grins at me as he stands before cutting his eyes to her. "No, ma'am. Just here for coffee," he replies, looking down at me.

I look away, flustered by how afraid and how aroused I am, knowing that I am playing at a game I do not yet understand.

"Enjoy your thing," he tells her before stepping away and striding through the front door.

Myrtle watches him go. "What was all that about?"

I stand as his car drives away. "Nothing I can't handle."

I turn around to push in my chair, ready to allow myself a sigh of relief, when the jingle of the door opening plays against my already frayed nerves. Looking over a shoulder, I see that it's *her*. She is unmistakable. The venery's matriarch has finally arrived.

Aunt Bella sits in her tufted leather wheelchair like a queen.

A mink hat is wrapped around her powder-white hair, a velvet burn-out shawl pinned over her shoulders by a pearl brooch. In her lap rests a wool blanket and a live hen, whose silky, orange feathers fan around her like a pom-pom. The hen is wearing a cloth diaper, I note. Behind her stands one of the women I recognize from Myrtle's photo, though she's far older now, with pale yellow hair combed elegantly back from her face and striking green eyes. She is dressed entirely in black.

I freeze, unsure what to do. But Myrtle kicks into high gear. "That's it," she hollers. "Closing time. Everybody out." She begins shooing people from the café, including Ed and some of the remaining guests.

"But it's only seven thirty," complains Amos, the other Drunken Moose regular who likes to come in.

Myrtle shoots him an impatient glare. "Which is already far too long to have put up with you," she hisses. "Now go on! Get!"

He and Ed scoot out the door with sour expressions, and she locks up behind them. The women who remain—eleven not counting myself and Myrtle and the little girl, Scarlet—look around the room at one another. They are the venery of bane witches, the last of our family, here to decide my fate.

Aunt Bella bends over and sets her hen on the floor, who promptly scurries off. "Rowena needs to stretch her legs," she croaks. When she sits up, her cold eyes fall on me. "The prodigal returns," she declares. "Well, let me see you."

Myrtle pushes me toward her, and I stumble forward, standing awkwardly, unsure if I should curtsy.

"Donna!" she barks, raising a hand over her shoulder. "My glasses."

The woman in black rustles through a handbag and pulls out a pair of delicately framed granny glasses. She hands them to her mother, who slides them onto her long nose.

She proceeds to look me over with agonizing fastidiousness, as if I am a prize mare to be ogled, giving nothing away. At last, she pulls the spectacles from her face without a word and holds them over her shoulder for Donna to put up. Then, she lays her hands in her lap. Everyone around me is achingly silent, hanging on her every gesture as if they dare not breathe without her permission first. I don't know if I'm supposed to keep standing there or step away or say something. But before I can figure it out, she speaks.

"Let the conclave commence."

15

Conclave

I am surrounded by women far deadlier than I, women whose understanding and experience of our gifts outweigh my own. They have a history, an unspoken accord, that binds them together. I see it in the way they look at one another, the heavy glances, the tiny gestures of brows and lips and hands. In their posture and proximity, the easy way they move around one another. The careful way they move around me.

It is clear—they belong; I do not.

I sit rigid in the dining chair Myrtle has provided as they circle with their own chairs, aware that I am in the hot seat, completely out of my depth. Aunt Myrtle speaks first.

"Piers came to me of her own accord," she begins. "Drawn by something we all share, clutching the memory of our meeting more than twenty years ago."

"Does that matter?" Scarlet's mother, Barbie, asks before Myrtle has barely taken a breath to continue. Her dark hair is glossy straight, framing her face in long layers, causing her gray-green eyes to stand out in contrast. If she's older than Azalea, it's not by much. "She's completely green, ignorant. And that's dangerous for us, especially at her age. I know it's not her fault, but I don't see how that makes a difference. I have a daughter to protect."

"We all have daughters to protect," the second-oldest woman in the room says sharply. Her hair is gray fizz around her face, skin mottled with brown, but there is beauty there in the largeness of her eyes and the puckered bow of her mouth.

I notice the way Myrtle drops her head at the words, daughter-less.

"Well, most of us," the old woman amends.

Barbie looks put out by the interruption. "Thank you, Lattie. But your daughter is fifty-one, and hers is already twenty-two." She nods to the two women I assume are Lattie's daughter and granddaughter, respectively. "Scarlet is six." She looks at me. "I thought the plan was to leave her be, observe from afar, and act in the interest of the venery should she malfunction. Isn't that precisely what's taken place? You said yourself, Myrtle, that her work was sloppy, amateur, lacking polish. There was a sheriff here just today asking questions. We can't afford that kind of attention. She's already put us at risk."

The threat behind her words is unmistakable, sharp enough to rip a hole in the room, bleeding tension. I shiver to think what acting "in the interest of the venery" actually means. I'd like to defend myself, but she's not wrong. I don't know what I'm doing. And that can't be good for anyone here, least of all me. And they aren't even aware that I've done it *three* times already. Not once, like they're arguing. Not even twice, as Myrtle knows. *Three* times. So it will happen again. It is only a matter of time. The question is, will I be ready? Can I be? Can I pull it off with the kind of grace they expect of me, and do I even want to?

"Malfunction?" Myrtle's eyebrows crinkle symmetrically like an accordion bellows. "She's not an android, Barbie. She's a person."

"She's a witch," the older woman in the pink slacks speaks up, the one who had been watching me with Regis. She rests a hand on Barbie's shoulder. "A bane witch, no less. If she were just a person, we wouldn't be having this discussion. And my daughter is right. The risk is too great. We let Lily's sad story play out and it has done nothing but cost us. It's time we end it."

Myrtle whirls on her. "She's one of *us*, Rose. She's family."

"Is she, though?" I turn to see Azalea has spoken from the other side of the circle. She cocks her pretty blond head and eyeballs me, her bright yellow dress swapped for a lean Missoni pencil skirt and a cropped tee that reads HATE BAIT. Her hair has been pulled into a high ponytail with a big, black bow over it. "I know she's Lily's daughter, but didn't Lily make it clear she was out of the venery? I still don't understand why we let her live after that," she says casually, as if ending my mother's life were as simple as returning a dress that doesn't fit. "Might have saved ourselves a trip."

A rush of heat rips through me, stealing my breath, and it takes a moment to register that it's anger. I feel defensive for my mother, the very same woman who left me clueless. It's so startling, I nearly topple from my chair. With effort, I force the feeling down. I cannot lose my cool when I am this outnumbered.

"With all due respect, Azalea," Myrtle cuts in, "you were three at the time."

Azalea shrugs nonchalantly and proceeds to slurp her Coke through a metal straw. If I don't make it out of here, I realize, she will fly back to her life of indie fashion labels and cold brew on the West Coast as if I never existed, relieved to have one less responsibility to think about. It's a chilling thought.

"She's right," someone says. I turn my head and take in the redhead in her forties, the soft turtleneck she wears, the delicate curve of her ear, the cut of hazel eyes so like mine in shape and size that I cringe when I see them.

"Thank you, Misty," Aunt Myrtle says, visibly relieved to have someone's support.

"No." Misty smiles sweetly. "I meant that Azalea is right. Lily renounced the venery. She renounced her family. She renounced her powers. She renounced our lifestyle. Everything that makes us who we are, keeps us safe. She didn't deserve our mercy, but we gave it to her anyway. I'm not inclined to do so again."

Myrtle frowns. "Lily was . . . a disappointment to be sure. But she never actually put us in harm's way. We had no reason to move against her."

"*No reason?*" The woman, Rose, is purpling under her collar. "We had *every* reason. Thirteen in this room tonight if I'm counting right. She was a wild card, uncalculated, unpredictable, a bomb that needed to be disarmed before she detonated. If we wait for the explosion, the damage is done."

Barbie's fingers toy with the green enamel locket on a long gold chain around her neck. I wonder what she keeps inside, probably nothing good. "Hasn't Lily put us in harm's way by leaving her daughter untrained, undefended in the world? Effectively and literally dumping her on our doorstep thirty years too late with a badly botched mark and a nosy cop sniffing around?"

"If we had delivered the last kiss, then it would have been preemptive. Premeditated, even. We don't kill innocents. I thought we settled this twenty years ago," Myrtle argues with exasperation, twisting in her seat.

"It would have been protective," Rose counters. "If you recall, several of us were opposed to your pleas for mercy at the time."

"And clearly still are," Myrtle shoots acerbically. She shakes her head, as if she's been stung. "We're arguing over something that is already done. Lily kept her word to the venery. When the relationship was no longer sustainable, she ended it. *For good.* She saw to his dispatch herself, and it shattered her. She knew it would, and she did it anyway. For all her faults, she was *loyal* in the end."

My mind reels at this morsel of new information about my mother and her death. It sits bitter on the back of my tongue. I assume they are talking about Gerald—her sole relationship for most of my life, implying that *she* killed him. But I can't imagine it. Can't envision all her years of misguided devotion to that selfish buffoon spilling out across the linoleum in a tide of excrement and vomit, the grisly issue of a well-timed kiss, a drop of sweat in his coffee, her lips around the neck of his beer bottle. But Myrtle's words ring with truth; it would have shattered her to do so. And suddenly, her suicide is coming into sickening focus. I grip the seat beneath me until my knuckles whiten.

"Yeah, and took herself out in the process," the only teenager in the group says. When everyone gawks at her, she tries to clarify.

"I mean, she did kill herself. She basically did our job for us. That counts for something, right?"

Myrtle's eyes slide to mine surreptitiously. I'm not supposed to know these things. Not yet. This conclave is revealing as much about the venery to me as it is about me to the venery.

I see Rose scowl at the teenager and the resemblance is suddenly undeniable—same long nose and small chin, same murky green eyes. This girl must be her daughter as well. "What Olea means to say is that Lily's betrayal *did* cost us. It cost us *her,* a powerful witch with a gift that might have strengthened our line, that might have ended dozens of marked lives and saved countless others. And here we are, still trying to clean up her mess after all these years."

She looks me in the eye then. Defiant, I hold her gaze, refusing to be cowed by these women discussing my mother's suicide like a political debate. Her lips curl on one side as she regards me before finally looking away.

"Lily was weak," Great-Grandaunt Bella finally interjects, Rowena nestled at her feet, quiet and still except for the occasional head bob. "Like her mother. A reality that confounded my sister all the way to her grave. In many ways, we can lay the blame for Lily's poor choices at Angel's feet. But with both dead, it hardly seems a fruitful road to tread."

Aunt Myrtle cocks a haughty *I told you so* brow at everyone. But Bella quickly checks her.

"Still, it cannot be overlooked that Piers is Lily's child, who was Angel's—a line that has proven itself to be tainted with malignant idealistic and romantic tendencies and an unchecked power that has demonstrated it is more blight than boon." She reaches down to stroke Rowena's feathered head. "If I were to take a vote now, where do you stand?"

Already? A quiver of concern lances through me.

She rises stiffly and settles her pouchy eyes over the room. "Those in favor of the last kiss for Lily's line?"

Hands clot the air. Rose's fingers jut out like iron railheads beside Barbie's, glossy under the lights. Their faces are cinched as I take them in, tight around their suspicions. Nearly everyone has voted for me to die. My chest caves like a sinkhole, the bloated mass of Don flattening the grass beside his own sick imprinted on my mind, and the smell of the man in the café, tables crashing, the fear streaking their eyes in their final moments. The man from my childhood, his weight on my shoulder and his leering smile, the drop of his body like a tree falling. Is this how it will be for me? A flurry of bodily fluids and flapping limbs, my face contorted in disbelief, as my body gives way to the poison? Have they fed already? Will they do it now?

My eyes go to the door, calculating. I'm outnumbered, but some of them are old. Maybe I could smash through them like a wall. But even if I make it out, they'll hunt me. And I've seen the way Myrtle's eyes shape themselves to the dark. How long would I last before they found me? Would I even see morning?

"Those in favor of mercy?"

Myrtle's hand is swift to rise and singular. Her eyes ring the room. "Oh, come on."

Olea, blessed rebel, asks Bella, "Do I get a vote?"

"Of course," the matriarch confirms.

Her hand barely lifts above her shoulder, a cheeky tilt to her head as she finds my eye. It is met with a whap to the back of her skull from her mother. She quickly lowers it.

"Azalea," Bella creaks out like an old door in the rain. "You didn't raise your hand."

"I'm undecided," she declares, as if she can't be bothered to form an opinion one way or another. "Besides, it's not a real vote."

Not a *real* vote? I feel the air punch out of me, leaving my body loose and rubbery. Will I live then? Who decides?

Bella points at a woman in midlife with a streak of gray coursing through her ebony curls who we had yet to hear from. "Ivy, when did you take your first mark?"

Ivy looks surprised. She points at her color-blocked sweater. "Me?"

Bella's eyes do not waver. "Did I stutter?"

"I was seventeen," she quickly replies.

The old woman nods once. "And you, Azalea? You were younger than your mother, weren't you?"

Azalea's eyes sparkle with pride. "Fifteen," she boasts.

Bella turns to Rose. "How about you, then? How old were you when you killed your first man?"

Rose doesn't hesitate. "I was sixteen, Grandma Bella. So was Barbie."

Bella smiles at her. Her eyes find Lattie next. "How old was Tina when she took her first?"

"Fifteen," she says proudly.

"Yes," Bella agrees. "I remember. You were sixteen, just like Rose and Barbie. And your sister, Donna, was fifteen. Isn't that right, Donna?"

"It is, Mother," she confirms. "And my third daughter, Misty, was sixteen."

The old woman's eyes narrow. She looks at me. "Olea took her first last year. And before we know it, Scarlet will be following in her footsteps. Verna, Tina's daughter, bloomed at seventeen if I remember correctly, and, Myrtle, weren't you only fourteen?"

"I was," Myrtle admits.

"So young," Bella comments. "Made my sister proud to see it. But Angel—she was the prodigy. Tell us how old your sister was when she took on the mantle of being a bane witch."

Myrtle clears her throat. "Thirteen."

Everyone gasps even though it is clear from their slack faces it's not news to them.

"And poor Lily," Bella finishes. "Your mother took her first mark at twelve," she tells me. "It remains debatable if she was truly ready."

What would they say if they knew my first victim died when

I was barely five years old? So much younger than anyone here. My mother had her faults, but maybe she was right to put me on medication. How might I have turned out if I'd been allowed to go on killing, too young to comprehend what I was doing and why? My eyes meet Myrtle's and the secret sparks between us. She will not tell them. She fears their reaction as much as I do.

I swallow the revulsion that has wadded itself in my throat. I belong to a family of murderers, *proud* murderers, who began killing *as children.* I don't know how to reconcile this with the kindness Aunt Myrtle has shown me, the goodness I see in her every day. The way she helps Ed and tolerates Terry and Amos, the free bananas and bowls of soup she gives to anyone who wanders in off the street without money to buy their meal. Her community may be rough around the edges, but Myrtle is certainly one of its pillars, someone the residents of Crow Lake can count on. Even I have spared a life against the three I've taken. Certainly, to that man and his family, I am a hero. I am good. If he only knew the savage truth. My stomach turns inside my ribs, as if it can outmaneuver these contradictions.

Reaching down, Bella picks Rowena up and settles the chicken in her lap, stroking its head with a finger. Its papery eyelids close in response as she continues talking. "I took my first mark at almost twenty," she says after a moment.

From the disks of their eyes, the wet, crater mouths, some of the younger women are surprised by this. They've not heard it before.

"Unspeakably belated for our kind," Bella elaborates. "I was, quite literally, a late bloomer. But I still remember him well, his high-waisted pants and little vest, even the width of his red silk tie. It was the very start of the war. The venery had all but given up on me. The Golden Gate International Exposition had people flooding into San Francisco's Treasure Island to commemorate the city's now storied bridges. Men, in particular, came to ogle the female attractions, like burlesque dancer Sally Rand and her so-called Nude Ranch."

She eyes each of us in turn before continuing. "I felt him coming three days on. I couldn't sleep. I couldn't eat. Couldn't do anything except wander the sea-swept hills looking for the lavender flowers and purple berries that called to me like a lover in the dark. I fed until my ribs ached and my head burned. And then I slipped on my mother's slinky green dress with the little buttons down the front, wandering the fair like a waif, trying to sift him from the throngs of horny, clownish men. They were all greedy, like half-starved children at a birthday buffet, but his fetor was laced with evil, the stink of a putrid wound. It called to me. It begged me to disinfect it." She sighs as if remembering a passionate embrace.

"I thought I'd never find him. It must have taken me two whole days. But when I did, he was so eager, so ready to show me what he was truly capable of. I let him lead me away from the crowds into the isolated back alleys. I could still smell the last woman on him. She probably wasn't more than fifteen. Certainly unwilling. Her fear clung to him, clouding the air like smoke. I was inexperienced, of course, and small framed. He tried to take me, his head turned away so I couldn't see his face. Had he succeeded, he still would have died, but I would have learned a painfully unforgettable lesson that scarred me for life—we are not invulnerable." Her eyes target mine, searching.

"Fortunately, he finally glanced down, and I spit in his face, saliva spraying across his eyes and nose. Maybe not so graceful as a kiss," she says, looking to Azalea. "We can't all be masters of seduction. But certainly, it was effective. He backhanded me before the poison could do its work, but it was the last hand he ever laid on a woman. I thought I'd never roll him off me."

Her gaze drifts to a place we can't see as she recalls the night in question. "When I found my way home, my mother took one look at her torn dress and began to cry. Not because she cared about the garment, or because she realized how close I'd come to being defiled, but because she knew I was saved. She'd been begging them for more time, you see. Some in our line had become convinced the gift had skipped me, especially when my sister, Laurel, was already showing the signs at fourteen. They weren't sure it was wise to leave a woman in the world who knew our secrets but didn't share their burden. I'll never know how close I came to receiving the last kiss, but judging by my mother's reaction, it was far closer than I ever realized.

"They found the man's body that same night. In the news report, they called him an alleged rapist, having been accused by no less than four women. It's hard enough to convict a man of sexual assault now, but it was even harder then. We can't say how many women he actually harmed, or how many I spared, but what we can say is that my mother was right. All I needed was time."

Her eyes twinkle behind the folds of skin that surround them, and her lips lift at the corners. "I've taken over a hundred marks since then, my last just this year."

Her story lands like a winter squall, stinging the skin. The meaning is evident.

I audibly exhale, my bones falling away from each other.

"What are you proposing, Grandma Bella?" the one who Barbie signaled to be Lattie's daughter asks, a woman of middle age with pale strawberry hair and a white, collared shirt.

"What I am proposing, Tina, is time. A trial period for Piers to show this clan if she can be trusted, if she has what it takes to be one of us, to kill swiftly and *discreetly*, without hesitation or misgiving." She fixes me with a vulpine stare.

I should feel grateful for her endorsement, if it can be called that. Certainly, a knot somewhere inside me unwinds. But it is quickly replaced by the slow burn of registering what this means, what they want me to do. The man when I was five, Don, the man in the café—these are only the beginning. This will become my whole reason for existence if I give them what they want, the slaughter of who knows how many men. Men with parents and siblings. Men with wives. Men with children. This cycle of hunger, feeding, purging, killing will mark my days from now on, repeated over and over. It is not the life I imagined for myself when I dared to envision one apart from Henry.

"She can stay with me," Aunt Myrtle offers before I can speak up for myself. "I can teach her. She's already showing promise, all she needs is the education, something Lily was never able to give her. But I can. I wasn't able to have a daughter of my own. Maybe this is why. Maybe this is *my* gift to the venery."

"Myrtle Corbin, you have already given much to this clan," Donna says from beside her mother's wheelchair. "Your territory provides us with a place for these gatherings, a place for bane witches to escape when needed, to disappear. And you mind our stores, keeping valuable provisions from all our territories in your underground sanctuary for when they are needed most. You play a valued and important role in our family. Never forget it."

I recognize the word "provisions" for what it truly is—poisons. The jars Myrtle had me hide. She dries and stores deadly plants on those shelves. Back stock, I suppose, for bane witches who need it in a pinch. Who knows how many ways there are to die down there?

Myrtle nods her appreciation for the elder woman's words.

"A trial period makes sense," I am surprised to hear Azalea of all people say. She scoots from her chair and waltzes over to Bella, scratching at the chicken's head before turning to appraise me. "If she stays here, she can learn from one of the best, hone her skills in the privacy of this backwoods establishment, then claim a territory of her own, one we all agree on. The Midwest is short of our distinguished services right now. But how will we know she's proven herself?" She winks in my direction.

Aunt Bella's wrinkles deepen, furrows plowed with every shifting expression. "She will take a mark," she declares. "Succinctly and without observation, bending herself to our edicts. Her performance will be graded on three points—accuracy, brevity, and confidentiality. The worth of her target. The precision of her delivery. And the stealth of her process." She ticks each off on a crooked finger.

"And if she doesn't succeed?" Rose asks.

Bella's smile is oiled, the efficient glide of a ventriloquist's dummy. It sets my teeth on edge. "Well, then the venery will get its last kiss after all."

"There should be some kind of limit to this experiment, so it doesn't drag out indefinitely," Barbie insists.

"Six weeks should suffice." The old woman scans the room, daring anyone to challenge her.

I see Myrtle's face wash a ghastly pale shade, like curdled milk. "But . . . she just bloomed, just killed. It's impossible to know when the cycle will—"

"Six weeks," Bella reiterates, bringing a clawed hand down on the end of her armrest. "If she shares her mother's precocious nature, that won't be a problem."

Rose snakes a hand down and squeezes Barbie's shoulder. My nostrils flare against the heat building in the café.

Bella turns her gaze on Aunt Myrtle. "But if she doesn't, Myrtle will call another conclave in order to see to her *retirement*. Won't you, Myrtle?"

Her eyes find mine over a shoulder. They are soft, pitying. She turns to Aunt Bella, still stroking her mild-mannered hen. "You have my word."

"And the cop," Tina adds, her blouse so stiff it's practically saluting.

The mention of Regis sends a spike of heat through my center, both passionate and protective. Surely, they can't mean for me to *kill* him? I recall Myrtle's statement that they don't kill innocents and allow my muscles to slacken a little. Regis is a complication, but he's an innocent one.

"She needs to take care of him. Get him off her scent or Myrtle will lose this territory we all prize so much," she finishes to my relief.

White is not her color, I think snobbishly, the designer in me never far from the surface. It bleeds the warmth from her skin like a tick on a dog.

"Agreed," Rose adds. "She will have to clean up this mess she's made to be permitted a place in the venery."

Bella's eyes narrow into thoughtful slits. Her mouth forms a languid, crinkly smile. "I've no doubt that she won't let us down." Her eyes sharpen on Myrtle's. "*Either* of you."

The room erupts into a chorus of exhales and sighs and sagging shoulders as the tension begins to dissipate. Several women rise from their chairs and shake Myrtle's hand like she's just won an important court case. Azalea turns to Barbie and begins discussing a hair mask she's been applying to her split ends with some success. All around me, they are buzzing and stirring, ready to move on to the cocktails and refreshments now that the hard work is over.

I remain in my chair, baffled, a disgruntled energy building behind my sternum like a white-hot breastplate of rage. I have six weeks to learn everything it has taken these women twenty years or more to master; to find, stalk, and kill yet another man without leaving a trace, and to convince Sheriff Brooks that I had nothing to do with the one who collapsed in the café, that all is well in the tiny hamlet of Crow Lake, despite the two murderesses living under his nose. It seems designed for failure, a ploy of planned obsolescence. Rose, preposterous in those pink slacks, gloats in the corner with Barbie at her side, a winning smile painted across her doll-like features.

They are milling about as if I do not exist, as if I am not right here. A few begin to stack chairs while others wander toward the door. Scarlet is begging her mom for a crop top like Cousin Azalea's. My own mother, the dead black sheep in a family of killers, got more airtime than me at this trial, which I have finally deduced is what a "conclave" actually is.

"Stop!" I screech, rising to my feet.

Around me, the room hushes. Everyone freezes and turns in my direction. Tongues still. Eyes widen. A few narrow with ire at my impudence.

Aunt Myrtle quickly steps over to me—more like between me

and Great-Grandaunt Bella—placing a placating hand on my arm. "Piers, dear. It's all settled. There's no need to drag this out."

But I shake her off, my eyes digging into the old matriarch's. I will not be set aside, looked over in my own family as if I am some kind of apparition rather than a woman of flesh and blood, desire and aversion. I did that with Henry for the last two years and it nearly killed me. I will not do it again.

I glare at her, challenging, and find a note of admission, even respect, in hers.

Choking back doubts, I find my voice and use it. "I have something to say."

16

Normal

The confusion is written across their faces. The offense. I have done what even Aunt Myrtle didn't dare to—ungraciously rejected their goodwill. Taken all their generosity and fisted it before dumping it back at their feet. But if I don't say this, say *anything*, I will hate myself for it.

They don't all return to their seats, not for me. A few glide slowly back, lower themselves down as I take the floor, but many remain, sticking to their respective places like pins in a corkboard, glowering in my direction. Azalea and Barbie lean against the wall, arms crossed, waiting. Rose spins on her heel, staring at me as if I've just lifted my leg and pissed the rug. But the only one who really matters, I suppose, is Great-Great-Aunt Bella, and she has not budged from her original place. Her daughter Donna, who'd moved behind her to direct her chair, takes a step back.

"I know you've made your decision," I begin, as a couple more find a seat. "And I'm grateful for your confidence in me, truly." We all know *confidence* is the last thing they have in me, but I'd rather not stomp on the hive after I've already angered the bees.

"Don't confuse charity with confidence," Rose interrupts, her lips pinched.

I swallow, ignoring her words. "But . . ." My eyes dart to Azalea, who is slowly shaking her head. I quickly look away. "What if I don't want it?"

Donna's brow creases. "Don't want what, dear?"

I take a breath. "*This*. Being a bane witch. The venery. All of it."

Beside Aunt Bella, Lattie breaks out into peals of high-pitched laughter, but Donna looks sick to her stomach. Myrtle grimaces in my direction with worried eyes.

"What if I just want a normal life?" I ask, frustrated by the looks of incredulity hemming me in.

"Here we go," Barbie says, throwing her hands up. "Just like her mother."

"A *normal* life?" Aunt Bella croaks out, ignoring Barbie's outburst. Her eyes peer up at me, flashing with outrage.

"Well, yeah," I tell her. "You know, without all the killing and hunting and poisoning and whatever."

A muscle under her left eye twitches as if it is trying to communicate by Morse code. "What do you imagine that to be, this normal life you will live?"

I wave my hands in the air. "I'll live here for a while until I find another job. And then I'll move wherever that is. I'll wake to coffee in the mornings and drink hot tea at night. I'll have a small place that I keep tidy, and a dog for company. Maybe, in the distant future, I'll date again. Maybe I'll find real love. A partner. Someone who really gets me. Who is easy to be with. Or maybe I'll live alone, able to make my own decisions about everything from what sweater to wear to what car to buy. But it will be *mine,* and that's what matters."

The old woman scoffs. "Donna, please tell our new recruit what her normal life will actually look like."

"Of course." Her daughter stands, the sleek paleness of her hair and sharpness of her cheekbones creating a lean, coyote elegance despite her advanced age. She smiles the way a cat might smile at a wounded bird. She clasps her arms behind her back as she begins pacing around me slowly. "You will, as you say, make your own decisions for a time. Coffee and tea and perhaps even the dog. If you're lucky, you'll land that shiny new job before the hunger kicks in. But you'll lose it the second the cravings overtake you. Unable to concentrate on your work, your performance will suffer. You'll begin missing days as the hunger drives you farther and farther to feed. Any friends you made will write you off as undependable, maybe even mentally unstable, when you stop returning calls, cannot explain where you've been or why, turn up at the edges of their property, your shoes lost and dress tattered, streaks of berry juice dripping down your chin.

"Resisting the urge to kill, you will condemn yourself to inevitable mental decline, slowly losing your grip on reality, on what is true and what is not. You will act and speak in ways that are unguarded, that leave you vulnerable and make no sense to the people around you, who will distance themselves over time. As the toxins you feed on build up in your system with no release, they will turn on you, devouring your mind. The extent of your unrest is anybody's guess. But it will be certain. And it will be disastrous.

"If you have a dog, it will cower from you once the cycle begins. It will smell your bloom coming and begin disappearing for lengths of time, pissing on the carpet, hiding under the bed. Perhaps it will finally run away for good. That is if you don't kill it first. Every date you go on will be a disappointment. Even if they aren't a mark, you will sense things about these men they never wanted you to know. Things *you* never wanted to know. If they are attracted to you, you'll never be sure if it's genuine or just the allure. You'll become paranoid, insecure. If you find someone patient or desperate enough to stick around, you will end up killing him by accident when you're in bloom—a thoughtless kiss, an erotic evening, even just a misplaced sneeze or falling tear. When he's gone, you'll learn that you're pregnant.

"You might think it a blessing until they are born. If you have a son, he won't be likely to live beyond infancy, not if he's in your care, and that's if you don't kill him in the womb first. You'll bury him, knowing it was your fault. Not in that way normal parents grieve a child, believing they could have prevented some terrible end. You will know with absolute certainty that your child died by your hand. And it will ruin you. If you have a girl, she'll live.

For many years you'll think all is well. And then puberty will approach. Her own cycle will begin. She'll bloom, potentially before her time if your line is any indication. And she'll kill some innocent in a daze of ignorance, traumatizing her beyond belief."

I swallow, my throat dry as old tobacco. Her argument is indisputable. I know what she is saying is true because I have lived it.

"There will be witnesses. She'll become a suspect or at least appear suspicious enough that you will feel compelled to flee with her to protect her life. Maybe you'll land somewhere safe for a while. But it won't last. Before you know it, she'll kill again. And again. Until eventually, you alert the attention of the community around you, where she'll be tried and executed in front of you, if they don't drag her out and murder her first.

"By this point, you are a shell. Life will no longer feel worth living. And we will come for you in the night, overpowering your senses, driving you to an early grave with a toxicity so powerful even God wouldn't have immunity to it." She pauses before me, her long arms crossed over themselves, her face punishing in the warm lights of the café. "And all of that is only if you don't manage to get yourself killed, which you undoubtedly will."

"Thank you, Donna," the old matriarch says. "That was very enlightening."

Her daughter returns to her seat, a smug smile crowning her long face.

"So, you see," Aunt Bella begins, leaning forward as she stares up at me, "what you want is irrelevant."

My mouth drops open, leaden. A bead of sweat is running along the curve of my neck, sitting atop my collarbone. I think I hear my pulse. Henry chides me in my mind, *Piers, show some dignity. Find your tongue.* "B-but that's not fair."

She falls back against her wheelchair, upsetting the chicken momentarily. "Was it fair when that man I told you about took some young girl's virginity without her consent? Or when the man you killed beat his wife into submission? Was it fair when your mother accidentally killed your father because she insisted on living out a romantic fantasy regardless of the consequences? Was it fair when Myrtle gave up her son to keep him alive? Or when Misty gave up two of hers? Was it fair when the first bane witch risked her life to save another's in childbirth, only to be thanked with a brutal rape by the noble husband, her own beloved babe ripped from her womb in a torrent of blood that left them both for dead?" She stops and shakes her head, amusement playing across her lips. "Humph. *Fair.* What a useless word." Her eyes dig into mine; they are hard as gems. "We're not interested in *fair* in this family. We are interested in *justice.*"

I suck in air as if I've been gut punched. Reeling, I manage to stay on my feet. "How can you call this justice?" I whisper, my voice quavering. "You're murderers! All of you. This is not justice. It's death."

She cocks her head, eyes crinkling at the corners. In her lap, Rowena ruffles her feathers. "Sometimes," she says wisely, "they are one and the same."

"How can you say that?" I blurt. "How can any of you say that?" I look around the room. The faces have hardened like salt dough. The smiles and chatter have dropped. They regard me coldly, a worm on a hook. "These aren't marks you're killing, they're men. They have lives. They have families. It's not for us to decide if they live or die."

"Then who is it for?" Bella asks. "Go ahead. Tell me. I'll wait."

My jaw works soundlessly before I arrive lamely at, "The courts. The judicial system."

She laughs, and they follow, snickering behind hands and into collars. My naivete thrills them. "How many women do you know who have been helped by the judicial system?"

When I can't answer, she continues.

"These magical courts you speak of, have they worked for you?"

I stare at her, stricken. "M-me?"

She nods. "Come now, you think we don't know, that Myrtle didn't tell us? About your man? The one who used you, who controlled and tormented you? Tell me, did the courts protect you from him?"

My eyes fill with tears, face reddening, a blister of shame. "No."

"No," she repeats, watching me. "I didn't think so." Her eyes travel the room. "Azalea, tell us about your last mark."

Azalea steps forward, radiant, a coy smile on her face. "Percell," she purrs, drawing out the *l* sound. "Such a charmer." Her sarcasm lights the room up with laughter. "He ran a multibillion-dollar corporation on the West Coast. He was a man of . . . how shall I put this?" She fingers the fruit charms on her enamel bracelet. "Discriminating tastes," she finally finishes. "He had a cannibal fetish. One his money and prestige allowed him to move from the realm of fantasy to reality. He only indulged in female meat," she adds when my face pales. "He had two sons also. I decided they were better off without that sick fuck guiding their lives. Now they'll grow up rich and sad but otherwise normal. They'll go to private school and work for hedge funds and maybe do a little coke. But they won't eat people."

"Thank you, Azalea." Bella looks disturbed. "That was . . . vivid."

Azalea nods and steps back, leaning against the wall as she grins.

Aunt Bella stares at me. "How would your courts handle that man? Hmmm? Where is his justice outside of this venery?"

"I—They probably wouldn't," I admit. "Because his money protects him. But that's just one person."

She smiles and raises a bent finger, pointing to Verna, whose pixie cut and boyish build make her stand out in the room.

Without a word, Verna begins. "My last mark was a judge in the district courts. He liked to film kiddie porn on the weekends for his hobby. When I found him, he'd already raped over seventy boys between the ages of six and fifteen, several of whom he paid for exclusive rights to after they were sexually trafficked. He was never going to stop," she says, giving me a hard stare. "*Never.*"

"But you stopped him, didn't you, Verna?" Bella asks.

She smiles bashfully. "With a tampon in his thermos."

Bella's eyebrows arch. "Creative . . ."

The young woman dips her chin innocently. "He was driving to his 'summer home' near the Canyonlands of Utah. He kept a special room there, a fitting place for him to die. They didn't find his body for many days. By the time they did, the thermos had been scrubbed with oxygen bleach."

Bella looks at me. "See? Even your judicial system is corrupted. But we are not. There isn't a woman in this room who has taken an innocent life. Not a one. If your mother were still alive, she would be the only exception."

Even I fall under this rule, I realize. Three men, every one deserving in their own way. But the urge to defend my mom, however new, beats hard in my chest. "Because she didn't want to be a killer."

"Because she didn't listen!" Lattie hisses before Bella can respond. "If she had done her duty, your father would be alive, and in his place countless predators put out of commission. But she was selfish, just like you. She wanted a *normal* life." She says the last line mockingly. I feel absurd.

My cheeks are wet, sticky with tears and heat; my mouth cannot form another word. It feels gummy inside, disintegrating. I'm so confused and sick and horrified I can hardly stand. I know when I'm bested.

"You stand there and judge us," Rose says acidly, moving toward me, corrosive and sparking. "Your own kind. But where is your judgment for the men who rape and kill and hit and take? Who barricade themselves behind money and power and a culture that protects them, champions their aggression and narcissism? You are sick with poison, but it's not ours, it's theirs. It spreads in you even now, tainting your self-image, the way you look at everything, especially other women. The men we kill are not victims. But *you* are. And you should know better."

Her words are like a chemical burn in my ears. I want to flush them out before they scar. Why is it easier for me to point a finger at these women than the men who provoked them? Shouldn't someone stand in contrast to the misogyny that has defined us for millennia? The vigilante in me has been hog-tied, wrists and ankles numb, circulation cut off. A banded appendage that fell off long ago. A vestigial tail.

Aunt Bella grips the wheels of her chair and rolls toward me. She raises a crooked hand to take one of my own. "We are products of their violence," she says softly. "As long as they commit crimes against our sex with such impunity, as long as the imbalance exists, so will we."

Myrtle steps forward. "Piers, I know this must be hard for you to swallow. Lily tried to shelter you from it, and it has only done more damage. But listen when we tell you, there is no other choice. It's not fair, but it's fact. You either live as a bane witch, or you die as one. There is no in-between."

The soft pads of Aunt Bella's fingers are cool against my own. "We have lost too many to count over the centuries," she says sadly. "Many casualties in the first, stumbling generations of our kind as we adjusted to the weight of our magic. Women who weren't careful enough, who miscalculated, who paid the price. Girls even, who simply paid for their mother's transgressions. And then came the fires and the burnings. So many innocents lost we could never cleanse the world of that bloodshed. But among them, so many of our own, too. Now we are cleaner and clearer and far more careful, but safety is never a guarantee. If we are hard, sweet child, if we seem cruel . . ." Her hand grips mine with a force and dexterity I wouldn't have known it still had, crushing my knuckles together. "It is because we have to be to keep you safe, to keep ourselves alive. There cannot be room for error without making room for death."

I stare down at Aunt Bella, knowing I cannot escape again. Henry was one thing, but how many bridges can I survive? Is there one tall enough to leave the bane witch behind? My mother tried to evade her fate, and she was a resolute failure. The only choice I have is to go down the same doomed path she took or forge my own.

"But I died," I tell them. "I died so that I could live on my own, *as* my own."

"You died to an illusion of weakness," Bella says to me, "so that you may live your strength."

Her words are the final swing of the hammer. My chest hitches and a sob erupts, laying my soul bare. I am cornered.

"It's time," the old matriarch whispers gently. "Take your place, Piers Corbin. You are a victim no longer."

THE CABIN FEELS stifling. Everyone is crammed in for the after-party, wedged into sofas and chairs, clumping around the kitchen and near the windows, sipping the hot toddies Myrtle keeps passing out and munching on finger sandwiches. A bowl of dessert mints sits on the low table in front of me, little pastel pillows that melt in your mouth, making this look for all the world like just another wedding shower or holiday. My hands are pressed between my knees. To my left, Verna is hanging over the arm of the couch, chatting Misty up about Pilates; to my right, Ivy and Tina are discussing canapés. I feel as if I have fallen into an alternate universe. I have to remind myself that only weeks ago, Misty followed a man back to his car and offered to blow him in an empty parking lot, then stood back and watched him die, and that Verna grows deadly wolfsbane in her garage. There will be a moment where these contradictions come together to form a complete picture in my mind, where Pilates and wolfsbane make sense in the same sentence and I won't wonder if the canapés are laced with shaved columbine root. But it hasn't happened yet.

When Ivy gets up to go to the bathroom and Tina wanders into the kitchen to help Aunt Myrtle, Azalea plops down next to me. "You look positively green. What's the matter? Is the pimiento cheese not agreeing with you?"

A plume of perfumed air rises to greet my nose, and I have to admit, she smells divine. "Is that the allure?" I ask, overcome. "That intoxicating smell?"

She giggles. "No, silly. That's perfume. It's called Jump Up and Kiss Me by Clive Christian."

I shake my head to disperse the fragrant cloud and gesture toward her. "How do you afford all this?" It's rude to ask, but I can't help myself. "You're so young."

She wrinkles her nose. "Don't you know it's impolite to talk about money?"

"Yes, of course. Sorry." I break eye contact, feeling like an ass.

She shoves my arm playfully. "I'm kidding! There are no secrets in the venery. Look, Myrtle probably hasn't parsed it all out for you yet, but here's the gist. We have money."

"We?"

"The *family*," she says under her breath. "Generational wealth, you could say. It's important that we have a way to take care of ourselves and to do what we're called to do. So, it's something they've been working on for a very long time."

"They?"

"Yes, they. *They*. The venery in perpetuity. The bane witches who've gone before us." She quirks a brow at me like I'm being weird but it's cute.

"Oh, right." I nod as if I understand.

"Rose and Donna are the biggest holders," she says, eyes darting to where they stand. "And of course, Great-Grandma Bella. But assets are distributed between us all. They just kind of stay on top of that part for everyone. Like, if you're playing Monopoly, they're the bankers."

"Oh." My eyes must widen because she tries to reassure me.

"Don't worry. Your needs will be met. We all do our part to add to the funds of course. And, you know, I have ways of taking care of myself." She flutters her lashes demurely.

"And where did this money come from? Or does?" I scrunch up my brow as I wait for her to answer. Henry never liked me involved in our finances, but I listened well and overheard enough. And I'd run a successful business for years before he showed up.

She turns her head toward me. "Where do you think?" And then she laughs.

"Right." I swallow hard. *From marks.* "But how does that work? I mean, I thought we couldn't, you know, have relationships or be connected to our . . . our victims."

"Aren't you full of questions tonight," she chides. "Look, it's complicated. So it's only ever taken on by a select few bane witches, and only after the whole venery agrees. But on occasion a mark might be coerced into marriage *if* he has substantial assets to be gained. We think of it as financial karma, an investment in justice to lift a bit of the stain from his soul. But it's incredibly hard to pull off; it takes enormous care, planning, and self-control. So don't go getting any ideas. Your mother could have done it, I'm told. That's what the venery had selected for her, but she refused. So, Rose took her place. Nearly got herself killed. It's left her a little bitter."

I nod slowly. "I picked up on that."

Azalea passes me a hot toddy from Myrtle's abandoned tray. "Drink. It'll help."

"Why are you being so nice to me?" I ask, taking a sip.

She assesses me a moment, then shrugs. "I like you."

I harrumph at that.

"Seriously," she insists. "You don't believe me?"

I eyeball her. "*How will we* know *she's proven herself?* You know, for a moment there, I thought you had my back," I reply with heavy skepticism.

"I did have your back," she tells me. When I don't look convinced, she keeps going. "If I don't point out the obvious, someone else will. We can't dance around the issues, Piers. We would never last that way. We have to confront risks head-on, the reality of who we are and what we do and how to keep ourselves safe. Myrtle says you're the real deal, that you're not your mother. That you just need instruction. And I believe her. I believe in giving you a chance to prove yourself. You may not realize it, but I went to bat for you in there. I gave them a reason to try. Parameters make them feel safe. You didn't stand a chance otherwise. I bought you those six weeks, so don't flub it up. And for what it's worth, I think what you did was brave."

"What *I* did?"

She rests a hand on my knee. Suddenly, in spite of the perky ponytail and the exposed midriff and the lime-green nail polish, Azalea seems decades older than she is. "Standing up to them," she whispers. "It was stupid, but brave."

I look down into my toddy. The caramel color is inviting, like being underwater in the Cooper River. "I'm out of practice."

This time, it's Azalea's turn to look confused.

"Standing up for myself," I admit. "I haven't done it in a very long time."

Her eyes glisten with amusement. "Oh, I don't know if that's true. According to Aunt Myrtle, that's all you've been doing since you left Charleston."

My eyes meet hers, and behind the party-girl glint, I see deeper things—sadness and pain. Innocence lost. Things that can't be spoken but must be carried. Things I understand intimately. "It wasn't Charleston I left."

She pats my knee and stands up, looking down at me after she finishes her toddy in one big gulp. "One demon at a time, cousin. One demon at a time."

17

Beth Ann's

I shouldn't be here. A bitter chill brushes against my skin in the bluing dark, the morning sun trying valiantly to crest the trees and chase away another long night. I couldn't sleep, rattled as I was by the conclave and the afterparty, not to mention Myrtle, Lattie, and Donna singing "Poison Ivy" by the Coasters at the top of their lungs at 3 A.M. Finally, just before dawn, I tiptoed into the kitchen where I pulled a quilted jacket over a hasty outfit and went outside. But the woods were as restless as I was, their leaves rustling loudly in the shadows, and the women of the venery still felt too close for comfort.

Burrowing my hands in the pockets of Myrtle's borrowed coat, I found the keys to her ancient Subaru and decided a drive would clear my head. Myrtle probably wouldn't be up for hours. She'd never even know I'd gone. I was circling the edge of town when the itch struck, a sinister yank at my gut. It felt similar to my poisonous cravings but with a powerful shift, like the wind changing direction. When I couldn't shake it, I parked along the narrow shoulder and walked down the lonely drive waiting behind the shelter of the trees.

It's only now, as I stroll up on the familiar firepit, that I realize where I am. But I have no idea why. I let my eyes crawl over the piled stones, the metal ring inside, the black patch of cold ash. Paces away stands her timber house, a muted blue with white trim, dark behind the windows, the front porch just high enough for a raccoon or a possum to slide under. It's silent. Empty.

Beth Ann—the last victim of the Saranac Strangler.

The trees are still around me, their branches dipping toward the ground like feathers. I look down. My dusky-green suede boots feel louder here, as if my feet are screaming my presence with every trespassing step. I've bound the laces too tight. I can feel the strain across the top of my foot. But I don't bend to loosen them. That would be assuming a vulnerable position. Unwise, I think, given the location. My arms prickle with apprehension.

There is a pattern in the dirt beside the firepit, as if it has been brushed one way and then another. I stare at it, wondering if she struggled, if they fought, if she was dragged like old lumber. Did she try to run? Did she bolt for the cover of the trees? I glance at them sidelong, a barricade of arms, and picture her blond hair flying. Her place feels suddenly like an arena. The stage where people go to die.

Did she even know what was happening?

My heart rate begins to pick up, and the longer I stare, all I can see is that clearing in the woods Henry drove me to. Everything around me transforms, shifting from morning to night, cold to warm, here to there. His long fingers press into my neck as he rocks against me, eager to see the deed finally done. His breath is stale—garlic for lunch, decaying meat. I wanted to believe, when I jumped off that bridge, that I left Henry behind forever. But I realize standing here that he will always haunt me. I've made a crucial mistake. I saved my life when I should have taken his.

"You shouldn't be here," a familiar voice calls from the drive, echoing my own thoughts.

Everything spins, South Carolina falls away. I startle and look over a shoulder to see Regis coming up, his uniform snug against his thighs and shoulders, the sunlight trailing behind him. When he reaches my side, he crosses his arms.

"You're up early," he says, taking in the sloppy state of my dress, the loose layers of my hair.

"I could say the same."

"This is a crime scene," he tells me. "And private property."

I clear my throat. "Sorry. I didn't mean to come here. I . . . It was an accident."

His eyes find mine, probing, as if they are always asking a question I can't answer. "You look pale. You okay?"

How can I tell him everything I've learned, the weight of it on my chest, what I've been asked to do? I worry he sees the three dead men in my eyes, that the danger inside gives me away, but he only looks concerned and my heart clenches.

"Motion sickness," I lie. "I just needed to pull over for some air."

He nods as if he believes me, but his eyes cut away. He knows there's more to it than that. The tether that allows me to read him gives him the same insight into me.

"I met her," I tell him, staring into the firepit. "On my first day here. She was . . . nice. She was more than that actually, but I never got the chance to find out what." When he doesn't respond, I ask, "Did you know her?"

"I know everybody around here." He looks at the ground.

It's not really an answer, but the truth floods into me like biting into a cherry cordial. "She was your girlfriend."

He stares at me, brows slanted, wonder collecting in the crease between them, then sighs. "Yes, when she first moved here. We hadn't seen each other in some time. It didn't end well."

I don't ask why. It's none of my business no matter how desperately I want to know.

"She used to bring maple-iced cookies by the sheriff's office sometimes with her cat, Snowball. Never knew anyone who had a cat that liked to ride in the car," he says with a small laugh. "Despite our history, Beth Ann was good people. This shouldn't have happened to her."

"Bad things happen to good people all the time, we just don't like to think about it," I say. Without thinking, I reach out to squeeze his hand. It's warm, smooth, more comforting to me than mine probably is to him. He doesn't let go right away. "I'm sorry."

"It's a small community," he finally says. "She'll be missed."

"Will he return, do you think?" I ask, casting a furtive glance around. "The Strangler?"

Regis purses his lips. The fine lines at the corners of his eyes deepen. "I hope so." Shock colors my face, and he rushes to explain. "I want to catch this bastard now more than ever. For Beth Ann. For Crow Lake. I don't want anyone else to die, but I hope he hangs around long enough for me to give him a taste of his own medicine." His body goes rigid. "You shouldn't be out here alone. You need to be more careful. He's not done killing."

I squat down and press my fingers to the dirt. I can feel something here, braille under the dust, an imprint left by the killer. The ground is saturated with it, like a lingering scent. Standing, I rub my thumb against my fingers and meet the sheriff's eyes. "He's circling."

He pauses, mouth opening. His lips come back together and then he asks, "Circling what?"

"Not what," I say. "*Who.*"

"His next victim?" The words are shallow, as if there's no breath behind them. A whistle sounds at the back of his throat. I realize it's fear.

"Possibly." Except the answer doesn't taste right on my tongue. Something in me is expectant, noncommittal, as if I am holding space for the *real* answer, which will arrive any minute. I feel a powerful urge to lick the ground, to understand.

"You some kind of psychic?" Regis asks. His brows lower as he squares his eyes on me, evaluating. "I wasn't much of a believer myself, but the department used one out of desperation. She lives in Rochester. Broke open a missing child case we had ten years back. I still can't explain it."

"I'm no psychic," I'm quick to respond. "I'm an interior designer—*was* a designer. Just have an eye for detail." The second it's out I want to swat it from the air like a fly. I cannot be *Piers* anymore, cannot have her career or backstory, her preference for dark chocolate, her fear of spiders. I must be Acacia now. Acacia who reads cheap paperbacks and eats bacon and wouldn't know Aubusson tapestry from crewel. My hand goes to my face, a quick swipe across the mouth, as if I can wipe the words away.

He takes a step back, regards me, his dark shirt casting a shadow up his face that swallows the sunlight before it lands on his skin. "You won't find that kind of work around here."

I flick my wrist like it's old news. "It's in the past. I don't do that anymore. I'm starting over."

Something sets behind his jaw, an opinion of me congealing, inflexible as concrete. The wind blows, swooping into our private glade, rustling his hair where it's grown a little long on top. *He's heard this before,* I think. *He doesn't trust a woman without roots.* I don't know where it comes from, this private grasp I have on the sheriff, but it sits at the base of my spine like a marble, wholly formed, irrefutable. Is it part of my power? There is no evil in him; I'm certain of that. He can't be my next mark. But still he whispers to me. Donna said that I would sense things about men I didn't want to know. But I want to know everything about Regis Brooks, from his size eleven shoes to the tiny mole above his right ear to the picture of the girl in his house, his sister.

"I want to study botany." The lie comes easily. Maybe because it's braced by a kernel of truth. I know in a way I shouldn't that this will impress him.

A tug at the corners of his mouth wrinkles his beard. "I was a forestry major myself when I started college."

He smells salty, a hint of aftershave about him like a ring of ambergris and mint. It makes me long for the ocean, July at Folly Beach, the taste of fresh crab. Without meaning to, I lean in. "I thought you might be a fellow tree hugger."

"Well, you couldn't have come to a better place," he tells me, opening, his face turning up to the sun, brows slackening. "The biodiversity in these forests is unlike anywhere else in the Northeast."

I arch a brow. "Like the mushrooms for instance?"

A laugh escapes him, riding an undercurrent of embarrassment.

He hangs his head, nodding. "Right. That's fair. I guess it makes a little more sense now."

The wind dies and he glances around, Beth Ann's house swinging back into view. He'd almost forgotten where we were. "We should probably get out of here." He seems to recover himself, a stiffness to the neck and shoulders, the mantle of authority.

We're about to leave when a low crunch sounds to our left, the snap of a twig in the hollow of the woods. Our necks jerk in that direction, and I see Regis's hand poise on the grip of his gun, a cat ready to pounce. His eyes scour the tree line. "Wait here."

I watch him step away, moving deliberately toward the forest. In his absence, something stirs, rising from the ground like vapor. It fills me with dread and a cold longing, a fleeting sense of dark need, like hunger and sex rolled into one, without the fever or friction of either. *He's close,* it whispers. A tide of nausea hits the back of my throat.

"Stop!" I call just as he enters the shadow of the trees. He pauses and turns, face etched with misgiving. He's suspended between us, unmoving.

I step toward him, fear urging me to do what's necessary to protect us, and also a quiet voice from within the danger—*Not like this.* "We should go."

Even from here I can see the ripple of uncertainty cross his brow, the way he struggles to trust me but also struggles not to. His shoulders tighten, resisting. For a second, I feel sorry for him. My eyes slide to the trees beyond. I can't be sure, but it ticks beneath my skin like a pulse, this presence. He's out there. Somewhere. Watching.

The Strangler.

"Let's go," I say, stepping back. The sound of leaves shuffling echoes from within the trees. We are both moving away.

Regis turns, begins to draw his gun, glancing back at me again.

I shake my head, moving toward the drive until I see his shoulders slump. I've won. Relief courses through me along with knowing I will meet the Strangler again. When Regis starts toward me, I turn around.

At the car, he takes my elbow, stepping closer than required. His eyes search mine for an impossibly long moment, lips parted, as if there is something he wants to say. I feel his body warm to me, like melting honey, a sliding tension between our hips. I could break it, this moment, with a word, like shattering a glass bulb. But I don't. I hold it between my breasts, between my lips, for as long as he will let me.

At last, he looks to the ground, clears his throat. "Let's get that coffee."

18

Coffee Date

I am playing a dangerous game, but I cannot stop myself. The shop is small, a handful of aluminum tables set too close. But the coffee is good—not over-roasted or chalky, like that silt that comes out of Myrtle's pot—with a selection of flavored syrups and a milk frother, local art on the walls. The girl behind the counter wears her dreads in a floppy bun, the tattoo on the back of her hand spreading and retracting as she moves through a flurry of motions. Regis steers me toward a table in a back corner where the light from the front window doesn't quite reach, retrieving our drinks once they're ready.

I sit, back to the wall, and stare at my hands. My weeks-old manicure has not held up. The white has chipped away from nearly every tip, leaving glossy flesh-pink patches in the middle; my cuticles are fringed with hangnails. I add *nail polish remover* to my mental grocery list.

He takes his seat across from me, passing me a wide-mouth cup of cappuccino. For a moment, I lose myself in the steam, wafting on it like a current back to the red brick and fig ivy of my favorite coffee shop in Charleston, those little blue plates of scones. Before Henry, I used to sit in there on a spring afternoon, listening to the muted conversations around me, the gentle patter of raindrops on the glass, phone down on the table, pretending I was no one, sinking into the stripes on the walls, pooling like cream. It was blissful then, my life. I wanted someone to share that feeling with.

"Been a while?" he asks.

My eyes flutter open. I have a habit of revealing too much to this man, same as he does me. I wonder if he knows that. I think he must. It only makes him more dangerous for me. "Myrtle wouldn't know a milk frother from a garlic press," I joke.

He grins, then looks down at his own caffè americano, letting the smile drop. His face takes on a deadly serious grimace, as if his thoughts cause him pain.

"Do you have more questions for me?"

There's a flash of hurt in his eyes, a quick tug of the brows. "This is off duty."

I relax into my seat, letting the small of my back round against it.

"You knew that man at the café was a domestic abuser. And just now, at Beth Ann's place, you said the killer was still circling. And then we heard—"

"It was a twig snap," I tell him. "We don't know what we heard." Admitting anything more would only embroil us further, leaving us both vulnerable in the end. And I can't be sure yet. I'm still learning, still adjusting to my senses.

He nods once and leans back, appraising me. "You don't really believe that."

I shrug, remembering Myrtle watching the black night outside her cabin with wild eyes before the deer stepped out. "There are a lot of things in these woods." Including her. Including me.

But my heart jumps momentarily in my chest, that animal feeling returning. There is an awareness behind my breastbone that wasn't there before. New life inside me. The stirrings of a primal intelligence. Causing me to flinch.

This inheritance—a curse, a power, magic, venom, whatever you call it—sits in me like a seed. A tiny sac of unknowns, dissolving. The witch unfurls. I worry she will squeeze me out.

"See, that right there." He leans forward. "You were thinking something."

"Was I?"

"It passed across your face."

I take a breath, try to school my features. *Behave.*

He shifts back, crossing his arms over his chest. "It's gone now."

I spin my cup on the table, take a sip, watch him over the rim. "Why are you so interested in me?"

His eyebrows lift, bottom lip jutting out. He glances over his shoulder and leans across the table. "Other than the obvious," he says, gesturing to indicate an appearance I apparently take for granted, "I wish I knew."

I set my cup down and level my gaze on him. "That's not very flattering."

His lips tug up. "I didn't think flattery would work on you."

He's right. Henry has beaten the joy of male attention out of me, the silky weight of it. It's excruciating now, like a deep tissue bruise.

He's eyeing me. "There it is."

"What?"

"The place you go when you're not here."

My knee begins to bounce under the table.

"Somewhere you left behind. Or someone. Who is he?"

I frown. "I'm not a turtle, Regis. I don't carry the past with me. You're making much more of this than there is."

He grins briefly and looks away. "So, tell me about him."

"Now who's the psychic?" I joke, then shake my head. "There's nothing to tell."

He abruptly grabs my hand, but his fingers are soft on mine, coaxing. I should let go. "Then tell me about you."

I almost laugh. "Not much to say on that subject either."

His eyes narrow but he doesn't pull away. "It's funny because Myrtle never mentioned you. And then you just showed up like a new star in the sky. Appearing out of nowhere with no history to speak of. I've known Myrtle a long time, my whole life really. Can't make heads or tails of it—why she kept you a secret all these years."

Our hands are still entwined. It's irrational, how our words and our bodies don't match up when we're together. I should pull away, stand up, leave. I'm not supposed to have men, touch men, kiss men. Especially *this* man. And why would I want to after all I've been through? I'm supposed to be getting him "off our scent." If the venery saw me now, I'd be damned. But they're sleeping off their hangovers, and all I seem to want to do since coming to Crow Lake is *have, touch, kiss* Regis. I stare at our fingers curling into each other and cough. "I thought this was off duty."

He smiles, a chuckle escaping, and presses his gaze into me like I am a smear on his corneas he cannot blink away. "Who are you?" His eyes are gravity, gray and grounding, they pull me in. "I want to know you."

"I'm Acacia," I tell him, unable to give him what he's asking for. "I'm no one."

"I don't believe that," he says, assessing.

"I'm not a secret." But the words come out hollow, little puffs of wind, idle. *Put your back into it, Piers,* I tell myself. I don't like lying to him.

He cocks his head. "Then why did you come here?"

There's an angle to his jaw, a flare of pulse underneath, that burns through me. Without trying, I see my lips there. Something warm gathers in my hips, at the base of my throat. I clear it away. "I told you; I want to study botany."

"Texas doesn't have plants?"

My lips press into a line. "Austin is . . ." I've been there a few times, weekend trips and once with a client. It's a place to go in the South, a mecca for style. Of course, I went. "Ungrounded. Too gentrified for me. It's lost something over the years, between all the yoga studios and vegan cafés and independent bookstores. A sense of itself, the roots. I felt adrift there."

"That's the most you've said about your past since I met you." His lips relax, a flash of teeth signaling his appreciation.

I feel relieved. It surprises me. I didn't know how much I

wanted to please him until this moment. "My past . . ." I begin, looking at him. "It's not really been a great life up to this point. My past isn't something I like to talk about because it's painful. I came here to study botany, but I also came here to start over, to leave my past behind. Crow Lake is my future, and that's what I'm focused on."

He nods. "Got it."

"What about you? What's your story?" I ask him.

"A common one. Boy grows up in the woods, falls in love with them, vows to do everything in his power to protect them. I switched from forestry to law enforcement because I realized it wasn't only the trees I loved here, it's the people. I wanted to do as much for the community as the land." He's almost sheepish as he talks—eyes cast down, fingers twitching. I haven't seen him this way before. He hazards a peek at me.

"No vengeful exes or Bertha Rochesters I should know about? Jilted lovers stalking you?" I say it with humor, but it sounds more intimate than intended. I almost blush.

He bites his bottom lip. "I'm told I have commitment issues," he says, finally pulling his hand away. "Repeatedly."

He thinks this will bother me. He has no idea how wrong he is. It's been years since I've been with a man and not a monster. I can barely recall what it feels like to open myself, back arched against the mattress, as someone pleases me. Sex with Henry became so traumatic, I didn't even realize I missed it. Safety, I realize, is a prerequisite for pleasure. Here, shielded by a massif of mountains, as another woman sitting across from another man, I feel the first churnings of desire in two years, like pins and needles between my legs. "How close is your place to here?"

His face shifts, posture straightening, an illicit response in his gaze. "Close enough."

I stand up and walk toward the door. When I turn, he's still at the table, uncertain, afraid he's misread the moment. *Bless him.* "You coming?"

He rises and follows me out to his car. As we get in, leaving the Subaru in the lot, he watches me from the driver's seat, something eating at him. Without warning he leans over, taking my chin, about to put his mouth on mine.

I lift a finger to his lips and press him back. After Don, it's not a move I can be comfortable with. After the venery, it's not one I should be. "Promise me something."

He swallows, eyes wide and hungry. "What?"

"Always ask permission first."

THE RIDE TO his cabin is short but blisteringly long. My fingers crawl over his thigh as he drives, and when we get there, I practically run inside. He closes the door behind me, and I jump. When I turn, he says, "We don't have to do this."

"I want to." I set my jacket and bag on his table.

He undoes the buckle of his duty belt, laying it beside my things.

A couple of lamps burn in their respective corners, but the trees block the sun from the windows, leaving the inside dark and cozy. Henry always kept the can lights on, not just a lamp or a dimmer, as if I were being interrogated. He wanted to see every ounce of pain written across my face, wanted to watch the color drain from my skin, see it bruise beneath his fingers in real time. I look up and note that Regis doesn't have a ceiling light in his living room, just a fan. I back into the room, waiting.

"The bedroom is this way." He gestures to the left, where a darkened doorway yawns. I know this already, but we are suddenly bashful, awkward with each other.

I shake my head. "I like it here."

Henry didn't tolerate sex outside the bedroom. Everything had to be ordered, exact, in its place. The few times he broke that rule, it was not for pleasure but for power, to hurt me. I don't ever want to share a bed again.

He lowers his eyes and steps into the room. "Okay."

We stand there, neither knowing which move to make first. Until finally, I take a breath and step up to him, pulling apart the snaps of his shirt one by one. I can't remember the last time I undressed a man. His body is tight beneath my fingers, a barely perceptible tremble running over him. I like that he lets me take my time without interfering. I slide his shirt off his shoulders and let the heavy fabric drop to the floor. Then I tug at his waistline, pulling up the dark undershirt, peeling it off him. He watches me as I trace circles across his chest, a thin map of hair over the lean muscles, trailing delicately down his abdomen. Our eyes meet and I lean forward, pressing my lips to one side and then another. He smells like soap and pine needles, fresh, an indefinable layer underneath, warm as baked earth. I run my hands over his shoulders and down his long arms, across the ridges of his stomach, and watch his flesh rise with goose bumps. By the time I unbutton his pants, his mouth is slack with need, his eyelids at half-mast, every contour of his body straining toward me. But still, he holds back, letting me explore.

As I unzip him, his blood rises, firm and ready, and when I slide my hand over his thighs, the bulge waiting there, he catches my wrist.

"Please," he begs, voice thin.

I tilt my head up, inviting, and his lips burn against my own. He undresses me slowly, grazing my skin with his fingers, as if I might shatter under too much pressure. Everywhere he passes my body comes alive beneath his touch, returning to me—the round of my left breast, the cinch of my waist, the stretch of my neck. Pieces that were taken in the night are brought back, restored, made new, as if he is stitching me together. The feeling returning to limbs choked off by fear, bloodless and numb. I am waking from a nightmare to a dream. I rub my skin against his, wanting to feel him everywhere, to wear him like a coat. He throbs against me, the pulse I do not have.

We stumble hungrily to the couch where he lays me back,

parting me down the middle like water, drinking me in. I evaporate in his mouth and reassemble, quivering like a fawn, a new woman.

When he finally slides into me, I have never wanted anything so much.

19

Four Don'ts

Their faces are slack and pale when I enter the room, white as chalk. They huddle in a semicircle around Aunt Myrtle's thirty-two-inch television panel, silent. I didn't realize they were up yet, or even still here. Though I suppose I didn't expect they would leave before 8 A.M., considering how many of those toddies Myrtle kept passing around. The news is on, but I'm not really hearing whatever the reporter is saying because I'm taking in the room—the long faces, the half-drunk cups of coffee, the occasional worried glance. Even Rowena, Aunt Bella's pet chicken, seems distracted by the screen, pecking feverishly at the air before it.

"Is something wrong?" I finally ask from the doorway to the kitchen.

They all turn at once, a theater of mimes, their eyes falling on me with mute accusation. Aunt Myrtle looks sick to her stomach.

"What is it?"

"Where have you been?" Rose hisses.

Before I can mumble an excuse, Donna tsks from her chair and shakes her head, and Azalea's wide eyes slip from mine to the TV screen. That's when the picture and audio come into focus.

"The death was caused by phytolaccagenin toxicity from pokeweed berries, a poisonous perennial once used medicinally by Native Americans. Doctors say the man would have consumed a sizable amount to experience such dramatic symptoms, though very little matter was found in his stomach, likely owing to the prodigious vomiting. Who took his car and why is still under investigation. Ted?"

"Thank you, Nancy . . ." Ted says with a plastic smile.

Don. I gulp and meet their eyes. "You don't understand—"

"Oh, I think we do," Rose says, rising.

"You lied to us," Lattie shakes out through clenched teeth.

"No, I didn't lie."

"Piers, how could you?" Myrtle asks. It is her look of disappointment that breaks me inside. I've betrayed her. "Why didn't you tell me?"

"I—I can explain," I try to tell them.

"There's no need," Aunt Bella cuts in, her voice sharp as slivered steel despite her age.

"There's not?" Barbie asks, as shocked as I am.

"No," Bella insists. "There's not."

"But killing an innocent is the worst offense a bane witch can commit!" Rose shrieks. "The girl is clearly guilty. She doesn't deny it."

"She's not guilty," Aunt Bella says, her eyes reaching into mine. "At least not of killing an innocent. Of lying by omission, perhaps. But that is another matter."

"I don't believe it!" Barbie spits, crossing her arms.

"He tried to rape me," I manage. They stop arguing and fall quiet. I place a hand on my stomach, breathe in, let it rise like bile. "That man tried to rape me. He wouldn't have died at all if he hadn't forced himself on me, pushing his—his tongue into my mouth after I'd eaten . . . I'd eaten . . . berries. Pokeweed. To make it look like I'd killed myself. I wanted my husband to think I was dead, so he wouldn't come looking. He's a dangerous man. Like the men you hunt. It was the only way. I might have died, actually. I jumped off a bridge, but the river spit me out. And then I needed a ride, a way out of town, to safety. That man, Don, offered to drive me to DC, but he pulled off the main road while I was sleeping. He wanted sex. In payment for a few bottles of water and a sandwich."

A ludicrous giggle vibrates up my throat. It's mad. The whole thing. My story. My life. My death. They'll kiss me now for sure, bury me in the soft moss beneath the Douglas firs. And I don't know if I care anymore. I'm so sick of carrying the wrongs of others inside me, on my body. Anger swells hot and salty like brine in my stomach. "I didn't know. I didn't know it would kill him. That I'd been feeding. That I had this . . . *power*. But I couldn't have stopped him even if I did. And I *did* try. He was big. My rib was broken. He brought it on himself."

"You poor dear," Myrtle whispers.

Words continue to tumble out, as if I need to hear myself say that it was not my fault. "I didn't know *that* would happen. At first, I didn't really understand it. But after the other night, the man in the café, I finally put the pieces together." I sit on the arm of the sofa, turtling into myself, wanting to disappear. I don't mention the man I killed when I was only five. Myrtle is keeping this secret from them, and I assume her reasons are good. "I know you don't trust me, and this looks bad. I know my mother let you down. But I'm not her. Please. You offered to give me a chance—six weeks. Let me prove I can do it differently." Six weeks was laughable last night. This morning, under the glare of the television screen, the flash of Don's headshot, it looks downright generous.

What's more—after the dust of the conclave has settled, after my experience at Beth Ann's property this morning, the weight of the killer still inside me like a parasite, a real entity needing to be put down—I realize that I *want* this. I messed up with Henry because I didn't know. But if I had, I would have laid him down a long time ago. Of that, I am sure. Yes, it is messy and gray and morally questionable, a responsibility and a burden, but it is real—action, solution, permanent. So much more than words. And the victims of these men, the women and children who are hurting, they deserve that.

"Too late," I hear someone mutter.

"Why?" I spin around, the speaker silent. "Whatever it looks like, that man got what was coming to him." I jab a finger toward the front of the room, to the reporter—Nancy—and her immaculate teeth. "He was in the wrong place at the wrong time trying to rape the wrong woman. It wasn't planned, but it saved me. I can't say Don deserved to die for what he was going to do, had already done to someone else, but I don't regret it. If it saved another woman after me, I don't regret it at all."

They stare at me like owls, eyes shining preternaturally, unblinking.

"I can do this," I say. "I can *be* this. Let me prove it to you." I'm not just begging for my life anymore, I'm begging for a chance, for a destiny that belongs to me.

"Spoken like a true bane witch," Azalea says, chin jutting. I see other heads begin to nod, Lattie and Ivy and Tina. I want to fall at their feet.

Bella strokes the chicken in her lap delicately. "Our arrangement stands."

My head lowers, eyes fluttering to a close, as I blow the anxiety out between dry lips.

"But speak true, girl. Are there any others we should know about?" She points to the TV screen where the news is still playing. "This is not our way."

My eyes dart to Myrtle's. She doesn't move a muscle, but there is a pallor in her face, a tightness to her jaw. I shake my head vehemently. "No, I swear. It won't happen again. Not like this. Myrtle will teach me. I can be discreet. I can be invisible."

They don't know it, but I've already had the best teacher. Henry forced me to smile against my pain, to put on a pretty face and hide the mess we were behind closed doors, to scream only on the inside. Now that I understand what's happening, I can be careful. I can act with intent. I can be the bane witch they need me to be. I can keep myself, Myrtle, and countless others safe.

"It better not," Donna says, rising to her feet. "Myrtle, we leave it in your hands. Don't let us down. We'll be in touch." She grips the handles of her mother's chair. "Come along, Mother. We have a flight to catch."

As Myrtle sees them to the door and helps Donna lower Bella's chair from the porch, I slump over my knees.

I feel a hand on my shoulder and look up into Tina's bright face. "There, there," she tells me with a wry smile. "The worst is over now. You'll see." It's the first brush of kindness she's shown me. She crooks a finger beneath my chin. "So much promise. Don't spoil it like your mother did."

"Okay," I say stupidly as she walks away.

They clear the room, each stopping to hug Myrtle goodbye and head out to their respective cabins where they will pack up and prepare for their journeys home. I can't help feeling like the person who farted at the party. I notice a tray of bagels on the table. I stick half of one in my mouth and begin gathering cups of undrunk coffee to take to the sink. Myrtle finds me there after seeing the last of them out.

"Put those down, Piers," she says plainly. "We have to talk."

Now I feel like a kid on the verge of being grounded. I let her lead me back to the living room. She clicks the TV off. "You want to tell me where you were this morning?"

I lower my head, unable to look her in the eye and lie.

She exhales forcefully, her lips forming a grim line. "You're lucky to be alive," she tells me, her eyes level and sincere.

I shake my head. "I don't understand. These women live to kill men like Don every day. Why am I so different?"

She takes a breath and sits across from me. "Consider this your first lesson in being a bane witch. We are the venery—all of us together, every witch of our line. And we act with mutual interest, you understand? We do not act alone. This is not an every-woman-for-herself mentality. We survive *together*. A witch on her own is a dead witch."

"*Those who hunt alone often starve.*" I repeat the words I heard her say to my mother so many years ago, words that sent my mother into a rage.

"That's right," she says. "It's a saying of ours. It means we are stronger together. *Safer* together. You understand?"

I nod my head.

"There are four things that are never tolerated in the venery." She raises a finger. "Men—no husbands, no sons, no long-term lovers." Her eyes bore into mine as if she can smell him on me, and she raises a second finger. "Secrets—full transparency is the only way we can know we are truly safe. If you are caught hiding something, you better hope it's worth dying for." She raises her third finger. "Exposure—we operate in the shadows. It's the only way. The world as we know it has long festered a hatred for women, let alone witches, a hatred for everything we are and stand for. There is nothing it despises more than a woman with power. We are everything they want to eliminate. And we exist by living and killing covertly."

I look down at my hands. A curl of skin sprouts beside my right index fingernail, parts of me peeling away. I pick it off and look up. "What's the fourth thing?" I ask, almost afraid to hear it.

"The killing of innocents." She appraises me. "You accused us of being murderers, and maybe by the standard definition that's true. But we take only a certain kind of life, the kind that's rotting from the inside, that breeds evil and pain and preys on those weaker than it. We do not take an innocent. To do so is to step away from being a bane witch and step toward becoming a monster."

This will be my future. A sun-parched horizon looms before me, loveless, without exclusive possession. I belong to the venery; nothing belongs to me. My mother's mulish assertion of independence, however damned, takes on a polished cast, like tarnish clearing from silver. Gerald, I am becoming achingly aware, was never the prize. Her own sovereignty was.

"Myrtle," I ask, knowing I can no longer afford to live in the dark. "What happened between my mother and the venery?"

"Do you really want to know?"

"I think so," I tell her honestly.

Her shoulders slump as her eyes fall from mine. "Your mother had a bright future with us," she begins. "Lily was strong, so much stronger than you give her credit for. And our numbers were dwindling. There was a second venery here in the United States, but they'd died out a decade before, unable to keep their line safe and fertile. So, when your mother showed such early signs of a power beyond what any of us had known, the venery was ecstatic. We believed we were being given the power to do the work of both lines. But my sister, Angel, was a poor teacher. She'd fallen in love young with a politician's son. It was a doomed match for many reasons, not least of which was his life in the public eye. She was persuaded to leave him against her will, but she came away pregnant. It was all the venery could do to get her to hold out for the birth, telling her this child would fill the hole her lover had left behind. Angel gave birth to twins—your mother and a little boy. She clung to him, even as your mother wailed in her bassinet. In the end, they had to pry him from her fingers. The loss sent her over the edge. She was never the same after that. She raised Lily, but her heart wasn't in it. And she did only the bare minimum to keep her own gifts from destroying her. Honestly, we should have taken Lily away, but we feared how Angel might react. She wasn't as strong or as early to bloom as your mother, but Angel was already more powerful than most of us."

I can't imagine how much longing and loneliness my mother must have felt, knowing she was always the consolation prize, the unwanted child. And yet, my childhood wasn't all that different. "And Mom? What did that do to her?"

"Angel filled your mother's head with all her fantasies of love and marriage and normalcy. She poisoned her against the venery, against her own self. Lily was mortified when she began to bloom. She tried to hide it, but you know how impossible that is. Eventually, she was convinced to ease into her cycle. But she was so young. I think it traumatized her. She met Patrick just out of high school. Like her mother, she fell hard. They tried to run away together. It was a terrible mistake. No matter how we pleaded, she wouldn't break it off with him. When he died, she was inconsolable. It was her fault, you see. It can happen so easily; all it takes is one careless second. She'd been feeding after months of starving her power because she was having violent nightmares, the cravings building inside her like compressed air. She tried to avoid him, hoping she could take her mark quickly and be done with it. She picked a fight, locked herself in another room, slept alone. But Patrick came to her in the night. By the time she woke up, he was lying beside her, kissing her neck. It was a hot summer that year. They were near the Gulf Coast. The humidity was through the roof, and they were a couple of kids with next to no money. The place they were renting didn't have air-conditioning. She'd been sweating in her sleep. You can imagine what came next."

"That was my father?" I asked, my throat closing on the word.

Myrtle nodded. "She renounced us after that. But then you were born. You were right about her wanting a boy, even though she could never have kept him. A son wouldn't have tied her to us. A son wouldn't have carried on our legacy, everything she hated in herself. A son could have had everything she wanted and never got. But she loved you in spite of herself. She wanted better for you than she'd had. It was misguided, but it came from a pure place."

"Why?" I ask her. "Why did the venery let her live? Why did they let her keep me?"

Myrtle shook her head. "We thought with time, we could win her over. Get at least the bare minimum out of her. We thought it would grant us access to you, allow us to carry the line on through you. But Lily never caved. How she found the will to hold so much back for so long without destroying herself and you in the process, I'll never understand. But the drugs played a role. It's a wonder neither one of you killed Gerald by accident in all those years."

"Believe me, I wanted to kill him on purpose plenty. I just never knew I could."

Memories drift back to me, like reflections on the surfaces of bubbles, tenuous and faded, the colors off, the symmetry transposed. Gerald's ashtray, always resting on the arm of the recliner, like a loyal pet. My mother treated it with reverence, a holy relic never to be touched. If I strayed too near, she would smack my hand. The dishes I wasn't allowed to wash. The piles of laundry she tended alone, her hands encased in lime green latex, like alien attachments. I never saw them kiss, or even hug. Twice I saw him press himself against her from behind, the kitchen counter biting into her midsection as if it might cut her in half. He liked her near, focused on him, like a lady-in-waiting. But he was too fixated on himself—his game, his beer, his meal—to want anything more than a servant or a security blanket. And she let that be enough for her. I understand why now. "Bad joke," I admit.

Myrtle gives me a lame smile. "The man you did kill, the bad thing when you were five—that's unheard of in our clan. Once that happened, I imagine your mother knew exactly the cross-hairs you would fall into. She didn't know how the venery would react, and she wasn't willing to take the chance. She had her issues, but she also did a lot of what she did to protect you."

"And you?" I ask her. "You never told them. Why?"

She smiles. "Because when I looked into your eyes that day, child, I saw the future staring back at me. There's a force in you, Piers. Something we haven't seen before. I knew you were a wild card, but I was willing to take the gamble. And I still am."

I reach out and squeeze her hand, grateful.

"Anyway, Lily threatened to expose us if we crossed her. In the end, it wasn't worth the risk. A witch like her, we knew she could do it and probably would. There was always a certain desperation to her, like a person living on the edge of a cliff. One shove in the wrong direction . . . We drew our line in the sand, and then we watched and waited."

"Gerald," I say plainly.

"He was a dull man. And cruel. I'll never know what she saw in him, other than a whisper of Patrick—"

"He was safe," I cut in, my voice threadbare. Narcissism coupled with stupidity made him oblivious. She was playing out a fantasy, like a doll. Middle-Class, Doormat Barbie.

Myrtle pulls her lips in, swallowing words. "Well, he caught on eventually. Your mother was careful, and she could go years in between, but she *did* feed and she *did* kill. And he figured it out.

How is anyone's guess. Or maybe she finally grew tired of his bull-shit. I don't know. I just know she upheld her promise and killed him before we had to. After Patrick, and whatever falling out you two had, Gerald was all she had left. I wasn't surprised when she took her life after. She probably thought we'd come for her any-way. She would have hated that—letting us have the final say. At least this way, she died the way she lived, by her own rules."

I take a deep breath, letting Myrtle's words wash over me, fill-ing in all the gaps that have lingered in my understanding of my mother. "Thank you for telling me."

She looks weary, as if telling me this has taken a little piece of her. I hate to press further, but there's still something I don't un-derstand. "Can I ask you one more thing?"

"Sure," she tells me, her lips pressing together.

"Why did the venery want access to me so badly? They didn't know about the man I killed. And you let me live all those years without knowing what I was. Based on what I heard at the con-clave, that was a risk the venery wouldn't usually take. I know you thought the drugs had managed to suppress my gifts, but I still can't reconcile that with everything I've learned over the last twenty-four hours. Why take that kind of chance?"

When Myrtle's eyes meet mine, they are fathomless. There is so much to this woman I still don't know. So much she can choose to share or not. But there is one thing I know for certain—whatever she is about to say, she means it.

"Because, Piers," she says, watching me as she lets the truth spill from her lips, "your power is stronger than your mother's ever was. Everyone can see that."

20

Impound

Reyes had to admit, she'd caught him by surprise. He'd a hunch the post office box would yield something enlightening about the Davenport woman, perhaps a bank statement to a separate account or a medical bill suggesting an injury, but all his expectations were in the realm of *mail*. After all, that's what post office boxes were for.

He took a step back and then another forward, shaking his head. Finally, he pulled out his nitrile gloves, dragging them onto his hands. Then, he grasped the only item in the PO box and brought it under the fluorescent lights. It was too thick and heavy to fit through the slot, which meant it was not delivered. She must have put it there. She had taken this box out solely to store this item.

It was wrapped in ruled notepad paper, held fast with a thick blue rubber band, a four-digit code scrawled across it. Unbinding it, he slipped the paper sleeve off, revealing an older model cell phone with the charging cord still attached. He pressed the power button, but the battery was dead.

Walking over to the counter, he smiled at the woman behind it. "Hi there, Cheryl. I need to come back and plug this in if that's all right with you."

She gave him a flat smile. "Suit yourself," she said, lifting the counter for him to enter.

He quickly located an outlet and plugged the phone in, waiting a bit before he tried the power button again. This time, the screen flared to life and he entered the code on the paper. Several seconds later, he found himself staring at the home screen. The wallpaper was a photo of her with the husband, Henry, on what he assumed was their wedding day. There was no veil, but she appeared to be wearing white. Her smile was radiant, except for a slight dip on one side, causing her bottom lip to look crooked—a hallmark of a fixed smile, one held with effort as opposed to naturally given. He was smiling with a closed mouth, his lips pressing into each other, his eyes staring at some invisible point in the distance, as if she weren't even beside him.

He checked the contacts and text messages, both were completely empty, scrubbed of whatever data they once contained. Reyes tried to slide to another screen, to look for any remaining apps beyond the most basic—games or video chats—anything that might explain why she hid this phone here, in a PO box her husband likely knew nothing about. But there was only one—*photos*.

With a hard swallow, he thumbed the image. A new screen flared to life. For a moment, he wasn't sure what he was looking at. The first few were so close they were nearly featureless, but after a moment he could identify a cheekbone or a rib, a stretch of her neck, the inside of her thigh. Eventually, he reached several where part or all of her face could be seen. Each seemed to be documenting an injury. The eye was dotted with blood, the arm black with a jab or pinch, the throat wrapped in a collar of spectacular bruising, aubergine and greening at the edges, deep black spots where the fingers had dug in. In one, her eyelid was so puffy he almost couldn't identify it; only her lashes gave it away. In another, the busted lip Henry's assistant had told him about. They went on and on, each image automatically dated. Her neck being the most recent.

Reyes's stomach turned. How many times had he seen injuries like these on his mother? How many baggies of ice had he gotten for her? How many mornings had he sat on the bathroom counter, helping her sponge makeup delicately over green or yellow skin? He remembered brushing her hair after each fight, after the tall man had stormed out in a rage, because it calmed her. And the sound of her sobs choking in her throat. The tremble of her shoulders. The smallness of his own hands, how powerless he felt, even as the rage simmered inside him with nowhere to go.

Mrs. Davenport was not his mother. He wasn't even related to her. But they were connected in a different way, and Reyes felt that same fury building inside. He took a breath, reminded himself he was no longer powerless, and schooled himself against the desire to beat the living shit out of Henry Davenport. He had other ways to fight now.

The pictures were graphic and certainly compelling, but without the context, he didn't know how much they might help him convict the man he believed had done this to her. Almost without thinking, he wadded the paper that had been circling the phone in his fist, the crunch of it against his palm reminding him to unroll it. He found her slanted writing staring up at him. He recognized it from the suicide letter, which a graphologist would be able to match conclusively, but if he had any doubts, she'd signed her whole name—Piers Corbin Davenport.

The letter read:

To whoever finds this:

This phone contains a series of photographs documenting my abuse at the hands of my husband, Henry Davenport, from October 2021 until June 2023. Please know, if you are holding this phone, reading this letter, then you are too late. Something terrible has happened. Henry has finally fulfilled his promise to me. Whatever he says about me, wherever he says I am, whatever he claims has happened or not happened, do not believe him. He is a liar and a bully. He is a killer. If I am missing, then I am dead. If my body has been recovered, know that he is to blame. I placed this phone here because I knew he was preparing to kill me—he's threatened it many times—and I believe it's the only way left to defend myself. The things you see in these images—he did those things to me . . . and worse. Take this and whatever else you can find and make him pay. But understand, Henry is a fastidious man. His hideaways will not be obvious. What you seek can only be found barking up the least expected tree.

Help a dead woman find justice.

Piers Corbin Davenport

Reyes stumbled back as the letter sunk in. This was circumstantial evidence still, not physical, but it was a doozy of an inference. It might not be enough on its own, but taken with the phone, with the footage from the bridge and the lab analysis of the plant matter found at the scene, on the letter, *and* in the yard, it was painting a devastating picture of abuse and foul play. If he were able to get his hands on some kind of material evidence that he could corroborate with this, something that concretely connected Henry to the scene at the bridge, he would have a rock-solid case.

Carefully, he wrapped the phone and letter how he found them, unplugging it from the post office wall. Making his way outside, he took a minute to just breathe. The sun was high and painfully bright, but its warmth on the back of his neck helped to settle his stomach. It didn't matter how many years passed, domestic violence cases still had the power to weaken his knees and set his hands shaking. Suddenly, he was a little boy, crouched in the corner in his Batman underwear, watching the tall man choke the life out of his mother with no way to help her or himself.

Almost as a reflex, he pulled out his phone and dialed his sister.

"*Hermanito!*" she chirped on the line. "What's shaking, baby brother?"

"You know I don't like you to call me that," he griped. He said it every time, though he never really meant it.

"Oh, that's right. I forgot. You're a big, strong man now with a gun and everything. My hero!" she teased.

Reyes frowned. It had been part of their dynamic for as long as he could remember for Lucia to rib him while he feigned irritation. Secretly, he adored his sister and her affections. But today, her lighthearted words struck a little too close to home. The pictures on the phone still had him rattled, memories beckoning from the dark of his mind.

"Emil," she barked when he didn't respond. "What's wrong?"

"Nothing," he insisted. "Why do you think something is wrong?"

"Because you are breathing into the phone like someone has been chasing you. What's your heart rate? Huh? Count it for me."

Nurses, he thought with an eye roll. "My heart rate is fine."

"Count!" she ordered. "Or start talking. One of the two."

He pinched the bridge of his nose. "It's nothing just . . . I keep thinking of Mama."

Losing their mother five years ago was hard on them both, but they dealt with it in different ways. Emil threw himself into his routine—work, run, eat, sleep—as if he could drive the grief out of his heart by staying busy. Lucia threw herself into church. She must have gone to mass more times in a week than there were days that first year. And even though he didn't exactly share it, he admired her faith. It made her resilient.

"I see." He could hear her deep inhale through the phone. "Is it another case?"

She knew him too well. "It started as a suicide," he told her.

"*Started?*" Lucia was nearly as shockproof as he was. It seemed the Davenport woman had a special knack for knocking people off their guard.

He blew out. "I had this feeling, so I decided to dig a little deeper. Turns out, the husband had been abusing her. I just came across a phone full of pictures."

"Breathe, *hermanito,*" she said softly, understanding. "You aren't back there in that house with the shag carpet. He can't hurt us anymore."

"I know," he told her. "I know."

"You can't save them all, Emil," she told him. "You have to

learn to make your peace with that. It's enough that you want to try."

He walked toward his car, something catching in his throat. "This one feels different. It feels . . . important."

"Why?" she asked.

He shook his head. "I know her, Lucia."

His sister emitted a small squeak, then asked. "A girlfriend?"

Reyes dated plenty, but he rarely made strong connections to women. He'd had a couple of steady relationships, but they hadn't lasted beyond a year, and he'd never brought anyone home, afraid of getting his mother's hopes up. He liked keeping the pieces of his life neatly ensconced, separate from one another. It was cleaner. He wasn't even sure he'd been in love, that he was capable of it. His sister said it was because of their childhood. But Reyes knew better. He understood the truth even if he couldn't quite explain it. It's like he was waiting on something, like his energy was being diverted, needed elsewhere for a task he hadn't encountered yet. It sounded crazy, and that's why he kept it to himself, but he just wasn't fully available to a woman until that moment passed. *A hero's complex,* a shrink had called it once. He didn't go back. "No."

She sighed and he could hear her resignation. "Who then?"

"*Her,*" he said emphatically. "The woman in the restaurant. The one who saved me from choking."

There was an intake of air on the other end. "What? No. She's dead?"

Reyes nodded even though she couldn't see. "Yes, we think. But we haven't found a body." It was his turn to sigh. "I don't know, Lucia. Something about this guy, her husband. He seems . . . *worse.* But not on the surface. On the surface, he's polished. He sets my teeth on edge."

"Polished just means sneakier," she told him flatly. "Better at not getting caught. You remember Jace—country-club poster boy on the outside, sadistic asshole on the inside."

"How could I forget?" Reyes climbed into the driver's seat and started the car. He still had nightmares where he beat the man's skull in, unable to stop himself. Jace was Lucia's last bad boy-friend, and by far the worst. Reyes had tried again and again to get her to leave him, until she stopped taking his calls. The night she finally phoned him from a motel room, her voice so low he could barely hear her, he worried he wouldn't get to her in time, that she would die before he arrived or that Jace would come finish what he started. Reyes had a lifetime of bottled rage at men like Jace, men who had used and abused the women he loved, men who were so small inside they had to hurt someone smaller to escape their own misery. His niece, Mia, didn't know her father, never would, and it was better that way.

But Jace was a small-time thug masquerading as a corporate square. Once you got past the porcelain veneers and the Ivy League haircut, it was obvious. Henry Davenport was a different beast—colder, crueler, leaner.

Reyes sighed. "This guy makes Jace look practically docile."

"That's terrifying," Lucia replied. "What did he do?"

"Nothing," he told her. "I mean, nothing I can point a finger at except kill his wife and make it look like a suicide. But I can't prove that. Not yet. He just feels *wrong*."

"Trust your gut, baby brother," she told him. "It's the gift God gave you."

He pursed his lips. He didn't know about that, but it did often lead him in the right direction.

"You said there's no body?" his sister asked, her tone ranging higher in hope.

"Not yet. It's probably in the Atlantic."

"I wouldn't count on it," she said. "Men like Jace, like this man—they're proud of their work. Too proud, if you ask me, to let it go unseen. Jace left me where someone would find me. He wanted the cops to know there was nothing they could do to stop him. If you don't have a body, she might not be dead. There might still be time, baby brother. I know she's important to you."

"What are you saying? That he's keeping her somewhere? Alive? Like a prisoner?" A scoff escaped him.

"If he is, it won't be for long," she suggested. "Or maybe she ran away. Maybe he's too ashamed to let people know she got away from him, that's he's not all-powerful."

"We have a suicide note," he told her.

"Maybe he wrote it."

Reyes shook his head. It was too convoluted. The truth was usually simple, the simplest thing staring you in the face. "We have footage of her jumping off a bridge."

"Then maybe she's finally free," his sister said sadly. "The only way to get an asshole like that off your back is if they think you're dead. I should know."

Reyes flinched. Lucia believed Jace had never come looking for her because he didn't think she'd survived that last beating. That's what allowed her to sleep at night. That, and the nine-millimeter she kept tucked under her mattress. A present he'd given her for Mia's first Christmas.

Her words burrowed into him. "I gotta go," he told her, feeling a powerful urge to return to the residence. He had to be missing something. Something that would nail this guy.

"Emil?" she said before he could hang up.

"Yes, Lucia?"

"Be careful. If this man is as bad as you think, then he's more dangerous than you or I could ever imagine."

"I WANT HIS car." Reyes dumped the cell phone and note onto Will's desk.

"What?" His partner nearly spilt the coffee he was slurping. "What's all this?"

"That," Reyes told him, "was in the PO box."

"A crappy old cell phone?" Will didn't look impressed.

Reyes reached over with a sigh of exasperation and plugged it into the outlet on Will's cubicle. He entered the passcode, then dropped it in his lap. "Turn it on."

Will looked from him to the phone. Setting his coffee down,

he did as he was told. The screen flared to life, the image of the happy couple. "I don't get it. There's nothing on here."

"The photos," Reyes told him. "Look at the photos, man."

As his partner scrolled through image after horrifying image, Reyes watched Will's face move from confused to shocked to disgusted. "He did these things to her?" he finally asked.

Reyes handed him the note in answer.

Will read it through the plastic bag, then set it carefully on his desk. He took a deep breath and rubbed his forehead. "Why his car?"

"Think about it," Reyes began, which is exactly what he had been doing from the post office to the station, the wife's words—*His hideaways will not be obvious*—pestering him mile after mile alongside his sister's. "Right now, we have circumstantial evidence. We have some physical evidence, too, but nothing that concretely puts him on that bridge. Just a fuzzy video that a judge is just as likely to throw out as admit based on insufficiency. If we find one thing that draws a line between these dots, we'll have him."

"And you believe that one thing is in his car?" Will asked skeptically.

Reyes cocked a brow. "Where's the first place he went after forcing her off that bridge?"

"I don't know. To work?" Will suggested half-heartedly.

"Yes, but how did he get there? He didn't walk. He didn't take the bus. That guy has probably never seen the inside of public transportation in his life. His assistant said he came in late that morning because of a flat, and we saw the spare tire on his car. So where was he between the bridge and his office?"

"In his car," Will supplied, finally seeing what Reyes was driving at.

"So," Reyes went on, "I want that car."

Will leaned back and crossed his hands over his belly. "Good luck getting it. He's not cooperating anymore."

"What do you mean?" Reyes asked. "He seemed real interested in what we had to say the last time we were there."

"Yeah, well, maybe he lawyered up. I don't know. We've asked several times for him to come down for more questioning and he's refused. Up to this point, everything has been voluntary. He doesn't even know he's a suspect or that we saw that footage. So, as far as he can tell, he's not obligated to do a thing more," Will explained calmly.

"Dammit." Reyes pounded the desk. "I thought we were careful not to tip him off, because we wanted his cooperation. The second he clams up, this case gets a thousand times harder to prove."

Will shrugged. "He's smart. And guilty. It's a tricky combination."

Reyes gripped the edge of his partner's desk and leaned into it, thinking.

"Look," Will said, "if he's already suspicious, then what difference does it make? You're not going to get anything else out of him without a warrant, certainly not his car. So, let's impound it."

"Do we have enough to do that?" Reyes asked.

Will held up the phone he brought from the post office. "This is probable cause, Emil. That video is probable cause. The labs on the berries in the yard and the ones from the bridge. We have enough to take his car. If we find something in it, then we go for an indictment, a warrant on the house and office, seize his computers and anything else we think might button this up."

Reyes blew out a long breath. "Once we take his car . . . that's a point of no return with this guy."

Will pursed his lips. "I think we're already there. Might as well cuff him and stuff him in the process."

Reyes pinched his lips together and nodded. "Let's do it."

THEY WERE AT his office parking lot the next day. It had rained that morning, but the sun was a mellow presence now, lighting the city up in soft beams. Reyes was glad the sun was out. He didn't want anyone in Henry's office to miss this. This small show of force, the ability to catch a man like Henry Davenport off his guard, to embarrass him *publicly*—it was personal for Reyes. He saw himself sticking it to the tall man every time he took one of these bastards down. And it felt good.

He shook the tow-truck driver's hand as the man lowered the wheel-lift to secure the sleek, black Jaguar. The nice thing to do would be to go inside and inform Mr. Davenport what was happening. But Reyes wasn't interested in being nice to men like Henry Davenport.

"You sure about this?" Will asked, turning to him.

Reyes smiled. "He's gonna know one way or another. Might as well inform everyone else in the process. Let them know they're employing someone who commits uxoricide."

Will's face scrunched up. "Commits what now?"

"A scumbag wife-killer," Reyes explained, and his partner nodded.

Reyes tapped the tow truck guy on the shoulder. "No need for a gentle touch with this one," he told him. "And be loud."

The guy grinned and gave him a single head nod. Walking over to his cab, he switched on the sirens.

Will laughed and did the same from their patrol car. Before they knew it, people were lining up at the glass walls of the building, staring out at the spectacle in the parking lot.

By the time the Jaguar was loaded and secured, Henry Davenport was storming across the concrete toward them, his face a red mask of fury, fingers clenched into fists at his sides.

"Just what do you think you're doing?" he spat. "This is my place of business."

"We're impounding your car," Reyes told him, stepping up to the engineer's tall frame. He enjoyed watching the man's face slip into a pall of bewilderment.

"Why? What right have you to do that?" he asked, still furious.

"Oh," Will said, stepping between them. "Maybe you didn't notice. You see, we're the law. We have *every* right."

Henry took a step toward Will and Reyes interceded. "Refusing to comply with a police officer is a misdemeanor. We can Mirandize you right now, if you like. In front of all these fine people watching at the windows."

Stomping his foot, Henry spun around and ran his fingers through his pale hair, visibly at the edge of his self-control. When he turned back, he had somewhat composed himself, cheek color moving from beet to tomato. "First, you do nothing to locate my wife. Then you harass me in my home with your inane questions and needless searches. And now this." His eyes darted to his car being raised on the wheel-lift. "I'm calling my attorney. You will both deeply regret this day," he growled.

"You do that," Will told him. He patted the trunk of the Jaguar. "And we'll give this baby a real thorough search. I imagine by the time we're done, you're going to need that attorney."

Henry took a dumbfounded step back. For a second, Reyes thought they were getting a glimpse of the real man. A man who was unused to surprises. For a guilty man, he seemed genuinely taken aback, as if he had no understanding of how he'd arrived at this particular moment, watching his car be hauled away by police in front of an audience of his peers.

There was something about a man like Henry caught off guard that made Reyes's blood run cold even as his chest puffed with pride. Cornering a man like that came with a level of risk. He reassured himself it was one he was willing to take. He wasn't a little boy anymore, and he had the build to crush a man like Henry in a fight any day. But men like Henry never fought fair, if they fought at all. If he chose to strike back, Reyes was likely to never see it coming.

"This is absurd," he told them. "You won't find anything because there's nothing to find! My wife—my wife . . ." Suddenly, his face slackened, his eyes and cheeks losing focus.

"Your wife is dead," Reyes told him. "And we don't have a body, despite our best efforts. But we have a few other things, things you might prefer kept private, things a man like you wouldn't want falling into the hands of the police." He moved toward Henry, determined and angry.

"That's enough," Will said, placing a hand on Emil's shoulder in warning. He turned to Henry. "Now, you can give us your keys, or we can pry these doors open with a crowbar. Your pick."

Henry glowered and threw his keys at Will's feet before they turned to leave.

Reyes had said too much, but it didn't matter. The wheels of justice were in motion, and not even Henry Davenport could stop them. They drove away behind the tow truck and the impotent Jaguar, watching him grow smaller in the rearview mirror.

WHEN REYES GOT to the impound lot the next morning, Will was already there, looking incredulous as he wiped his fingers on a garage towel.

"It's clean," he told him.

"What?" Reyes couldn't believe his ears. "What do you mean it's clean?"

Will shook his head. "I mean there's nothing there. The guy's a squeaker. He's meticulous."

"That can't be true." Reyes pulled on a set of gloves, opened the back passenger door, and leaned inside. "Did you check behind panels? Under the center console? Inside the fuse box and spare tire? Shit like that?"

Will rubbed a hand over his stomach while he nodded. "I'm telling you, we made a mistake."

Reyes stepped out of the car and faced his partner over the top of the door. "We did not make a mistake, Will. This guy is guilty."

"Then he's a professional because there's nothing inside that car."

"What about outside?" Reyes asked moving around to the trunk.

"Obviously I checked there," Will said with a frown. "Even preschoolers know that."

Reyes circled to the driver-side door. He opened it and pulled the safety lever for the hood, walking around to slide his fingers beneath the front and pop the latch, raising the hood to look underneath. Will joined him.

"I've been over it more than once, Emil." There was a note of apology in his voice. "Maybe we're missing something. Maybe it's not what we think."

"Just . . . let me look," he said, trying to bite back his temper. He refused to give up on the Davenport woman. He would deliver her the justice she deserved. There must be a reason he'd been called to this case.

He spent the next forty minutes combing that car for anything remotely out of place, anything admissible as evidence. But like his partner, he came up empty-handed. There wasn't even a bit of lint on the floor mat or spare change in the cup holders. He finished back where he started, slamming the hood closed as he cursed.

"It's not here," Will told him as Reyes stepped away from the Jaguar. "Maybe he scrubbed it. He beat us."

But Reyes couldn't abide that. "We're not giving it back."

Will looked stupefied. "Uh . . . We have to give the man his car back, Emil. You know that."

"Not yet," Reyes snapped. He walked around the vehicle one more time, studying it, asking himself, if he were a violent psychopath with a brilliant tactician's mind and a murder to cover up, where would he hide his evidence? He tapped his chin, an idea beginning to form. The second-to-last line from the letter hammering at his brain—*What you seek can only be found barking up the least expected tree.* "We need a dog."

"I'm sorry?" Will asked.

Reyes turned to him, hands on hips. "A canine unit. A sniffer."

Will looked exasperated. "We don't even know what we're searching for."

"Yes, we do," Reyes told him. "Give him the pokeweed and that dog will tell us where the evidence is in this car."

Will didn't look convinced, but he was staring at Reyes with less concern than a moment ago. "We'll get the dog," he said after a moment. "But if the dog says the car is clean, then it is."

"Deal," Reyes agreed.

They had their canine unit—a German shepherd named Glover—by that afternoon. Used to sniffing out cannabis, cocaine, and methamphetamine, Glover had a glowing track record for everything from narcotics to cadavers to missing children. His handler, Deborah, insisted he could find a rat turd in a barrel full of coffee grinds if she asked him to. She held the berries they'd taken from the Davenport residence in front of him in one hand, while her other was fisted around some treats. Every time he sniffed the berries, she rewarded him. In no time, they'd moved on to placing the berries inside a box that she set on the ground. After a few rounds where Glover correctly indicated the box and got his reward, she felt confident moving on to the car. She let Glover sniff the berries a final time, then passed them to Will, leading the dog to the Jaguar.

"You guys stand back," she told them. "Let him work."

Will leaned over and whispered in Reyes's ear. "This better work."

Reyes swallowed. In truth, he didn't know if he was chasing a shadow or if he was really onto something. He'd felt so confident before, but the car search had him rattled. For once, he prayed the way he'd often heard his sister do, begging God for a break. *Please, God,* and he added at the end, *don't let this asshole win.*

Just then, shrill barking rang out. Glover had reached the side of the car behind the front passenger-side tire and his tail wagged frantically as he indicated the spot again and again.

"Gotcha," Reyes whispered.

Beside him, Will's arms fell to his side. "Well, I'll be damned."

Deborah gave the dog a treat and called them over. "It's here," she told them. "No question."

Reyes raised the hood and studied the area near where the dog had gotten so excited. The cap for the windshield wiper fluid reservoir caught his eye. Lifting the container, he leaned over to look inside. "Bingo," he told his partner and the handler. "We got the bastard."

They used some long-handled tongs they rustled up from a nearby grill store to wiggle it free. When they finally got the whole thing out, Reyes couldn't believe his eyes. The ziplock bag had been tightly rolled around whatever was inside, all the air squeezed out so it would fit. Emil laid the bag on the ground.

"Open it!" Will insisted.

Reyes glanced up at him, then carefully split the seam, opening the bag and pulling the item out. It was dark, black, probably cotton fabric with a single zipper. He shook it free and held it up for him and Will to see, feeling his stomach drop as he registered what they were looking at.

"The black hoodie," Will said with awe.

"Is that what you boys were after?" Deborah asked them.

"Oh, yeah," Reyes told her. "This is exactly what we were after."

He checked the right pocket. Inside was a paper towel wadded around several dried berries.

21

Flos Mortis

The light is thin in this part of the forest, dreamlike. It haloes the uppermost branches as if we are on sacred land. The black-throated wail of a loon rides the scattering fog from nearby Crow Lake, and I can picture those red eyes splitting the morning like heralds of hell. Myrtle leans down over a tangle of tree roots, her long hair sliding over a shoulder, ends grazing the dirt. She looks like some ancient earth goddess with that green knit scarf about her shoulders, a grandmother of trees. She points and turns her face to mine, smiling. "Yellow wart."

I step closer and study the small mushroom, a golden scepter marked with rough patches. It is unassuming, a child's toy among giants. Hard to imagine it's just a part of something larger, something vast sleeping underground. A network of dread.

"An amanita. To be avoided at all costs. Except by us of course." Her grin is infectious. It's easy to forget we are plotting someone's murder. "Most amanita are poisonous, though the effects vary. Still, in a pinch, an amanita will do. You can recognize them by this tell-tale collar—the annulus. When they grow, this tears away from the veil as the cap opens to expose the gills." She tickles the fleshy skirt of the stalk with a finger. "They also have a volva near the base. This cuplike structure here that they erupt out of."

She straightens, her mouth screwed up to one side, thinking. "The man in the café succumbed rather fast, even for a destroying angel exposure. I don't typically get results that quick, and I have a certain affinity for *Amanita bisporigera*. Tell me again what happened in the car with that man."

I sigh. I'm tired of recounting the details, of flashing back to the look of horror splashed across his face. But Myrtle attends with tedious scrutiny, as if she is a conductor listening to the homogeneous tones of the orchestra tuning their instruments, searching for that one off-key. "I told you. He forced himself on me, pushing his mouth over mine as I was struggling. A moment later he started wheezing. It all happened so fast. He turned purple and kind of seized up. He got out of the car and vomited. Then he was dead."

She regards me thoughtfully. "I believe you might have a gift for concentration that is unique among our kind. Your work in the café was fast, but Don even more so, likely because your fear, your need to defend yourself, further amplified your magic. With my first mark in the deli, I had to sit there for nearly an hour waiting for the affliction to take hold. It's not always ideal. I have since learned ways to achieve more immediate results, but it takes effort for me. Clearly not for you. Though, there are occasions where prolonging the effect is better. I know how to accomplish that, too. You will need to learn. You can't be standing idly beside every mark that falls or you will start to look guilty by association."

I gaze down at the mushroom, a sickly sort of gold now that I really look at it, like jaundice. The man in the café teeters in my mind, yellowing like an onion. "You call what we do magic, but magic is an art; it requires something on the part of the wielder, the right word or gesture, an elaborate ritual, a set of special tools. Knowledge or skill. Even TV witches have cauldrons and brooms and black cats to do their bidding. This doesn't feel like magic to me. I don't feel like a witch. I feel like a freak of nature."

"Oh, Piers, you're wrong," Myrtle says, stepping toward me. She wraps her cold fingers around my arms. I feel them through my jacket like bands of ice. "We carry an ancient magic within us. You've only just begun to experience your power, but you'll find there's as much knowledge and skill involved in this as any other esoteric craft. Your body is the instrument, yes. The plants your ingredients. You don't have to speak an incantation, it's true, or point a wand. But your abilities will grow as your understanding and experience do. Your learning will inform your craft, just like any other. Do you think if you'd swallowed a fistful of radishes before that man kissed you that it would have had the same impact?"

I shake my head briskly, conceding her point.

She places a hand on my stomach. "When you feel that gnaw in the pit of your belly for something noxious and death-dealing, where do you think it comes from? That is your magic speaking to you, waking up your senses, your awareness, informing you of the things that move between sight and sound, the unseen world. That is your power, your teacher, your god. If you don't trust it, if you don't partner with it, you will not survive." She drops her hand, stepping away. Her eyes are clouded, hard to read. "No, we don't fly on brooms or work through black cats, but we aren't normal witches. We're *bane* witches—a different breed. Our magic is unparalleled, but it has its limits."

A snuffling sound catches my ear, and I look over to where Bart, the black Lab, is pawing ferociously at the earth, having caught the scent of something beneath the ground. He presses his nose into the shallow hole and snorts, drawing back. He looks at us, ears cocked.

"And we always have Bart," she adds with humor. "Though, I will say, he's a sad excuse for a familiar."

As if on cue, he twists away, hearing something in the distance, and bounds off into the underbrush. I hide a smile.

"There are unique gifts among us, specialties that come to light in time with care and practice, things only one or a few of us can do. Yours are only just beginning to show themselves. But you will learn. And then you will see, this *is* a calling, not an accident."

"I see things, *women,* in my mind. You told me when I was a kid that if I thought very hard, I would know the man I killed had hurt someone else. And I did know. I saw her before he died, when he touched me."

She smiles, her cheeks ruddy with life. "The sight is common among our kind. It is a kind of psychic connection with our marks. It's one of the ways the magic has of revealing them to us, and of making sure we don't take an innocent life."

"Is any life truly innocent?" I mumble dryly.

Myrtle peers at me. "Yes, Piers. Whatever has happened to you, you must never forget that there are predators and there are prey. We hunt the former, not the latter."

"I know," I tell her, chastened. "Do you see them, too? The victims of your marks?"

"Sometimes," she tells me, eyes scanning the forest floor. "Sometimes I hear their cries, smell their blood. It's different with every mark, but I always *know*."

"What about the ones who haven't come to pass? The ones they will hurt or kill in the future if you don't stop them?"

Suddenly she stands stick straight, eyes boring into mine. "What do you mean? You see *future* victims? Potential victims?"

I nod. "With Henry I did."

She snorts, a blast of air from her nose ruffling the leaves on the ground.

"Do you?" I ask her.

"No," she says shortly. "No. This is unheard of."

My breath hitches in my throat. "You mean, no bane witch has ever seen the victims their mark *wants* to kill, will kill, but hasn't yet? Not a single one, ever?"

She bends over the ground. "Not a single one. Ever. Until now." When I don't respond, she says, "I told you, Piers. You are special. We are evolving. You are the key to our future."

She squats beside the yellow mushroom and plucks it from the ground with a flick of her wrist, bringing it to her nose and breathing deeply. "*I* can identify any species of mushroom in these woods on smell alone. Did you know that?"

When I shake my head, she goes on.

"Rose can shift her allure to make herself smell like any flower she wants. Sounds simple, but it's come in quite handy. No need for perfume. She's even used it to disguise her presence before. Verna can grow just about anything regardless of the conditions. I've seen her sprout morning glory seeds in pitch darkness. And my mother, Laurel, could make her marks see things that weren't there. She stopped a man dead in his tracks one time by making him think an enormous tree had erupted in his path."

"What about Azalea?" I can't help asking.

Myrtle glances at me, a smile playing with her lips. "Azalea's allure is so strong she can make any man fall in love with her in less than five minutes. They give her anything she wants, marks or not."

I can't say I'm surprised.

She turns away, pocketing the small cap before pointing out a striking copper-brown mushroom nearby. "Deadly cort," she says happily. "Full of orellanine toxin. As bad as it sounds." She plucks and pockets it as well, then points to a colorful patch of ear-shaped fungus on a nearby tree trunk. "Turkey tail. It's medicinal—an excellent digestive aid. Useless to us except when used to slow our poison down."

I want to ask how, but she's already moved deeper into the trees, peering through the half-light, and I stumble to keep up.

She stops and points again, this time to an unassuming taupe mushroom jutting up through the moss. Its cap fans out across a slender stalk, and I can't make out any truly distinguishing characteristics. "Tawny grisette. Another amanita, but unlike the rest, this one does not come with the annulus I told you about. And it's not likely to kill anyone. But when dehydrated and combined with other amanita species, it can greatly increase gastrointestinal distress, speeding up expiration. The spew I've witnessed from such combinations is positively torrential." She says this last bit with wide eyes, the way your grandmother might describe the size of a watermelon from the supermarket.

"Combined with other species?" I recall her mortar and pestle in the room above the café.

"You know, *eaten*," she says. "Though, when I find a blend I like, I do sometimes mix them together in one of my jars for easy feeding."

"Right." I take a breath, my shoulders falling. "Am I supposed to remember all these?"

She watches me as she collects the tawny grisette. "Not right away. But it will help to know what's around you. You will find the cravings come easier—"

"Easier?" I step toward her, hopeful. I have no desire to experience the intense "feedings" of my youth, deadly potations that were all-consuming.

"Softer," she says with a sympathetic smile. "When you are ignorant, the plants must work extra hard to draw you to them. The magic compels you to eat with such intensity because without it, you never would. But when you know what you are, what you do— when you *practice*—it gets easier. Less force is required to direct you. The cycle informs, it doesn't demand. Do you understand?"

"I think so."

"Here." She holds the tawny grisette out to me. "Take it."

I let her drop it in my palm, light and damp. "Do you . . . do you want me to eat it?"

Her hair wafts around her as she shakes her head. "No. Just feel it."

I look down. The cap has split into ridges along the edge where the gills are. I run my fingertip against them. "There was a mycology club at my college," I tell her. "Maybe something like that would help."

"No." She curls my fingers around the mushroom, holding my hand in hers. "You can never be seen with your *flos mortis*, Piers— your *flower of death*. Do you understand? The risks are too great. If a kill is traced back to you . . . They have no mercy for our kind." She shudders, as if remembering the heat of a pyre personally. "No books. No classes. No clubs. No internet. Not even a misplaced documentary. You must learn from here." Her hand goes to my chest, over my heart. "And here." It drops below my navel. "And here." A finger between my eyes. "Let the magic teach you. Or another bane witch. Never the outside world."

I swallow anxiously. How many times have I stood beside pokeweed with admiration in my eyes, chest swelling with longing? How many mistakes have I made? The suicide note I left behind for one. Don's death for two.

"Now," she says. "Close your eyes. *Feel* it."

At first, it's hard to vacate my mind, the jewel-bright berries I love so much like Christmas lights beside the shabby, nondescript exterior of this mushroom. I must wait out my thoughts, my breaths. Until finally, like a light in the distance, I begin to feel a moldering undercurrent beneath my ribs, velvety and unobtrusive, nuzzling. My nose fills with the aroma of fresh rain, a passing draft against my skin, and my tongue tingles along the sides, expectant. It's not a voracious hunger but a cultivated appetite, the simple, grounded knowing that if I ate it raw, I would savor something delicate and terrestrial, with a bitter, buttery twinge. Until the stomach cramps set in. Which, of course, would never happen for me, but could put another through an unfortunate evening at best, and result in a trip to the ER and possible organ failure at worst.

I open my eyes and meet Myrtle's. She has seen it find me, her smile echoing my own wonder. "And now you know," she says, scooping the mushroom from my hand.

"Is it the same for you?" I ask. "How it feels; what it does?"

She grins, eyebrows lifting. "Finally beginning to ask the right questions, are you? There are *variances* among us. How the toxins manifest in a mark can shift from one bane witch to another. But we don't alter the fundamental properties of the plant. You can think of it like two people getting the same virus but displaying differing symptoms. One may run a fever. Another's cough may linger. You get the idea. The marks themselves can have impact, too, depending on their current physical condition. You will find you feed more when your mark is young or strong."

A patch of sunlight draws me like a spotlight to red stems. A shrub, chest high with flat, green leaves and white berries—I want to scratch my fingernail down to the pith, watch it bleed, suck the sap. Myrtle comes to my side.

"You found poison sumac. Go ahead, pick some," she says.

I break off a stem and hold it to my chest, the wetness on my fingers a strange comfort. "It would take a lot of this to kill someone," I tell her. "Unless . . ."

She cocks her head and waits.

"It would be extremely irritating to the mucus membranes and could lead to dehydration. Properly concentrated or combined with a diuretic or allergen, it could do the trick."

"You learn fast," she tells me. "That's good." She plucks the stem from my hands and folds a leaf into her mouth like its chewing gum. "Delicious."

"It's okay even if you aren't feeding?"

"We're never vulnerable to the plants' toxins, but when we're in bloom, we're driven to them so they can build in our system, discharging as soon as we kill."

She's started back to the cabin when I place a hand on her elbow, tugging her to a stop. "At the conclave, when they gave me a time limit, you started to argue. You said I'd only just bloomed, just killed. That it was impossible to know something about the cycle."

Her face falls.

"Tell me," I insist.

"We can't dictate when a mark will come to us. The bloom is not something we force. The cycle tells us when to feed, when to kill, not the other way around. And I have a suspicion about your *class*." She pulls the scarf tighter about her shoulders, like a hug.

"My class?" I dart between her eyes, as if one will give the secret away over the other. "What is that?"

"It's like having a type. The way certain women choose certain lovers again and again, specific traits and features of physicality or personality. We tend toward a particular kind of mark. It's not a hard and fast line, mind you. You will deviate from it, taking the marks the allure calls to you. But you will find a kind of pattern begins to emerge." She scowls, as if this annoys her. "It takes time to reveal itself, but I have a theory when it comes to yours. And if I'm right . . ." She shrugs the rest off like dead weight.

"What's your theory?"

She doesn't answer at first, but her eyes pucker at the inside corners, pitying.

I yank her arm. "Myrtle. What's your theory?"

"Your husband." It comes out like a huff, like she's pushed him through her nostrils.

"Henry?" I step back, wanting the shadows, the dapple of light, to camouflage me. As if speaking his name has brought him here, to this hallowed place, infecting it. "What does he have to do with any of this?"

She puts her hands out, trying to calm me, but her fingers spread like webs, and I flinch away. "Hear me out, Piers. What if you didn't choose him? What if you *called* him? What if your power, strong as it is, was still trying to work through the drugs and the ignorance? What if he was never supposed to be your husband but your mark?"

I grip the sides of my head, shaking it. It's a thought I've already had, but when it arises it distorts everything I know. All my memories, my feelings, the suffering I endured. It somehow becomes worse, *wrong,* in a way I can't tolerate. As if I did it to myself. "I don't want to talk about this. I don't want to talk about *him.*"

The trees elongate, suddenly menacing, beasts with leaves. The air gathers close, rushing into my mouth and nose, an invisible swarm of molecules. Why did I come here? This forest will suffocate me.

"It would mean your class is an uncommonly dangerous one. Not just domestic abusers—killers." Her fingers clench the air. "*Stranglers.*"

There is a long pause between heartbeats where my chest flattens out like pie dough, something rolling over me. The feeling in the clearing at Beth Ann's surfaces, foreign and familiar—*his*, mine—when the twig broke.

"Piers!" Myrtle is in front of me, shaking. "Are you all right? Piers?"

I realize I am clutching my chest, that I've stopped breathing. My eyes meet hers and I inhale. The woods stream into me, powerful and antiseptic like medicine. My lungs burn with life. "It's me."

She blinks, eyes round and bright like an owl. To our left, a flutter catches the air. A ruby-crowned kinglet alights nearby. His red patch makes him look scalped.

"It's me," I say, turning to her. "That's why he's here, isn't it?"

"Who?"

But she knows. I see it written in the veins of her eye, gliding behind the fissures of her iris like a doe in a thicket.

"The Saranac Strangler."

Her arms drop to her sides.

"I'm the reason Beth Ann is dead." I have committed the venery's ultimate sin. I have killed an innocent.

"No." She puts her fingertips to my mouth. "No, you mustn't say that. He was here. She was alone. It was too easy."

"But he came for me? Didn't he? *I* drew him to Crow Lake. My allure." There is a high-pitched buzz between my ears, the onset of tinnitus, like mosquitoes in the brain. For a second, I think I might pass out.

Myrtle toes the ground, looking everywhere but at me. She couldn't act more guilty if she tried. "That's my suspicion, yes. Your allure was probably working on him before you ever started eating pokeweed in Charleston, moving him in the direction you would take rather than the one you were in. It's a funny thing—our magic. It often knows us better than we know ourselves."

I feel Henry's fingers curling around my throat, stripping me of the safety of the trees, the miles between us. The Strangler may be a different person, but he's the same man I left behind. And he's here. *For me.* My insides quake with panic. The longer he is here, the longer I endure him, our connection like twine laid across the forest, the closer Henry feels. I have a sudden urge to shake him off like a dog with a tick.

I hold out my hand. "Give me the yellow wart."

"What? No." The shock sits crooked on her face, like it doesn't quite fit.

I tear off into the brush. I'll find more.

"Where are you going?" She chases after me, plucking at my jacket. "Piers, stop!"

"I'm going to kill him." It's the only way I can be free. A hemlock branch palms me. I smell bracken, a break in the trees. Somewhere a marsh is idling, spotted with geese. I can sense it all. "Two birds with one stone. He can't hurt anyone else because of me, and I'll get the venery off my back." And I won't feel Henry's shadow stretching across five states to persecute me.

She forces me around. "You're not ready."

"I have to be." I can't let another woman die in my place. I can't let Henry win. Even if I'm terrified. I try to brush her off.

"Don't be rash!" she hisses, her grip tightening like talons on my wrist. "You can't let your fear guide you, Piers. Not anymore. You must let the witch guide you now. And the witch is fear*less*. She is power and she is cunning. She is instinctive, not impulsive."

I inhale sharply, unsure if I can manage that.

She shakes my arm. "Listen to me. He is not killing because of you. He would be doing that anyway. He is only killing *here* because of you. Which is fortunate, whether you're smart enough to see it or not." She lets go of me, certain I won't stalk off again. "You wouldn't even know where to find him."

Part of my bottom lip sucks in. I pick at a spot of lichen on the slender trunk next to me.

She steps so close I feel her breath on my face. The stale coffee of the café. I suddenly long for its warm, orange lights and cedar tables. "Would you?"

"Something . . . *happened*," I admit. I tell her about being at Beth Ann's place, leaving Regis out of it.

She grips her elbows, walks a few steps away. With her back to me, she says, "The hunt has begun, then."

"So, I'll be okay? I mean, with your guidance I can get him before the venery comes for me, right?"

She turns to me. "He's dangerous, Piers. Practiced. Experienced in ways that you aren't. This isn't Henry, the man you left behind. This is Henry ten, twenty years from now. A man who's gone from toying to executing. Who has made killing his life's work. A master of *le jeu sombre, the dark game*. He won't be easy to take down. Not in six weeks, not in a year."

I peer at her. "You don't believe I can do it."

"I don't believe anyone else can," she replies.

Suddenly Bart comes crashing through the darkness, tearing up the earth as he lopes toward us. There's a fresh scratch on his face beneath one eye, a new battle scar from a match with a fox or a raccoon. He grins from ear to ear, tongue lolling, unaware he is the loser.

Myrtle reaches down to rub his head. "What mischief have you been up to, huh? Come on, Ed'll have a coronary if I let anything happen to you." She turns to go, the dog at her heels.

"Myrtle!"

She stops and angles toward me, face hidden behind her hair.

"If you're right, if my allure called Henry to me, but I didn't know it, then what happens now?"

Her face turns to me slowly, the dark curtain of hair hiding one eye.

"Will it call him again?" My heart is peppering my chest with adrenaline, pumping panic through my veins. The idea of Henry in these woods frightens me more than the Strangler ever could, and that's already turning my guts to jelly. It would make no sense to someone else, but I *know* Henry. The way the Strangler kills is clean, orderly, violent but efficient. Henry is not interested in efficiency. Henry likes to draw it out. He lives for the suffering. Maybe he hasn't taken the final step to committing murder like the Strangler has, but what lives in him is even darker, deadlier. I've seen it.

"I don't know," she says. "We've never had a witch spare a mark before."

22

Feeding

I hear her in the night, scratching like a rat through the kitchen cabinetry. At first, I try to roll over and ignore it, but after a couple of softly muttered curses, I throw the covers back and walk to the kitchen. When I flip on the light, she blinks at me like a wide-eyed baby doll, all lashes and surprise.

"What are you doing up?"

"I was going to ask you the same thing." I take in the room, every cabinet door standing open, the fridge light spilling onto the floor as condiment bottles begin to sweat. Her long nightshirt in blue and green plaid sags forward from bending over. Her braid has begun unraveling. "Looking for something?"

She purses her lips.

"In the dark?"

She turns away, contemplating how much to tell me. Finally, she says, "Poet's daffodil. Azalea brought me some bulbs when she came for the conclave, but I can't remember where I put them." Her shoulders hang off her spine in despair. "I must have left them in the shelter." Her eyes dart to the windows, thick with night.

I close the refrigerator unceremoniously. "You're feeding." It hits me like a splash of lemon in a cut, the sting of truth, of knowing that she is more than the kind old woman who's taken me in, the granny in the woods. She is deadly. She has killed and will kill again.

She watches me close each cabinet door, resignation lowering over her like a theater curtain. "Yes."

"Since when?" I sit at the little table.

"I first felt the hunger this morning," she admits.

I nod. "Our lesson in the woods, that wasn't for my benefit, then?"

She sighs, a world of feeling slipping out on her exhale. "Yes, of course. But also, I was searching."

"*Flos mortis,*" I whisper. *Flower of death.*

She does not meet my eye.

"Why not eat the yellow wart you collected?"

"It wouldn't do."

"The tawny grisette then," I suggest. I've seen her stores, over-flowing with specimens from around the country. Even without them, she must have dozens of options living out here in un-spoiled wilderness, no one around for miles to catch her foraging except the occasional moose or porcupine.

"No, it's even less useful," she says with more force than needed. Her jaw grinds. It's getting to her, the craving, the need to feed. "Besides, no fungi. Not this time."

I pinch the bridge of my nose. "Why ever not? It's abundant and effective. You said so yourself—" And then it sinks in. Because of me. Because of the man in the café.

She sees the truth steal across my face and throws out a hand, letting it slap her thigh as it drops. "Exactly. I can't risk alerting Sheriff Brooks with any . . . *overlap.* This kill must look wholly un-related. He's already got mushrooms on his mind. This will need to be cleaner, less obvious. Poet's daffodil is unexpected, not terri-bly toxic. I can combine it with another emetic and something to draw them both out. With any luck, they'll pass it off as a terrible case of food poisoning. We're miles from any hospital out here. It wouldn't be the first time someone died of an otherwise perfectly treatable condition in these mountains."

"Who's the mark?" I ask, willing my voice not to cave.

Her eyes slide to mine. "I don't know yet."

"You said we often have a class, a type. What's yours?"

She folds her arms beneath her breasts, clutching her elbows.

"I have two." Her eyes flicker away and back again. "Most of my marks are incestophiles."

I drop my head into my hands. "Like the man who built your shelter?"

"Yes." She drags the chair across from me out from under the table. The legs make a loud juddering sound against the wood, echoing my discomfort. She sits down. "And my first mark. The one in the deli."

There's a sick twist of poetic justice to an incestuous father being killed by a girl barely old enough to have entered puberty. But the weight of her life's work sits over me, ugly and squalid and stinking, a carcass of deeds. The horrible things she must have seen in their eyes, in her own mind. "Oh, Myrtle."

"Don't feel sorry for me," she's quick to say. "I have no qualms about what I do. I put an end to a particularly virulent strain of suffering for many children that will not come any other way before they reach adulthood. In some cases, not even after."

My stomach flops and my mind starts looking for exit points. "You said *most* of your marks."

"I have a second class," she admits, a touch wary. "It's unconventional."

I laugh humorlessly. "Isn't all of this unconventional?"

Her smile is tight, hovering at the height of her mouth. "It's not a class any other bane witch has shown a leaning for. It's a first among our kind. So, it's been controversial, you could say."

I imagine Rose and Barbie and the rest gathered in some back room raking Myrtle over the coals for whatever she's about to tell me. "Go on."

"Mercy killings."

I don't know what I was expecting—pipe bombers, dog fighters, those guys who put rat poison in envelopes and mail them to government buildings to create anthrax scares—but it wasn't that. I blink, too stunned to comment. After a long pause, I gather my wits enough to mutter, "I don't understand."

"It goes against the nature of our . . . *creation.* We are defenders, protectors of the vulnerable. That has always been women and children. Some have argued that killing a man for his *own* sake, to end his own suffering, is a distortion of our duty," she tries to explain.

"Let me guess. Rose?"

She looks taken aback. "No. Rose has been a staunch supporter of mine, in fact. It was my grandmother, actually, who protested the loudest—Hellen."

Her own grandmother? The betrayal had to slice deep, but she sits before me, discussing it as if it were a disagreement over a family pot roast recipe. "And you? What do you say?"

She shrugs as if it's simple. "Remember how I told you we were evolving? All species do it. They adapt to survive. Why shouldn't we? We no longer live in the time or country where we began. Our justice system may leave much to be desired, but it certainly deals out more punishment than was seen in thirteenth-century France. Women enjoy freedoms unheard of in past centuries. Including access to defenses once inconceivable to them. Obviously, there is still work to be done if our venery continues. But we've seen one line die out already. And perhaps it is time for some of our gifts to shift, to meet the calling of the times."

"But these men—the mercy killings—they're innocents, right?" I blink at her.

She smiles softly, as if remembering a caress. "Yes. They are effectively innocents. Maybe the most innocent of all. Wounded, hurting, chewed up by the world and spit back out. Desperate for release. I give that to them. The rules are different, of course. When the intent changes, so do the parameters. Never too young, too strong. The life force must have already waned to an irrecoverable point."

"And you can sense that?"

"Yes." Her eyes drift over to me. "I told you it was unconventional."

But I know Myrtle. I know her kindness and her humility, the strength of her resolve, the largess of her heart. Were it anyone else, I would certainly question the motive, the discernment. But because it's her, I don't. Instead, I ask, "Is that where bane witches started—thirteenth-century France?" I recall Bella's brief and passionate reference to the first bane witch, her rape at the hands of a nobleman, her miscarriage after.

"So it has been said for as far back as anyone can remember," she answers me. "And so we shall go on saying. Women killing in self-defense, particularly with poison, is hardly unique to us. Who can say when the first battered wife or angry mother dosed someone's cup or meal? There have been widely documented cases of course, primarily in France and Italy, but those women didn't invent the wheel, they just gave it a good turn. Neither did we. But we are a distinctive instrument of delivery, and as such, we do have an origin story."

"I'd like to know it." I imagine fireside chats, multigenerational, the glow on a grandmother's face, girls cross-legged at her feet, staring up, riveted. The way all stories are passed on, family legends, myths told and retold. An ache opens up inside me yet again for the childhood I missed. The camaraderie. The sense of tribe. But then what sits at the heart of ours burns through it, and I think maybe I was better off alone.

"She was a cunning woman," Myrtle begins. "The first of our kind—a midwife and a healer in her village. And worse, a widow, having lost her husband to side sickness the season before, what we now call appendicitis. Late one evening she was called to the bedside of a noblewoman who'd gone into early labor. The child, sadly, could not be saved, but the woman was spared thanks to the healer's efforts. Her husband, however, was not so grateful. Drunk and enraged at the death of his son, he raped her brutally and turned her out. She staggered to her horse to ride home, clutching her womb, but never made it. She hemorrhaged, falling unconscious, the horse wandering deeper into the woods with her draped over its back.

"She would have died if the old witch hadn't found her. A grizzled old woman most avoided, but that the midwife often left food for." Here, Myrtle's eyes begin to sparkle, the storyteller inside waking up, stretching her limbs. "But when is a witch ever just a witch? This one was a fée—a fairy or woman of herbs and stones. Or a demoness, depending on who's telling the story. What's clear is that she was not human. She recognized this healer who'd shown her kindness and chose to grant her a dying wish. The midwife did not ask to recover, or even that the life of her unborn child be restored. Her dying wish was for revenge. And so the bane witch was born, resurrected with a potent, toxic ability, the nobleman her first and most deserving mark. But like many gifts of the fay, this one came with a terrible cost. For generations her daughters would be born killers, sons poisoned in the womb or soon after unless given up, with gifts both feared and hated. We've had to hide for hundreds of years or be driven from our communities, even savagely murdered for daring to deliver justice where it is due."

It seems too glossy to be real, spun a little too tight. I whistle low, teeth buzzing with the sound. "That's some story."

She gives a small dip of her head and smiles broadly. "It may sound like a fairy tale, but mark me, Piers, it's all true. We're the living proof."

Certainly, there must be truth *in* it. But I imagine unseemly details lost over the years, like jagged edges sticking out, catching at loose skin. Perhaps not food but offerings the midwife left, seeking the power of life and death. Or maybe *fairy woman* is a euphemism for something older and more sinister, a Lovecraftian presence brooding among the trees, slogging from the swamp, pestilent and hungry. A Faustian bargain was struck, something traded away from the eyes of men, the prostitution of the soul. In any case, it is *my* story now, the origin of my kind. The notion of my trading places with Myrtle someday, sitting in her chair as I retell it to another, ignorant and disbelieving as I am, strikes me with such violent clarity that it forces the wind from my lungs, and I double over.

"Piers?" Her voice is high, worried.

"It's nothing," I say, pushing myself up, head in a daze. "Just a passing sickness. I'm fine."

She studies me as if she can smell the lie but leaves it alone. "I've kept you long enough," she says quietly, admonished. "You need to sleep. Your hunt is more important than mine."

That's not what she means. She means more dangerous. More exhaustive. More precarious. But I listen just the same. "What will you do?" I ask, rising. "To feed?"

Her eyes twitch toward the window as if the darkness sets them itching. "I'll find the bulbs," she says, patting my hand. "Don't worry about me."

Stepping to the wall, I hit the switch, and we both stand in sudden shadow, staring across the house to the uncovered windows, straining to see what lies just beyond our sight. We are so still even the dust begins to settle, silence thick enough to drown thought, the tick of our hearts syncing, keeping time. Who knows how many minutes pass, our eyes adjusting moment by moment, pupils growing large enough to swallow stars. Somewhere beyond the cabin, I feel him, gazing back, locked in a stare down, holding until one of us breaks. I think he is too far to see me, but I know he feels it, the thing that ties us together, like gossamer twine.

Myrtle would call it *magic*. I call it *death*.

Something slides around inside me, slippery and unmoored, a slug in a jar. "Don't go out there," I whisper. "Not tonight. Wait until morning. Promise me."

I see her throat bob and glide as she swallows her nerves. She nods once. She will stay inside tonight, but she's right. The hunt is beginning, and my prey is out there, hunting me in return.

THE NEXT MORNING, I find her at the table with a cutting board and a utility knife, slicing up daffodil bulbs like they're shallots and eating them raw. Her flannel hoodie is partially unzipped like she forgot what she was doing halfway through; her hair isn't yet pulled back. Fleshy, lavender pockets bulge beneath her eyes. The corners of her mouth are cracked and bleeding.

"You found them."

"I trekked to the shelter this morning," she says without looking at me. "But I waited for the sun to rise."

"You should have waited until I was awake," I scold, but she goes on eating, untroubled. I watch her from the corner of my eye as I set the coffeepot and wait for it to brew. Normally, she would have done this already. "Has anyone opened the café?"

"I told Ed to unlock the door and put the cereal and bowls out. I programmed the coffeepot last night." She pops a final papery, brown nub of bulb into her mouth and chews like it's a piece of homemade caramel, licking her fingers.

"I can go over and make some oatmeal," I tell her. "Let you . . . finish here."

Her eyes finally snap to mine. "I can do it. This will last me for a while."

Coffee steam invades the air, bringing the cabin to life. I pour her a cup and add milk, setting it before her. "Shouldn't you refrain from . . . you know, *handling* things for a bit?" I say, gesturing at the empty jar with the pot. I wonder how she's done it all these years, alone in this untethered circle of mountains, overcome with hunger and the need to take a life while still maintaining her Pollyanna presence in the community.

She grunts, lifting a limp pair of white cotton gloves. "That's what these are for. Everyone thinks I have palmoplantar psoriasis. When they see the gloves come out, they assume I'm experiencing a flare-up."

"Let me help. It's the least I can do." I wiggle my fingers. "I'm toxin-free at the moment, safer than you."

She picks at a gap in her teeth, then agrees. "Fine. I'll head over in a bit. Just need some time to get myself together." She looks down and notices her zipper, tugging it up.

"Will that be it?" I ask her as I sip my coffee. "Or will you have to feed again?"

"Don't know," she says, rising to set the jar in the sink, fill it with soapy water. "Hard to say when I don't know who it is yet. But he's close." She turns to me, gaze down. "I can feel him nearby, dull and ever present, like a sound that's always been there but you're only just becoming aware of. The daffodil won't be enough on its own anyway. I need to visit my stores one more time, make a couple of adjustments, eat more."

"I hope he comes soon," I tell her, a shiver tickling through me. I don't like seeing her this way.

"So do I," she says. "So do I."

WHEN I MAKE it to the café, I find Ed inside reading the *Adirondack Daily Enterprise* while he eats Cheerios out of the box, stooping to feed one to Bart every now and again. I walk over and pat Bart's head, giving him a good scratch around the ears. "No dogs in the café," I tell Ed with a warning tone. "You know how Myrtle feels."

"Isn't anybody here," he complains. "He's a good boy. You know he is!"

I give Ed the side-eye, fighting back a smile, and park myself behind the counter, getting a pot out for oatmeal. "It's Myrtle's place, so it's Myrtle's rules. But I won't tell if you don't."

"Rules," he grumbles, folding his paper up as he approaches one of the barstools. "Where she at anyway?"

"Just a little stiff this morning," I tell him as I fill the pot with water. "She'll be in soon."

"Well," he says begrudgingly, "I gotta clear some downed limbs from that last storm. She's been after me to take care of them for weeks."

"Okay." I turn and give him a bright smile. Ed is a lot like his dog. He doesn't always mind, and he can be a bit smelly—and Myrtle's right about his drinking too much, though he tries to hide it—but something about him grows on you. I can't imagine the motel and café without him. He's a fixture, and I'm grateful he's been here for Myrtle over the years when no one else has. If I thought he'd like a scratch behind the ear as much as Bart, I'd probably give him one. "Will I see you later?"

"Gotta get my dinner from somewhere, don't I?" He lifts a

small resealable baggie from his front overalls pocket and waves it at me. "Hope you don't mind. I made myself the lunch special to go."

"What are we serving?" Yesterday's foraging trip seems to have thrown me off schedule. I can't remember what Myrtle had in store, even if I did run the last trip for groceries.

"Ham and cheese," he tells me, waddling to the door. "With mayo! *Mm-mmm!*"

I watch him leave, Bart prancing beside the stains on Ed's denim overalls, before turning back to the stove to get the water boiling. I like the café when it's quiet. If it weren't for all those tables, I could pretend it was my own little hut in the woods. But a prickling sensation lingers behind my skin, like ants on the inside, and I can't get comfortable. The door sounds and I assume Ed has forgotten something important. Most days he wanders off without his keys or glasses. He's left his phone behind for whole afternoons.

"What did you forget this time?" I call out, stirring the oats into the water with a knowing smile. "Huh, Ed?"

When he doesn't respond, the baby hairs at the nape of my neck begin to rise. "Ed?" I turn just as the door sounds again. The café is empty, the front clear of anything but spotted grass and a few paved parking places outside, the clear morning sky. Whoever came in has left.

I grab a kitchen knife, feeling suddenly naked. The weight of it in my hand—the dry wooden handle sanded smooth, the cold lip of tang—is something to hold on to. I should walk to the front, check outside, see if a guest needs help. But I just stand there while the oatmeal congeals, wishing I weighed a hundred pounds more, that I was foot taller, that I'd taken up martial arts as a hobby a decade ago.

Not only is the Saranac Strangler circling—circling *me* if Myrtle is to be believed—but another mark is coming, any day, any minute now. Someone who has tortured children and would feel nothing about hurting me. I think of Azalea in her platform heels and cat-eye sunglasses and understand her bravado. This life requires an iron spine, the ability to look death in the face again and again without flinching. Not only theirs but yours.

It takes me a long time to turn back around. By then, the oatmeal has clumped together, sticking to the bottom in an umber crust. I have to scrape it out with a metal spatula and start over. I'm just getting my second pot going when the door sounds again. My skin lights as if it's electric, every pore tingling. I hold my breath, but like before, there's no cheerful greeting, no heavy footfalls. Only that noiseless knowing that I am not alone.

I reach for the knife I'd set down between the burners so I could stir. Holding it stiff before me, I spin around, nearly slicing Regis open from one oblique to another.

"Shit!" He jumps away before the blade can make contact.

Something ejects from my mouth like a scream, but there's no sound to it. I stand there gaping as if I expect it to arrive late, unable to draw a breath.

He reaches out and plucks the knife from my hand, clattering it on the counter. "You trying to gut somebody?"

Oxygen finds me all at once, and I suck in a pitchy, terrified breath as if it will be my last. "You shouldn't sneak up on people," I squeeze out. "Not with that maniac running around, choking women."

He leans down, elbows on the counter, and blows out. "Sorry. I didn't mean to scare you. I wanted to see you, is all. You left so quickly the other day, after . . ."

I glance toward the oatmeal, the heat of our exchange "the other day" riding up my legs, filling my belly like warm honey. I don't know where to put my eyes. It all happened so unexpectedly, the rush of want and the press of skin on skin, a desire I didn't know I could still feel. And then it was over, and I was scrambling to pull my clothes on, unable to look at him on the drive back to my car. I didn't think about *after*—the uselessness of words when bodies have been joined, the pretense that there is nothing more between us than investigator and witness, the utility of sex without commitment. A soft pop sounds and I look down to see the oatmeal forming opaque bubbles that burst into creamy craters. I grab the spoon.

"Are you sorry that we—" he starts to ask.

I stick the spoon in the gruel and turn to him. "It's not that."

Relief plays across his lips, causing them to curl like pencil shavings, a little unruly. "I was afraid maybe you didn't like it." The words jam together on their way out of his mouth, so that I have to decipher them.

My toes ball in my shoes, the grooves that separate his muscles coming back to me like a landscape I want to get lost in. I slide a finger between the buttons of his shirt and look up into his eyes, like the feathers of a great gray owl. "I liked it very much."

His hands slide up and down the tops of my arms. "I like *you* very much." He bends slowly, letting his lips glance over mine before closing the space between us, folding over me as our mouths greet each other again.

I put a hand on his chest and push him away, breathless. "Not here."

I don't want Myrtle to see. It's not just the venery, the risk. There's something possessive in me, a need for custody over my own heart and body. I want him to belong to me in a way he cannot belong to anyone else. I want what we do to exist in an autonomous sphere, like a snow globe, a world under glass, perfect and separate, outside of time. A place only we can enter. When he is with me, he's not the sheriff, and I'm not the bane witch. We are private entities, reborn in each other's arms, regenerated everywhere our bodies touch. Every meeting an introduction, an act of creation.

The door chimes and we leap apart, my fingers easily finding the spoon, stirring the oatmeal as if it is my whole purpose in life.

"Sheriff Brooks," I hear Myrtle croon. "What lucky turn of events has brought you to our door again?"

He clears his throat and my mind flashes to the pattern of stubble where his beard meets his neck, the trace of my lips across it like a surveyor drawing a boundary, careful not to miss a step. I take a steady breath and relegate the image of him naked and trembling beneath me to a dusty corner of my mind. That I can fool Myrtle, keep what is between us to myself, is lunacy. But I have to try. Because I cannot tell her, and I cannot refuse him.

"Learn anything else about what happened to Beth Ann?" she asks.

He eyes her warily. "I can't discuss the details of an active case. You know that."

"Well, we all know who did it," Myrtle carries on unhindered. "That Saranac Strangler's getting a little too close for comfort."

I pour a cup of coffee and hand it to him. "You don't have any idea who he is? These are small towns. Surely someone's seen a strange face around."

"Tourists pass through here all year," Myrtle tells me before Regis can answer. "Most of the houses in the area are empty, but they're not for sale. City dwellers like to buy up the real estate and save it for vacation or rent it out to travelers for passive income."

"Unfortunately, she's right," he agrees. "Whoever this guy is, I don't think he's local, but he's got a home base, somewhere he's lying low between murders. A place he's renting seasonally or even squatting in. Some of these homeowners don't come up here for years. They'd never know if a person was living on their property temporarily." He sets his cup down without taking a sip. "Ladies, I better get going."

I open my mouth to say something, but the words glob inside, and he stalks out as I stare after him.

"Damn shame we don't have anyone here who could help that man by shedding some light on this mysterious killer," Myrtle says flatly.

I look at her. "Do you mean *I* should help him?"

She eyes me sidelong. "I mean that he should help you. The more you get out of him, the greater your advantage over this monster. And you need every advantage. But you gotta scratch a back around here to get yours scratched in return."

"Who says he'll believe me?"

She shrugs. "Don't overthink it, dear. Chalk it up to women's intuition. Besides, something tells me he'd believe just about anything that comes out of your mouth. Better hurry," she adds dryly. "He's leaving."

I drop the dish towel I'm holding and rush out the door, throwing myself at his patrol car before he can back away.

Regis rolls his window down.

"Let me help you," I tell him, panting.

He looks bewildered.

"You said the other day . . . I mean, I did *feel* something when we were at Beth Ann's place." I take a deep breath. "Take me to the other crime scenes. Maybe I'll get something else—a sense or a premonition. You don't have to tell anyone. We can keep it unofficial, off-the-record. But it might be useful."

He looks pale, jaw flickering with tension. "You're some kind of psychic after all, aren't you?"

"In a way."

He sighs.

"I *can* help," I insist as he quietly deliberates. "Let me prove it to you."

"Acacia, it's not that I don't believe you . . ." he starts.

I squeeze my eyes shut and burrow deep within, feeling for the pulse that isn't mine, the flicker of another presence, dull but persistent, like a clock ticking through a very thick wall. I put myself back at Beth Ann's place, the way I found it that morning, littered with the invisible debris of what occurred there. The first flash is dim, muddled in a way I don't understand, but I can see her tromping down her porch stairs through the branches, unaware she is being watched. Suddenly, the shift in his MO makes sense to me. I open my eyes. "It was an accident," I blurt.

"What?" Regis looks confused.

"He wasn't looking for another victim when he found Beth Ann. He came upon her place by accident. But the need was so strong, and the opportunity presented itself—he couldn't resist."

It spurts out of me like a balloon deflating. I grip Regis's door and sigh. My eyes meet his. "He's losing control. Slowly, incrementally, but still. He's going to make a mistake soon. You need to know what to look for, or you might miss it."

Regis stares at me like I've just confessed to killing Beth Ann myself. After a moment, he relaxes.

"Look, I don't know what this is, this thing you've got. Maybe it's a gift, maybe it's all bullshit. But I know you're not a liar. I know you believe it. I have some time this afternoon. I could take you to one of the spots, but it would have to be just between us. Understand? I wouldn't even consider this if I wasn't so desperate to catch this bastard—if he wasn't so good."

I glance back to the café. I shouldn't leave Myrtle to tend the guests alone. Not when she's feeding. No matter what she says or how long she's managed without me, but if I can convince her to close early, I can leave without worrying. "Can you come back around four?"

"It's a date."

THE SIGNPOST PROCLAIMS TRAILHEAD & PARKING in golden autumn lettering. Beside it, a matching bit of police tape is lying on the ground. Regis bends to scoop it into a pocket. An old road stretches before us, linear, parting the trees like a plow has been driven through the forest. The air is nippy, bright, laced with a smell I can't place—old paper and ash.

"The fall colors will arrive soon," he says to me.

I look up to see browning leaves, speckled and dry, ripening to sunny yellows with orange frill. "Aren't they here?"

He laughs. "No. This is just a primer. In another couple of weeks, you'll think you fell into a Willard Leroy Metcalf painting. It's like fireworks going off all over these mountains."

I walk over to the sign and place my finger in a groove, running it along the grain. It swings gently with the pressure. "Where are we?"

He squints. "About ten miles out of Malone. This is where we found the last victim." He points down the trail. "She was there a ways. Not out in the open like this but in plain view for anyone on a hike."

I turn away from the sign and step to the center of the trail, staring down it. I can feel him here, the Strangler, like a memory. He hunches over this place, an umbrella of fog. It belongs to him now, he thinks. This road and these trees. The night when it happened. He's made it his. I see the trail leading before me like an arm, an extension of the man, his lost appendage. He leaves a little drift of his essence behind at every one—a time stamp, something he can follow back. It pours into me like wine, feeding me what I need to know. I see a glimpse of her—short hair, brightly colored windbreaker, a tube of lip balm in one pocket—and then I get my first real glimpse of him, a burst of movement from the edge of the trail like a mountain lion pouncing on its prey, so fast I can't distinguish anything in the poor light.

"She came late in the day," I say out loud.

"Yes. How did you know?" He steps toward me, studying my face as I stare down the dirt tracks striping the earth.

I glance upward. "Because he took her at night. The moon was almost full. She was visible between these trees. That's why he chose this trail. It's wide here; he could see easily without being seen." I take a step, wait, take another. Slowly, I make my way down the center of the trail until I feel his energy dissipate. I step back into it, like crossing a fence, and turn to face Regis. "She came late, and he watched her pass. He took her on her way back to her car. By then it had grown dark. He likes the cover in this region. The way people trust the landscape even when they shouldn't. The beauty puts them off their guard. It makes his job easier. He could kill a hundred women out here and people would still show up to these trails. They can't resist what nature has wrought. It's a playground for him."

Regis lifts a hand to his head. He looks troubled, as if I've said something incriminating or nonsensical, eyes narrowing, mouth tight. "You got all that from taking a few steps?"

I can feel the killer's appreciation for this spot like a rug burn. It is etched into the land around me, the leaves, the cool brushes of air. A flame ignites in my chest, like hunger, sex, adrenaline, but it's none of those. It is its own fuel, an acute drive bordering on pain, the need is so great. I want to bite down on my knuckle until the taste of blood, warm and metallic, fills my mouth. If Regis weren't here, I'd scream. I'd tear my clothes off and race down this trail, frothing at the mouth. The nearness of the Strangler incenses me. To step where he stepped—the hunt dilates my veins, a flood of instinct. "Do you believe me now?" I ask Regis. "That I can help you?"

"I believe that you have a . . . an ability. Some kind of knack for this. I don't know what it is. I'm willing to listen, though."

I nod. There's a turkey vulture circling overhead, gliding on invisible hoops of sky, blotting out the sun in lazy turns. Its wings are scarecrow straight, a boomerang returning to the same point again and again. Something died here since the woman. "So, what can you tell me?"

"Tell you?" He looks confused.

"He doesn't use his hands," I say frankly. "What is he strangling them with?"

His eyes jump from mine. "Parachute cord. He ties it like a tourniquet using a stick so he can tighten the loop with one hand. It gives him total control over the victim."

I nod, press my lips together, scent the air around me like a bloodhound.

Regis continues. "We assume because he's using his hand for *other things.*" He looks like he's bitten into something foul.

The truth floats around me now, the smell of his sweat. "He masturbates," I blurt with enough objectivity to curdle milk. "He holds something around their necks with one hand while he gets off with the other." My lack of squeamishness inculpates me. I see the way Regis's brows rise with alarm, the part of his lips at my uncanny criminal insight. I'm a far cry from the nervous woman he questioned that day in the café.

"Yes, that's true. But we never find any biological evidence at the scene," he informs me.

"You mean semen?"

Regis turns a funny coral color across his nose and cheeks, a wave of strawberry passing under his beard. "He likes to clean up after himself. Which is why we think he's chosen such out-of-the-way locations like this one, so he can take his time, tidy up the crime scene without risk of being interrupted. But it's like you said—something has changed since Beth Ann's murder. Something pushed him, tipped him over the edge just enough that he abandoned his usual penchant for planning and order."

I know what that something is. My allure has been at work all right.

"It hasn't caused him to make that mistake you promised yet, but it's only a matter of time," Regis continues.

"And why this trail?" I ask. "There must be hundreds of 'out-of-the-way locations' like this one out here."

His bottom lips juts out. "We're pretty far north," he says. "Fewer tourists up this way. But . . ."

My brows arc, waiting.

"It's easy. One of the more moderate climbs with stairs at the worst part, which means he doesn't want to work too hard for it." Regis stands beside me, glancing around. "He's not into the chase. And he's not from here. Not used to the elevation, the terrain. He's protecting himself."

"He likes to watch," I tell Regis. "Not run. It's the power he's after. Watching makes him feel powerful. Running reminds him of his humanity, his mortality, his limitations. He's probably not a large man. Not small necessarily, but not an athlete. The woman wasn't small in stature, but she wasn't large."

He shakes his head. "Not especially. But she was a bit older, in her late fifties. And she had an on-again, off-again limp, arthritis in one knee that sometimes bothered her, which is likely why she chose this trail. She was looking for easy, too."

I breathe in the faint aroma of lemons, too sugary to be real. Likely a shampoo or detergent. It's not her I'm smelling. It's his memory of her smell breaking off, drifting back to me, like a trail of dandelion seeds. "He likes to find the ones with a weakness. Wolves hunt like that."

"Because they're easier to kill?"

A snaking grin slides across my face. "Because they make him feel more powerful." I turn to Regis. "Did Beth Ann have any physical disabilities? Anything that would have slowed her down, given him an advantage?"

He frowns. "No. She was strong. She took care of her body— worked out and ran. She was in good shape."

I push aside my own niggling sense of comparison and self-doubt. "He's gaining confidence."

"Getting bolder, sloppier," Regis agrees.

I shake my head. "No, not sloppy. This is arrogance, not care-lessness. His confidence is gained from experience, but he's not infallible. He grows with every kill. Beth Ann was a kind of lev-eling up, like in a video game. He's training himself. You under-stand?"

"I think so." Regis glances behind us to where a young cou-ple are starting up the trail, laughing. Her leggings are a jaunty red, his cap a little offset. They've foregone backpacks for a small utility bag and a water bottle between them. They don't expect to sweat. As they pass with easy smiles, greeting us, unaware that they are treading on a murder scene, Regis tips his hat.

"Just don't underestimate him," I say once they're out of ear-shot. "This is not just a man becoming impulsive. This is a killer getting better, more efficient. This is a boy becoming a man."

Regis doesn't look comforted by my help. His teeth grind be-hind his beard, eyes pointing into the trees, sharp as blades. His drive to catch this man is nearly as raw and eager as my own. But there's purity behind his motives, altruism. I wonder if his version of justice is really so different from ours. Why should this man live when he has killed so many? I don't believe Regis wants to spare him, but he will because he is a rule-follower. His nature is to color inside the lines. Mine, I realize starkly, is to stand just outside them, stuffing my face with forbidden fruit.

Maybe I am like the venery after all.

23

Ed

Something isn't right. I feel it like a tickle beneath my breast-bone, a hum of anxiety that can't be explained or brushed aside, my heart alerted to a change that hasn't shown itself yet. The sun has rolled beneath the mountains, leaving the sky the color of compost, black with possibility. I lean against the seat back and feel the ground moving below me, a blur of territory in my wake. Beside me, Regis is quiet, everything that passed between us on the trail percolating in his mind, a simmer of data about our shared target both horrific and impossible. When we pull up in front of the café, the lights are still on. Myrtle's sitting just inside by the windows. She looks up, her face rounder than I remember, more vulnerable.

"What's she doing still open?" he asks. "Shouldn't she be at the cabin by now?"

"I don't know." I slide out of the vehicle and get to my feet just as she's pushing through the door toward us. The concern is printed like a birthmark across her face. Wrongly, I think it is for me. I spin around and bend down, ducking back into the car. "Just go," I tell Regis. "I'll deal with this."

"You sure?"

"Go," I tell him, straightening and heading toward her, fearful that I've committed some cardinal sin of the venery I don't know about.

She approaches as he backs away, the headlights washing out

her face. The nearer she gets, the more I realize I am not the thing to blame for her worry. Her face stays painfully drawn with angst.

"What's wrong?" I ask, reaching for her elbow.

"It's Ed," she tells me, eyes plated with tears, reflective. "He hasn't returned for dinner, and he's not in his cabin." She scans the trees rearing behind us, monuments to Mother Nature, as if she'll suddenly spot him there at the edge, overalls hanging by one shoulder, an empty bottle in his hand. "He's not answering his phone."

"Could he be in town? At the Drunken Moose with Terry and Amos?"

She shakes her head so vigorously I want to hold on to her neck to stabilize her. "I have a bad feeling," she whispers. "You don't think the Strangler . . ."

The impossibility of it is swift, dumping over me like ice melt. "No. He only hunts women."

Myrtle nods, but the tears drop from her eyes, landing on her cheeks like pearls.

"We'll find him," I tell her. "He's around here somewhere."

The crush of leaves and breaking sticks scampers toward us in the dark, the approach of an unknown entity. I go rigid, every muscle preparing to fight, my mind bracing itself for whatever horror emerges from the trees. Beside me, Myrtle crouches, a bobcat ready to pounce. She has fed, at least. It is the last thought I have before the brush parts.

Something barrels in our direction, coat slick with night, the flap of ears audible, the beat of paws.

It's Bart. And he's alone.

IT'S UNUSUALLY COLD tonight, well into the thirties but not yet freezing. A howl of wind beats through the tree limbs, causing me to hug my arms to my chest. Ahead of us, Bart keeps tearing off into the hobblebush, littering the ground with scarlet berries, and Myrtle has to call after him. I strain in the dark to see, worried we'll overlook Ed somehow, despite the moonlight. If we don't find him soon, hypothermia could set in. I watched him leave the café this morning in nothing but his shirtsleeves.

"Ed!" I call out, fingers freezing as I cup them around my mouth. The ensuing silence hangs like a curse.

"Damn dog," I hear Myrtle grumble as she tries to keep up with Bart, who is leading us—we hope—down the most direct, if not the clearest, path to his owner.

"What's he doing way out here?" I ask her, stumbling over a tree root but catching myself.

"Who knows," she bellows. "Foolish old man. Can't tell the difference between a bullfrog and a rattlesnake."

"He said something about clearing tree limbs around the property." I fist my hands together in front of my mouth, blowing on them.

"Must have been gathering them for firewood," she says, trudging forward. "No other need to worry about deadwood this far in. Half of it's too wet anyway. I've told him that a million times."

Bart picks up speed, darting to the left, refusing to loop back when Myrtle calls him. "Ed! Can you hear me?" she shouts this time, her voice pitching lower than my own. "We must be close."

A soft moan sounds nearby, like the earth is sighing beneath our weight, and Myrtle thrashes toward it, knocking branches out of her way until suddenly Bart is there, nose down, tail wagging, a pathetic whine filtering from his snout.

Beneath him, Ed lies prone in a spread of fallen leaves and pine needles, his face barely clear of the ground, one eye swollen shut. Myrtle is on her knees in an instant, hands fluttering above his back, his skull, his arm. The ground is wet, seeping through my jeans as I kneel beside her. I think the darkness across her palms is dirt until I realize the damp around Ed is blood.

"Ed! What's happened to ya? It's Myrtle. Talk to me. How long have you been out here?" She presses her face low by his so she can hear his replies. He responds with great effort, struggling to form even a word.

"Moose," she barks, sitting up. "He says a cow trampled him. Never even knew she was there. Must have had a calf nearby."

I think I should feel relief, that a flood of oxytocin should cascade through my body at the word *moose,* which to my mind must be better than *bear* or *mountain lion.* So, I can't understand when my jaw clenches and my nostrils flare, fingers curling into fists I want to beat on the ground. "Will he be okay?"

"We need to turn him over." She grips his shoulder, only touching the cloth. "We're gonna turn you over now, Ed!" she shouts at him.

His words are thick, pouring from his mouth like molasses, barely audible. She leans down to hear. When she sits up, tears slip conspicuously down her cheeks. She swats my hand away. "Can't do it," she explains, wiping at her nose with the back of her hand. "Says his back is broken. *Again.*"

An owl calls with a hooting purr, invisible in the canopy, like a warning from God.

"We need an ambulance. The paramedics can secure him," I tell her. "I'll call nine-one-one and wait at the café for EMS to arrive. You stay with him." I straggle to my feet, but she clasps my hand. Her eyes squeeze together, ringing out tears, and her head shakes from side to side. When she opens them to look at me, they are huge like the moon.

"There isn't time. His lung is punctured—that's why he looks so gray—and he's lost too much blood. We'll lose him before they can get him to a hospital."

My jaw drops, mouth gaping with uncertainty. "I don't understand. What are we supposed to do?"

Her grip is so strong on my hand that my thumb feels like it might separate at the joint. "There isn't time," she repeats. "We can't *save* him. You understand?"

"No." I would slap her if I thought it might make a difference. The weight of what she's considering drops like an anvil in my lap. "Not that."

Beside us, Ed moans again, and it is not soft but rigid with pain. It is only then I register that he is hurting. His injuries blaze across my understanding at once, like scattered embers. The punctured lung. The gash across the back of his head. The crack in his skull. The arm bent wrong. The back shattered once again. Contusions pepper his insides like mold. He's had two teeth knocked out, and his right leg is broken in two places. He's been out here a long time—too long—Bart afraid to leave him. He's dehydrated. His core body temperature is dropping. And he's lost a lot of blood.

She's right. In the time it will take me to find my way back to the motel, where there's cell service, call an ambulance, wait for them to arrive from the nearest town with a hospital, and then pick my way back here with the paramedics, he will have succumbed to oxygen deprivation, hypothermia, or simply bled out.

I find her eyes in the dark. They are childlike, pleading, wretched. "Your mark," I whisper.

She nods slowly. This is what her cycle was preparing her for. Not an incestophile—a mercy killing. Not a stranger—a friend. Not a murder—a release from misery. She bends low and listens as he mumbles to her, nodding, whispering back, shushing him. Her fingers hover over his cheek and hair, the hand she'd like to take in hers. When she rises, she says, "He's begging us to shoot him."

My brows lower, refusing to hear it. "You can end this," I tell her. "But not like that."

"He is suffering." The words are pressed between her teeth, bitter and hated. "I did not feed to end a life quickly. If I poison him, he will waste out here, his suffering increasing until he finally gives out. I can't do that to him, not after he's been out here so long. If we'd found him sooner . . ."

The dark is obscuring her words and time has stopped. I cannot seem to comprehend what's happening, what's being asked of me. Bart nuzzles the side of my face, his nose slick and clammy as a fish.

"You have to do it," she says to me. "Please, Piers."

"No!" I scrabble back on my hands and feet. I can't do what she's asking. Not him, not this way. I know Ed. I *love* Ed. This is not what I am here for.

She takes my hands in hers, nails digging into the fleshy mounds beneath my thumbs. "He's in agony," she implores me. "You can end this. Please."

"How?" I haven't fed. I'm not prepared. This isn't what my cycle responds to.

She swallows a sob, tries to steady her voice. "The deadly cort. It's in the kitchen at the cabin. In the canister marked TEA."

I jerk away from her, stumble to my feet, bracing my hands against my knees. I cannot save Ed, not his life, but I can rescue him from his pain. I can send him to the wife he misses. I can spare Myrtle the agony of watching him die slowly and miserably. I can make it quick. It is not the kind of superhero a girl dreams of becoming, but it is something. It is all I have to offer. And it's time I stop withholding it from the world. I can do some good with this magic of mine. I can deal death where death is due. It doesn't make me evil; it makes me powerful.

I suddenly understand men like Henry and the Saranac Strangler so much better. They're seeking power because deep down they feel power*less*. But power is not their issue. The best they can manage when they kill is control. That's why they keep killing. Because they're chasing a moving target—it's always a step ahead, just out of reach. They are a poor reflection, a mirage, a copy of a copy. But the venery, the magic flowing through me, *that* is the truth.

I sniff and rise to my full height. She must see the surrender in my face because something in hers lifts. "There's just the one."

"It will be enough," she tells me. "For you."

I nod, glancing over my shoulder.

She points east. "That way," she says. "Almost a straight shot. I have my phone. I'll keep the light on to guide you back. Go!"

The trees seem to shrink away as I dash through them, as if the forest is on our side. Bart is on my heels. He must believe Ed is okay with Myrtle there. I do my best to keep a continual line eastward. When the doubts arise—the voices that tell me I could get lost out here and never be found, that the Strangler may find me before anyone else—I push them aside. Because Ed is waiting. Ed is hurting. And I can stop it.

That's all I know.

The cabin emerges from the black shrubbery like a beacon, windows pouring light into the woods around it. I stamp up the steps into the kitchen and snatch at canisters, ripping off lids until I find it where Myrtle said I would, a bit shriveled but otherwise recognizable. It goes down easy like pudding. In a bite or two it's gone. I swallow the yellow wart, too, for good measure. When I turn to leave, Bart stands in the open doorway watching me. I think he knows what I intend to do. His eyes are unreadable, but he doesn't growl or lower his head. He just stares before bounding down the stairs. I follow him into the night. He is fast but not frantic. Myrtle's phone begins to shine before us like a fairy light. I wish that it were.

When I reach them, Ed is breathing faintly, his pulse a whisper. Myrtle scoots to one side so I can get close to him. She has been careful not to touch him, not to risk a tear splashing across his skin. Her cries are soundless. She tells him it will not be long; his wife is waiting. He tries to open his injured eye, to look at her one last time.

I kneel over him, my hair hanging to one side. He taps my knee with a finger, one arm still mobile. I turn my ear and lower it so that it nearly touches his lips. "Thank you," he whispers.

My eyes well. I lift up and look down on him. "Goodbye, Ed," I tell him. "Sleep well." And then I lick my lips and place them on a gash at his temple.

THE WALK BACK to our cabin is a disheartening slog through pitch-dark wilderness. Even the cheerful glow of lamplight as the cabin looms into view doesn't stir our spirits, though it will feel good to get warm. I reach down and squeeze Myrtle's hand; it hangs there limply.

"In the morning, I'll report him missing," she says, weary, voice thinner than sheet metal with the same brisk edge. "They'll find him within a few hours."

I follow her up the stairs. At the door, she waits, holding it open. "Come on," she says to the dog. "You sleep here now."

Bart emerges from the shadows. He lifts his head sadly and peers past us into the house before tucking his tail and scooting slowly inside.

The little house is a welcome refuge after our trauma in the woods. I make hot tea and slice lemon wedges, fingers still numb from cold and dissociation. Myrtle runs a bath, washing off the blood and soil, the dank, midnight stink of the wild, the crushing grief. She comes to sit beside the fire I've kindled in the stone hearth, hair wet and eyes lowered, her robe tucked tightly, holding her together. Bart curls up in front of her chair, claiming his new owner.

"With any luck, they'll assume he died of his injuries and forgo an autopsy." Her eyes are mossy in the firelight, a green that goes on for miles, mirroring the country around her. They reach into me. "What you did for me tonight, Piers . . . Thank you. I only hope I can repay you someday."

"You already have," I tell her. "I came here with nothing, and you took me in. Despite the risks, my questionable past. Besides, I really did it for Ed, so he wouldn't . . . linger. Will you tell the venery?"

She rubs Bart with a foot, thinking. "Do you want me to? It might be better if it stays between us."

"Doesn't it count? Wouldn't it mean I passed their test?" I'm not necessarily proud of what I did, but I'm not ashamed either. It feels mysteriously humbling to take a life with intention this time. And the grief is swift and immediate, like blood flow after a cut, the sense of waste. More so because he was a friend. But thinking I did it to *help* someone makes it easier. I want it to matter, to get me off the hook with the other bane witches. Maybe because that will make it all feel less pointless. Maybe because I don't want to kill again for a long while.

Myrtle shakes her head. "I don't know. They want to see you move through a complete cycle. This was rushed, not really an examination of your own instincts. Besides, your mark is still out there. Your hunt is on. Soon, the hunger will set in. Would you really leave that man in the world to take more innocent lives?"

I'm ashamed to admit how much I want to walk away from the Saranac Strangler, from being a bane witch, and live a life that's uneventful. I killed myself to get here. I killed one man to keep from being raped and another to spare his wife, one for reasons so blurry and lost to time I can scarcely remember them if I ever knew at all. And now I've killed someone I cared about so his pain would end. I shouldn't have to kill anymore. But after what I saw, what I learned on that trailhead today, I know I can't walk away from this fight. If I don't take the Saranac Strangler down, who will? If I don't fulfill my cycle, I'm risking Regis's life along with so many innocent women. They all deserve better than what the Strangler will give them. The world deserves better.

"I want you to tell them," I admit, knowing that it means I'm admitting the shame is alive in me, a stowaway in my heart. "But only so they stop breathing down my neck. I will kill the Saranac Strangler regardless. I know now that's what I'm here to do."

She leans her head back. "Your courage is as plain as the color of your hair."

I wish I could smile. The praise is a bit of salve on my weary heart. But Ed's loss hangs over us like a heavy cloud, and smiling will feel wrong for a while.

When I don't respond, she continues. "There probably isn't

a one of us who wouldn't want to walk away if given the chance, to be with sons and lovers long since lost to us. Except maybe Verna—she's ruthless. That tampon trick . . . But there's a mighty cost for our freedom, and we'd be asking others to pay it." She sighs. "I suppose they can't really argue that you've fulfilled your obligation. And perhaps it will look good that you came to my rescue."

Relief washes over me, leaving my limbs with a shapeless, stretched-out sensation, the way I feel after yoga or too much weed. The future wipes itself clean, a smooth and gleaming shingle of potential outcomes, blank but fertile, waiting for me and no one else.

I sip my tea, watching the flames leap over one another and listening to Bart snore beside me. When I look up, Myrtle is fast asleep, hands slack in her lap. I get up carefully and go to the bathroom, undress, and wash the stain of guilt off my skin. Unfortunately, the soap won't penetrate deeper. I crawl into the bed in only my underwear, covers pulled practically over my head, as if even the weight of my pajamas is more than I can bear tonight, a feather too many on the scales. I decide to dream of flower crowns, will-o'-the-wisps, and fairy processions, the spun-sugar fantasies of my little-girl self, what populates the woods beside predators, impenetrable shadows, and deadly plant matter.

But when I close my eyes, all I can see is the split of Ed's bulging eyelid, lashes matting against gray skin, and the motionless slab of his back, gummy with blood that has stopped flowing. The trauma won't let me sleep, and after many long, painful minutes, I finally get up, tug on my jeans and a flannel shirt, and tiptoe back through the kitchen, pulling Myrtle's car keys from the jacket pocket I found them in before. Bart lifts his head as I open the front door. I press a finger to my lips, and he lowers it again, content to stay by Myrtle's side.

I'd like to say it's somewhere on the road that I decide where I'm going, but the truth is, I've known all along. The hands of men have not been kind to me. I should distrust them, like wildlife, unpredictable and misleading. *Don't feed the animals.* But Regis's hands are nothing like Henry's—those long spaghetti fingers and scrubbed nail beds shining in the light, pale as filtered beeswax, mean as hornets. In the early days, when we were still dating, I remember how he would touch me, deliberate or not at all. The way he always held my hand a little too tight, his weight in every pat and stroke. A hardness behind the smallest of gestures. At the time, I saw it as a sign of strength. Henry was implacable, solid like steel, incorruptible, I thought. I didn't know the putrescence was already inside him, shielded by that impregnable manner while it festered.

Regis's hands are slow, methodical even, not calculating but ponderous. They choose their course with care and a sense of wonder, every touch receptive. I can't imagine him making a fist, though I'm sure he has. He holds me lightly with no desire for constraint, as if it is enough to simply pass over my skin and be left wanting. As if I am liquid and pour through him.

It is Regis's hands I need.

When I pull up and get out, I make my way to his door. The night is aging like fine wine, rich and layered, impenetrable, steady. There is only one way I can scrub my mind clean tonight. This is my forgetting. And Myrtle insists I'm no longer a danger. She made a point to remind me how early I needed to be up to food prep in the café, that I would have to feed again—and soon—for the Strangler.

My knock is urgent, ringing out with need. He answers it with sleepy eyes, a question in his expression. "Acacia? Your eyes . . . Is everything okay?"

My irises must be the color of poison apples by now, green as peridots. I have no explanation. I don't give either of us time to speak. If I open my mouth, it will all come spilling out, the ugly truth of who I am and what I've done. Sobs I cannot cry for Ed will pour over, and he will know. Regis will know it was me.

Instead, I press myself against him, my lips finding his in the dark, my body speaking for me—asking, *begging.* He pulls me in, shutting out the world around us, drawing me deeper into him, tangling. The hush in his living room is like a buffer from the brutal reality of our respective worlds. We move inside it like butterflies, lighting on each other in a hundred places, breathing the same air, the same need, drinking each other in sips and swallows, little nips of gratification. He is more confident this time and less rushed. He moves with leisure, a man with eternity in his pocket. He takes my breasts in his mouth like candied apples—something to be savored for long hours before the heart is breached, the pulp extracted. I melt beneath him, unable to hold my tongue, my composure, a thought or form. Climax ripples over me in waves, the undulating expression of things undone, like water or sound.

We lie on the carpet after, loose as old boot strings, shameless as dogs.

He says, "You're not like any woman I've ever known."

Some women might be troubled by that, the implied comparison, the undertone of quantity. Perhaps I should be. Perhaps I am too languid to care. Even Beth Ann feels light-years away. He has no idea how true his statement is. "No. I don't imagine I am."

He presses up on his elbows, smiles down on me. Appreciation kindles in his eyes. I like my body when he looks at it. There is nothing out of place. "Why is that?"

This is why we don't speak. Because talking inevitably leads to the things I cannot say, the secrets I can't tell. With my thighs, with my lips and neck and the palms of my hands, the swell of my hips, I can speak unhindered, enunciate every feeling I wish to communicate. My body is articulate in a way my mouth can never be. An ache catches in my throat behind the larynx. "You tell me."

He sighs, brushing the hair away from my shoulder with his fingertips. "You're a mystery to me, but you're more present than anyone I know."

"That's because I don't have a past. I can only exist in this moment." Out of uniform, Regis has become boyish, simple, a teasing edge behind his smile, his hair too short to be messy but still rumpled. "I'm not the only mystery around here."

He grins as if this pleases him.

I reach up and tug at a strand of his hair, not curly, but definitely not straight. "You're nothing like they think you are, are you? Does anyone truly know you?"

He blushes. "I'm just me," he says. "No mystery here."

My hand drops. This is categorically untrue. "What about her?" I point to the picture of the girl, the one I saw the first night I stayed here.

Surprise pulls him back.

"She's important to you."

"Tanya," he whispers. "That was her name."

"What happened to her?"

His eyes pinch together, unbearably sad. "We don't know."

I sit up on an elbow, stare at him.

"She disappeared many years ago. We were on a family camping trip. She wanted to walk over to the lake one morning before our parents were up, but I wanted to sleep longer. So, she got dressed and went alone. We never saw her again."

My lips part, disbelieving. "But the police—"

"Came and went. Did their level best. And closed the case once it had gone cold. There was no trace of her left. Nothing for them to go on. No one saw what happened, who took her. They dragged the lake, but it was clear. For years my mother swore Tanya was still alive. It's the only thing that kept her breathing. But Dad and I knew after the first few months that she was probably gone."

I rise and walk over to her picture, skate my fingers along the frame. Little flutters wing through my mind—rubber soles on a dirt road, the sun like yellow gossamer in the air, the blue truck rumbling up behind with the dented fender. They turn dark, sour, like ash as they drift away. Regis is right. She didn't live long. When I turn to him, he is watching me with big, tender eyes, unsure what I will tell him, if he wants to hear it. "She loved you very much," I say, choking back a tear. "And she never blamed you for it, so you should stop blaming yourself."

His face crumples, and he ducks away from me until he can school his features. I watch him, thinking this is why my family does what it does. For girls like Tanya. To stop the countless men in blue trucks with dented fenders shadowing little girls. To save someone as pure as Regis from such unbearable pain.

"I've never told anyone about her before," he says once I've returned to sit next to him on the floor. "Not about giving up on her after those first few months, somehow knowing she was gone, we were already too late."

"Not even Beth Ann?" I ask.

"No." He glances toward me. "I didn't take you for the jealous type."

I hug my knees to my chest. "You misunderstand. I'm curious. Not about her—about you. About why you hold back, even when it's unnecessary."

He rolls onto his back, stares at the ceiling. "Are you sure you weren't a shrink instead of a designer?"

I give him a playful shove.

His smile is nimble, a flash of teeth, but genuine. His hand wanders across his chest. "Beth Ann was nice. She was really nice."

"But?" I know one is coming.

He shrugs. "That's the problem. I don't know what was missing exactly. I never do. But I can feel everyone's expectations flung over me like a net. That I should marry, settle down. That someone like Beth Ann should be enough for me. What more could I possibly want? Especially up here. What do I expect?"

"What more *do* you want?" I question. His openness is startling. I'm not sure I've earned it.

He laughs. "I wish I knew. I just keep thinking I'll know it when I find it." His eyes meet mine, and for a second, they are so frank it's unsettling. He sits up and kisses me tenderly, then pulls away and says, "Why don't you want more? From me? *Than* me?"

I swallow. The ice is thinning, every step precarious. "I had more," I tell him finally, voice soft as a rabbit's foot. "It didn't agree with me."

He cocks his head, appraising, runs a knuckle under my chin. "Whoever he is, I don't like him."

It might be charming to someone else, but I don't need to enlist one man in my fight against another. I'm not looking for a hero. Regis knows that. I think he does. "Neither do I."

"But you must have," he suggests. "Once."

I clear my throat, sticky with emotion. How to explain the Henry I first met, to reconcile him with the Henry I left? The first is a man of culture. The second, not a man at all. "He was impressive in the beginning—brilliant, refined, successful. The complete opposite of the men I'd known growing up." I cringe as Gerald comes to mind—that collared velour shirt he always wore with the cigarette burns pocking the sleeves, cans of flat beer covering the coffee table. "I felt flattered by his attention. More than flattered. *Chosen.* It made me feel special to be on his arm."

"And later?" Regis asks.

I hug my knees closer, shrug once. "I found out he was just another bully."

He is compassionate, but not pitying. He doesn't scoop me up or wrap me in platitudes. He doesn't rush to make it right or alter my feelings. He just sits beside me, leaning back on his hands, a borderless land.

"I should get home," I tell him, rising to find my scattered clothes. Dawn will come, and Myrtle must find me in bed.

He pushes himself up and pulls on his underwear and pants, his T-shirt. I can't help but feel we look like mollusks redonning our shells, the pieces we have adapted to suit the world.

At the door, he stops me. "My sister . . . Did you really get that from touching her picture? That message?"

That and more, but the rest shouldn't live inside him, so I will carry it instead, beside the danger, the cruelty I have been forced to witness, felt firsthand, even delivered. "Yes."

"How?" he asks.

It is another question I can't answer. His sister's victimhood is my line to her, her abductor's memories like leaves scattered on the breeze—but to explain would be to go into secrets that aren't mine alone to share. Instead, I lay a hand over his on my arm and give him the truest, simplest answer I can. "Magic."

24

Autopsy

Of course, it is Regis who responds to Myrtle's call. I feel childish for not having anticipated it and twice damned for the role I've played in this calculated drama. Somehow, it seems more sinister with him here, less straightforward. I can barely look him in the face, our stolen hours in the night still creeping over my skin like lingering kisses. But this is Sheriff Brooks, not the Regis of last night, and there is a wary tilt to his chin, a quiet reserve that says this may not go down as smoothly as we'd hoped.

I feel a fervent and misplaced hope that he won't find the body. The proximity of Ed's death to the one in the café is enough on its own to make any law enforcement officer do a double take. There is no way to explain that I killed Ed out of kindness. In the harsh glare of the morning sun, I realize my questionably good deed may not go unpunished.

He stands outside the café with stiff shoulders, hiding his assumptions behind the mirrored rounds of his inscrutable sunglasses, a hand resting on each side of his belt. "You say you tried calling?"

"His phone is dead," Myrtle explains. She is presentable as ever, hair neatly plaited down her back, face scrubbed to a high shine. Even the whites of her eyes seem brighter, every inch of her polished. "It was still ringing last night. Maybe up until around midnight. I found Bart outside of my cabin this morning. That's when I figured I better call you."

"If he wasn't answering as late as midnight, why didn't you report this then?" he questions as I bite my lower lip. I resent that I can't see his eyes, as if he is deliberately keeping them from me.

Myrtle lets loose a mocking laugh. "Come on, Sheriff. You know Ed as well as I do. Man could drink himself into a ditch at night and be up bright and early for coffee come morning. There hasn't been a day that he didn't turn up at these café doors for opening since that time I found him sweating out a fever in his cabin three years ago."

I watch Regis press his lips together until the pink disappears. He believes her. Or at least he believes he *should* believe her, but something about it doesn't sit well with him. There is an under-current of suspicion that ripples off him in waves like a bad smell. "Which one of you saw him last?"

"I did." I step forward, hoping to ease Regis's doubts. I want to believe that what exists between us when there is no one around will protect me. That a trust has formed like a ridge of bone, linking us together. "He said he was going to take care of some downed limbs yesterday."

"Did you look for him in the woods?" He addresses this to Myrtle. The rebuff offends me, like spit in the face. I try to focus on the fact that the less I say, the better I feel.

"Wanted to," she tells him. "But you had my niece detained till well after dark. Didn't seem smart to wander out there on my own, what with this Strangler business going on."

"No," he agrees, checked. "Of course." He scans the woodland behind us, the measured oscillation of his face the only giveaway. I wonder if he expects to spot Ed there on the brink, like one of those pictures where you have to find the hidden images—*Do you see the mitten? The teapot?*—as if he's been there all along, just waiting for someone to bother looking. "Let me call in some help. We'll get out there and take a look. Probably sleeping it off under a tree somewhere."

Myrtle smiles, sweet as cream, as if she fully expects this to be true. "I'll put the coffee on," she says, throat raspy. "I'm sure he'll need it by the time you drag him back."

Regis heads toward his patrol car when Myrtle goes inside, leaving me standing there, a nonentity on the edge of their conversation. Impulsively, I reach out to stop him. "Wait."

I don't know what I intend to say. I can't stand the thought of Ed's body lying out there during this charade, as if he is refuse dropped on the ground, forgotten like last year's leaf fall. I can't tell Regis anything of substance, but maybe I can at least point him in the right direction. I also just want him to see me.

He stops, face still obscured by the sunglasses.

"Can you take those off?"

He slides them from his nose, and when his eyes meet mine, they are as apprehensive as a stray cat backed into a corner. I almost stumble over the unexpectedness of it. "You got something to add, Ms. Lee?"

I clear my throat, unsure of the words trying to fill it. "Regis?" *It's me,* I want to say, but it's not my voice he's familiar with, it's my body.

The edge of his gaze softens, and he drops it, as if he can't bear to look at me as a man and not a cop. "I'm on duty, Acacia," he says flatly.

"Right." I take a step away, regroup. "I just . . . I saw him enter the forest there, beside that tamarack tree." I point to the stubby conifer clad in its shaggy, yellowing coat of needles at the edge of the forest.

He follows my finger, a flicker of some unexpressed emotion glancing his jaw. "Thanks. I'll remember that."

I watch him walk away to radio in for backup, wishing I could be anywhere but here when they haul Ed's body out.

He waits in the car until two other officers arrive. They huddle on the pavement as he debriefs them, the occasional glimpse toward the café breaking their cloister. Eventually, they dismantle at some mysterious signal and move in unison toward the back of the property, vanishing into the thicket behind the cabins.

Myrtle ignores her cardinal rule and keeps Bart in the café for a change, where he lies under one of the tables, watching the door like Ed will step through it at any moment. I bus the tables and wipe the windows with protracted fastidiousness, squinting through bubbly streaks for some sign of what's happening. When the glass is clean enough to disappear—a sure trap for the local birds—I turn my attention to refilling all the condiments and saltshakers, hands trembling the whole time, spilling more grains than I contain.

Myrtle is cooking breakfast as if nothing is happening—a sausage and egg casserole—as if she expects Ed to return, hungover and famished, with Terry and Amos in tow. She catches me flubbing the salt and admonishes, "Steady, Piers. It's all downhill from here. Maybe leave the more dexterous tasks for another day, hmm?"

I have an abrupt desire to take up smoking or knitting, anything to keep my hands occupied. The sole guest from cabin seven comes in for coffee and a bit of toast, as does the old guy who runs the Drunken Moose—a *Bill* somebody. I don't need the extra eyes—their presence makes me clumsier—but the distraction of a full crowd is sorely missed. When I run out of things to busy myself with in the café, I grab the caddy of cleaning supplies and head out to work in the bathroom. I've never been so preoccupied with porcelain.

About an hour later, Regis leans in the door. "Can you step outside for a minute?"

His hat blocks the light, casting me in dismal gray. I stand, an overworked sponge gripped in one hand, and meet his eyes. They lack the usual sincerity I have come to admire. "Sure." I strip off my cleaning gloves. "Be right there."

He nods and steps away, letting the sun back in.

I peek at myself in the mirror, a disheveled mess of flyaways and unbuttoned sleeves, my cheeks a ruddy tone from the chill and zealous scrubbing. I'd put myself together but there's no time, and it'd only make me look more obvious. The best I can do is button my cuffs as I step outside.

Myrtle is already waiting.

Regis exhales, keeping his eyes on the ground, a thumb hooked in the front of his belt. "I have some bad news, ladies."

Myrtle uncrosses her arms, pretend shock stealing across her expression like ice forming on the water.

He looks at me, then her. His reluctance is palpable, a watershed of resistance. When the words come, they are heavy with implication. "We found Ed."

"You did?" Myrtle places a hand over her heart.

"We were too late." He blinks slowly, lips sucked in. "He'd already passed."

She lowers her gaze like a shade being drawn, a vision of misfortune sinking in, fingers white-knuckled.

"I don't understand," I tell him, following her lead. "He was fine when I saw him yesterday."

He draws a long breath. "Looks like an animal attack."

"An animal?" I glance to the trees, my unease playing as alarm. "What kind of animal?"

He shrugs. "Hard to say. Bear, maybe. Or moose. The coroner will be able to tell. In any case, I'd stay out of these woods for a while."

I open my mouth to breathe like a cat in shock. *Coroner* is not a word we were hoping to hear.

"Is that necessary?" Myrtle speaks up. "He's got no one but us. I hate to see him sliced up over semantics."

Regis's nostrils flare like he's picking up a scent trail. "Not semantics, Myrtle. Not when we're dealing with the safety of this community. It's important to identify what kind of animal did this so we can be sure it doesn't happen again. Can't go out there shooting at anything we see. We need to be certain."

The notion of guns so soon after last night causes me to rock back on my heels. "I'm confused. Who said anything about shooting?"

Regis looks at me as Myrtle frowns. "They may want to put it down," she tells me. "If a bear did this."

My stomach drops. Another life lost on my account. I can't abide it. "Surely that isn't necessary?"

"It's my property," Myrtle argues. "And I'd just as soon leave it be. Can't have you all out here scaring off my customers with gunshots."

"I'm afraid that's not your decision to make, Myrtle. I've got the ME on the way. They'll haul him out and get him down to the morgue. Meanwhile, keep people out of the forest. No spontaneous hikes today, you got it?" He squares his shoulders and tilts his head back, looking down at her. There's no room to protest. He's invoking the full mantle of his authority.

It doesn't sit well with my aunt. "You don't have to tell me twice," she says before stomping back into the café, swinging the door open and closed a little too hard.

I swallow as he regards her, narrowing his gaze. His scrutiny stings. "You'll have to excuse her. She loved Ed like a brother. Anger is just her version of tears."

His gaze slides to mine. "Keep an eye on her," he says before walking away.

The words fill me with an ominous buzz, like stinging insects. They ring inside my head the rest of the day. As I slop mayonnaise onto sandwiches and pour glasses of water and empty the café dishwasher, even as I lean against the sloping metal roof of the A-frame, trying to grab a breath. *Keep an eye on her* punctuates my every move like the tempo of a metronome. I catch myself stealing glances at her throughout the day. It's not until dusk when they finally roll a stretcher out of the woods, the white sheet draped over it rising and falling with Ed's contours, that I realize it's not his words that have unsettled me, but his tone when saying them—clipped, flat, ringed not with concern but command.

Keep an eye on her.

Regis isn't worried *for* Aunt Myrtle. He's worried because of her.

MORE THAN TWENTY-FOUR hours pass without a word. Somewhere they have Ed's body on a steel table in a cold room, one of those scales hanging over it like you see in the produce department. He will be inventoried like back stock, every piece accounted for. Like it or not, I am also in that room. I wonder how I'll be accounted for—in the necrotic liver tissue, the engorged veins, the mess of internal bleeding? The anticipation is unbearable, a slow, tortuous grind that wears away at me like an acid dip. I am lowered inch by excruciating inch into the vat, unable to either grease or stick the gears.

Myrtle is exceptionally quiet. She avoids my questions, throwing herself into cooking like we're expecting a state convention to descend on us. She bakes muffins in the morning and fries up grilled cheeses for lunch, with real home fries on the side. As if one casserole isn't enough, she makes two for dinner—one with chicken, another with pike. She follows that with a chocolate silk pie and a giant bowl of pistachio pudding. All washed down with pitcher after pitcher of tea, even though we're past the summer months when people ask for it.

Like a spell, her efforts seem to conjure diners from all over, wafting in on the scent of her latest creation. The café fills up by ten in the morning and stays full the whole day through. Non-stop serving, bussing, and cleaning being the one small mercy I'm afforded. Myrtle nestles into the steady flow of company like an owl in the hollow of a tree, gabbing and laughing, surrounding herself with a fortress of people.

It's practically closing when Regis turns back up, half our tables still full of stragglers. Terry and Amos are arguing over a game of Scrabble, washing their sorrows over Ed down with their second slice of pie. Myrtle is ensconced behind the bar, mixing fresh waffle batter for the morning. If Regis is surprised at the bustle, he doesn't show it. Thankfully, he's no longer wearing those aggravating sunglasses, and his hat's been left on the dash of his car. He catches my eye as I lean down to stack a bunch of plates from a table that was just vacated. But before he can get to me, Myrtle hollers, "Want some pie, Sheriff? We're feasting in Ed's honor today."

He pauses as if she's seized him and he is somewhere he doesn't belong. Recovering quickly, he pushes his chin out. "I'm all right, thanks."

She nods as if it's no skin off her nose, but her eyes are narrowed to dashes above her cheeks, the look of a woman playing a dangerous game she believes she's winning.

But Regis is not easily taken in, and I'm not sure her confidence is warranted. I suddenly understand the pull of customers, the gobs of food, the exaggerated laugh at someone's joke. It is a tableau, a stage set, everyone a prop that proclaims her status in the community, their love for her—her innocence. It strikes me as both brilliant and foolish. The attention it draws to her will only engage his obstinacy. There is a stubborn lift to his lip already.

When he reaches me, he bends to my ear. "Can we talk?"

I want to melt where I stand. Has the frost of the day before shifted? But when I brush past him toward the door, he shrinks away, my touch something he fears. Like a subluxated rib, something has slid quietly out of joint between us. I feel the ache of it between my shoulder blades, the misplaced pressure, the decreased range of motion.

The raucous night is an improvement over the noise in the café, less grating, the stirring of nocturnal creatures growing on me like an overplayed melody. I drag him from view around to the side where the slant of the roof blocks out the motel lights. We wash monotone as night swallows us.

"Is everything okay?" I ask when he doesn't immediately start talking. I suddenly wish I had a necklace on, something with a thin chain and a pendant I could fiddle with. I don't know what to do with my hands.

"I got the autopsy report," he tells me.

"So soon?"

"It's preliminary. The full report will take some weeks to come out, but they shared their findings with me. It's standard procedure."

"Oh." I stand there, not knowing quite how to respond. When he doesn't go on, I ask, "And?"

His face is pinched, eyes darting away. "I shouldn't be talking to you about this, but . . ." When he meets my eyes finally, he looks sad, sadder than I've ever seen a man look. "I don't know what it is about you. I can't seem to help myself. I want to protect you so badly."

"Protect me? From what?"

"I care about you," he says now, as if it comes as a surprise, like ants in the sugar jar. He sighs, the sound of it heavy between us, weighted. "It's not good, Acacia."

My heart rate picks up, stuttering into overdrive. I wipe my palms on my thighs. "Was it a bear, then? Should we be concerned?"

He sighs again, as if he expected this but still hoped for more. "A moose, but that's not what I mean."

I clear my throat, try and hide the anxiety shooting through me like a drug. "It's not?"

His hands go to his hips, elbows out, a wall I cannot breech. "The coroner found traces of orellanine toxin in his bloodstream, and amatoxins. Do you understand what I'm telling you? *Poison,* Acacia. Mushrooms. Another amanita plus something else."

I deflate but am careful not to collapse in front of him. "Is that what k-killed him?"

"That's not the point," he tells me. I feel like a mouse in a very small field with a very large cat. There is nowhere to hide.

"I see," I say, stalling. "How do they think he got—"

"Oh, come off it," he barks, swearing at me. He takes a few steps away, hangs his head, pinching the bridge of his nose, and walks back. His lips barely move as he says, "I don't know what you two are playing at. But since you got here, we've had two deaths and two mushroom poisonings inside of a week. And this isn't the first time someone has died of suspicious causes around here. My first year in the department, we found a young man at a campground, lifeless. His heart had stopped the night before, and his blood was chock full of amanitins—deadly amatoxin compounds. Coroner couldn't make heads or tails of it. Last place he was seen alive was this very café. At the time, I believed your aunt when she said he wasn't acting right when he came in. Said he seemed to be high on something. We wrote it off as a case of mistaken identity. Boy was probably looking for psychedelic mushrooms and got confused, especially if he was already on something." Regis glares at me. "He was twenty-one, Acacia. Twenty-one years old."

I can't imagine Myrtle taking a life that young, but how much do I really know about the venery? About Myrtle's history? I scrabble for words, but none come.

"Despite my best instincts and the obligations of my job, I'm out here telling you this because . . . because . . ."

I widen my eyes and cross my arms. "Because?"

"Because you matter to me, and I don't want you to go down for her . . . *deeds.*"

"What exactly are you implying about my family, Regis?" My eyes narrow, and I can practically feel them blazing with green fire.

He leans in. "You told me you were here to study botany. Is that true?"

"Yes," I tell him, refusing to look away. If I don't stand by my story, he will never believe another word I say.

"Well, then you better start interviewing attorneys. Because if I go any further with this, you are in a heap of legal trouble. Is that clear?"

Fear crests over into anger, years of being told who I am, who I should be. It froths inside me, threatening to spew. I came here for freedom, independence, a chance to live beyond the reach of Henry's control and bloodlust, but between the venery and this, I am starting to wish I'd never made it out of that river. "Perfectly."

This should be the point where he stalks off unburdened of the responsibility of me, his message delivered, but he doesn't. He just stands there, like he can't believe what he's hearing. After a second, I realize he's waiting for me to say more, anything that might absolve us of what his instincts are telling him we're guilty of. His chest heaves, every breath a prayer that I can make this right.

I take a step toward him. "What's clear, Sheriff Brooks, is that you think I not only slipped toxic amounts of poisonous mushroom into a stranger's coffee for no apparent reason other than the satisfaction of watching him die a brutal, grotesque death in front of a room full of my aunt's customers—in an amount that would be physically impossible to disguise in eight ounces of liquid even if it is that bitter swill Myrtle serves for coffee, I might add, *and* at a time that would render his symptoms remarkably, improbably swift—but that I then turned around and did the same thing to a man I considered a friend, who showed me nothing but kindness, who was old and vulnerable and not a threat to anyone. In the middle of the woods, likely at night no less, while a serial killer stalks women in the area and we have been repeatedly warned to stay indoors after dark."

His jaw grinds even as his lips part, so that he looks like a cow chewing cud. A series of rapid blinks attack his eyes, lashes wrestling for dominance, but he is utterly unable to respond.

I step toward him again so that I am only inches from his face. I want this part to sink in. I want him to know he has lost. Myrtle would be proud. "Good luck making that fairy tale stick in any court of law from here to the Mexico border."

He closes his mouth and the color drains from his face, turning him a wan, sickly blue in the dark.

"You can think whatever you want, *Sheriff.* But that doesn't change the truth." I step back and give him an icy once-over. "Maybe they were right about you. Maybe you're terrified of commitment after all."

I stalk back inside, leaving him to his presumptions, the callous night, and the ugly pall of defeat.

25

Delivery

"Sit!" I command Myrtle and Bart as we enter the cabin. I whirl around to be sure there is no one slinking in the darkness before I close the cabin door, making sure to lock the deadbolt. When I clomp to the living room, I see they have taken my command to heart. She is poised in the armchair like a scolded child; he rests on his haunches beside her, cowering.

"What's the matter?" She watches me start to pace, eyes gliding left to right and back. "What'd he say to you to get you so shook up, our morally superior sheriff?"

I round on her. "Regis is not the enemy here, Myrtle. You better stop thinking that way if you want keep your little outpost in the woods for the venery."

Her eyes widen, cheeks suddenly pale. She looks older, smaller, as if she has been shrinking day by day. My words have rattled her. "What are you talking about?"

I sigh. "The autopsy. He got Ed's autopsy results."

"And?" She leans forward, fingers clutching the rounded arms of the chair as if she might launch herself at me.

"And they found the amatoxins in his system. He *knows*, Myrtle. He's been onto you for a long time, I suspect. He's been watching you. After the man in the café and now this . . . Well, he's put two and two together. And it adds up to you and me." I feel suddenly dizzy and squat down, bringing my hands in front of my face as I try to breathe.

She sits back in the chair, thinking. "They can't link the ama-toxins to us. He's got nothing."

"They found Ed on *your* property! That's something."

"Circumstantial," she quips. "Why would I kill Ed? Everyone in this town knows I loved that man. He's family. I depended on him. It would be shooting myself in the foot. He wouldn't be able to rustle up a single character witness against me."

I fall back on my rear and drape my arms over my knees, look-ing up at her. "Even if he can't prove it in court, this should scare you. He's onto you, and he's waiting for you to slip up. Somewhere there is a file with your name on it. Don't you get that? It's only a matter of time. You can't stay here."

"Like hell I can't stay here!" she bellows. "I ain't leaving. I was here before that man was born. This is my town, not his."

I rub my hands briskly over my face. "This was a mistake. We should have let him die naturally."

Her eyes narrow, lips puckering around her wrath. "Leave that man to suffer, to die cold and alone in a puddle of his own piss and blood all because Sheriff Busybody has a bug up his ass?"

I stare up at her, weary.

"Even if I wanted to, I couldn't have left him out there. The cycle wouldn't have let me."

"Yeah, but I'm the one who killed him. So, you didn't fulfill your cycle anyway." All the food she prepared today comes back to me—the gooey casseroles and creamy pudding, the skillet po-tatoes with onions. What else did she put in those dishes? I shud-der, fearful. "What have you done?"

Her eyes glance to the vacant firebox, a black hole in the room.

"Myrtle . . . what have you done?"

When they slowly drag to meet mine, her eyes are proud and contrary. They will not bow down or apologize. "Never you mind. It's a little trick I learned a long time ago from my mother, a way to spread the toxin out over many doses to many people when you need to unload without a mark. The allure draws 'em in by the handful."

I jump to my feet. "Are you kidding me? All those people in there tonight? Are they gonna die?"

"Sit down," she demands. "No one is dying tonight. I fed on a blend, remember? To draw out the poison. Dilute that between so many servings of food and drink distributed to so many people, and the worst you can expect is a high demand on the town plumbing."

"I don't understand. I thought you said no bane witch has ever spared a mark?"

"They haven't," she confirms. "But over many centuries there have been a few near misses. Marks who died before the hunt was over, of natural causes or some unforeseeable mishap. Marks who suffered a fatal accident in the pursuit, usually because the witch bungled it, ending up in a physical fight for her life, using whatever was available to her. We're not perfect, Piers. This is not a science. It's magic. And sometimes magic is messy."

My brow rumples. It sounds like the out my mother was looking for her entire life. "Why couldn't we just do that then? Someone like my mom at least, who wanted a murder-free life?"

Myrtle chuckles, reaches into a candy dish and pops a peppermint into her mouth. "Ah, see, that's the rub. It only works once. I mean, you can employ it more than once in your life, but not in succession. The next time I feed, were I to try it again, the consequences would be dire. We're talking about fay magic, Piers. The Aos Sí. The nøkken. The People of the Threshold. The Hidden Ones. There isn't a loophole, so don't go searching for one. They're tricksters, you understand? They think of everything before you can even blink an eye. They made us what we are. Embrace it."

"I'm trying," I spit out, but even I hear the whine in my voice. "It's a little hard with Regis telling me stories about you killing men as young as twenty-one years of age. I thought we weren't supposed to be savages. I thought killing an innocent was our highest crime. We're supposed to operate by a code!"

She draws her hair over a shoulder, the long line of her neck like a column of marble, an exclamation point. "Yes, I remember him well."

"So, you admit it?" I fume. "You did kill him. How could you? He's practically a child."

Her ire is immediate. It stings my eyes like a flash burn. "That *boy* you speak of had been raping his two younger sisters since the age of fifteen. The eldest girl was nine when he started, but the youngest was only three. He wasn't sorry or even ashamed. He liked it. He liked it so much that he began raping the girl down the street, a seven-year-old whose mother dropped her off from time to time for babysitting. By the time he made it up here, he'd already abducted and raped two other young girls, one of whom died from a fatal infection of injuries sustained in his assault."

I swallow my blame. I should have known better. Regis didn't know the full story. How could he?

"They come in all shapes and sizes, Piers—the monsters we fight, the demons. All ages. All ethnicities. From all walks of life. But if you think for one second that I enjoyed stealing the many years he had left, then you don't know me, and you may as well walk out that door right now. I fed for two weeks before I found the courage to do it. Two weeks wrestling with my own conscience, knowing that if I didn't, more little girls would lose their innocence, their security, even their lives. So, you tell me, who should I have chosen, him or them?"

I lower my gaze. "So, what do we do now?"

Her lips purse as she draws a deep breath. "We wait."

When I glance at her, she elaborates.

"We let him sweat it out, the sheriff. Let him think what he wants but stay out of his way. Whatever was between you two— don't bother denying it, I have eyes, you know—it ends now. We'll tell the venery Ed was my doing. That way, if Brooks does come for us, they'll blame me. You can't afford any more heat. With any luck, my cycle won't begin again for some months, maybe even a year or more. Gives me time to sort my next move. But you have your mark, the Strangler. We'll focus on sourcing new material for your feed. No more mushrooms."

My mind flickers to her shelves in the bunker, lined with jar after jar of toxic herb, flower, berry, and root. "There should be something suitable in your hideout, right? You said I had a gift for concentration. Surely anything you have on hand would work. They can't all be mushrooms, can they?"

She looks worried, and that worries me. "No, they aren't all mushrooms. But we're suspects now. I loathe the thought of using anything that grows naturally within a thousand square miles with your boyfriend so hot and bothered to put one or both of us behind bars."

"He's just doing his job," I defend. "You have to consider what this looks like from the outside. He's sworn to protect his community."

"So am I!" she insists bitterly.

"I know that, but he doesn't. How could he? You can't expect him to just take your word for it."

She rolls her eyes, lips tight. "Well, in any case, maybe I can get something carried in."

"Carried in?" A shipping trail of toxic plant material sounds like a bad idea.

"Poisonous vegetation from a different region, hand delivered by another bane witch. It's something we do from time to time for one another, inside and *outside* of the venery."

"Outside of the venery? You mean—"

"A separate venery, another family of bane witches. I told you before, we aren't the only ones of our kind."

My mind spins as it takes this in, dissects it, tucks it away in aptly labeled boxes. "You said the only other venery in North America died out years ago."

"And so they did," she tells me. "But there are two in France, one in Italy, and another in Barcelona. Maybe as many as three in South America—Venezuela, Brazil, and Ecuador—but we lost communication with the Quito clan over fifteen years ago, so who can say anymore? And at least one more, vast as I understand it, in Eastern Europe, spread over several countries—Hungary, Romania, Bulgaria, and who knows where else by now."

My skin erupts in chills, dotting with goose bumps as the numbers increase. How many lives have we taken? How many more have we saved? "That many?"

Myrtle smiles, lips curving like a sickle. "Did you think there was only one angry, vengeful woman in history? Only one fée in the world, disguising herself as a hag, a woman of no consequence? Haven't you learned anything since you came here, dear? Look around. The world is not what you think it is. It never was. There are more things hidden among the spheres than you or I could ever name. Start getting used to it."

I HEAR HER on the phone with Donna, Bella's daughter, the next morning. "Do you think I wanted to do it? I didn't know it was him until the final moments. I did what I had to—what my magic was calling me to do."

She is silent for a moment, listening. Her face scrunches up, prickly with irritation. "Oh, don't give me that, Donna. We've been over this. I know mercy killings aren't everyone's cup of tea, but I don't make the magic. I didn't create the cycle. We don't set the rules, we just follow them. Remember? Take it up with our creatrix if you're so sore about it."

After a pause, her mouth drops. "Of course I realize it was a risk! You think I'm stupid? What choice did I have? I'd been feeding for days. And heaven knows he's the last man alive I'd want to take. He meant something to me. But the magic already knew. It determined who my mark was, whether you or I or anyone else likes it."

She nods as she listens, her face falling a little. "I couldn't add to his suffering. I made a snap decision. Maybe it was the wrong one, but it's done now. And it won't happen again. You can be assured of that."

Her eyes roll and her hand flops. "No, Piers had nothing to do with it. She wasn't even here. Her hunt has begun. She was chasing her own mark."

She nods impatiently. "Yes, yes. The one I told you about. It's as we thought. Fitting, I suppose. But it will be tricky, even with her power. He's no small fish—he's dangerous—and she has so little proper experience yet."

A pause followed by an audible inhale. "Well, of course they're all dangerous. Don't you think I know what we do? I just meant that he's *unique.* Her class will be challenging. She'll need support. That's why I was calling you, in fact."

She waits, pulls the phone away from her ear a minute. "We'll need a hand delivery. We can't rely on mushrooms with that sheriff breathing down our necks. It's about as obvious as a fingerprint at this point. I don't even want to get into our stores. If it grows on this continent, that sheriff will trace it back to us somehow. We need something from farther afield. Something they wouldn't even know to look for."

Deep breath in, slow breath out. "I don't know what I'm going to do later. Let's just focus on what's right in front of us. The deadline wasn't my idea, so don't get testy with me. She couldn't possibly meet it like this without one."

Finally, the sag of relief washes over her. "No, I think Barcelona. It's as good a place to start as any. Paris is so rigid. And those arum leaves Bryony brought us from Venice a few years back were old. Misty had to eat gobs of them. Of course, some manchineel would do nicely. But do you still have a contact for Venezuela?"

She nods emphatically. "Uh-huh, uh-huh. Okay, keep me posted. I'd send her on a scouting holiday, but I think he'd notice and then where would we be?"

She takes a deep cleansing breath. "Thank you, Donna. Hunt well."

She hangs up the phone and stares into space, lost in a mesh of thoughts, eyes watering as the seconds tick by without a blink.

Finally, she says, "Piers, stop hiding. If you have a question, come ask it."

I step gingerly into the room. "I couldn't help but overhear."

"It's okay," she tells me. "There are no secrets in the venery. You can eavesdrop all you want." Her eyes meet mine. "You're beautiful; do you know that? So like your mother. She positively glowed when she was younger, all that soft yellow hair and flawless skin. Her eyes were big and round as headlights. Once she locked Patrick in them, he didn't stand a chance, poor man. I know you're well over thirty, but you look like a child standing there. At least to me."

I don't feel like a child, I feel like a crone in a fawn's body. But it's nice to be regarded as one, to be the recipient of maternal affection. Myrtle would have made an incredible mother. What a shame that she couldn't raise her own son.

"It'll all be fine," she declares. "Donna is reaching out to our international contacts now to get something potent carried in for you. She understands what's at stake."

"Okay."

It's bright out this morning. Frost laces the windowpanes, and the chill air seeps into the room, drying out the cabin. Regis said the fall colors will be upon us in a week or two, autumn leaves littering the forest floor like confetti. I hope I have the Strangler by then. Once the snow and ice set in, my chances will wane to nothing. If I didn't have the venery riding me, I could wait out the freeze, get him in the thaw. But they won't wait that long. And neither will he. He will be gone by the first true snowfall, if his survival instincts override my allure. Off to find a place where he can stalk and kill without the natural elements getting in his way. Everything is riding on the next few weeks.

We walk over to the café together to open it up. Myrtle plugs in the waffle iron and pours our coffee, while I straighten the tables. We've barely had a chance to set the cereal boxes out when Terry bursts through the front door.

"Did you hear?" he asks, his gaze bouncing between us.

"Hear?" Myrtle lowers the dish towel she's holding to the counter. "Hear what?"

"It's the Saranac Strangler," he says, breathless as if he ran the whole way. "He's killed again."

Myrtle turns to me, a look of betrayal in her eyes. Can't believe I didn't see it coming. Neither can I. Killing Ed must have interrupted my connection to the Strangler, crossed marks so to speak, because I never felt or saw this looming. I thought I had more time. That, or else he's just that good. Either way, this is bad.

"Who?" she asks Terry.

He gulps air and sidles up to the bar. "Kathy Miller—Bill's daughter."

"Yeah, I know her," Myrtle confirms. Her eyes slide over me, a nervous calculation in them.

"Daughter?" I ask, eyes narrowing on Terry. "How old was she?"

He peers at me as if he's taking his first real good look. "Not so young. About your age in fact. Your height, too. Same hair color. Same build. Same fair skin. Could almost pass for you come to think of it. Heck, you probably even wear the same shoe size!"

My stomach rolls, threatening to eject my morning coffee.

"We get it, Terry," Myrtle snaps. "When did it happen?"

"Last night," he tells us. "In the parking lot of the Drunken Moose."

26

Feather

Kathy is gone, bagged and loaded, headed to the coroner's office for postmortem, but her killer is not. I'd be lying if I said I wanted to get here in time to see her discarded on the corroded concrete, face ashen and still as stone, maybe not so different from my own. But I see her anyway, as *he* did, eyes fading to a lifeless horizon, a heap of parts.

He's still here—the Saranac Strangler—in the earth, in the air, in the weeds that grow in the cracks of the parking lot. And he's hungry. His appetite has doubled, tripled in the last few weeks, and he can't understand why. It unnerves him, makes him feel out of control. And that makes him angry. Kathy's death was more violent than the rest, more brutal. I see it play behind my eyes in cinematic flashes. He didn't stop squeezing until the skin around her throat began to split and her eyes bulged from their sockets like balloons. Her lungs are swimming in fluid, her skin freckled with hemorrhages. And still, he is not satiated. The craving is overpowering him. He thinks that makes him weak, but it only makes him more dangerous.

In answer, my own cravings begin to kick in, a tickle at the back of the throat, the memory of destroying angel on my tongue, the bitter spores of yellow wart. It's time for me to feed. He's so close, so present, it could be any day, any moment, when we collide.

Police tape wraps the back lot, strung between the building, a patrol car, and a couple of traffic barrels they've set up. I look for the little plastic stands used to mark evidence, but there aren't any.

Which means our Strangler, true to form, left this scene as clean as the last. I skirt the edge of the yellow tape, scanning the ground, the cars, the back wall of the Drunken Moose with its pitiful gray siding, and scrutinize my surroundings, examining the faces of everyone nearby.

There are a few curious onlookers—a woman and two men—too unabashed to realize how inappropriate their presence is. The woman meets my eyes, impassive. Her nylon jacket has faded from a deep cranberry to a sickly lavender over the years, and the coffee-stain of her boots has been scuffed tan on the toe. She's a nosy resident, nothing more. I break eye contact with her and study the nearest male—in his seventies and leaning on a quad cane, too old to be a threat. The second man is wearing a thermal under his T-shirt and a stupid grin across his face. He's still in his twenties. This is probably the most exciting thing to happen in his hometown for years. He doesn't have enough life experience to know he's making a spectacle of himself.

If the Strangler is still nearby like I believe, then he's not letting himself be seen.

I stare at the concrete and think, *this* is what Henry was becoming. *This* is what he wanted more than anything. Who will he asphyxiate now that I have gone if my plan fails? What woman will suffer Kathy's fate, the one meant for me? What a disservice I have done the world to kill myself and leave him alive.

"Acacia?"

I look up and see Regis walking toward me from the other side of the police tape.

"What are you doing here?" he asks.

I lift a shoulder. "I was drawn."

He glances behind him where an officer is snapping pictures of the ground.

"I didn't know if you'd be here," I tell him.

"Crow Lake is very small," he says. "Makes more sense for them to contract with us than maintain their own police force."

I should have realized as much, especially with all his trips to the café. But Myrtle's place is at the edge of town. The Drunken Moose, however, is located squarely in the center of it. It's another departure for our killer. He's closing in.

"You shouldn't be here," he tells me. His lips depress into a thin line behind his sandy facial hair. His eyes remain wary.

"Shouldn't I?" This is a prime opportunity for me to collect as much information on our common foe as possible, while the scene is fresh. He had to know I would come.

His head dips, eyes cast down. "Look, about last night—"

"Don't," I tell him before he can go on. I don't blame him, knowing what I do, what he doesn't. It sits at the surface, ready to tumble out of me, the truth. For a second, I think it might. My mouth opens, lips poised, tongue stiff with it, and his eyes are on mine, searching, waiting. I bite it back. It's impossible. Why would he ever believe me? And yet, there is something between us already, an unspoken understanding, a yoke of intuition. "I know how it looks from where you stand, but I promise you, Aunt Myrtle and I—we're not the enemy here. We're on *your* side."

He hangs his head, then lifts it to cut through me with those impossibly gray eyes. The officer behind him calls his name and he waves over a shoulder. Turning back to me, he adds sadly, "You should go."

I cross my arms, annoyed to be shut out when we both know I could tell him more about this murder than any of his officers could. "I hear she looked like me, the victim."

Irritation flashes across his face. "Who told you that?"

"Terry."

He rolls his eyes. Everyone knows Terry can't keep his mouth shut to save his life. "Maybe a little," he says impartially. "Same age. Same coloring. Similar hair. But it's coincidence. You have nothing to worry about."

I have plenty to worry about. "We all have something that keeps us up at night." The words are so loaded they drop like bullets. I hope he understands. I *need* him to understand. We are hunting the same person.

His eyes are penetrating. I can feel the pressure building in his chest, his hands, creeping up his neck. "I guess we do."

"I'll go," I finally say. "But I'll be back tonight, after your officers are done here."

He sighs. "It's not safe. Especially so soon."

I sharpen my gaze on his. "One A.M. See you then?"

His nostrils flare, and his Adam's apple bobs against the restraint of his throat. There're so many things he wants to say to me, all fighting to get out at once. "Miss Lee," he says instead, dipping his chin.

"Sheriff." I turn and walk away.

A STING SHARPENS the midnight air, already brisk by day. I glance around, make sure no one is looking, and duck easily beneath the police tape. The Drunken Moose will stay closed tonight, but by tomorrow those barstools will be topped with denim-clad rear ends, the lights over the pool table giving off that amber glow, the buffoonish chatter of men like Terry drowning out the crickets outside. This is my only chance.

I kick at a pebble, shuffling my feet as I walk, so I don't overlook anything. The soft light of my phone illuminates a tiny circle around my feet and nothing more. I'd use the flashlight, but I don't want to alert anyone to my presence. I don't know what I'm looking for. I only know that I don't believe our resident serial killer truly leaves nothing behind. Maybe the sheriff's department thinks that, but it's only because they don't know what to look for. They're trying to find the usual suspects, the typical evidence one might find at a murder scene like this—hair, semen, a broken fingernail, clothing fibers. But our Strangler isn't typical. His cleanliness has made them complacent, too willing to accept that he will have outsmarted them. But he's too controlling to leave nothing behind. The places where he kills belong to him. He will mark them as such, somehow. Just not in a way a cop would notice. I know because I know Henry.

Shortly after we moved into the new house and his mother died, I took on the role of designer for our space. I used all the professional skill at my disposal to perform the job I had excelled at for years for us as a couple. I wanted to impress him, to show him my work carried a quiet importance. Maybe not the obvious prowess of an engineer, but it was more than the frivolous, superficial "hobby" he'd deemed it. Spaces impact us, define us even. Who we become inside them is an art I had mastered manipulating. I took pride in that, in the way I lingered at the edges of the rooms I designed, influencing their occupants. I thought if I could do the job with enough splendor, he would *see* me, love me again, that he would return to the man I first met.

But I was wrong.

They were small, the things out of place. I noticed the first one on a shelf in our living room—a bronze paperweight, pre-mid-century, smaller than my hand and in the shape of a naked woman. She was on her back, legs spread, knees up. Tiny breasts marked her chest, and a slit ran between her legs. The patina was thick, and she was crudely formed but a collectible, nonetheless. When I asked him about it, he said casually, "Don't be invidious, Piers. It doesn't suit you." But his eyes were ice chips.

A few days later, I found the banana salt and pepper shakers in the kitchen. Vintage ceramic and completely out of place, they stared me down as I stood at the gas range, stirring the spaghetti sauce. This time, I didn't ask any questions. When he said, "Let's eat at the bar," I sat beside him, both of us facing the counter where they rested, shiny and golden, centered in our view.

It went on like that for days, one item after another, like a strange game of hide-and-seek. There was the melting desk clock that turned up in the study, a Salvador Dalí wannabe. And the soap dispenser shaped like a rubber ducky in the guest bathroom. And the garden statue of a toad that appeared in the garage. At first, I didn't understand. They were harmless enough, but there was something sinister in the way he placed them one by one, drawing it out, never mentioning them. Henry was not the sort of man to want a duck soap dispenser or banana salt and pepper shakers. It was over a week later that I realized what the message was—he was mocking me. My work, the pride I'd taken in carefully curating our home. It was a joke to him.

And he was reclaiming the space as his, despite my presence in the design, daring me to remove what he'd placed there, reminding me who was in charge. Soon I began to find them in my own personal space, and they got darker—less overtly funny, more threatening. The bullet-shaped lighter on my nightstand beside my favorite candle. The coffin decal on my bathroom mirror. But the worst and final one was in my closet. A palm-sized windup skull. It went off on its own one afternoon when I was folding sweaters, nearly scaring me out of my skin. I snatched it down from the shelf where it was perched and threw it into the bathroom trash. The next day, it was there again, staring at me with gaping sockets and hideous, happy teeth.

So, I know, standing here in the dark as I am now, that the Saranac Strangler has left something behind. Something only I will recognize. Because, like Henry, he believes he is in charge, and though he must remain hidden, he desperately wants everyone else to know it, too.

The light of my phone pours over two small stains on the concrete, rust in color, opaque, like liquid brick. It's her blood—Kathy's—a little piece of her here. I want to bend down and set my finger atop one, feel her last moments, the fear coursing through her. But it's not her I'm after. The dark presses in on me, squeezing. I feel it washing down my throat, pricking my eyes. He is in it, the dark. If I breathe in, he'll slide into me like a spirit, take possession.

The hunger gurgles through my abdomen, nips at my ribs, insistent as a puppy. It doesn't want me to be caught unawares. It is growing inside me, the appetite for death; I won't be able to resist it much longer. I shouldn't, even if I am able. It's only the thought of Regis's lips on mine, his skin sticking to me on his living room floor, that holds me back now.

I shine my phone out, drawing a line with the light from my feet to the edge of the lot. And then I see it, just beyond the pavement. It is sticking up from the dirt at an angle like a tilted gravestone, the iridescence catching the light, flashing green. I walk over and squat down beneath the police tape. The feather can't be more than three inches long, its shaft thrust forcefully into the ground. Among the leaves beginning to fall, it's easy to miss. The posterior vane is the same drab gray as the siding of the bar. But it's the anterior vane that dazzles, black to green, shining in the light like a miracle. I reach out and brush the barbs with a finger, tiny threads of silk, and I pluck it from the earth.

The second my skin makes contact with the shaft, the world tilts. *I see her clearly now, lying underneath me, so tranquil. It calms and infuriates me. I want her to rise up, to resist, to push back. I want to kick her and watch her body bounce off my shoe. But there is no time to play cat and mouse, and it's no fun when the mouse is dead. The plastic baggie around my penis has slipped, leaving marks in the skin where the ridges of the zip closure are, but I don't care because the release is so spectacular it hardly matters what comes after, and the petroleum jelly has smoothed the action so that I didn't even notice. I seal it carefully and tuck it into a pocket next to the rebar and electrical wire I used. This one might have fought harder than the rest, might even have landed a blow or two, clawed grooves into my skin, but she was too drunk. And so surprised she hardly knew what was happening before it was over. Still, it's progress, and I have brought something to mark the occasion. I bend at the edge of the lot and plug it into the ground with a black-gloved hand, cut resistant and coated in nitrile. I've no sooner stood up when the scent finds me, like cinnamon cream and homemade dough, the breakfasts my aunt Esther used to make. I can see the sheer pink fabric of her robe now, her breasts like withered apples underneath, and feel the smarting slap across my cheek, bloodying my lip, when I dared to reach for them as she leaned over me. It was a game with her, always a game. To look but not to touch. To shame me for the erection she deliberately caused. To beat me when she caught me masturbating into her pantyhose. To wrap those same nylons around my throat and squeeze the tears from my eyes.*

The corners of my mouth dip down as my cock stiffens. This one was close, but she's still out there, the one I'm really seeking, the one that will make Aunt Esther finally disappear. And when I find her, I'll destroy the power she has over me, once and for all.

I drop the feather and gasp, stumbling back a couple of steps.

"Acacia!" Footsteps stampede behind me as Regis runs up. He's in civilian clothes tonight, a black fleece pullover and jeans. "What happened? Are you okay?"

I stare at the feather where it fell, the green gleam calling to me, taunting. "I—I'm fine," I tell him as I turn. "You came."

"Of course, I came," he says, almost angry with himself. He spots the feather where I dropped it. "What's this?"

"Something he left," I tell him. "A kind of signature."

He picks it up with a tissue and rises beside me, spinning it in his fingers. "It's from a green-winged teal, a species of duck. Both the males and females have these beautiful green stripes on their wings. They're transient here, passing through on their migratory route in the spring and the fall." He looks to me. "What does it mean?"

"That we are a detour on his journey. And . . ."

Regis wraps the feather in the tissue, puts it in his pocket, and it's like a line snaps, freeing me, the fish caught on the hook. "And?"

"He's looking for a mate. That's what this is, a search."

He runs his fingers back through the short waves of his hair and forward again. "A *mate*? Are you kidding me? How is that possible?"

"This one was close," I tell him. "The closest he's come. He thinks if he finds her, if he kills her, it will put something to rest inside him, something a woman he knew stirred in him as a child and fanned into a roaring fire."

Regis faces me with his hands in his pockets, elbows angling out like wings. "How do you know?"

Fatigue zaps through me, taking my need to convince him with it. "I don't have the energy to explain. Believe me or don't. Take it or leave it. It's all I've got."

As much as his logic begs him to hold out against me, his expression is more resigned than angry. He's caving with every encounter. The allure plays a role, sure. But the allure isn't the only thing drawing him to me. There are deeper things forming there now—respect, admiration, feelings. They tell him I am worth listening to, even when everything else says he shouldn't.

"Why do you care so much?" He looks around the empty parking lot as if he'll find the answer there. "No one else is out here at one A.M. risking their ass."

I sniff. The cold has stiffened the tip of my nose and it tingles. "If I tell you, you won't believe me."

"Try me," he dares.

"Not here."

He pulls a hand free and grabs my elbow with it, leading me to his truck. When we get to it, he opens the passenger door.

"Where are we going?" I ask him.

"Where do you want to go?"

I stare into his eyes until my own burn and tear, until the reticence leaves me like a virus vacating the body, until I am as certain of my answer as I am his. "Your place."

IT'S TIME FOR the truth. As much as I can reasonably give. Here, in his space, with the rest of the world shut out, I feel it pressing against my teeth. I cannot continue to hold so much back. Not when we are alone, when the tender shape of him lies against me, when those eyes brush against my heart.

"I was married before I came here," I tell him as I walk slowly around his living room, scanning the varnished cypress wall clock, the brass brads on the arm of the suede sofa, the places we made love. I turn and sit down across from him, perched on the edge of an armchair. "I told you that already."

"You did," he agrees. "You implied it."

I smile, but it skates off my face like snow on glass. "He wasn't a kind man."

"You implied that, too," he tells me, leaning forward on his sofa, elbows to knees.

"Did you know that it only takes ten seconds of cutting off someone's airway to cause unconsciousness? That fifteen seconds can cause a stroke and thirty, cardiac arrest? Within minutes a person can die. But even if they don't, lasting damage—fatal damage even—can be done. Permanent damage to the brain—vision changes, seizures, memory loss, tears in the arteries—these are just a few of the side effects someone might experience for years to come after one, seconds-long event. And even with all of that, there are rarely glaring signs of injury. Bruising can be minimal, visible only under the skin, or take days to show up." I level my gaze on him, green on gray, and wait for a response.

"We learn some of this when we go into law enforcement," he says quietly. "Those aren't facts the average person is aware of though. How do you—"

"Seven hundred," I say, cutting off his question. "Domestic violence victims who have been strangled are *seven hundred times* more likely to be killed by their abuser."

He's quiet, but his brows raise in the middle, giving a sad slant to his eyes. His hands rub together slowly because he doesn't know where to put the energy cresting inside him, the anger he feels, the useless desire to protect when it's already too late.

"It's funny, because I remember when I first read that statistic. I was in a coffee shop with Wi-Fi and a couple of free-for-use laptops zip-tied to a hickory-wood bar. I don't know what possessed me to type *strangulation* into the search engine. Maybe the burn in my throat from the night before, or that one tiny vessel that ruptured in my eye. But I didn't actually need a website to know that Henry would kill me, that he wanted to. He'd already made that clear so many times before."

"Jesus." Regis rubs his hands over his face, tries to absorb what he's hearing.

"He's brilliant, my husband," I tell him. "Really. I'm not just saying that. He's tactical. He'll think of things you never will. I think that's what drew him to me in the beginning—my eye for detail. He liked that I noticed. He didn't want his particular brand of genius to go unrecognized. It's hard when you specialize in destruction because so often you must operate in the shadows. I was his shadow for two years. He practiced on me. It made him feel strong, omnipotent. But my time was running short."

"How did you break free?" he asks, barely able to speak.

"I took a leap of faith, you could say." I look down at my hands, knotted in my lap. "And now I'm the one who operates in the shadows. You asked why I care so much about the Saranac Strangler. I care because I know him. He *is* Henry. He is every man who needed to squash the life in a woman in order to feel like a man. I left Henry behind—he is my past—and I came here to start again. But Henry will never stop being Henry. Another woman will take my place. She will suffer and she will pay for my escape. I can't go back and bring Henry to justice; there is no justice for men like him. But I can stop this man, this killer, because I understand him in a way you never will. I am that woman you found on the pavement behind the Drunken Moose. And the one along the trail. And the countless others men like this have left in their wake of self-discovery. And I have the power to make sure there are no more after me. I intend to use it."

He doesn't fully understand what I'm referring to. My power, he likely thinks, is akin to parlor tricks, a keen eye for the little things, honed by years of interior design experience and the bad fortune of being married to an exacting, inhuman man. He doesn't know a huntress lives within me, a predator born of untold magic and unspeakable violence, who must kill or die. He doesn't know that when I say I can stop the Saranac Strangler, I don't mean it euphemistically, but literally. That I will take him in hand, lips to lips, and watch him as he convulses, the existence draining out of him, sinking into the forest floor.

But he doesn't need to. He only needs to know that I have ample reason to be interested in this case. That I am here to help.

Regis stands and moves toward me slowly, kneeling at my feet.

He looks up into my eyes as he kisses one knee and then the other, taking my hands in his, placing the palms to his lips. "I will never hurt you," he tells me.

And I know it's true. I feel it in him like a nougat center, how soft he is for me. My eyes flood with tears. "What about Ed?"

He looks at me, the fear he once displayed abandoned. "What about Ed? Ed is not here. But you are. And I am. What happens out there, it can't touch us in here. In here, there is no past, no future. In here, we're no one."

He leans toward me, kisses me slowly, waits for me to unzip the pullover he is wearing, slip it over his head. Piece by piece, we shed our identities until we are nothing but skin and bones and heat. We press our bodies together like pages in a book, a story unfolding line by line, each in the telling of the other. And when we are done, we lie in the dark a long, fragile while, listening to our breathing, praying the night will never end. Because out there we are hunters, and a killer is waiting, hoping we will make a vital mistake.

At last, he rises, drags his pants on, sits beside me. "Can I ask you something?"

I nod, curling to one side.

"You said the Strangler left that feather. Do you think he takes something, too? Lots of killers keep mementos from their murders."

"No. To keep something of theirs is to give them power over him. He would never allow it."

Regis scowls, thinking. "If power is what drives him, then why women? Wouldn't killing a man make him feel even more powerful?"

I brush the hair back from my face with my fingers and look up, thinking of Henry's mother. "Because it was a woman who made him feel small in the first place."

27

Life Vest

Reyes wasn't sure what he was looking for. He combed the docks, searching. He'd been on his way to get Will, arrest warrant for Henry Davenport in hand, when he made an abrupt change in course, swinging back toward the shoreline, his sister's words buzzing in his ear like a gnat: *The only way to get an asshole like that off your back is if they think you're dead.* What if she was right and by some miracle Piers Davenport was still alive? It was absurd, and yet he couldn't let it go. He didn't know what he expected to find, if anything. And maybe that was why he'd really come, to prove Lucia's words weren't true, however much he might hope they were.

They'd been over the shore multiple times along the river. There was still no sign of a body, and his eyes scanned the watery horizon knowing she had to be out there somewhere, at the bottom of the Atlantic, like an old ship. But the marina kept calling him, with its crowded nearby resort and unparalleled view of the bridge. All those pretty boats undulating in their slips on the water. Maybe this wouldn't be a wasted trip. If someone had seen something, maybe they could confirm the husband's presence on the bridge with her. Maybe they could even identify him. Didn't yachters usually keep binoculars on board? It was a long shot, but he wasn't opposed to searching a few haystacks for the occasional prize needle.

A young man sauntered over, his polarized sunglasses obscuring his eyes. "Can I help you?"

Reyes gave him a friendly smile, flashed his badge and ID card.

"I'm looking into a missing persons case," he told the boy. "We think she might be a jumper." His eyes went to the bridge spanning the water and the boy's head followed.

Reyes held out the cell phone with the image of Henry and his wife on the home screen. "Do you recall ever seeing this woman?"

The boy removed his sunglasses, staring at it. "No," he said, but he hesitated, and it gave Reyes hope.

"You sure? It would have been a couple of weeks ago. August fifteenth to be exact. Early morning hours, around dawn." He held the phone up for one more look. "Were you here that morning?"

"I'm not usually scheduled that early, but I was helping a guy prep his boat to take it out. It was quiet, though. The water was like glass. I saw a manatee."

Reyes squinted. "A manatee?"

The young man ran his fingers through his hair. "Well, that's what Tom—Mr. Young—called it. But it was so fast, who really knows what it was."

"Sure," Reyes agreed with a slow nod. "And how would I get a hold of this Tom Young? If I wanted to ask him a few questions?"

Suddenly, the boy looked scared. "We're not in any trouble, are we?"

Reyes inwardly kicked himself. He should have brought Will along. "Not at all. We're just asking anyone in the vicinity who may have witnessed something. Really, even the smallest detail that seems unrelated can make a difference, so . . ."

The boy nodded. "Oh, okay. Well, in that case. I'll give you his number, but you'll have to follow me to the dock office."

"No problem," Reyes said. "Lead the way."

As they neared the bright red roof and clean taupe siding of the dock office, the boy added, "We did find something that day you might be interested in. I mean, it's probably nothing. But you said, any small detail."

Reyes raised his brows, a striking sensation running along the length of his back. "Oh?"

The boy flashed him a smile. "It's just a life vest, but it was left sitting on one of the docks last month and no one has claimed it. I can look up the exact date inside."

He opened the office door, and they stepped in. At the desk, he quickly jotted the name and number of the man he'd mentioned and passed it over.

Reyes smiled. "Mind if I take a look at that life vest?"

"Sure." The kid brightened. Reaching into a lost and found cabinet, he pulled it out. "It's a woman's fit, that's for sure."

Reyes reached for it slowly. It was covered in a pale green nylon across the front with black buckles. But it was the familiar purple-red stain near a bottom corner that had his hand trembling ever so slightly.

"It's a shame, too," the boy said with a twist of his mouth. "Looks brand-new."

Reyes gripped the life vest, disbelieving, and met the boy's eyes.

"You know," the kid told him now, "come to think of it, it might have been a woman that morning instead of a manatee."

REYES CARRIED THE vest back to his car and sat for a long while, sun beaming through his windshield, staring at the tiny stain smaller than a dime. He had to take it to the station, clip the fabric for testing, but he was too stunned to move. Had his sister been right when she claimed the woman had just run away? Did Mr. Davenport suspect as much? Reyes glanced out at the bridge, hazy in the distance. Could she survive that jump? Did she intend to?

His eyes focused on the unmistakable stain against the cool wintergreen color of the vest, certainty washing over him.

He couldn't imagine that kind of courage, what it took to stand up there and risk it all. But after witnessing what happened to his mother and his sister, he could imagine that level of desperation.

When he finally found the wherewithal to start the car, it wasn't the station he drove to. It was to the man, Henry.

He pulled into the drive, catching Mr. Davenport home on his lunch break, blocking his rental car as he was attempting to leave. A Toyota Corolla, Reyes noted with a smile, utterly ordinary.

Reyes climbed out of the patrol car, leaving the door open, and strode toward Henry, who was tossing a briefcase into the passenger seat of his own vehicle.

"What are you doing here?" Henry barked at him, a contemptuous curl to his upper lip. "Are you going to impound this one, too?"

Reyes resisted the urge to gloat. "No, sir. Though we appreciate your cooperation in the matter."

Henry practically snarled. "Well, I'm done cooperating, I assure you. You can speak to my attorney if you have any further questions."

"Just one," Reyes told him. "It won't take long." Before Henry could protest, he pulled the life vest, bagged in clear plastic, from where he'd been holding it behind his back. "Have you seen this item before?"

The effect was immediate. Henry's body went rigid, his chin drew back like a snake ready to strike. His eyes, so pale already the irises were barely visible, turned white with rage, the pupils retracting into themselves. He stepped forward once, a man entranced, then twice. "May I?" he asked cordially, as if he wanted a closer look at a prize jewel.

Reyes shrugged and handed the vest to him.

Henry took it in his hands, fingers tensing around the sculpted plastic foam, and turned it over as if it was a thing of beauty, perhaps the most admirable thing he had ever beheld. "Where did you find this?" he asked quietly, voice rapt with awe.

"The Charleston Harbor Marina," Reyes told him. "Are you familiar with it?"

Like Reyes had, Henry zeroed in on the small stain near the bottom. His thumb rubbed over it ruefully, as if it might be a magic lamp and grant him the wish of his wife's return from a watery grave. "I know of it, yes."

"Do you have a boat there, Mr. Davenport?"

Henry looked at him, truly seeing him for the first time. "No."

Reyes nodded. "Perhaps you or your wife frequented the marina? Is she friends with someone who keeps a boat there?"

He clutched the life vest, unwilling to part with it. "No."

"You mean, not to your knowledge?" Reyes clarified.

"I mean *no,*" Henry said plainly.

Reyes took a breath. "Mr. Davenport, is this your wife's life vest? Because if it is, this could mean she survived her fall. Do you understand? She could still be alive."

Henry looked down one last time, his expression nostalgic, before holding it out for him to take. "No, Officer," he said, shifting to the all-business persona Reyes was already so familiar with. "I've never seen it before in my life."

REYES PINCHED THE bridge of his nose as Will examined the life vest. "That color is unmistakable," Will told him with a sigh. "We'll see what the lab has to say, but if you ask me, this belonged to our girl. I mean, what are the odds? This vest is found within plain view of the bridge the very day she jumped *with* a stain that matches those poisonous berries?"

Reyes shook his head. "I just don't understand it. Why would she take that risk—the jump, the berries? Either could have killed her. I've heard of people faking their own deaths before, but not like this. Not by actually committing lethal acts. We saw her vomit on that CCTV footage. She ingested those berries without question. And we saw her jump. We have the hoodie from Davenport's car and the man on tape. What did we see if not a man forcing his wife over that bridge? Would they have a reason to be in on it together?"

Will shrugged. "You never know with these types. Insurance money, maybe? Who can say. The bottom line is, until we get results back on this vest, all we have is the evidence against the husband. I know this changes things. If she's alive, it can't be a homicide. But we need to take him into custody until we know for sure. The arrest warrant still stands."

He paced before Will's cubicle, hitching his pants up, a nervous gesture. He blew a long and steady exhale up into the air, stalling.

"Emil," Will insisted.

"I'm thinking." He rounded on his partner. "Where would she go? She ate a mouthful of toxins and jumped into a river. Where do you go after that? We need to check the local hospitals, emergency clinics, anywhere she might have turned up. She had to have been sick, possibly injured."

Will rolled his eyes. "Emil, none of that is here or there right now. Let's get the results on the vest first. Then, if they prove something, we'll go after her. In the meantime, we need to go get this guy."

Reyes didn't tell Will that he'd already confronted Henry with the life vest. His partner would scold him. It was sloppy police work. He fully expected Davenport to confirm that the vest belonged to his missing wife. Reyes'd thought that would wrap it up, shift them from homicide into missing person, perhaps even tampering with evidence for the planted hoodie. But Davenport had looked him straight in the eye and denied it, leaving himself squarely on the hook for the murder of his own wife. It made no sense.

"Fine," he told his partner, caving. "Let's go get him."

Only, it wasn't so simple. When Reyes checked with Johanna, Henry Davenport's administrative assistant, she said he hadn't been back to the office since that morning. He hadn't even called, which was wholly unlike him.

Deciding to try the house, Reyes and Will pulled up to find the same rented Corolla parked in the drive. When he arrived earlier, Henry had been about to leave. Had he changed his mind? They got out and started toward the front door.

Reyes peeked in the Corolla windows. The briefcase he'd seen Henry put inside was no longer there.

On the porch, his partner Will was already ringing the bell, pounding his fist against the wooden door. "Hello?" Will called. "Mr. Davenport? Are you in there?" He turned to frown at Reyes.

"Force entry," Reyes said, joining him on the porch. "We have the warrant."

Will pursed his lips. "We should call for backup first."

"Move aside," Reyes told him. He was tired of playing the Davenports' games. Reyes didn't like being made a fool of, having someone play on his emotions. Not that he believed *she* would really do that, the woman who'd saved his life. Or that they could have known about his past, his history with domestic abusers. His head was hot right now, the exact opposite of where it should be for this, but he didn't care. He wanted answers. With a deft, powerful kick, he blasted the front door from its hinges as Will pulled his Glock from its holster and unlocked the safety. But the house only echoed the bang of the door, and all the lights appeared to be off.

Will entered first and Reyes followed, but he didn't draw his weapon. The house was empty. They moved slowly around the first floor of the residence, looking for anything that might allude to where either of its owners had gone.

A biting chill began to steal over Reyes, the harbinger of dread. His confidence was sinking with every step they took, even as his certainty grew. He'd fucked up—royally. And now she would pay for his mistake. Unless he could find a way to protect her. He owed her that much.

"He's not here," Will said at last, putting his gun away.

"He fled," Reyes said, defeated.

Will turned on him. "Why, Emil? How would he know we were coming for him?"

He hung his head. "I might have come by before the station, questioned him about the life vest."

His partner groaned. "Goddamnit, Emil. We've talked about this. You can't go off half-cocked like that. It's not professional."

His little, unannounced visit earlier had tipped the husband off. Henry Davenport now believed his wife to be alive, and he'd gone in search of her.

Reyes mounted the stairs. He had no defense for his actions.

His hunger to know what had happened to Mrs. Davenport, to find her alive, had clouded his judgment. In his rush to save her, he'd put her in harm's way. He wandered through the second story, guilt and duty riding him. When he entered the master bedroom, he found both closet doors open, clothes strewn across the floor, a suitcase on the bed that Henry must have decided against taking. He entered the wife's closet where the destruction was far worse. Shattered wooden shelves littered the floor. Blouses had been ripped from their hangers and torn apart then cast aside. Jewelry speckled the carpet in sparkles.

Reyes sighed. The man had not gone after his wife because he loved her. He wasn't out to save his marriage. He'd gone after the woman who betrayed him, duped him, and tried to frame him for her murder. He wasn't out for reconciliation. He was out for revenge.

And Reyes was the source that tipped him off. Piers Davenport would not be safe, wherever she was. Her crime, however illegal, was not to serve an injustice but to right a wrong. To imprison the man who had hurt her and would do so again if given the chance. To protect herself and every other woman besides.

Wouldn't he have done the same to the tall man if given the chance?

He owed it to her to find Henry and stop him for good. But could he get to him in time? The only way to find him was by finding her, but how?

Looking down, he spotted a plastic toy, a skull with little feet that walked when it was wound up, making a chattering noise. He stooped to pick it up and saw the carpet, the corner where it had been pulled back. Beneath it lay a small wrapper, white with a gold seal and Chinese lettering, curling at the corners where it had been wrapped around something. Reyes picked it up and turned to find Will standing in the doorway.

"I need to show you something," Will said.

"What is it?"

He sighed, turning a laptop around in his arms. On the screen, an article flared to life, the image of a body lying next to a field crop. The headline read, *Man Found Dead from Poisonous Pokeweed Berries.* The opening line continued, *Don Rodgers had been traveling for work, his wife confirmed, when he turned up dead along this secluded road in Virginia from an ingestion of pokeweed berries. Authorities are puzzled as to where he got the berries or why he consumed them. Suicide has been written off due to theft of his motor vehicle along with other valuable items. His wife verifies his last point of contact was a call from his hotel room in Charleston before leaving, more than forty-eight hours prior to the discovery of his body.*

Reyes met Will's eyes. "We need to get the name of that hotel and find that car."

"You were right," Will said. "She's alive, and she's on the move."

28

Ring

I am painfully aware that I've just spent my last night with Regis. Soon I'll begin to feed, and he cannot touch me then. No one can. I haven't yet determined *how* I'll keep my distance, maybe fake an illness or a trip. Considering the complexities swirling in our relationship, it shouldn't be too hard. I only hope that once I begin, I find the Strangler soon, and finish him.

I return to the cabin and soak in a long, hot bath. When I get out, I crawl into bed and immediately fall asleep. In my dream, I am on a trail, light twinkling through overhead branches, as I follow a man with a hiking pole. His back is ramrod straight, eyes never straying from the path, steps as regular as the hands of a clock. I study him, the creases in the back of his shirt, the curl of his fingers on the rubber grip of his hiking pole. Something doesn't feel right, and the feeling gnaws at me, adamant and disturbing. I gain on him, certain this must mean he is the one I'm searching for, the murderer I am meant to kill. As I get close enough to touch him, a scent warns me off, both familiar and repulsive, a cologne I know and detest. But it is too late, I am laying my hand upon his shoulder and spinning him around, ready to make my move. Only it isn't the Saranac Strangler. It is Henry, and in my shock, I am too slow. One hand reaches out to throttle me as the other raises the pole, the sharpened carbide tip aimed at my heart.

I wake to Myrtle shaking me feverishly. "Get up, Piers. *Now.* You need to see this."

Groggily, I rise from bed and follow her into the living room, registering that it is early morning. "What time is it?" I ask with a yawn.

Her eyes pierce mine as she directs me to the TV screen. Don's car, abandoned in the Syracuse cemetery, is emblazoned across it, and a reporter is explaining how it was found to be in association with the roadside death of a Washington, DC, man in Virginia, poisoned with pokeweed berries. "Police now suspect foul play," she is saying gravely, "and are asking anyone who has seen this woman to come forward for questioning."

A fuzzy video of me, frantic and with a fresh dye job, fleeing the hotel lobby in Charleston in my crappy *Miami* T-shirt plays on a loop in the corner of the screen.

"She was seen leaving the victim's hotel with him in Charleston, South Carolina," the reporter explains. "A ring was also missing from the victim's belongings; an anniversary present from his wife, commissioned for him only last year. Stolen, they believe, by the person responsible for his death, and possibly the key to finding the truth."

An up-close image of the signet ring I took flashes across the screen in all its unique detail. Myrtle waltzes over and turns off the set. My stomach bottoms out.

"You let yourself be recorded," she admonishes.

"I didn't realize. I didn't even know any of this then. It was an accident. I was trying to get a ride out of the city before Henry—"

"The venery will not like this, Piers. Not one bit." She paces back and forth, practically wearing a groove into the thick boards at her feet.

"Any chance they won't have seen it?"

She shoots me a look that could turn anyone to stone. "If it's playing on the news *here,* then I doubt it. You brought that car across state lines to New York. Do you know what that means? FBI will be involved. He was a political consultant, a high-profile figure in Washington. You've turned this into a national manhunt."

"I had no other way to get here!" I counter. But it doesn't matter. Myrtle is right; I'm screwed whether I deserve it or not.

She comes over and rubs my upper arms briskly, as if she's trying to warm me up. "Shhh . . . It's okay. We'll figure this out. I've just got to think. I need a defense planned before they call." She turns to stare out the window, as if the answer is waiting in the dark. What I can see of her face pales. "What if Sheriff Brooks sees this?"

I crumple to my knees as I recall the night that I arrived. I'd put Don's ring on the counter as payment to anyone who would take me to Crow Lake. He'll recognize it. The second he learns about Don, he'll put it together with the man in the café and Ed. He'll never believe me again.

"At least your hair is different," she says. "We can recolor it. Something close but not quite so red. Men never notice those kinds of things. He'll think it was always that way. And the video is just bad enough. If he says anything, refute it. Deny, deny, deny." She glances back, sees me on the floor, and rushes over, lifting me by my elbows. "You did nothing wrong. No matter what it looks like. They won't be able to prove this. No one up here will even place you in that video besides the sheriff."

But Regis is not the only person I am worried about. There is someone else who will know my face, my build, instantly. It won't matter that I colored my hair or put on new clothes. If Henry sees this report—which is surely playing in Charleston now that I've been connected to Don and the hotel—he will know everything. That I didn't drown, didn't die. That I fled. That I planned it all. That I am here, in New York.

And he will come for me.

"He saw the ring," I tell her. "I stole it from the car, and Regis saw me with it, Myrtle. He'll know. The second he sees this, he'll know."

Her lips pull tight with fear. "Then you must convince him you are innocent, Piers. Use your allure, his attraction to you, your insight into the Strangler case—whatever you have to. But make him believe they got it wrong. Because they did. They always do."

I shake my head, tears beginning to spill over. "I don't know, Aunt Myrtle. I don't know if I can do that. I'm not like you. I'm not good at this."

She wipes them swiftly away, cupping my cheeks in her hands. "Of course, you can," she tells me, summoning a confidence I know she doesn't feel. "You're a bane witch. Never forget it."

MYRTLE WOULD NOT approve. She wanted me to wait until he confronted me. She wanted me to deny it. She wanted me to overpower him with my allure, as if I even know how. She wanted me safe. But I can't sleep. And I can't keep lying in bed, wondering if he knows, if he'll show up tomorrow with handcuffs and drag me away. I don't want to wait, and I'm tired of running; I've been running since Charleston. Running since Henry and I first met. Running since I left my mother and Gerald behind. Running since I was that little girl eating pokeweed berries under a full moon. I don't care what happens to me as long as I can finally *be* me, as long as I can belong to myself.

It must be after three in the morning when I pull into his drive. Myrtle was snoring in the next room, so I took the car, a habit I am getting stupidly accustomed to. I expect to find him in bed, dead asleep. Expect that he will answer the door with mussed hair and bleary eyes like he did a few nights ago, a note of vexation at being woken, summoned at such an ungodly hour, by me no less.

But when I pull up, he's in the harsh glare of an overzealous outdoor light, chopping wood in his long underwear and a loose flannel shirt, his boots pulled up to his calves, sloppily laced. Even in the frigid night, there is a gleam of perspiration at his hairline. I turn the car off and get out.

"We need to talk," I say.

He casts a bitter glance at me, swings his ax, and brings it down hard on the block of wood he's splitting. "I think you've done enough talking," he says.

I know then that he's seen. And he hates me for it. For lying to him, he believes. For killing the innocent.

"Regis, you have to let me explain." I take a step in his direction.

He holds the ax at arm's length, pointing it at me. "I don't have to do anything of the kind. I've given you so many chances, Acacia. So many chances to let me in, to tell me who you really are, to prove you're not . . ." He can't finish. The ax falls limply to his side.

"That I'm not *what*? A murderer? Is that what you were going to say? Is that what you believe I am?"

He looks at me from the corner of his eye, tormented, distrusting. "It's generally what we call someone who kills someone else."

I nod my head, press my lips between my teeth. "I'm not a murderer," I tell him. "But I am a killer."

He faces me now, aghast that I've said it so plainly. His jaw can't quite form the words.

"The problem," I go on, "is that there isn't a word for what I am exactly, not in your circles."

"What circles are those?" he shoots back.

"Legal ones—law enforcement, government."

He swings the ax again, splits the block into threes, tosses each piece onto a pile off to the side. Then he turns in my direction, leaning against the tree trunk. "So, in what circles is there a word for you?"

I look down at my feet and try to clear my mind before answering. When I look up, he is waiting, face skeptical, arms crossed, as if he can't imagine what I'll come up with this time. "Secret ones," I reply.

He shakes his head and turns for the house. "I'm not listening to this."

I grab his arm. "Please. Just hear me out. It's not a story; it's real. Haven't you wondered *how*?"

That gets his attention. He pulls my hand off and my heart shudders in my chest.

"The man who took your sister," I begin. "He wasn't very old. Late twenties maybe, early thirties." I watch his eyes widen, the lids shrinking back with shock, his curiosity more than he can refuse. "Looked like a regular young man, someone that could have sacked your groceries. He drove a blue truck with a dented fender. I bet you're wondering how he got her inside, aren't you? I bet it's eaten at you all these years."

Regis just stares at me, a film of tears beginning to wash over his eyes.

"She loved kittens, didn't she? Your sister, Tanya. He didn't know that, but he knew most kids came running where animals were involved. He had a box of five-week-old kittens on the seat, a litter he'd gathered from a junk lot near his house. Told her there were more nearby, that he'd give her one for free if she helped him catch them."

The tears slide down his face and he staggers on his feet. I rush to his side to make sure he doesn't fall. When I know he's steady, I place a hand over his chest. "I'm sorry. I didn't want to tell you. I just didn't know how else to get you to believe me."

"She'd been begging my parents for a cat for years, but our mother was allergic," he finally manages. "It's hard to explain that to a child, though. And Tanya was more stubborn than most."

"We should go inside," I tell him. "Get out of the cold."

He nods wearily, opens his door for me. "After you."

Inside, he heats two mugs of water, digs out fresh tea bags, sets them before us. "When, how did she die?" he asks once he's gotten the courage.

The scenes spark through my mind, grisly and devastating—the duct tape, the reddened hammer. I shake my head. "She didn't last long," I tell him quietly. "Not even twenty-four hours."

He winces, stares down into his cup, stirs it absently with a sugar spoon.

I lay a hand on his arm. It's the only comfort I can give. "It was fast," I tell him. "And that was a mercy."

He doesn't ask for the details, and I am grateful. "If he were still alive," I tell Regis, "I'd kill him myself."

"I wouldn't ask you to do that for me," he's quick to reply.

"I wouldn't do it for you," I tell him. "I'd do it for *her*. And for all the others like her who could have been spared."

He studies me, thoughts shuttered away where I can't read them. After several long minutes, he says, "Are you part of a secret society, is that what you're telling me? Some kind of underground network of female assassins? Vigilantes?"

His accuracy smacks me in the ribs. For a second, I can't draw air. "Actually, yes. That is what I'm telling you."

His eyes squeeze shut. "I thought you were going to be honest with me."

"I am," I answer. "As honest as I can be. I am part of a circle of women—all related—who kill men guilty of horrific crimes. My mother, my grandmother, Aunt Myrtle—it's who we are."

He rubs at his face. "You poison them?"

"Yes." I don't look away as I answer. I want him to see the truth in my eyes.

"With mushrooms?"

"With our bodies." I don't even blink.

He starts slightly, scrutinizes me to see if I have a tell, if I am giving myself away somehow. But I am as still as the lake itself. "You mean you—"

"We eat the mushrooms, yes. Or the berries. Or the roots or leaves or stems or flowers. We happily eat whatever part is most toxic, and we transfer that poison to our victims."

He blinks. "Are you sure you want to be telling me this?"

"Yes," I respond. "No. I'm not supposed to tell anyone, least of all you. But . . ."

He waits patiently.

"Lying to you is impossible," I say with a sigh. "The other night, when you warned me about the autopsy—you wanted to *help* me because you care. Well, that's what I'm doing now."

"You're warning me?" he asks.

"I'm trying to help because I care," I clarify. "Maybe it would be better to keep you in the dark, only you won't stay there. You're stumbling blindly into something you don't really understand. And that could get dangerous."

"For me?" he asks now, a little incredulous.

"For both of us," I emphasize.

He frowns. "I don't understand. How does it work? Do you build up a tolerance? Is it genetic?"

"It's magic," I say simply.

He laughs. "Right."

"Do you want answers or not?" I sip my tea, return the mug to the table.

"You're serious." He doesn't ask, he states it. He sees it as plainly as the mug before him.

"Deadly." I give him a small smile. "The man in the café? I spit into his coffee after I saw what he did to his wife. Don, the man from the news reports? He forced himself on me, tried to rape me. It happened when he kissed me. I don't take credit for his loss. He did it to himself."

Regis looks like he can't believe what he is hearing, and yet he must, because he just sits there, staring, trying to piece it all together in his mind. "And Ed?" he asks.

My eyes water. "Ed was different. We found him on the brink of death already, suffering. His pain was so great. We knew help would never arrive in time. I promised to give him relief, and then I kissed him goodbye."

"Jesus." He spins his cup on the table, processing. When he looks at me, his eyes are sharp as flint. "Acacia, tell me the truth. Did you kill your husband?"

"Henry?" I laugh bitterly. "No. A missed opportunity I will regret for the rest of my days. Of everyone, he is the one I should have taken out. But there was so much I still didn't understand then, and I was desperate to escape. That's why I'm helping you, I suppose."

"Helping me?" He looks confused. His chin tucks. His brow crinkles.

"To get the Saranac Strangler. A kind of penance, I guess, for leaving Henry alive to possibly hurt someone else."

His eyes narrow. "You said 'get,' not *catch*. You don't want to help me arrest him, do you? You want to kill him."

"Doesn't he deserve it?" I ask.

"That's not for us to decide," he says firmly.

Ah, the *good cop*. I see myself in him now as the venery must have seen me—the naivete, the ignorance. I smile. "Isn't it? This is our community. You're an authority in maintaining law and order, and I'm a female victim of domestic and sexual violence. Surely, there is no one more qualified than us."

His mouth opens silently and hovers there. It takes him a long moment to collect himself. "You know that's not how it works."

"Maybe that's the problem," I tell him calmly, sipping my tea. "Maybe it doesn't work as it is."

He shakes his head. "This sounds like a confession, but what you're telling me is preposterous. By all accounts you're either lying or mad. I can't take this into the department without being laughed out of the building, but I can't let you walk away. Tell me what I'm supposed to do here, Acacia."

"Piers," I correct him. "That's my real name. You might as well know it, though you likely already do by now. I would appreciate if you keep up the pseudonym for public appearances. No point in confusing everyone. And Henry is still out there. I'd rather not give him any opportunity to find me and finish what he started. It's enough to have one killer on my trail."

"Are you saying the Strangler is after you? Aca—I mean, Piers, did something happen? Did you see him? Did he confront you?"

I hold the hot tea under my chin, enjoying the comfort of the steam. There's no point holding back now. "Not yet, but he will soon. And when he does, I'll be ready for him."

He scratches at his head, frustration mounting as he tries to complete the picture without all of the pieces. "Why would he come after you?"

"We call it the *allure*. It attracts our victims to us, like a magnetic force. He's been circling me this whole time, closing in. I can't let another woman fall in my place. The next encounter must be mine, and I must be ready. It means I'll have to begin feeding." I lay a hand on his wrist. "There can be nothing more between us once that starts. Do you understand? I can't risk harming you. I have to save my strength for the Strangler."

He wants to think I'm crazy. That would be easier to swallow. But he's the sheriff; he's seen psychosis and delusion, psychopathy and hallucinations. He knows what instability looks like. By comparison, I am rock steady, firm as the mountains encircling us and just as sure. He can read my conviction even if it challenges his understanding of reality. And he knows, more than anything, that what I told him about his sister is true. He knows it in his heart.

"I can't stay," I tell him, rising.

He gets up. "You're leaving? You show up here and deliver this outrageous story, expect me to believe you, to do nothing, and then just pull out? Am I supposed to pretend this didn't happen? Let you risk yourself chasing this perpetrator? Not report your previous crimes—three counts of murder, fraud when you faked your own suicide?"

I stare at him. Cautiously, I take a step in his direction. When he doesn't pull away, I lean in and place my lips on his. The heat floods my chest and face. Lower still, my nerves beg for more. His lips part against mine, and despite his misgivings, his body cannot deny its truth—he wants me. Even now.

When I pull away, I am filled with sadness. I caress his cheek before stepping back. "I can't tell you what to do or not to do with the information I've given, only this—stay out of my way."

His face reddens as if slapped. "Piers . . ."

"I'm not your enemy, Regis." My eyes burn through his. I feel Myrtle's words in my veins. I *am* a bane witch. And I will never forget it. "Don't become mine."

"Wait." His arms shoot out, strong hands gripping mine. "Let me help you."

Now it is my turn to stumble in shock.

"If I can't stop you, what other choice do I have? We both want to bring this guy down. What you and your aunt are doing, it's not my way. But my way didn't save Tanya, and it didn't save whoever came after. This community is everything to me. I won't let him rip it apart any more than he already has. And more than that, I need you safe. I know what's between us is new and complicated, but . . . Can't you see the effect you have on me? I want this. I need you in my life."

My lips part, and my heart catches in my chest.

"I can't believe I'm saying this," he continues, "but maybe we can work together. *This* time."

I take in every morsel of him, from the sincerity in his gaze to the firmness of his bite, the square of his shoulders, his steady hands. He means it. Every word.

"What did you have in mind?"

29

Hostage

Our plan is good, sound, better than I would have come up with on my own. It fills me with a quiet confidence as I drive back to the motel. The sun will rise soon, and I have only a couple of hours to prepare, to dress and feed. I intend to hike to the bunker and ransack Myrtle's stores since I'm short on time. I can repay her later by doing some foraging.

The handcuffs are heavy in my coat pocket. A precaution only, like the pepper spray—he insisted. I didn't have the heart to tell Regis there likely wouldn't be time for either, that if I am face-to-face with the Strangler, there will only be time for death. His or mine. But he knows how this works. I made no promises about a tidy ending. Only to *try*.

The sky is still dark around the edges when I return to find Myrtle sitting on the porch steps, her long hair coursing down her back, the flannel of her gown peeking beneath the down fill of her parka. Out in the brush, Bart is snuffling at the ground. He takes off after something, the sound of him crashing through the leaves echoing back to us.

"You should be inside," I tell her as I approach. "It's not safe."

She purses her lips. "I'm old. And the benefit of getting old is that people stop telling you what to do." She shoots me a pointed look, the warning implied. "Where were you?"

"Nowhere," I tell her, trying to pass to the door.

She follows me in. "Does nowhere wear a gun and a badge on duty?"

I roll my eyes at her. "I know you mean well, but I'm a grown woman, Myrtle. I come and go as I please."

She folds her arms and watches me as I get a glass to fill with water. "You are grown, that's true. But you do not belong to just yourself anymore. You are part of a whole. And there are no—"

"Secrets in the venery," I recite. "Yeah, I got that."

She sighs. "I only want to keep you safe."

"Then talk to them, not me," I shoot back. It's unfair and I know it. She's been nothing but kind to me. But I feel childish and sulky, my heart stampeded by the look in Regis's eyes, the impossible truth of who I am, the reality that this simple existence—a life in a fairy-tale cottage in the mountains with a big-hearted man—can never be mine.

Her eyes narrow dangerously. "You aren't yourself," she observes. "What have you done?"

I glance at her and turn away. "Nothing."

"I have defended and protected you, but there are things I cannot save you from, including yourself. Do not make your mother's mistakes, Piers. And do not underestimate me or the venery. I love you—I do. But my allegiances are with my clan *first*, with the whole."

I turn to face her, a boldness I don't recognize coursing through me, wrapping my spine in steel, my heart in quills. "What are you trying to say? Do you want me to leave?"

"I want you to be smart," she hisses. "I want you to think of yourself and your kind. I want you to be better than your mother ever was. I want you to win, dammit."

"I will," I spit out, "if everyone will just keep off my back."

"Everyone?" She nears me, eyes thin as cracked windows.

"Look, I don't know why you're upset. It was your idea after all, that I use my allure, that I convince him of my innocence, paint him a picture. And that's exactly what I did."

She startles, wheels turning. "You were supposed to wait until he came to you. How can you be innocent if you go to him, throw yourself at his mercy? What have you told him, Piers? What does he know?"

"Nothing," I lie, voice laden with irritation. "He knows nothing."

"I don't believe you."

"You don't have to," I tell her. "He won't do anything."

She falls into the nearest chair, her head dropping into her hand. "Oh, Piers, what have you done?"

I lean against the corner of the counter. "I haven't done anything."

She looks up at me and her eyes are spidery with veins. "He's a good man. You know that? You've doomed a good man."

"I haven't doomed him," I argue. "He's not going to tell anyone. He's not going to do anything about it." I haven't even had a chance to tell her about our plan to catch the Saranac Strangler together, but considering her reaction, it might be wise to keep that bit to myself.

She chuckles dryly. "You think you know him? You think it matters? He's a risk we can't afford to take. Don't you understand? Every day he breathes he is a threat to us. To me, to Tina, to Ivy and Verna. To Azalea and little Scarlet." She rises from her chair. "They will not forgive this. Not this."

Panic begins to claw at me from the inside. "You don't have to tell them," I insist. "It can just be between us."

She looks defeated. "I thought you understood. I thought you were learning. Maybe they were right. Maybe the seed of your line is too toxic to overcome."

"What are you saying?" My heart races inside me, barreling toward an end I can't see. "Are you threatening me?"

She reaches over and takes my chin in her fingers. "Precious girl, I don't have to. They'll overrun me. All I can do now is damage control."

"Damage control?"

She looks full of immeasurable grief. "If I act fast, if I'm lucky, then perhaps they won't take it out on me as well."

"*You?*" The truth begins to dawn in sickening shades of red. "You mean, they'll want to kill you? Because I told Regis?"

She studies me. "See there? You are learning. Just not fast enough."

"But you didn't do anything!"

"I sheltered you. You are my responsibility. There will be a heavy price to pay for this violation. We will all have to pony up—him, you, me." She picks up her boots and begins to drag them onto her feet, grabbing the keys from the table where I dropped them.

"What are you doing?" I ask her.

"Trying to fix it." She glares at me. A sickener mushroom lies on the table between us, something she must have gathered on a recent walk. Before I can move, she scoops it up and shoves it whole into her mouth. When it slides down her throat, she says, "He will suffer. This is your fault."

"No," I insist. "Myrtle don't. It doesn't have to be like this."

"Our rules exist for a reason. They are all that has stood between us and the anger of men for hundreds of years. They're not arbitrary. All you had to do was follow them."

"I will," I assure her. "I won't make another mistake. He won't tell a soul. No one has to know, I swear it!"

She looks at me and sighs. "Sweet girl, you have already made one mistake too many. Now, I must clean up your mess. If we are very lucky, very clever, it will be enough. I can concoct a story that they'll buy, and he'll pay the price for us both. But I must act fast."

I hurl myself between her and the door. "No! I won't let you. Don't do this, Myrtle, please. It's my fault. I can't take another person dying because of me. Tell them it was me. Let them deliver the last kiss. Just spare him, please."

She grips my shoulders with talon-like strength. "Stand aside, Piers. Sacrificing yourself won't change anything, so I don't recommend it. As long as he knows, we are not safe. Be glad I am not making you do it. It's more than your mother got."

She shoves me aside with a bullish strength I didn't know she possessed, and starts out the door, but I throw myself at her, catching her by an ankle as she descends the stairs, causing us both to fall to the ground in a heap of limbs. I recover first and pull myself up her body, reaching for the keys, clawing them from her fingers.

She pushes me aside and leaps up, starting forward at a determined speed. After a moment I realize that she intends to walk. It would take her hours to reach him on foot, but still, I can't allow that. I cast about looking for a way to stop her when I remember the oars crossed over the doorway inside the kitchen. I run in and wrench one free, darting back out. Myrtle is booking it toward the café, but I scramble behind her, swinging the oar and clipping her across the shoulders. She goes down hard, the wind knocked out of her, and I leap on top before she can get up.

Prying her arms back, I slip Regis's handcuffs from my pocket and lock in one wrist, then the other, before dragging her back to the cabin and depositing her onto the sofa. She glares at me as if she can kill me with looks alone.

"These weren't supposed to be for you," I spit at her. "We had a plan! Now, if you'll sit tight and let me handle it, everything will work out like it's supposed to. You'll see."

I rip the shoelaces from her boots near the door and tie the cuffs to the sofa's heavy frame beneath the cushions. Then I dig through her pockets and take her phone and spare key.

"Who's *we*? You and Sheriff Brooks?" She eyes me venomously.

I stand back, crossing my arms with a huff. "Yes. Regis and me. We're working together. It was your idea, after all."

"Not like this," she hisses.

I sigh and drop to a crouch before her. "I love you, Myrtle. But you're wrong about him. You told me that our roles are changing as society changes, that we had to evolve. What if that's what this is? What if there *are* men we can trust with our secret? Men who can help."

She scoffs. "Please. You sound pathetic."

"Fine," I say, rising. "Have it your way. But I'm going to go out there and get my mark, *with* Regis's help."

"I'll believe it when I see it," she says sourly.

"Good. Because you will see it. And once we're done, we're

gonna come back here and talk—calmly and rationally—about how we can make this work. Maybe it was stupid for me to take the risk, but I'm willing to give him a chance. You said yourself he is a good man. An honest man. He'll keep his end of the bargain. And once you see that, you'll believe me, and we can keep it between the three of us. No one else has to die."

My heart is hammering with fear even as I speak, terrified that I've crossed a line I can't come back from. Not with the venery. I've attacked one of my own to protect a man I have no business loving. In their eyes, I have become my mother, plain and simple. Worse, because in the end even she had the decency to do what was required of her. But if I can just get Myrtle to see the truth, then maybe we can fix this without them ever knowing.

She stares up at me, petulant as a child.

"I'm not your enemy, Myrtle."

"You've handcuffed me in my own house," she points out.

"Only for a little while," I explain. "So you can see we mean it. Please, give me a chance here."

I want to believe the twitch at the corner of her mouth is a sign her resolve is softening, that the deep breath she takes means I am getting through to her.

"What choice do I have?" she finally replies.

I exhale and head for the door. "I'll be back," I tell her. "Just sit tight."

"Piers," she calls.

I glance back.

"Hunt well."

The last thing I see before locking the door behind me is the wry smile crowning her face, savage and proud.

THE CROW LAKE trail was Regis's idea. It isn't a big tourist draw, thanks to it being a flat hike less than four miles long and bordering one of the smaller lakes. Anyone visiting the mountains will head for the myriad Instagrammable options that pepper this region like buckshot. They'll probably never even notice Crow Lake on their map. But that's why it's perfect for him. It's the kind of quiet, easy, out-of-the-way spot he loves. That, and it's close to me. Taking Kathy Miller in the back parking lot of a local bar was unadvisedly risky, out of character, but that's my fault. He's stalking me like a heat-seeking missile. Regis thinks, given the chance, he'd gladly keep to the recesses, the cover of wilderness. He just needs the two to come together. Me and this morning, this trail, are precisely that moment.

Of course, he doesn't know I'm the one he wants, the one with the power to silence Aunt Esther's laughter in his mind—*he thinks*. In a way, he's right. I have every intention of shutting Aunt Esther up for him, just not in the way he's expecting. But I can't do that if I can't figure out who he is. Hunting a ghost is proving impossible, and the last thing I need is another man like Henry getting the jump on me. I'm petrified to face him, after everything Henry put me through. Looking a darker, more mature version of my husband in the eye is not my idea of a pleasant afternoon. But I'm tired of waiting for him to show up for coffee and a waffle while other women, better women, die.

I make my way down the silent slip of trail between the trees, sniffling, wiping my nose hastily with the back of my hand. "Regis?" I whisper, but there's no response. I'm early, I realize. I shouldn't be here for another thirty minutes. The fight with Myrtle sent me springing this way too soon, before I'd checked the time, before I'd even fed. In response, my stomach gurgles, a searing hunger awakening in me. I swallow it down.

He feels close, so close, closer than he's ever been. He's coming for me. I can feel his pulse quickening at the notion, at his nearness. A flash of leaves and limbs crosses behind my eyes. He's out here somewhere, stalking. My allure must be working on overdrive thanks to Regis's good luck charm. I reach into my pocket and feel for it, pull it out to make sure it's there, silky inside my fist—the green-winged teal feather. The only thing we have that the Strangler has touched. It ties me to him like electric wire. I feel his presence in it, humming, and my body—no, my *magic*—responds with a crackle inside me. As if the man himself is touching me.

I think of Myrtle locked in her cabin, tied to her couch, and grimace. This feather is probably as much to blame as anything else for my reaction to our quarrel. My whole body is on high alert, senses sharpened to a razor edge, radiating with the need for action. It's unthinkable to have hit her with that oar, to have made her a hostage in her own home. I remind myself that I acted out of desperation, that when I left she was rooting for me, and I can fix everything. With the Strangler dead, the venery will be happy, and Myrtle will be safe. I'll send Regis away. I'll talk sense into Myrtle. I'll make them all see.

But I can't do what I came here to do if I don't feed. I need to forage something toxic off this trail before Regis gets here, or worse, the Strangler. I sit on the bench facing the lake and stare out across the surface of the water, smooth and contained like a spill, watching the ducks on the other side. I probably walked half a mile already. I could keep going, but I'm not stupid. Getting too far in, too isolated before Regis is here to back me up, would only put me in peril. I don't want to give our common foe any ideas, not before I've fed.

A smell, musty and sour, finds me like the steam coming off a fresh-baked pie. I practically drool in my lap and twist around trying to locate it. When I can't see the source, I get up and stumble blindly into the trees, pushing switches out of my way as I scour the earth like a chicken looking for worms. The lake shines through the brush to my right, but its beauty is lost on me. Even my original intention in coming here, the plan I had with Regis, shifts, relegated to a place of lesser importance. We were supposed to meet at the trailhead. But only one thought consumes me now—finding the source of that heavenly smell.

I am close to giving up when I spot the red cap through the moss, winging up like a saucer of blood, stemmed in white. I fall to my knees before it and breathe deep. It takes all my self-control not to bend down and lick the cap like a Popsicle. It's another sickener mushroom—*Russula emetica*—known for its nauseating effects on the stomach of anyone foolish enough to eat one. Not typically deadly, but my nose tells me it would be in my system, that my magic would heighten its effects with such acuity my mark would be dead in a matter of hours. I'd prefer something fast acting, but beggars cannot be choosers, and I can't resist the cravings anymore. I pluck the mushroom from the ground and hold it under my nose, then take my first bite. Everything inside me dilates—my veins, my pupils, my chakras. I feel a charge of energy course through me, hot and cold at once, and I chew greedily, swallowing before I am finished so I can rush into another bite.

This is different from the feedings of my childhood, lazy summer nights under the moon. This is ecstasy, the rush of a divine high. I lose all sense of time and place, the lake fading to nothing, the trees stretching to oblivion. I nearly forget myself, the Piers I am used to less important, less significant than the witch inside me, the drop of faery blood I carry far outmatching the gallon of my own. I merge with the mushroom, with the forest, with the magic. Cells and roots and streams all running into each other like lengths of yarn, knitting into a landscape, unrecognizable but achingly familiar, here and nowhere. There is only this feeling and its source and the hunt it calls me to.

When the last bite is swallowed, I scatter the leaves searching for another. There has to be *more.* That is what I'm here for. That is what I want. And then something swells in me, like air, a life force, and I am lifted from the ground, buzzing inside with a kind of desire I've never known before, as wanton as sex, as vital as thirst. He feels so close now, so near, that he's practically inside me. I crush the feather in my pocket. *Come,* my soul sings to him, my destiny, my allure. *Come now.*

I'm getting to my feet, brushing off my knees, when I hear a crunch. I spin and duck, crouching low as an animal, peering through the brush to see a pair of legs walk briskly by, a long hiker's pole beside them. My nightmare lances through me, of the hiker who was Henry, and I recall Regis telling me the Strangler uses a stick of some kind to control his victims in their bind, tightening the garrote until they perish. A hiking stick, I realize, would make a sturdy, inconspicuous choice.

I tumble forward, trying not to make too much noise, until I am squarely on the trail. But the man is already paces ahead and not slowing down. A burn rips me from lip to loin, and I nearly groan as I stumble forward, increasing my speed until I am matching him step for step. He's tall, but not large, the right build. His arms are pale and thin, sleeves short even in the brisk cool. They aren't explicitly hairy, another tip-off, and the hair on his head is short, hidden under a wool beanie. Wool is fibrous, a choice that could shed evidence, but our killer takes his time, cleaning up at the scene. He doesn't move like an inexperienced hiker, but then again, this trail is easy on a bad day. There is a wedding band on one hand. Does our killer have a wife? Not likely. Though it would make a perfect ruse.

I speed up, not wanting to lose him. But I misjudge my steps and soon I'm practically breathing down his neck. He doesn't seem to notice. My heat, my steps, magically cloaked even in his proximity. Another flash of forest flickers behind my eyes, the sweet relief he feels at being so close, but it confuses me, like an image laid over this one, not quite syncing up. I take a deep breath, but only smell tobacco and citrus, the notes of a lingering deodorant or body spray instead of the stench of death, the iron tang of blood, the sweet croon of rot. I cool inside, the intensity ebbing, the high of my feed dropping like a fever in an ice bath. For a moment, I can't understand it. The sensation disorients me, brings me back to where I am, *who* I am. Regis . . . I was supposed to meet Regis. But the sickener courses through me, and the man ahead is so close. My dream looms large in the forest beside me, everything such a perfect match, from his shirt to his pace to the tip of his hiking pole. That can't have been coincidence. I have to know.

I am reaching out when I hear his voice shout, "Acacia! No!"

Regis, I become aware, is behind me. This is all wrong. I was supposed to wait for him. To pick a place inside the trees—a bench—where he could lie low, keep a visual on me, have his gun ready in case. We were supposed to do this together. But I botched it.

Myrtle . . . *Oh, Myrtle. Please forgive me.*

I want to turn to him, to apologize, to explain, but the man is right in front of me, and my fingers are inches from contact, and I can *feel* the Strangler like a second skin intersecting with my own. This must be him.

"Piers!" I hear Regis call as I clamp down on the man's shoulder. The touch . . . The touch should tell me everything. But it is empty, like gripping sand. It runs through my fingers, this moment, and vanishes.

This isn't right.

Henry. His name is like a beat of my heart. Just one, the last, before he gets his happy ending.

He spins around, and my other arm raises instinctively to block the blow from the pole, but it is a blow that does not come. The man's face is wrong. It is not Henry's, not long and pale and taut with hate. And even though I've never seen the Saranac Strangler, it is not his either—I know this to be true. His five-o'clock shadow and bushy eyebrows don't add up, the streaks of gray in his mustache, the panicked bulge of his eyes, the flare of his nostrils. He looks stricken, as though I've beat him, taken my fist to his face instead of grabbing his shoulder. He is afraid, I register a second later. Of *me.*

Suddenly Regis is beside me, his gun gripped with two hands, his legs powerfully spread.

The man nearly swoons with fear. "P-p-please, don't shoot. Don't hurt me!" He pulls his wallet from a pocket and tosses it at my feet. "Take whatever you want. Take it all! I have a wife, a family."

As Regis bends down to grab the wallet, the man takes off running. Regis flips it open, quickly shuffling through the contents, then holsters his weapon. "Wait here," he admonishes, frustration deepening his voice, and takes off after the hiker. "Sir! Sir, your wallet! Please, wait. I'm a cop!"

As he brushes past me, I stagger, dumbfounded, bewildered, a daze of toxins flooding my system. It was him. I *knew* it was him. The dream. The feeling that he was near, that he heard my call. The flashes of forest like the one I'm standing in now. I shake my head to clear it, turn at the sound of a duck's call from the water, blink in rapid succession.

Something isn't right. My instincts keep pumping adrenaline through me, but the wires are all crossed, the signals wrong. I stare off dumbly down the trail where Regis went. And then I turn slowly until I feel a shudder deep inside. I realize I am facing the direction of the motel, of Aunt Myrtle. Dread rises in me like vomit, and I run.

30

Hiding

I am gasping as I trek to the cabin behind the motel, a sensation I don't recognize slicing through me like heartache. The flashes of forest I saw in the park gain eerie familiarity with each step. The burn to kill is still so alive in me it hurts, and the hunger is returning already, a craving for more poison than I can keep down, as if I could eat my way through this entire forest. But there's a fresh spasm of misery I can't trace. My eyes must shine like traffic lights, the witch in me so consuming she can no longer be contained.

I'm alarmed to find Bart at the base of the porch stairs, his head resting on his paws, eyes heavy with unspoken emotion. The front door stands open above him. I know I closed it behind me, left it locked. Did she escape? *Please,* I think. Tell me it's not worse, not what I think, what I feel like acid bubbling in my heart.

"What's the matter, boy?" I ask, tripping up to him, but he doesn't wag his tail or lift his head. He just cuts his eyes at me, round and dark and sad.

"Myrtle?" I call as I stomp up to the porch, step quietly inside. "You still here?" It's a silly question, one that implies she was in here of her own free will, but I don't know what else to say. I have resolved not to fight her this time. She can kill me if she wants, if she must. As long as she is safe. "Myrtle?"

I round into the living room and see her, legs sprawled and

bare, half off the couch where I left her. All that dark hair dripping over the side like syrup. Her face is turned up to the ceiling, eyes wide and unblinking. A thin red line ropes her neck just beneath the chin like a scar, a necklace of angry flesh.

I step closer and see the feather, sparkling green along one side, laid atop her breastbone.

My hand plummets into my pocket, hoping against hope, but the feather I had is there, a little crushed from my palm but whole. This one is new. An answer to my call.

My eyes fall closed. I am too late. The Strangler heard me, came for me, but I wasn't here. The mixed signals I felt by the lake snap into suffocating focus. Instead, he found Myrtle in my place, bound and helpless, an easy victim because I left her that way. Alone. Defenseless.

She is dead. The venery will come for me now to perform the last kiss. There is nothing I can do to save myself. It is what I deserve.

And then I hear Regis calling.

I rush out of the cabin and down the steps, throwing myself at him, pushing with all my force, my hands flattened against the polyethylene plates across chest, the vest he wore beneath his shirt for protection.

He looks baffled, pained. "Acacia, what the—where did you go? I told you to wait. I told you to meet me on the trail. We scared that man half to death."

He tries to pull my hands off him, but I jerk them away and step back.

"You have to leave," I blurt.

"What are you talking about?" he asks, brow wrinkling in confusion.

"Leave!" I shout, twisting my hands together. "You can't touch me anymore. I'm not safe. Go anywhere you want. Just not here. Not for a while, a *long* while."

He looks stricken, and I realize I must sound and look unhinged, with my radioactive eyes, hair tangled around my face, knees and hands dirty from the forest floor. "What's happened?"

I take a breath, steel myself. "He beat us."

Regis's eyes narrow. "What?"

"The Strangler, Regis! The man we were hunting, *together,* has won. Okay? He beat us. He was ahead of us the whole time. I don't know how, and right now I don't care. I will take care of him. But you can't stay here."

He peers over my shoulder toward the cabin, to Bart's lonely silhouette on the porch.

"I was wrong to bring you into this," I carry on, ignoring his confusion. "I thought we could help each other, but I see now that this is something I have to do on my own."

"What are you saying?" He focuses back on me.

"You're a distraction," I tell him. "One I cannot afford. One that has already cost me too much. I love you"—the words come as much of a shock to me as they do to him—"but my love is deadly, and I have a job to do. It's time I stop playing games."

"Piers," he says quietly. "Don't do this. Don't turn away from me, from *us.* It's the only place either of us makes sense."

I shake my head, tears hot and bitter on my cheeks. "I don't make sense anywhere," I tell him. "With anyone. I see that now. But I *do* love you, and I can't do this if I don't know you are safe. Do you understand? If you don't do what I ask, then he will keep winning—they all will, men like the Strangler, and Henry, and the guy with the blue truck—and we will lose. Both of us. Permanently."

He stands before me, disbelieving, his chest heaving with emotion.

"Pretend someone in your family is sick," I tell him. "And you've been called away on an emergency. You have to care for them. Make whatever excuses you can."

"In the middle of the most important investigation of my life?" he argues.

"Forget that now!" I fume. I need him to understand, to listen. "I will take care of it. You have to save yourself. Don't come back until I'm gone."

The thought of facing the Strangler alone—without Myrtle, without Regis, without support of any kind—is enough to topple me, but I can't let it. I can't let her death be in vain. I can't let anyone else get hurt because of my cowardice. It is enough that I left Henry in the world to do more damage. I must face this stronger, deadlier version of him. I must win. It is my only hope for redemption. Maybe not in this life, but in whatever comes next.

He walks over and tries to grab my arms, but I sidestep him. "Calm down. Tell me what this is about."

"They know!" I screech, fingers curling into claws. The venery doesn't know yet, but they will soon enough. "Aunt Myrtle . . . she's perceptive. She figured it out. She was on her way to kill you when I stopped her."

He shakes his head. "She knows what exactly?"

"That I told you! About her, me, *us*!" I pull at my hair, infuriated, the feathers, the toxins, the grief driving me over the edge. "Did you not hear anything from our conversation earlier? There are rules, Regis. We're not supposed to tell. Especially not a man. Myrtle won't harm you now." My voice catches on her name. "But it's only a matter of time, and I can't protect you from them all."

He grips the sides of his head. "Who? Piers, what did you do? Is Myrtle okay?"

I double over, my hands grasping my knees, the tears falling fast like summer rain. "It's not her you need to worry about," I choke out. "Not now."

He glances between me and the cabin, the truth dawning finally. His face goes slack. "You mean she . . . ?"

"Please don't make me say it," I beg, unable to form the words with my mouth. A sob burbles in my throat, and I choke it back.

He digs his teeth into a knuckle. "Fuck!" he shouts, tearing his jacket off and throwing it on the ground.

His emotion surprises me, but it shouldn't. Myrtle has a way of creeping under everybody's skin. She is irreplaceable. "Now you understand," I say softly. "You have to go and not come back."

He looks at me. "I'm not leaving you. Not now."

Inside, I crater. "You must. Because if you don't, you won't even see them coming. Do you hear me? There won't be time or a way for you to defend yourself. We're deadly! Don't you get that? I'm not the only one." I brush at my face and stand up, staring at him. "You can't protect me, Regis. But I can protect you, and this is how."

"Your family," he says with a question in his eyes.

I nod. "We are many. Not nearly enough to wipe out the evil in this world, but enough to keep a man like you—a good man—from ever standing a chance. They guard our secret fiercely. By telling you, I've violated everything that keeps us safe. They'll punish me for that once they realize. And then they'll come for you."

He swallows, the slow bob of his Adam's apple a punctuation.

"I've painted us into a corner," I tell him apologetically. "Please, just listen to me. Please leave. Once I'm gone, maybe then you can come back. But not for a long, long time."

He takes a deep breath. "Okay. If it will calm you down, make you feel better, I'll go. For a little while. But you have to promise me something."

I heave a sigh of relief. "Anything."

"Do not go after the Saranac Strangler on your own. You understand? Let my officers and lieutenants take care of it."

This is not a promise I can make. He has to know that. My life depends on this kill. Other women's lives depend on it. But I need him to believe me. I need him to leave. So, I swallow my truth and hold my gaze steady. "Deal."

He does the same. "Deal."

Watching him walk away is the second hardest thing I've ever done, next to killing Ed. Jumping off a bridge was easier by far.

I sigh and turn toward the cabin when he is gone at last. At least I will do some good before I die.

Again.

SHE'S HEAVY. MUCH heavier than I anticipated. I resume my grip around her ankles, one to each side, and lean forward, pulling with everything I have. It took me hours to dig the hole. I wasn't sure I could even do it, but something kicked in after the first couple of feet like adrenaline, a kinetic power that drove me on, chopping through tree roots and bringing up shovel after shovel of dirt. Thank goodness the soil here is rich and moist, easy to move. She will lie under a blanket of ferns when I'm done. A fitting resting place for someone who loved this land so much.

When I finally reach the grave, deep into the shadows of the conifers but close to the bunker, I lay her down beside it. Bart has followed the whole way. He seems to know I mean no harm, or at the very least that it's too late to do any further harm. Regis would seethe to see me cover up the Saranac Strangler's crime, but he's long gone, and I can't have his officers snooping around. Can't have her body discovered and splashed across the news for the venery. I need time to lie in wait. He'll return—the Strangler. Myrtle won't have satisfied him. He was there for me.

I kneel beside her, trying to drum up a few final words. My eyes are long since dry, though I know I'll cry again. She was more a mother to me in these last few months than mine ever could be. I'll miss her. And the guilt is an angry wasp, returning to sting my heart over and over. "I'm so sorry, Aunt Myrtle." I sniff, brushing the long strands of her hair away from her face, closing her eyes. "You deserved better. I promise to make it right. He *will* pay. And once he does, I'll turn myself over to the venery. I'll tell the truth of what happened to you and where you are. Of the blame I share in it."

Beside me, Bart lies down, poking his nose underneath her cold arm. I risk a rub to his brutish head. There must be some ceremony, some special way bane witches bury their own. It pains me that I don't know, that she won't receive it. A tart scent gusts past and fills my nose, like molded lemons. I turn and spot the small clump of destroying angels nearby. Rising, I gather them in one hand and return to the graveside. I lay one solemnly on her chest, folding her hands beneath it, and push the other two in my mouth, chewing until they slip easily down my throat.

My eyes meet the dog's. "Ready, boy?"

He looks up at me, head cocked, uncertain.

I purse my lips and wiggle my hands beneath her, rolling her over into the waiting grave. The thud of her landing sickens me, but I push my feelings aside as I begin to shovel the dirt back in. There's nothing to do for it now. And I am an old pro at living with the unlivable.

When I've patted the last of the dirt down over her and pulled fern fronds across the obvious disturbance, I get to my feet and brush off my hands and knees. Bart and I walk back to the cabin together, careful to erase and obscure our steps, the tracks where I dragged her in. Inside the little house, I set everything right, so that it looks like maybe she's just in the café or popped out to run a quick errand. I take a long hot shower in the bathroom, knowing it will be my last for a while, and dig a backpack out, stuffing the clothes she bought me inside. In the kitchen, I fill a reusable grocery bag with basic food items—peanut butter, bread, a block of cheese, cans of tuna. I turn off the overhead lights but leave the lamps burning, locking up as I depart. A few paces away, I stop and turn back, taking in the quaint cabin, its glowing windows and cheery appearance. This was home to me for a while, the closest thing to a home I've known. And it was her favorite place on earth. He took that from us both.

I will spend the coming days deep in her outpost in the ground, feeding. I don't care if the mushrooms give me away to investigators, Regis too far away to protect me. I'll eat whatever I can find, building her stores up in my body for the moment he returns for me. Then I will make this right.

Maybe I made some mistakes, took chances I shouldn't have and left us vulnerable, but he stole the best of what this life had to offer each of us. I will make him pay for that.

Myrtle would be pleased, I think as I walk away, the dog shuffling beside me. I am finally proud of my heritage, finally glad that I'm a bane witch.

31

Collision

Bart whines incessantly, pulling me from a heavy sleep, laden with disturbing dreams—Henry coming up behind me in the café, Myrtle's ghost walking the forest at night, Regis dead in a pool of vomit with Verna standing beside him. It's as if every fear I have is being projected across my sleeping mind, made all the more vivid by the mushrooms I keep eating. I know we aren't subject to a plant's poison as bane witches, but I no longer believe they have no effect on us. Or maybe it's just that I've been doing nothing the past three days but lying down in the dark, like an animal, chewing everything she left behind. It's overkill, I know, but I don't want to be caught off guard ever again.

It was a mistake bringing the dog with me. The constant trips to the surface to let him out put me at risk of being found. But he stood outside the door barking until I let him in, so I didn't have a choice. I don't dare pet him, for fear the toxins will leech out of me and into his skin. But he seems to understand, cowering in an opposing corner, watching with those big, soft, empathic eyes. And it's been nice to have someone to talk to, even if he can't say anything back. Apart from Bart, I am more alone in the world than I have ever been, which is saying a lot for someone who has lived my isolated past. And caring for him in whatever limited way I am able has given a modicum of structure to my days and nights, keeping the human in me alive, even just a bit, so that the witch cannot have all of me. But to be safe, I limit most of his potty breaks to after dark, feed him beans and tuna directly from the cans.

This time however, when I crack the door and he darts out, I see that it's morning. That early, diffuse light is setting the world aglow like something from a dream. "Bart!" I try to whisper-yell as he springs into the underbrush after a squirrel, but he ignores me. I have to remind myself as the irritation sets my teeth on edge that his independent streak, annoying as it is, is the only reason this living arrangement works at all.

I cross my arms over my chest and look around, trying to find some calm. The woods are magical at this time, though the chill is beginning to seep beneath my jacket. In another couple of months, this shelter will become miserable without a heat source, dangerous. Something tells me—a niggling beneath my ribs, the feathers I keep in my pocket, a matching set—that I won't need to be here long.

I cup my hands around my mouth and blow, duck back into the dugout to grab a mug of water. The carboy is nearly empty. I grab it by its plastic neck, the remains of my water supply sloshing in the bottom, and begin to climb back up. I can refill it at the cabin before it gets any later and the risk of being seen increases. Though I do not relish the idea of hauling it back alone.

Nearing the surface, I'm startled by a strange sound. I pause, clinging to the stairs, and listen. At first, I think it's the hum of a distant engine. But it's too early in the season for a snowmobile, and they don't allow motorboats on the lake. Then I realize it's much closer, much lower than that.

It's Bart . . . *growling.*

I roll my eyes and heave myself up the last few steps. Stupid dog must have spotted something bigger than a squirrel this time, like a fox or a buck. At the top, I climb out, the carboy before me. Once I get fully to my feet, I start to scold him. "You goofy dog, there's nothing that can get us all the way out—"

The words fall from my lips like pebbles, dropping to the ground.

He's standing about twenty feet off, eyes focused on me, a curious look skirting his face. He is fixed, so still that the backdrop of swaying green needles and falling leaves is the only thing that makes me aware time has not completely stopped. I know without a doubt who he is, though I've never seen him before. The latex cap is slick to his head, not that it matters. It's clear he shaves. Not just his head, but his whole body. I can smell the coconut fragrance of the women's shaving cream he uses. He's wearing some kind of green waterproof suit—vinyl or PVC—zipped up to his chin, legs tucked into strange rubber boots with the soles melted down. He has a pair of tweezers in one pocket and a plastic bag lined with petroleum jelly. From his hand, the paracord dangles in a colorful loop. It's new, a piece he's been saving just for me.

His face is pink, pinched, soft around the brows with eyes set too close together. But beneath the tender flesh, his bones are hard and cold like galvanized steel. They cry out for blood. On the outside, he's a stranger, oddly put together, a fish out of water in this environment. But on the inside, he is menacing, deliberate, removed. On the inside, he is Henry to the core.

The tremble begins at my feet, knocking my knees together as it travels up my legs and spine, setting my teeth to chattering. The fear is sharp, strong—it overwhelms me, all my brave ideas about killing this man melting at my feet like frost in the sun. The years that Henry tortured me rise up from the forest floor, taunting. I feel the weakness inside me cowering. I am just a woman after all.

But then I see Myrtle's fierce smile as I left her that morning. *Hunt well.* And the woman transforms, gives way, for something far older and far darker to take over.

I drop the carboy at my feet, the last of the water spilling out onto the ground. We are locked in each other's gaze, suspended by the experience of finally materializing that which we have hunted for so long, like bugs caught in amber. And then I do something he wasn't prepared for.

I charge him.

It takes a split second for the alarm to register on his face, for the signal to move from his brain to his feet, and in that time I am gaining speed, ground. My teeth gnash the air, every part of me committed to tearing his flesh from his bones. I will savor his death like wine, like that expensive Riesling from Alsace Henry couldn't shut up about.

But then he does something I am not prepared for.

He runs.

I tear through the forest behind him, certain he cannot outpace me, or at least not Bart, who has bolted past me in pursuit. But he's faster than I anticipated, and he's scared. His adrenaline spikes are fueling him even as my body burns to catch up, the magic driving me on.

I lose all sense of direction in the chase. Branches and limbs slap past me, tearing at my hair and clothes. I am certain to be striped with scratches when this is over, but I don't care. I can taste him on the air, that acrid bile of fear, the deep rot inside him like a tumor, the tang of all his sins. It sings to me, his flavor. It makes my blood throb in my veins. I am so close now, so close that if I spit it might land on him. But I want the satisfaction of seeing him die. I don't want to hurl my poison loosely in his direction. I want to sink it into him with my own teeth.

I stretch a hand before me, reaching for the hood of his jacket, when a collision from the left sends me spinning to the ground, so hard I feel my shoulder give beneath me and think it might be dislocated. Dirt grinds into my teeth, and my head swims even when the world stops moving. I blink again and again, trying to clear the bright spots before me. As soon as I can, I get to my feet, pushing myself up slowly, shakily.

He is only a few feet away, hands already on his knees, heaving like he might vomit. When he looks up, it startles me. I know his face, but I'm not sure from where.

"Are you all right?" he asks, breathing heavily.

I stumble back a step. "Stay away from me."

He stands to his full height, hands on hips, that chiseled jaw like a magazine ad. His hair is a ribbon of black, glossy like polished granite. His shoulders those of a linebacker. He's beautiful, really, but he's an unknown variant, a piece that shouldn't be on the board in a very deadly game. "Mrs. Davenport? Are you Piers Davenport?"

The name has struck me speechless, and he doesn't look like he's truly asking. He looks like he already knows.

"Who wants to know?" I ask, wiping the dirt out of my mouth.

The muscles behind his eyes slacken with relief, making him look sleepy and happy at the same time. He steps toward me.

I put a hand out. "I meant what I said. Stay back."

His brows cross over his eyes, but he quickly shifts gears. "My name is Investigator Emil Reyes—"

"Investigator?" I scrutinize him. Those biceps and that overall air of authority. I should have known. "Are you a cop? Did Regis send you?"

He seems confused. "Regis? I'm sorry. I'm from Charleston. South Carolina. We've been following your case."

"You've been following me?" I take another step back.

"Investigating," he tries to say.

"Where's your uniform? Your ID?"

He looks down at the sweatshirt and jeans he has on. "Investigating and then following. Please, Mrs. Davenport, I'm here to help you."

"Stop calling me that," I growl at him. "That's not who I am anymore."

"Can we go somewhere and talk?" he asks, eyes pleading.

"Not until I see your badge."

He pulls it out for me, holds it up.

"Toss it there," I tell him, pointing at the ground. "And then step back."

He debates and finally acquiesces.

I approach the shining emblem warily, keeping one eye on him at all times. Only when I am standing over it do all the pieces shift into place like a motherboard firing up—that face, so handsome and helpless at once, the name, the job. I know this man. Almost as intimately as I know Henry or the Strangler. His isn't a life I'm destined to take, but one I was destined to save. He's the cop who was choking that night, the one I rescued in the restaurant. What he's doing here is a bigger mystery than what I am.

Convinced he is who he says, I walk back several steps, sighing. "Pick it up," I tell him. "I recognize you."

He looks relieved, a flash of something akin to fondness in his dark eyes. "I owe you a debt," he tells me. "It's why I'm here."

"Well, you should have stayed in Charleston," I tell him, hearing Myrtle's own sass in the tone of my voice. "Hasn't anyone ever told you no good deed goes unpunished?"

"What?" His eyes narrow, perplexed. I guess he thought I'd be *happy* to see him.

"Nothing," I say. "Come on. I have somewhere we can talk. But you have to walk in front of me. And no matter what, you can't touch me. Not for any reason."

His eyes practically cross with the questions hovering between them, but he nods in agreement. "Okay. Lead the way."

I point south. And he begins walking.

I WAIT FOR him to deposit himself in a chair at the table, and then I get a glass of water, trying to keep my eyes from straying to the living room, to the sofa where she was. "How did you find me?"

He clasps his hands on the table. "Wasn't easy. Instinct, I guess. And a bit of luck. You left a few clues, bits of evidence in your wake. Once I figured out you didn't drown but fled, it was just a matter of following them."

I tug at my lower lip, annoyed. "I thought I was so careful."

He gives me a tight smile. "You were, but everybody leaves something. They found your life vest in the marina. There was a stain—same color as the pokeweed berries from the note and the bridge. And then the report came out about the man in Virginia, and the video from the hotel lobby, the car in Syracuse. I found the shirt you left behind in the cemetery there. The neck was rimmed with hair dye. I asked around campus and a girl admitted to driving you to the bus station, said you mentioned Crow Lake. From there, it was just a little detective work to find your aunt, connect her to you through the same maiden name. Birth certificates and census records confirmed the relation, and I came here. But the motel and house were empty, so I—"

"Risked getting yourself hopelessly lost by stumbling around the woods?"

He grins. "It was a hunch."

"A pretty good one," I admit.

He shrugs. "I heard the dog, followed the sound, ran into you chasing that man."

"Literally," I add.

"I saw my chance and I took it. I didn't want to lose you. Who was that guy anyway?"

I try to hide my annoyance at having been intercepted. It may be his fault, but he didn't do it on purpose. "A squatter. They get 'em up here all the time." I take a deep breath and square my shoulders, setting the glass on the counter beside me. "What are you doing here, Detective? Come to haul me away? Arrest me for jumping off a bridge? If you're good enough to put all that together, then surely, you're good enough to put together *why*."

"I know why," he's quick to confirm, and his eyes lower respectfully. "I may not know everything he's put you through, but what you didn't take a picture of, I can imagine."

I lean back against the counter by the sink skeptically. "Can you?"

"We have a connection, you and I," he says, watching me.

He's not wrong, but if he's operating on some misguided principle that he *knows* me, knows what I need, then it's my job to set him straight. "I appreciate your gratitude. I do, truly. And I will always be glad that I was there for you at that precise moment and able to act quickly. But don't let coincidence cloud your judgment or delude you, Detective. There is a wealth of information about me that you can never know and that I am not at liberty nor under any obligation to tell you. Besides, I haven't got the time."

He only smiles, which is not exactly the reaction I was expecting.

"I got into law enforcement because of my mother," he tells me. "She was a victim of domestic violence. The things I witnessed growing up, they stayed with me." He taps his chest with a finger. "In here. You can't unsee stuff like that. It burrows into you, changes you. Not always for the better. She got out finally, no thanks to the police or anyone else for that matter. Just fear and willpower, and the grace of God, according to her. But the tall man altered us all, and I'll never forget or forgive him. You're not the only one with a Henry, Piers, and you're not the only one who knows what it is to run."

I close my eyes, hating the idea of his face, younger, smaller, lined with worry and panic. "I'm sorry. I didn't know."

He shakes his head. "How could you?" Leaning forward on the table, he says, "I know my appearance here is uninvited and must come as a shock, but believe me when I say, I came to warn you."

The confidence I felt earlier chasing the Strangler, the killer instinct, seems to puddle at my feet. "Warn me?"

"You're not safe here," he says, brutally quiet. "If I found you, so can he."

My fingernails dig into the counter's overhang. *Henry.* My stomach burns and I clutch it helplessly, the fear a living thing in my body. *Henry is coming.* "When did he leave?"

"Before me. He won't have some of the things I did at his disposal, but I've met your husband. He's smart. Smarter than he deserves to be. And very little escapes him. It was brazen, what you did, trying to frame him for your murder. I can admire that, even if it is illegal. But it's backfired. You have to know what that means."

"I know," I tell him quietly. "And I appreciate your concern, that you came all this way. But I can't leave. Not now. Not yet."

A troubled expression crosses his face before he presses his lips together. "I'm here unofficially, but I can take you into custody, ma'am. I'll do that if it's the only way to keep you safe."

"Are you threatening me, Detective?"

He doesn't respond.

I level my gaze on him. "You can't keep me safe. I appreciate that you want to try, Emil. I do. You're one of the good ones. And I know you feel like there's some kind of score to settle between us. But you have no idea what you've stepped into the middle of. You're in over your head."

"With all due respect," he says confidently, "I'm not afraid of your husband."

I smile at him. "I'm not talking about Henry."

Slowly, he reaches into a back pocket, pulls out a set of handcuffs, lays them on the table between us.

"Those look pretty official to me," I tell him. When he frowns, I say, "I get that you want to be the hero here, but I don't need you to save me." Carefully, I set my palms against the tabletop and lean down. "I've had enough of the male ego to last me a lifetime. Thank you for giving me a heads-up, but let me give you a warning in return. If you lay so much as a finger on me, I promise you will seriously regret it."

He sighs, wiping his palms across his thighs and looking away. When he turns back, the hard lines of his face have softened. Beneath the testosterone-fed exterior, I realize a little boy is lurking, wounded, afraid, empathetic. "You know, it was my sister who told me you weren't dead. But even if you were, she didn't think I should feel sorry for you because it meant you were finally free. And she would know. My sister is the one who got it the worst out of the three of us. She grew up with a twisted sense of what love was supposed to look like, fell into one bad relationship after another. The last one nearly killed her. Without my help, I don't think she or her beautiful daughter would be here today. I did what I did for her not as a cop but as a brother. And I'm sitting here before you now, not as an investigator but as someone who cares about what happens to you, who is concerned for your safety. You don't have to listen to me, but aside from him, I'm the only one coming for you."

"I wouldn't say that's true."

The voice is such a shock that the water glass slips from my hand, shattering into dozens of jagged pieces across the floor. She stands in the doorway of the cabin, leaning against the frame. How she opened it without anyone noticing, I'm not sure. But an edge of wariness steals over me, the knowing that among our kind there are gifts, unique abilities that can't always be explained, like Myrtle's night vision.

Her hair is pinned up at the base of her neck, a soft golden-streaked knot of smoothed-over curls. The suit is Chanel. Black and white, with a long skirt and pockets she will never use. The leather boots gather up her calves, heels like ice picks. But it's her eyes I can't look away from. One second blue and the next green, radiant, as if backlit, impossibly large. They are set into her caramel skin like beryls. She smiles and the sun seems to rise with the corners of her mouth, brightening the cabin.

Emil Reyes immediately scrambles to his feet. He holds a hand out, but she doesn't take it. "Have I seen you before?" he asks, eyes scrunching up.

She puckers a lip. "Perhaps," she says mysteriously. "They are always taking my picture without permission, plastering me in the magazines and papers. Who can say?"

I glance from him to her and back, noting the way his eyes widen as something registers behind them.

"I have seen you!" he says with a snap. "You're that Spanish film star! My sister loves your movies."

She gives him a cursory nod. "That was many years ago in Barcelona," she tells him demurely. Her eyes lock suddenly on mine, as deep and unforgiving as the sea. "I've brought your aunt a gift."

32

Rabbit

I am afraid to be alone with her. I nearly reach out for Emil Reyes when he politely excuses himself before remembering that my touch could destroy the very life I once saved. But his lingering gaze tells me he doesn't intend to leave the area. Not until he ensures my safety. I follow him to the door and point to the ring of spare cabin keys Myrtle keeps hanging on the rack. "Pick one. They're all clean. You can stay on-site as long as you promise to keep away from me." It might be a foolish, split-second decision, but this way I can keep him close, instead of worrying when he'll turn up unannounced. His presence might at least keep Henry at bay, if he finds his way up here.

He slides one off the ring—*three*. Holding it up, he tells me, "Think about what I said." Then he steps out the door.

"You do the same," I reply, watching him go.

I turn to stare at the glamorous figure so elegantly out of place in Myrtle's rustic kitchen. The Barcelona venery must be doing quite well for itself. Somehow, her presence is more unnerving to me than the Saranac Strangler's. She carries herself like a panther, sleek and self-assured, the world parting as she passes. And her beauty, however undeniable, is like that of an ice sculpture—as unforgiving and inhospitable as deep space. But it is the secrets I must keep from her that leave me breathless in her presence. I wasn't ready to confront the venery—*any* venery—yet. My work is still undone.

"How old are you?" I ask her.

"How old do you think I am?" she returns. This is something she's good at, this game of questions. The flirtation, the coy dance. They are likely part of her specialty.

"Thirty-five? Forty at the most," I reply, crossing my arms over my chest. "But you made it sound like your acting career happened a long time ago."

She smiles and moves slowly through the kitchen to the living room, looking at the odd decorative item, picking up the old photo of Myrtle and the other bane witches, taking in the view from the windows. "I have lived more years than my face has recorded," she says with a laugh. "And acting careers are very short for women." She turns to face me, the sun beaming in around her silhouette. "I age exceptionally well. It's in the genes."

"You're the contact from the venery in Barcelona, the one they wanted to carry in a delivery?"

"You can call me Emilia." A small purse on a gold chain hangs from one shoulder. She slides it off and opens the clasp, pulling out a brown paper bag that's been rolled closed.

"Not *Daisy* or *Rose* or some other flower?" I ask flatly.

She grins. "Americans are so strange. We don't hold to such traditions where I'm from. Our venery is older, less bothered by such details." She passes the bag to me. It's then I notice the black gloves on her hands.

"You've been feeding," I note as I take it from her.

Her smile is wicked. "I am always feeding."

I unroll the bag and glance inside. A spate of red berries greets me, glowing orange in the light. "How did you get these on the plane?"

Her eyes follow my every gesture, independent of the rest of her. "I have my ways."

I bet she does.

She stalks around the room and takes a seat on the sofa. I don't correct her, even though everything in me is screaming for her to get up. I make a vow to take that sofa out and burn it in the woods. Myrtle would understand.

I lower myself into the armchair across from her. "They let you *act* in your venery? Have a career in the public eye?"

She draws a breath. "I told you, we are less paranoid. Besides, do you think I was going to keep this face hidden for long? My venery has made my career work for them. It has served us well."

I open my mouth to ask another question, but she cuts me off.

"No. Now you will answer a question for me. Where is your aunt?"

I see a glint in her eye that tells me lying will be futile. "She's gone," I whisper, the emotions rushing up my throat so that the words come out shaky and faint.

Her brows lower like thunderclouds hovering over her eyes. "Gone?"

I dash at the tears as they fall. "My mark. He came for me, but I wasn't here. He killed her instead."

"He came for *you*?" Even riddled with confusion and concern, she is stunning.

I nod briskly. "I hunt killers," I tell her. "Serial killers. It's my class."

Her lips tighten around a muttered string of words in Spanish that I don't recognize but sound an awful lot like curses. "We will drink to your aunt in the Barri Gòtic, beneath the spires of the Holy Cross. I promise you that. Please give my condolences to your *hermanas oscuras,* your *dark sisters.*"

I should tell her that they don't know yet, but I'm afraid of what she will do. Her face is as fresh as a peony in spring, but her spirit is older than the city she calls home, gnarled by what it's seen. And her alliance is with them, not with me. Should they stand against me, it's not my side she would choose.

"I must go," she says. She rises and I do, too.

"Wait." I duck into the kitchen, pilfering through cabinets and canisters until I find the browning remains of a couple of yellow warts and a third mushroom I don't recognize. Walking back into the living room, I hand them to her. "An exchange," I say. "You came all this way. I'd hate for you to go home empty-handed."

She cups them in the buttery lambskin of her designer gloves, eyes glinting with interest. "Gracias." Without hesitation, she pops one into her mouth and quickly swallows it. Noting my surprise, she says, "I told you. I am *always* feeding."

"Your class must keep you very busy," I remark, thinking it must be something far less specialized than mine. Date rapists maybe. Child abusers. The cavalier way these terms now flit through my mind should sicken me with cognitive dissonance, but it leaves only a residue of disturbance.

She laughs as if I have said something spectacularly clever. "My dear girl, they are *all* my class."

"All?"

Her eyes narrow in an instant, like slivers of glass. "If history has taught us anything, it is this—powerful men never tire of abusing their positions. There is much work to do still." She relaxes, smiles languidly, her shoulders sloping gently down her back. "And you know what they say—*a very little poison can do a world of good,*" she adds with a wink.

Myrtle's voice that day in our garden comes slamming into me at her words, Myrtle's long twist of hair, her towering presence, her knowing gaze. It hurts so much I have to fight the urge to cry out. But beneath the pain, a current of family and advocacy and magic. Beneath the pain, Myrtle is there. In the words. In the room. She is guiding me still, I realize. She is on my side.

Her hand tightens around mine holding the bag. When she speaks again, her top lip curls. "Black bryony," she says. "From Majorca. Enough to take down ten strong men and sicken a couple of arrogant bastards in need of a lesson. A little Spanish flavor for your *conejo.*"

I make a face, unfamiliar with the word.

"It means 'rabbit,'" she tells me, grinning. "When you find him, give him a kiss from me."

❧

I SIT ON the sofa where Myrtle died and stare into the paper bag long after Emilia is gone. I want to press the berries into my mouth and chew, tasting the high Spanish sun and the breezes of the coast in their tart skin. But I don't need them. Not with so many amatoxins already coursing through my system. I just didn't want to tell Emilia her travel was in vain.

When Bart yowls at the door, I roll the bag tightly up and set it on the table, to let him in.

We should return to the bunker, huddle there in the darkness and wait. But I can't bring myself to leave the cabin yet. *One night,* I think. I will stay one night. For Myrtle. For me. For the dog. I will take a shower and rest my bones on the soft padding of a real bed. I'll cook on a stove, eat a legitimate dinner, hydrate without rationing. By now, I'm sure the regulars have seen the CLOSED FOR TRAVEL sign in the door of the café. A couple of brave ones maybe even skulked back here, hollered her name for good measure before straggling back to town, contented for the time being. They'll let it rest for now. But in another week or so, when they circle back around and nothing has changed, that's when they'll call someone. The sheriff's department will descend on this place like a swarm of locusts. Maybe they'll find Myrtle's body in the forest. Maybe they won't. I won't be able to say because I won't be here by then. If Emil Reyes is to be believed, I may not be alive at all. Between the Saranac Strangler, Henry, and the venery, I have too many enemies willing to finish the job Henry started.

So, one night, *this* night, shouldn't matter.

At least, that's what I tell myself.

THE WATER IS so hot I feel like my muscles are melting beneath it when I hear the bang. I quickly turn the faucet off and stand there, dripping, the shower head still steaming above me as I listen. It was difficult to hear over the rush of the water, not loud like a gunshot but softer, like a door closing or a drawer being slammed. I strain to hear if Bart is making any noise—his presence in the house with me my only comfort. But silence echoes back, the hush of the gloaming.

My fingers curl stiffly around the edge of the shower curtain, tugging it back as I cringe at the sound of the rings scraping against the rod. I step out and pull Myrtle's Southwestern robe on, not bothering to tie it. My hair drips a fountain of water down the back, causing the fabric to stick to my skin.

I pause with my hand on the doorknob and set my ear to the crack. Nothing.

There are so many people after me that I have no idea who I might find on the other side. It was a mistake staying here. I should have returned to the shelter. But the Strangler knows where the shelter is now anyway. Still, the odds against one are considerably better than they are against three or more.

I turn the knob so carefully; it scarcely makes a sound. Pulling the door back, I poke my head into the hallway. The light from the living room filters in, enough to see the corners are empty of moving shadows.

I step out and inch toward the living room. Bart is lying at the foot of Myrtle's chair, his head on his paws. He looks at me as I enter, tracking my movements with his eyes. Then, they slide eerily toward the kitchen.

I follow his gaze, gliding around the furniture with the quiet of a ghost. When I finally have a view of the kitchen, I find it empty. I turn to the dog, "Hey, buddy. Everything okay in here?"

He lifts his head, curious, and I sigh. I check all the doors and windows meticulously before turning out every light in the house, pulling on some clean underwear and a tank top, and climbing into bed. My imagination must be getting the better of me, with good reason. But I need to keep my head. The next few days, next few hours, are too important to lose my focus. Even the smallest miscalculation could have deadly consequences. I've already witnessed that.

An hour later, I decide I've done such a good job battening down the hatches that I've shut sleep out as well. I flop from one side to the other on the springy mattress and soft cotton sheets. I should be enjoying this, but I can't settle. Bart is curled on the floor, attempting to ignore me.

And then I hear a rustle from the next room—*her* room.

I bolt upright in bed and slip from the blankets. This time, I move so slowly, so soundlessly, that my own breathing roars by comparison. The door to her room is open a crack, and soft light spills out. I am certain it was closed when I went to bed. As certain as I am of what I heard in the shower. My throat tightens as the fear creeps higher.

When I reach her door, I nudge it open, every muscle bunching inside me, ready to spring into action. It squeals on its hinges as it swings. The room is empty, the window closed. But the lamp on her bedside table is on.

I did not leave that lamp on.

"Myrtle?" I feel instantly foolish but can't help myself. When she doesn't answer, I open her closet door. Inside her flannels and overalls hang side by side, a rustic curtain. But there is no one there, and the space is too small for them to hide from me.

My shoulders sag as tears begin to gather beneath my eyes.

Regardless of how I felt earlier, all I can think now is that she probably hates me for what happened. She's probably haunting me because I was too stupid to listen. Spinning around, I stalk back to my room and gather my things, tying her robe tight at my waist and pulling on my boots without lacing them. "Come on, buddy," I tell the dog. "We're not gonna get any sleep here."

At the door, I don't even bother locking up. The cabin has rejected me. It was foolish to expect otherwise. I won't come back here.

The thought of the shelter cot gives me instant leg cramps, and the long walk in the dark concerns me. Can I even find it like this? What if I get stuck out for the night? A chilly breeze gusts up the hem of the robe in response. I stand on the path under the trees, looking left to right. The futon Myrtle kept in the café loft suddenly rushes to mind. I can make the walk to the shelter tomorrow. For now, the café is closer and a lot more appealing. The dog and I head for it.

At the entrance, I look around, but all is quiet. The two guests we had have presumably left, the parking lot empty save for Emil's car, a sleek Dodge Charger. They probably felt like they won the lottery when there was no one here to square up with. I let Bart and me into the café and head toward the staircase. The familiar sight of the tables and stacks of chairs, the bar and kitchen at the back where Myrtle always positioned herself, bring fresh tears. This time, I let them fall, let myself feel the hurt and betrayal, the deep, penetrating grief of losing a life I was just starting to love. I climb the spiral stairs with a heavy heart, and pull the futon out, a small, tinny note of gratitude for her constant preparedness ringing through me.

When I lie down, I drift off almost instantly, the firm futon cushion grounding my sorrow as Bart finds his place on the floor at my side. I don't doze. I don't dream. I simply fall into a puddle of black, thankful for an hour of reprieve and a warm, safe room, the chance to let go and forget.

It must be the witching hour when I hear it again, the same soft bang, like a cabinet door closing downstairs. I jolt awake, eyes dilating in the dark, and hover at the doorway, looking down the stairs. But I can't see anything amiss.

Behind me, Bart is on his feet, ears perked, as if he knows something I don't. But he is quiet, and that gives me some comfort.

"Stay here," I tell him, closing him into the loft room.

One step at a time, I spiral down to the café floor. The room is dark, except for the moonlight that trickles in the front windows. The tables and chairs loom like giant mushrooms, shadowy heaps sprouting from the floor, the forest creeping in.

I tighten the tie of the robe and walk toward the door. For a moment, I just stand there, staring out at the moon, a half-eaten disk in the sky. It reflects the state of my heart, a cookie with so many bites taken out it's almost unrecognizable. Somewhere in the far distance, Regis is stretched out under a blanket, waiting for the chance to come home. At least he is safe, I think with some pride. At least I have done that much.

I place my hand on the door handle before turning back, a quick tug to check that it's locked. But instead of resistance, the door swings toward me, letting in a draft of frigid night air.

It takes a split second for the truth to register—the key from the laundry. He has found it, let himself in. And then I catch his reflection in the glass—the slightest movement, a flash of refracted light on rubber, right behind me.

There is very little time to react. The cord is around my neck before I can even turn my head. My only stroke of luck is that I've put a hand up in front of my throat. The nylon bites into my fingers, pressing my knuckles into my larynx. From this angle, I cannot defend myself. All the poison stored inside me will stay there unless I can turn around.

There is a quick yank on the paracord and I realize he is knotting it behind me, and the heavy scent of iron as he slides the rebar in. With one turn, I feel my finger crushing against me. I can still breathe, but only just.

My free hand lashes the air, looking for something to seize. And then I remember the plastic and petroleum jelly I scented earlier that morning and know I will have one small window to save myself, if I stay conscious.

I hear the zipper of his suit slide down and my heart rate kicks up. *Typical man,* I want to think with a laugh, if only I could find the air. *Can't resist pulling his dick out.* I know this game already; I've played it before.

In another second, I hear the plastic rustle, and that's when I swing my arm behind me, before he can get the baggie open, and grasp his naked member with my free hand, squeezing the tender flesh mercilessly, digging my nails into the skin until I feel the blood wetting my quicks.

His cry is agony, but it sounds like victory to me. In a desperate struggle to pull my hand away, he loosens his hold on the tourniquet—the piece of rebar hitting the floor with a metallic clang—and I twist around, but not before he manages to wrench my wrist over, nearly snapping my elbow.

A wail of pain escapes me, and then he is on me again, both hands at my throat as he backs me against the bit of wall between the door and the window. I should be afraid; his fingers are unforgiving as they choke me. But all I feel is rage, magma hot and twice as thick. It pools in my limbs, beneath my tongue, like fire in my cells. I gather it under the roof of my mouth and spit it into his face.

His eyes squeeze shut against the assault of saliva, but he doesn't let go. A shrieking intake of air begins to sound in the back of his throat. My vision starts to blacken at the corners, and I feel peace. I may not make it long enough to watch him die, but at least I will go knowing he is soon to follow.

And then the blast rips through the glass of the door beside us and knocks him back, his right shoulder flinging to the side as he hits the floor. Emil Reyes pushes through the door, his gun pointed at the Strangler. He turns and sees me holding my throat, gasping for breath. He reaches a hand toward me, but I stumble away.

"No, don't touch me," I manage to wheeze out. "Not yet."

I've fed so much that I can still feel the venom mingling with my bloodstream, even though I should have already discharged the magic when I spit into his face. With time, it will ebb away, but I won't risk Reyes.

A gasp from below sounds, and we turn to see the Strangler sliding back from us, pushing with both feet, trying to turn over, trying to find the strength to run. I can't let that happen. I won't.

Without thinking, I leap on him, one hand pressing his head against the floor as I lick my other hand from palm to fingertip and dig into the bullet hole at his shoulder, blood gurgling over my fingers as he screams.

The cop's arms come around my waist, lifting me off and tossing me to the side. I catch myself in a crouch and spin back in time to see the convulsions begin. The Saranac Strangler jerks and flops like a landed fish, vomit erupting from his mouth like lava from a volcano, the latex cap slipping off his head.

The cop goes to kneel beside him, to try and lift him up so he doesn't choke on his own vomit, but I smack his arm away. "Get up!" I yell, giving him a hard shove, being sure not to touch his skin, though I feel the magic already dissipating within me. "Leave him!"

"He's choking!" His eyes practically cross with alarm. "He's going to die!"

"I said, leave him." I grind the words out through clenched teeth.

A sputter interrupts us, and we look over to see those close-set eyes roll to white, blood vessels bursting across them, before he goes still.

Again, Emil starts toward him, but I step between him and the body.

"I should check his pulse," he says angrily. "Record the time of death."

"You should turn around and leave this place," I tell him. "And never come back. Thank you for saving my life. Consider your debt paid. Go home, Detective."

He takes a step away from me, the venom in my voice enough of a warning. "Who is he?"

"No one to you," I say quietly, turning to look down on him. At least now, when the venery comes for me, I can die in peace. "But someone very, very important to me."

"What happened to him?" he asks now, stepping beside me, but careful not to overstep.

"I did," I say. "The same as I did to Don."

He looks at me, perplexed. "I don't understand."

My eyes meet his—sorrowful, resigned, exhausted. "It's better that way."

He moves to the wall and pulls a chair from one of the stacks, sits in it, legs spread and elbows on knees, trying to gather himself. "What now?"

"Now I call the sheriff and report a break-in. You leave before they get here. I'll probably get arrested. If not tonight, soon. But, then again, I've done them a favor. Maybe they won't investigate too hard."

"How will you explain the gunshot wound?" he asks, challenging my plan.

I can't think straight. I lean against one of the tables. "I won't. It really won't make a difference anyway."

He watches me for a moment, sits up. "I'm not leaving."

I start to argue but he cuts me off. "You can just say I was a customer, someone passing through. And I'll tell the truth. I'm a cop. I heard a scream. Came out and saw you struggling, shot him through the glass door. He fell and I have no idea what happened after that. Looked like he had some kind of reaction."

I smile. "They've heard that one before."

His brow gathers like a folded sheet.

"Never mind. Suit yourself, but I'm giving you the chance to clear out of this before things get worse."

He purses his lips defiantly.

"If you're worried about Henry, the place will be crawling with cops soon enough. I'll be safe. And that's *if* he's even managed to figure out where I am, which I doubt. I never told him anything about my family."

"Make the call," he says calmly. "I'll wait."

33

Last Kiss

"You shouldn't be here," I say angrily, staring down the man who has my heart despite how many chunks have been taken from it.

Regis glances at the deputies he brought with him. They circle the body like ants, carefully recording every detail. Grabbing my arm, he pulls me several steps away. "Did you honestly think I would just go off to save my own ass and leave you behind at a time like this?"

I work my jaw. "Yes. I did. And I haven't seen you, so I figured it worked."

He frowns. "I've been out here every day looking for you, but it seemed like you just up and vanished. Where were you? What happened here?" he says under his breath.

"A man broke into the café and attacked me. By the looks of it, he's the Saranac Strangler." I lean in and mutter, "You can thank me later."

His lips pinch with agitation. "Obviously. But how did he find you? And how did he end up with a bullet hole in his shoulder?"

I shrug, too tired to give him the details. "One of our customers shot him." I would have expected a little more concern and little less interrogation, but once a sheriff, always a sheriff. I should have known he wouldn't leave, not really. "Thankfully, I'm okay," I say sarcastically.

He eyes Emil Reyes, where he sits in the corner being questioned by a lieutenant. "Kind of an odd tourist for these parts."

I glance toward Emil, our eyes meeting briefly, and away. "Oh,

I don't know. He's fit enough to hike these mountains. Said he was looking for some peace and quiet."

Regis glowers. "He's from the South. I don't trust people from the South."

"I'm from the South," I remind him. "And he's a cop. That should score some points with you."

"From Charleston," he adds under his breath. "Am I supposed to believe that's a coincidence?"

"You can believe whatever you want," I tell him. "I've told you the truth. Or as much of it as I'm willing to tell at the moment."

He sighs, frustration tightening the muscles in his jaw, causing him to rub his eyes. "So that's him," he says, eyes pointed at the man lying dead on the floor.

"Yes. You'll find the plastic bag and Vaseline he used to jerk off over there," I say directing him with a finger. "There are tweezers in his pocket. The paracord and rebar are obvious. And this." I lift my chin and point to my neck, where angry red skin circles it. "This should be evidence enough."

"You need to go to the hospital," he tells me.

I shake my head. "No. Not tonight." I don't explain that I'm still worried about my toxicity levels. That I fed so much I fear I'm not completely safe yet, even though I felt the magic draining away. That I don't want to be poked and prodded by doctors ever again, knowing now I'm as much witch as woman. "I'll go in a few days. I need a break."

"Why were you in here in the middle of the night?" He looks down at me sternly, like I'm an unruly child.

"I couldn't sleep at the cabin. It felt weird without Myrtle." This, at least, is the truth.

He ducks his head, placing his hands on his hips as he stares at the floor.

"What are you going to do?" I ask. "About him?" I nod toward the Strangler.

"My job," he says simply. Then, seeing the hurt in my face, he adds, "Don't worry. I'll keep them from digging too deep. Once we positively ID him, there's a very good chance they'll drop their questions. On the surface, it all adds up well enough. I'll chalk the vomit up to shock from the gunshot."

"What about the coroner?" I ask.

Regis looks down. "I don't know what he'll say is the cause of death. Certainly not a gunshot wound to the right shoulder. But I have no intention of pursuing it further. We got our guy, and that's all that matters. I can protect you from this much."

EMIL STOPS ME on the porch as I am reaching for the front door-knob of Myrtle's cabin. "You sure you don't want me to stay with you tonight? You've been through a trauma. It might help you feel safe."

I smile wearily at him. "My whole life has been a trauma," I remind him. "Tonight wasn't my first rodeo."

He stands back, slipping his hands into his pockets, shaking the fabric of his sweatpants nervously. "Okay. But just so you know, I'll be keeping watch from the front of the property in case your husband turns up."

As if Henry would be stupid enough to pull straight into the parking lot for anyone to see. But I don't say that. I just nod and give him my thanks, desperate to lie down.

As he walks away, Bart dances around his legs, looking up at him adoringly. "Bart!" I call. He stops, cocking his head at me, then dashes after the handsome investigator, smitten.

"Stupid dog," I mutter, knowing I can never stay mad at Bart, the same as Myrtle could never stay mad at Ed. I thought they were supposed to be *loyal* animals, but I can't blame him. There is something unabashedly charming and boyish about the Charleston cop when you get past that crusty exterior. Maybe it's his larger-than-life heart, the kind of compassion that makes a man drive across the country to protect a woman he barely knows from her demonic husband. I'm doubly glad I saved Emil now. Between saving him and taking down the Strangler, I've left the world a little bit better than I found it.

Inside, I close and lock the door, leaning back against it with the smallest of smiles. For a while, I just close my eyes and breathe. When I open them, I think I feel her in the room with me, a quiet presence. Maybe I'm forgiven. "We did it, Myrtle," I say out loud. "We got him."

I push off the door and slip the robe off my shoulders, slumping it over the back of a chair. My eyes fall on the table where the brown paper bag full of Spanish berries had been sitting, but I don't see it. Knowing traces up my back, from my ankles to my scalp, setting my skin alive with electric fear. I have only a second to register its meaning.

"Looking for this?" he asks.

When I turn, he is standing with his back to me across the living room, staring out the un-shuttered windows. He turns slowly and holds the bag up, now open.

"You seem to have a thing for berries," he says flatly. "I never knew."

I swallow the bile threatening to rise, and my throat aches from it. "There's a lot you never knew about me," I say quietly. I will not give him the satisfaction of a reaction.

"Apparently." He tosses the bag onto a nearby table and despite myself, I flinch. "I underestimated you, Piers. Forgive me." There is a mocking note beneath the words. He must realize how much I longed to hear something of the kind for the last two years. It delights him to dangle it before me now, knowing he doesn't mean it, knowing I know it, too.

"What are you doing here, Henry?" I want to hear him say it.

"I'm your husband," he returns. "Aren't I?"

I shake my head. "Not anymore. Piers is dead. I killed her myself. I'm not the woman you remember."

"You belong to me!" he spits, the words flying from his lips on a spray of saliva.

I shut my eyes against them. When I open them, he is still there, still fuming, still ready to pounce. "I belong to no one," I say pointedly. "Not you. Not the venery. I am mine and mine alone."

The strangeness of the word catches him off guard. I see his composure slip, something closer to shock peeks through the rage. He is trying to maintain control in a world he does not recognize, and he knows it. "What are you talking about?" He circles toward me slowly. "You're not making any sense."

"I told you, there's a lot that you don't know," I repeat.

His head cocks the way a bird's does when it's listening for worms underground. "Like what?"

"Like the fact that there's a room full of sheriff's deputies three-hundred feet from here."

He smiles like it's a joke. "My funny wife. You lie."

I glare at him. "Do I?"

"Why are they here, then?" he asks coyly, enjoying the game, thinking he's still a step ahead.

"To investigate a murder," I tell him plainly.

That stops him in his tracks. His confidence falters for a moment, the look on his face contorting.

"A murder *I* committed," I continue, just to watch him squirm. Now it is my turn to begin circling. I step into the living room, moving away from him and toward the back wall, the windows and table where the bryony berries wait.

"I don't believe it," he tells me. "You're too weak. Too pathetic. You don't have it in you."

I laugh. I can't help myself. The irony is just too rich to ignore. The sound unnerves him. "Oh, Henry, you can be so incredibly blind where your ego is concerned. I've killed four men since I left your side. At first, it was hard for me to swallow, too. But now, it's becoming second nature." I pause beside the sofa and meet his glare, leaning against it as I tell him, "I made one of them actually shit himself first. I take a little pride in that to be honest."

His eyes narrow and his head shakes, sending wispy blond

hairs floating on the charged air. He doesn't know what to say. His speechlessness empowers me, makes me bold with triumph.

I move on. "And what have you been doing since I left, hmm? Pining? Standing over that empty grave in the forest with your cock in hand, wondering who will satisfy you now that I'm gone? Who will play your willing victim?" I grin at him. "It's going to take a lot more than a windup toy to frighten me now. I'm not your Lady Mother, Henry. I don't give a fuck about being respectable in public anymore."

"Who are you?" he hisses as he moves opposite me, the couch now between us, my back to the windows where he once stood.

"Don't you recognize me?" I ask, inching toward the table. I don't want him to see what I'm after. The second he knows, he will do everything in his power to stop me. Regardless of my earlier concerns, if I want to be sure I can kill Henry, I need to feed more. "I'm your darling wife. The woman you raped and beat and tortured for two years. I am what you made me, Henry. What's the matter? Don't you like what I've become?"

For a second, I think I see a flicker of remorse in those fathomless blue eyes, pale as glaciers and even colder. But no sooner do I recognize it than it's gone, replaced by a seething fury he will never be free of. Not until I free him.

"No more talking," he says slowly. "I'm going to kill you now, Piers. I'm going to squeeze you until the life flows out like juice across my fingers. And then I am going to fuck your corpse like you always deserved. Do you understand? You will die here in a puddle of your own piss as I watch, and it will be the best sex of my life."

"You can try," I tell him acidly. "But I'm betting it goes the other way, minus all the corpse fucking because *ew*. You see, I made a mistake in Charleston, one fatal miscalculation when I plotted my escape."

"What's that?" he asks between gritted teeth.

"I should have killed you instead of killing myself."

He lunges at that, grabbing the sofa and leaping over it even as he pushes it aside. I spin and reach into the bag, gripping a handful of berries in my fist, but before I can get them into my mouth, he's knocked me to the ground with the flat of his hand. Sparkling red spheres spill across the carpet like rubies. I scramble toward them, gathering them up, but he clutches my ankle and yanks me back, flipping me over as he pins me down, a hand on each wrist, his knee digging into my solar plexus.

His eyes burn down at me. If he could, he would make me combust right here, a bomb of a woman, a torch to his perversion.

Despite myself, the vulnerability of my predicament, I start laughing. A thick, heady, rhythmic sound flowing out of me, wetting the corners of my eyes, causing my chest to heave.

"Shut up!" he screams. "Shut the fuck up!"

"Or what, Henry?" I ask. He doesn't have me where he wants me yet. And he knows that I know it. He will have to let one of my wrists go to choke me. And it won't matter which. I have berries clutched in each hand. Either way, I will feed and he will die.

It infuriates him that he isn't sure of what's happening, that I know something he doesn't. The insecurity eats at his insides. It has been eating at him since the day they first put him in his monster mother's arms. He lifts my wrists and slams them against the floor, causing my bones to shudder in agony as several of the berries fly from my grip and the rest crush against my skin, their juice running into the creases of my palms. I howl with the ache and the loss.

He rises, grinning, releasing my wrists, and slaps me hard, my cheek cracking with the force, my ear ringing. Great tears betray me, rolling from the corners of my eyes at the pain. The feeling of triumph causes him to let up the pressure on my chest just enough for me to squirm and jerk my leg up hard into the soft meat of his groin.

He unleashes a furious howl, sliding off me as he grips his crotch, and I roll over licking skin and seeds and juice from my hand, scrabbling to my feet and making for the kitchen door. I tumble down the porch steps, and a moment's hesitation—should I bolt for the café full of law enforcement officers or make a run for the underground shelter full of dried, toxic stores?—means I hear the scrape of a table leg, the crash of a lamp as he finds his footing and comes after me.

Without another thought, I head straight into the woods, hoping I can lose him in a thicket of conifers or across a stream, hide beneath the swell of a mossy boulder. The meager drops of bryony juice I licked from my hands aren't enough, even with my gift for concentration, to kill an evil like Henry. Without feeding, I have no hope of winning this fight. Hiding from it is all that's left. But I haven't traveled more than thirty feet when he tackles me, bringing me down hard against the knot of an exposed tree root, filling my mouth with loam and blood.

I spit dirt, my vision swimming as a white, waxy knob focuses it—the immature cap of a destroying angel mushroom emerging from the earth right in front of me. Myrtle's voice rings through my heart—*a very little poison can do a world of good*—and I know this button has risen for me, my magic calling it forth when I needed it most, just like the pokeweed in Charleston.

Henry is already twisting my arm behind me, but with my other hand, I snatch at the mushroom, letting it fill my mouth, every bite a mix of relief and excruciating pain.

He grabs me by the neck and pulls me up, spinning me to face him. His hands rest there, tight but not constricting, not yet, as he glares at me in the early rays of morning.

"Come on, Henry," I tell him while I still have my voice. "Don't you want to kiss me goodbye?"

His fingers dig into my skin. For the second time tonight, I can't breathe and begin to lose consciousness, blackness creeping in from my periphery like ink spilling in water. Everything in me fights to stay awake, alive, long enough to finish him. As he watches my eyes flutter, my face purple, he can't resist. This was when I was always the most beautiful to him, the most irresistible.

He leans in, refusing to let up on my windpipe, and presses his papery thin lips to mine. With the last ounce of strength I have, I push my tongue, coated in blood and saliva and tiny fragments of mushroom, into his mouth.

The gesture startles him so much he releases me. I cough and wheeze, hacking to the side and stumbling, barely holding myself up on my feet. When I glare back at him, he is wiping his mouth, spitting out bits of white flesh.

"What the fuck is this?" he whines. He always hated a mess.

"Don't be such a crybaby," I grate out. "I saved it just for you."

That creaseless brow buckles as something rumbles inside him. He places a hand on his chest, long fingers splayed, every nail manicured to perfection. "What have you done to me?" he asks, belching noisily.

As the air pours into my lungs, I can feel the tissues of my throat knitting themselves back together, the magic inside me undoing years of damage even as it undoes Henry in front of me. I suck in oxygen like water in a heat wave, coughing out all the fear and self-loathing he planted, years of shame that was never mine to carry. When I am able to rise to my full height, he is on his hands and knees, back arching like a cat, as vomit streams out of him, panic warping his face. He finally collapses on his back, his hands crumpled against his chest as stomach cramps seize him again and again.

I move to stand over him, looking down at the face of my nightmares. For the first time, I see a man before me and not a demon. Such a shame he could only show me that at the very end. "Goodbye, Henry," I tell him, his eyes blinking with understanding come too late. "I can't say that I'll miss you, but you taught me an awful lot. Thank you for that. It'll sure come in handy from now on."

One gnarled hand raises toward me, as if to plead for help, but I knock it aside.

"Now, now," I chasten him. "We mustn't resist our destiny." When his eyebrows crumple with confusion, the painful surprise of where he finds himself, I realize I feel nothing for him anymore—not fear, not empathy, not even pity. He's just another

mark, one of many. I watch with detached interest as the life va-
cates his eyes like an incandescent bulb dying, the bane witch
inside me finally taking her full form, blossoming like a flower
toward the sun.

I kneel down with a cruel smile, kiss my first two fingers and
place them over his lips in a final farewell. "Sleep well, little rabbit."

34

Azalea

When she steps into the café, she seems to absorb all the light. My heart speeds up in my chest, and it must show on my face, because Regis slowly lowers his coffee cup and twists to look over his shoulder.

She is radiant in a Barbie-pink trench coat, low-rise cargo pants, and patent leather combat boots that lace up to her knees. A devilish smile coils across her raspberry lips as she sees me, tucking her wild blond hair behind an ear. "I came dressed for the occasion," she says, approaching the bar I am positioned behind, a forgotten ladle of waffle batter in one unmanicured hand. "Oh," she adds, slapping a fistful of foxgloves wrapped in brown paper on the counter. "And I brought these." She looks down at Regis where he sits on the stool beside her and smiles coolly. "Hello."

I am tempted to reach over and close his mouth. "Sheriff Brooks," I say instead. "This is my cousin Azalea. You remember I told you I'd have some family coming in for the holiday?" Halloween is just days away.

His eyes slide to mine, and he suddenly regains his composure. "Ah, yes, that's right." He clears his throat and smooths the shirt of his uniform. "How is Myrtle doing?" he asks casually, like I taught him.

Azalea beams a killer smile at him. "Wonderfully, or so I'm told. She's living with our aunt in Boca Raton, soaking up the sun and mai tai after mai tai on the beach."

His expression falters—likely the uncanny image of Myrtle

Corbin in a bathing suit on the beach—but he manages to get his bearings. Donning his hat, he smiles at me. "Well, I best be going. Got a vandal at the local high school I need to see about," he says easily, but his eyes relay the fear he feels at her nearness, the proximity of her power not just to him but to me.

"See you around, Sheriff," I reply, hoping he picks up on my coded reassurance.

He tips his hat brim to us and saunters out, but I notice he sits in his patrol car a beat too long, backing up slowly and rolling down the road below the speed limit. He won't go far, of that I'm sure. Not that there's anything he could do to save me. The thought sends a nip of alarm coursing down my spine. It was the same with Emil—he wanted to protect me from Henry, but in the end, I had to save myself. And send the handsome investigator back to Charleston with my blessing. "Hunt well," I told him before watching him drive off.

I drop my ladle and gather plates from the tables, ushering Terry and Amos out the front door until lunch, much to their consternation.

When the café is finally empty, I turn to her. "Are you ready for this?"

"Are you?" she asks.

I nod briskly. "As I'll ever be."

The woods are shadowy as we walk, leaving the café, the crescent of kitschy cabins, and the illusion of safety behind. Despite the sun and snow, they are haunted and deep, full of secrets, but the cold feels fitting, a reminder that life is fleeting, precarious, only a breath away from being snuffed out entirely.

I'm glad they sent her, out of everyone. I liked her from the beginning, I realize. For someone who doles out death like a bartender slings cocktails, she's so full of life, more vivid than anyone I've ever met. And it's not just her clothes. It's something nestled inside her—the magic, sparking like live wires.

"I hear you met someone from the venery in Barcelona," she says, making unnecessary small talk.

"Emilia," I tell her with a smile. "She was . . ."

"Magnificent?" Azalea asks like some kind of vigilante fangirl.

I laugh. "Yes, and terrifying. I understand now how the ancient Greeks must have felt in the presence of one of their goddesses. Too beautiful to be real, too capricious to be trusted."

She bumps my arm. "Oh, don't give her too much credit. She's still just a woman."

"None of us are just women," I reply as Bart bounds toward us from whatever hole he was digging in the forest, lips and ears flapping. He regards Azalea with the dazzled awe for a movie star and the healthy respect for an adder, prancing around her with excitement but careful not to get too close. I watch him, curious. "Are you feeding already?"

"Of course," she's quick to answer. "I wanted to get an early start."

I breathe deeply in through my nose and steady my nerves. I knew this day was coming, but somehow I still don't feel prepared. After several long minutes in silence, I tell her, "It's just a bit farther."

She nods but doesn't speak.

At last, we come to stand before a colony of zealous ferns, thicker here than I've seen them anywhere in these mountains. Among them, clusters of mushrooms in every variety surge from the earth, like a garden of fungal delights, the last vestiges of Myrtle's magic. Somehow, it all seems more fitting than a churchyard cemetery or an urn on someone's mantel. "Here we are," I tell her.

She takes a quiet step forward and kneels, laying the foxgloves among the ferns as she bows her head. After a moment, I realize she's crying.

"I'm so sorry," I tell her, squatting beside her on the ground. "She was special, and she deserved a better ending than what she got. I miss her every day."

Azalea wipes at her tears. "She was the best of us. Truly." She gets to her feet, and I rise beside her. "She would love this, you know," she tells me. "It's exactly where she would want to be."

It's my turn to wipe away a stray tear. "I can't say I feel good about it—not yet—but it does feel right, in a way."

Azalea places a hand on my arm. "You did the right thing," she says in earnest. "The hunt must always come first."

"Thank you," I tell her. "That helps."

"That's precisely why Great-Grandma Bella decided to spare you," she says as we turn back. "Well, that and the enormous aptitude and courage you showed in dispatching two marks of such a challenging class in the same day, all while keeping that sheriff under your thumb and squashing any suspicion. It's remarkable how far you've come, Piers."

My shoulders sag with relief. Even though I'd been told as much already, I wasn't sure until this moment whether I could believe it. I did exactly as I promised Myrtle, calling the venery myself and telling them what happened before they saw it on the news. I confessed to Myrtle's untimely death at the hands of the Strangler *and* to burying her in the woods so I could hunt him down. The only part I kept to myself was our fight, how in my rush to protect Regis and the fever of the hunt, I'd left her vulnerable. In the end, it was Myrtle's own words that convinced me I didn't need to share it—*would you really leave that man in the world to take more innocent lives?* If I told them I'd attacked her, however unhinged the hunt had made me, however unintentional her death, they'd come for me. And it would all have been for nothing—her investment in me, her loss. Countless men would continue to hurt those weaker than themselves, men she and I should have put down. In the end, I believe this is how she would have wanted it.

"I owe it all to Myrtle," I say, our steps slower, more relaxed. But I can't help but seize on Bella's implied veto from their gathering. "I take it the conclave didn't go completely in my favor."

Azalea laughs. "It wasn't all bad. Rose and Barbie will still need some convincing. You'll win them over with time. But everyone else was in your favor, believe it or not. Well, except for Lattie, who withheld her vote. But in the end, it's always Bella's decision. And she was on your side from the beginning."

"You voted for me?" I ask, peering at her through my lashes.

She stops walking and turns to me. "We may be witches, Piers, but we're still human. We're not perfect. We make mistakes. No one expects you to get everything right, they just want you to understand what it can mean when you don't. And to try your best, for all our sakes."

Muscles in my stomach that have wrought themselves into knots since Myrtle's death finally begin to unwind. "Now what?"

She lights up, taking my hands in hers. "You're a bane witch without a post." Her eyes arch overhead and back to mine. "And this is a post without a witch."

"You don't mean . . ."

"If you'll have it," she tells me, grinning.

"Of course," I manage to spit out.

"Good," she says, dropping my hands. "This is what Myrtle was grooming you for, after all. It would make her proud. And nobody can handle that sheriff as well as you can apparently."

I blush despite myself, despite the caution I feel discussing Regis with her, the protectiveness I have around our secret relationship.

"I wondered if that was the case," she says quietly.

When I start to back away, she reaches for me. "Relax, Piers. I'm not here to hurt you. To be honest, no one much cares how you keep him happy so long as you do and we get to keep this place in the venery. But you have to know, your mother's arrangement still stands."

"My mother's?"

"If he turns, if he decides to blame you or us for any reason, if at any time he becomes too great a risk, it's your duty to protect the family first." She's not smiling anymore. This contract is binding.

I nod. "I won't risk the venery," I tell her, and I mean it. I love Regis, but I have a purpose now. We all do. And I won't let anyone take that away from us. Fortunately, Regis loves me. He has no desire to stand in my way. His only focus, apart from protecting this community at my side, is protecting me.

"Excellent," she says. "Because it looks like I'll be staying for a while."

My eyebrows raise dramatically as I cock my head in her direction. "Pardon?"

She shrugs, sniffs like it's no big deal. "You could use a little more training, and I could use a place to lie low." Before I can panic, she goes on. "Nothing to worry about. I'll be back in Portland before the snow melts. It's just smarter to not be there when the news breaks on my last mark. I was careful, covered my tracks. But he's a big fish, bound to get a lot of media attention. It's purely precautionary."

"The news?" My eyes round as I look at her. "Who did you kill?"

"A Hollywood mogul with a habit of date rape."

"You mean a Weinstein?" I ask, incredulous.

"Worse," she declares as we start forward again. "If you can fathom it. This one liked to keep sex slaves in a secret basement room—the last one he tortured for weeks before she finally succumbed to her injuries."

I can feel my face going green.

"Besides," she says brightly, the snow beginning to fall in soft flurries around us, freckling her trench coat in ice. "I heard you might be able to use my help with your latest mark."

My latest mark. As much as I'd accepted my fate, it was something I didn't like to think about. It had only been a couple of months since I'd taken Henry and the Saranac Strangler. I thought I'd get more of a break before another predator began to prick at my magic like a cactus needle. But a couple of weeks ago I began to sense him, like a bad dream that hangs around after dawn. And then I caught wind of the news reports. He likes to hang his victims in their own homes, from ceiling fans, wooden beams, even towel racks, using whatever is at hand—belts, tights, bras, bedsheets—but his favorite is shoelaces. He'd been active in the New Jersey area for weeks, only recently going underground, silenced for reasons no one can understand. Except me. My allure is drawing him north. And when he gets here, I'll have work to do.

"You mean, hunt together?" The idea had never occurred to me, but it would be a relief to not have to face this one alone.

"Unless you think I'll cramp your style," she's quick to say.

I take in her glowing hair and immaculate complexion, the dark wings of her eyeliner and the uncanny shade of her coat, the boots that must have cost her twelve hundred dollars, and laugh. "You're the last person who would cramp anyone's style," I tell her. "In fact, I'd like the company. Bart's not much of a conversationalist."

Just then, an intoxicating stench finds me like an arrow in the dark. My nostrils flare and I make an abrupt left, stooping to pull a golden-orange umbrella-shaped mushroom from its unseasonably sprouting pod. "Autumn skullcap," I tell her as I hold it high then gobble it down. "He must be close if it's feeding time."

Tonight, I'll call Regis from the cabin, tell him to keep his distance for a while.

Azalea hoots with enthusiasm. "Well, I'll be damned. Seems I've arrived just in the nick of time."

I grin like a child, a little mad with the energy flowing through me, the snow caking the ground around us, the sun high overhead, trees dancing in the wind as the forest bends to our will. Inside me, the witch is stretching, uncoiling her limbs, ready to make a new notch in her belt.

The hunt is on.

ACKNOWLEDGMENTS

I wrote this novel in a fit of fantasy and fear, pouring so much love and detail into these characters and their dark magic. But I could not have made this book what it is all by myself. I am so incredibly grateful to every individual that had a hand in its journey, that also saw my crazy vision of poisonous witch assassins and cheered me on.

I must thank my agent, Thao Le, who never shies away from my ideas, no matter how dark or convoluted they get. I am beyond lucky to have an agent I adore working with and respect and trust so much. And, of course, my editor, Vicki Lame, who completely got it from day one and never once made me feel bananas for pitching witches with toxic bodily fluids. Her candor and support were immeasurably valuable to me as I dove into the world of this magical thriller, feeling a little more unhinged with every page.

Of course, a hearty shout-out to the entire St. Martin's Griffin team, who took the frenzied draft I handed them and turned it into an *actual* book—Anne Marie, Brant, Olga, Chrisinda, Layla, and Janna. To Vanessa, Kejana, and Sara, a special thank-you for being the ones with the answers when I need them most! And to my copy editor, Martha, I'm sure I owe you a drink—or twenty—for saving me from the tidal wave of things I missed. To Olya and Kelly, many, *many* thanks for delivering the cover and interior design of my twisted, fungal dreams. You are genius.

On a personal note, I am forever grateful for the support of my beloved family, who listens to my wild ramblings and absurd ideas without judgment. My ride-or-die rock of a husband, Nathan, who is the inspiration behind every love interest I write. My daughter, Zoey, the true creative talent of our family, who is always ready to help me talk my way out of a writing pickle and gaze at cover designs. And my brilliant son, Ben, who fielded all my panicked texts about the Adirondacks and let me pick his biologist/botanist brain many times over during the course of this novel (as well as letting me live vicariously through all his nature adventures). And to my forever-eighteen daughter, Evelyn, who is the spirit behind everything I do and the light in all our hearts.

There are countless friends, extended family, and other authors who lent their encouragement and advice along this road, who showed up for me in ways big and small, who are sources of endless support and positive influence. And so many women whose stories I read or heard or watched while researching this novel, whose courage and strength are the real inspiration behind Piers and the bane witches. I am grateful beyond words for all of them.

ABOUT THE AUTHOR

Zoey Sweat

Ava Morgyn grew up falling in love with all the wrong characters in all the wrong stories, then studied English writing and rhetoric at St. Edward's University. She is a lover of witchcraft, tarot, and powerful women with bad reputations, and she currently resides in Houston, surrounded by antiques and dog hair. When not at her laptop spinning darkly hypnotic tales, she writes for her blog on child loss, hunts for vintage treasures, and reads the darkest books she can find. She is the author of *The Witches of Bone Hill* and the YA novels *Resurrection Girls* and *The Salt in Our Blood*.